C000291667

MIND
WALKER

MIND WALKER

KATE DYLAN

To Siân,
DO NOT SURRENDER
CONTROL!

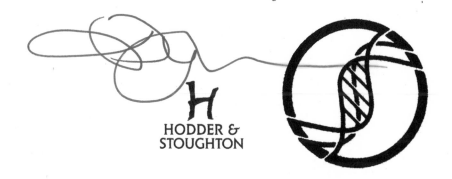

**HODDER &
STOUGHTON**

First published in Great Britain in 2022 by Hodder & Stoughton
An Hachette UK company

1

Copyright © Kate Dylan 2022

A CIP catalogue record for this title is available from the British Library

Hardback ISBN 978 1 529 39268 5
Trade Paperback ISBN 978 1 529 39269 2
eBook ISBN 978 1 529 39270 8

Typeset in Sabon MT by Palimpsest Book Production Limited, Falkirk, Stirlingshire

Printed and bound in Great Britain by Clays Ltd, Elcograf S.p.A.

Hodder & Stoughton policy is to use papers that are natural,
renewable and recyclable products and made from wood grown in sustainable
forests. The logging and manufacturing processes are expected to conform
to the environmental regulations of the country of origin.

Hodder & Stoughton Ltd
Carmelite House
50 Victoria Embankment
London EC4Y 0DZ

www.hodder.co.uk

To Kevin,
for giving me the push I needed to write this book.

CHAPTER I

It's impossible to ignore an alarm that's going off *inside* your head. Which is probably why Syntex put it there instead of on my bedside table. The blasted thing screams across three different octaves, growing so loud and relentless it rattles the nerves inside my teeth. *Christ-that-was.* I curse and throw a pillow over my face, half a second before I remember why that's a terrible idea.

Too late.

The jolt of electricity surges through my brain. It's only the tiniest bit of current, barely even a spark. But damn, it hurts. Every single time. You'd think I'd have learned my lesson by now: urgent alerts aren't optional.

Jarvis has already turned the lights on in my room and their glare is bouncing off the bare, white walls, brighter than is polite for . . . *argh*, 4.14 a.m. It's no wonder I feel like death is tap-dancing inside my skull. Lena and I were drinking until past one.

"Status report," I bark, because there's no point wasting words berating the computer in my head. Most of the other Walkers don't even bother naming their units, but I've never liked the term *it* much, and CIP—short for Cerebral Intelligence Processor—felt too clinical for me. So I named him after the AI bot from this pre-Annihilation movie Dad and I used to watch, back before my decision to join the program drove us apart. I downloaded the actor's voiceprint and everything, so that they'd sound the same. Peter something, I think. Or maybe it was Paul. In my defense, I was eight at the time, and it seemed like a good idea.

"Incoming mission," Jarvis tells me. "Confirm clearance code to commence data stream."

And just like that, I'm fully awake.

"Walker designation W914." My legs grumble in protest as I slip into a pair of shorts and a loose tee. Technically, no one can see me right now, not unless you count the cameras, which, somehow, I never do. Still, this isn't the kind of thing I like doing in my underwear. Jondi likes to do it naked, and he likes it more when some unsuspecting soul happens to walk in on him. He's just that kind of special.

The second my voiceprint is recognized, the screens along the back wall flicker to life. My performance stats on the left, my host's personnel file on the right, and the mission details in the center. *Damn.* I shake off the fuzziness as the full scale of his predicament hits. Not only has Lieutenant Cole Risler gotten himself stuck inside a classified server farm, he's gone and done it on the wrong side of the Demarcation Line. Which is a problem since everything west of Texas and the Dakotas belongs to the totalitarian militia that cleaved the United States in half. Now, we're divided into the United American State and the Western Block. And yes, they hate the name almost as much as they hate us spying on their technology.

Judging by the information populating my ocular display, Risler's chances of breaking out of there alone are pretty much non-existent. He's trapped in a closet, security outnumbers him four to one, his gun's showing as empty, and it looks as though his on-board computer—a sub-skin unit with a holographic screen in his wrist—has been damaged, so he's lost access to most of his tactical mods.

He's out of options, basically.

They usually are when a Walker is tapped.

"Secure channel ready?" I ask, tying my hair back into a messy bun.

"Affirmative. Beginning transmission."

A familiar click sounds in my ear and then panicked breathing fills my mind.

"This is Captain Sil Sarrah of Walker Division Nine," I say. "You've been recommended for immediate extraction. Please speak your consent to authorize the Meld."

A pause and then, "Are you *defective?*" Risler's words ooze contempt. "I don't need your help."

Oh good. He's not just stuck, he's in denial.

I mute my transmission for a moment, squeezing the bridge of my nose with two fingers. I'm too hungover for this. "Jarvis, prepare to initiate neural link."

"I'm sorry, Captain"—he flashes me a giant permissions error—"but the Lieutenant has not yet consented."

"He will," I mutter, familiarizing myself with the building. Risler might not want to admit he needs a teenage girl to save his incompetent ass, but he's going to let me inside his head for the same reason he let Syntex put Meld structures there in the first place. He doesn't want to die today. And he knows I'm his best chance.

I unmute the line. "Lieutenant, your odds of evading capture are at 14.96% and dropping. Authorize the Meld."

"Piss off, Junker bitch."

It's not the worst thing I've been called, but I *really* hate that word and I'm running out of patience.

"12.47%, Lieutenant."

"*Shit.*" The indecision in his voice rings clear, equal parts desperation and disgust. He's moving towards the inevitable right on schedule. "What are your stats?" he finally asks, because field agents are nothing if not predictable.

We so don't have time for this. We never have time for this, which is why I know at least three Walkers who flat-out refuse to answer that question. Lena, for one, tells these entitled pricks that her stats are the best they're going to get so they can either suck it up or die.

But since my record is perfect, I have no reason to hide it.

"I'm at six hundred and fifty-seven missions and a hundred percent," I say, knowing full well it'll impress him. No other Walker in the history of the program has ever scored that many wins without a loss—let alone at eighteen. I beat the last guy's streak over a year ago.

"But we're fast approaching the point of no return here, Lieutenant," I add. "Security are headed your way."

"No. I can't do it." Despite my credentials, Risler won't relinquish control. "Just talk me out of here."

"You know that's not how this works." Sweat beads a chain around my neck, my pulse quickening. Before Syntex perfected neural link technology, Walkers *were* expected to just talk field agents to safety, which made for a terrible rescue strategy since the idiots refused to trust our judgment and do as they were told. So now we take over completely. That's what they sign up for when they opt in to melded extractions. And what they promptly forget the moment they've messed up bad enough to need one. "Now do I have your permission or not?"

"Screw you."

"You've got five seconds to reconsider that answer, Lieutenant. Once your odds drop below 10%, I get to write off this mission guilt-free." When the carrot fails, I reach for a lie and a sharp stick. Because there's no way I'm handing Miles a report that says we're down an agent thanks to my lack of persuasive skill. And there's *absolutely* no way I'm letting Lieutenant Stubborn here single-handedly ruin my stats.

"Four."

Risler's breathing intensifies; sharp exhales whistling down the line. An alarm echoes somewhere in the distance, along with faint yelling I can't yet make out.

"Three."

He lets out a colorful string of curses. He's creative; I'll give him that.

"Two seconds, Lieutenant."

"Okay, do it. Do it now!"

"I need you to say the words."

"*I give you permission! Christ-that*—" His next curse cuts off as Jarvis initiates the Meld.

All at once, my vision goes dark. I've heard other Walkers describe the experience as hurtling through a tunnel filled with bright lights and synthesized sounds, but I think they're just bigging up the tech for the Reggies, because I've never seen jack. The process is quite seamless, actually. One second I'm standing in my room, then the next, I'm in a broom closet, in Lieutenant Risler's body, looking at the world through his eyes.

It takes me a moment to adjust to my new reality. Risler's a foot taller than I am, and close to twice as wide, nothing but solid muscle packed under his clothes. Not that his size much matters. Once the neural link connects us, I literally *become* my hosts, irrespective of their sex or stature. So Risler's hands become my hands, his arms moving readily at my command, grazing a stack of shelves that's crammed full of cleaning products. And wow, is Lena gonna flip when she hears about this . . . I bite back a giggle. This grown-ass man really is hiding in a broom closet.

I quickly take stock of his—sorry, *my*—condition and supplies. The unit in my wrist ate a bullet, so that's the bulk of my scanners and audio enhancers out. Weapons-wise, I'm down to the knife sheathed at my ankle and the sedative darts implanted in my thumbs, but those are only helpful in close combat and that's something I'd like to avoid. The door to the closet is locked, though, and judging by the mass of bodies running past it, security doesn't know I'm in here, so that's good news. As is the slim case of nanodots I find in my pocket. Risler brought along enough to hold about ten terabytes of data, and they're all flashing full.

Not as useless as you look, then . . . I tuck the case into my boot for safer keeping. Classified server farms are where the militia keeps the good stuff. Records of their military assets, citizen health data, projects in active development . . . everything our government wants to know about how the other side lives. Helping them spy on the Western Block isn't just one of Syntex's most lucrative contracts; it's how we prioritize our own R&D and beat other tech outfits to market. Being first means being the best and being the best means we're better placed to influence legislation.

Which makes the files on these dots every bit as important as Risler.

The Lieutenant keeps quiet for now, but no doubt he'll start backseat driving in a minute or two, once the shock of the Meld wears off. Why my hosts bother having an opinion, I don't know. Letting me into his mind has already spiked Risler's survival odds by a factor of ten, and that number will continue to rise as Jarvis pushes me new information. Blueprints, security feeds, known guard rotations . . . whatever we have on this facility. Before his wrist unit was damaged, Risler had access to this stuff too, but without a CIP to process and analyze the data in real time, he's nowhere near as effective.

Hell, if we weren't so damn valuable, Syntex would probably cut out the middleman altogether and send us into the field, but the reality is, we're far too scarce a resource. On a good year, only twenty-odd kids test into the program—it takes a specific combination of DNA markers and blood morphology to withstand the Walker-level tech, otherwise the implantation process kills you, or hardware rejection does—so once they make us, they like to keep us close.

Outside the closet, the alarm drones on, a piercing cry that echoes down the neural link. I wait for the survival odds Jarvis is calculating to spike above 85% before stepping into the corridor, treading lightly on my new size thirteens. From here it's a straight shot down the hall, then two lefts and a right; three entirely deserted corridors according to the cameras. After that, well, things will get trickier.

"You're heading the wrong way. The closest exit is behind us." The Lieutenant's found his voice again.

Super.

"We're not taking the exit," I say, pressing my back flush against the wall. Every time I run an op I find myself wishing they'd give us a mute button for the hosts, but the last time Syntex tried that, it almost ended in a mutiny. So I'm stuck with him.

Risler's outright screaming by the time I make it to the stairwell.

What he doesn't know is there's an old ventilation shaft on the third floor. And what I don't want him to know is he'll be jumping down it. The shaft lets out on top of the dumpsters, so unless they've been throwing out old machinery or knives, his body will survive the fall, give or take a few minor injuries. Based on my projections, it's the escape route with the greatest chance of success. And since I'm steering this ship, it's the one he'll be taking.

I leap the stairs three at a time—it's easy in this body; Risler's in excellent shape—then pull to a stop behind the door, consulting the camera feeds again. One security guard left on this floor. Armed. I wait for him to disappear around the corner before edging out into the corridor.

The access panel is exactly where the schematics show: snuggled between two rooms, low to the ground and sealed shut by a few rusty screws. In my own body, I'd fit through this shaft comfortably; as Risler, it'll be a tight squeeze.

I reach for the knife at his ankle, turning the blade into a makeshift screwdriver. The Lieutenant quiets down once he realizes I have a plan, though I'm sure that'll change the moment I unhook this grate and he gets a glimpse of what he's in for. Then he'll really let me have it.

The first couple of screws give easily, but the last puts up a fight. By the time I tease it free, the guard is halfway through his next sweep of the floor.

"You're not seriously thinking of jumping?" Risler asks as I poke his head into the shaft. He was probably expecting a network of ducts to crawl through instead of a steep, dark drop. The seemingly endless abyss is a terrifying sight, unless you know what's waiting at the bottom.

"It's the safest route out, Lieutenant."

"Like hell it is! Find a different way!"

I ignore him, throwing a leg over the rim. But before I can compel the other to follow, a sharp pain lances through my skull and my vision blurs at the edges, flickering to black. Then I'm back in my room again, my mind filled only with silence.

For a second I stand there dumbly, watching the words *neural link terminated* flash across the screens.

Terminated? That doesn't make any sense. Terminated *how?* By *who?*

There are only two ways to terminate a Meld: either I give the order to kill it, or the host I'm melded with dies. But I'd have felt it if Risler bit the dust on my watch. By all accounts, it's quite the memorable sensation.

Dread chills a path up my spine, seeping into my bones like a nuclear winter. "Lieutenant?" I call out, though I already know Risler can't hear me. The faint hum I've lived with since my CIP was implanted is gone, and without it, I have no idea what to do. When you spend your life filtering out the noise, silence is the true nightmare.

"Jarvis?" I try to reach him too.

No reply.

Shit. I swallow a mouthful of bile. Jarvis can't ignore a direct command. Even if I'm not actively using him, he's always there, standing by in case I need something. Which means the problem isn't on Syntex's end, it's with me. My systems are offline.

So get them back. I will myself to action, trying every fix I can think of. The connectivity options on my screens, recalibrating my CIP through the online console, the restart button behind my left ear.

Nothing.

Double shit. That means it's a power issue, though why my backup hasn't kicked in, I don't know, and right now, I can't spare the time to figure it out. I left Risler with one foot dangling over a three-story drop and a security sweep only seconds from his location. If he dies, my perfect record dies with him. And I've worked too damn hard to let that happen.

I lunge at my desk, throwing open each of the drawers in turn. The few possessions I own crash to the floor, scattering loudly across the cold tiles. "*Christ-that-was.*" The curse rips from my throat, half whimper, half growl. Where the hell did I put my hard line?

I finally find it hiding at the back of my closet, tucked behind an old box of family holoforms. I must have thrown it in there during one of my cleaning sprees. Mess makes me feel untethered, and it's not like I expected to need it anytime soon.

I *shouldn't* have to need it.

Not yet.

I tear the plastic film open with my teeth, but my hands are shaking so hard it takes a couple of tries to snap the cable into the port at the back of my neck.

Come on, come on, come on. My foot taps a staccato rhythm against the bedframe as I wait for the system to reboot. Seventeen whole seconds go by before the Syntex logo—a double helix forged of bone and metal—dances across my retinas, and then finally—*finally*—Jarvis breaks the silence.

"My apologies, Captain. I appear to have experienced a temporary shutdown."

Yes, like I didn't fucking notice.

"Get me the Lieutenant now!" I scream at him.

"Yes, Captain. Neural bridge will be back online in thirty-eight seconds."

Argh. This so can't be happening. I rake both hands through my hair. While I wait, I check the camera feeds from the facility. Tracking shows Risler is still inside, which means the idiot didn't jump or he'd be halfway to safety. Damn. This one's on me. I should have told him what was waiting at the bottom of that shaft. Syntex always says transparency is key to getting our hosts to trust us. And sure, I see their point, but given all the abuse the field ops throw our way, can you really blame us for toying with them a little?

"Opening secure channel in five"—Jarvis has always loved a good countdown—"four, three, two, one . . ."

Risler's panic fills my mind again, his breaths coming hard and fast. Since security has him on his knees behind the guard station, he can't give me an earful without also giving away the game—though I very much doubt he wants to. He's unarmed, surrounded, and his wrist unit is a dead stick. When I ask for his consent he mutters *yes* without hesitation. He even throws in a *please*.

The Meld launches me back into his head, and naturally, there's a gun pointed at it. I don't stop to offer him an explanation; I simply use his body to incapacitate his captors. Gun or no gun, it's easy to gain the upper hand when your tech shows you what everyone else is gearing up to do. And when you've studied a dozen martial arts since you were eight. And especially when the guy threatening your life is too busy screaming *who do you work for?* to have noticed the shift behind his prisoner's eyes.

He'll definitely have heard of Walkers—every tech outfit in the world has been dying to get its hands on our CIPs since the program first launched—but we're rare enough that the Reggies never suspect we're running an extraction until their analysts crunch the numbers after the fact.

We are a myth, basically. Thoroughly modern ghosts.

By the time Gun Man gets off a shot, I've already ducked clear of the barrel and the bullet hits one of the control panels instead. Good. A sharp elbow knocks the pistol out of his hand and then I feign left, drawing back in time for two of my captors to slam into each other. While they're off balance, I take out their legs, sending them both crashing to the ground, their limbs tangled together. The third guard I tackle, pitching a knee to his groin. Given Risler's size and strength, he won't be getting up anytime soon. Or having kids. Which just leaves Gun Man, who lunges at me full pelt.

Big mistake. With a pinch of my thumbs, I activate the sedative darts buried beneath Risler's skin. Then all it takes is a split second of contact and security is down for the count. The entire fight—if you can even call it that—lasted maybe a minute.

"Where the hell did you go?" The instant it's over, the Lieutenant's attitude returns.

So much for gratitude.

Dick.

With security on this floor incapacitated, the main door has now become the safest route out, though this extraction is no longer clean. The guards had a body scanner, for one, and they might well have had time to catalogue Risler's mods, so that's a bit of a cluster. Keeping proprietary tech out of competitor hands is why Syntex developed the Mindwalking program in the first place. It's never really been about protecting their agents; they're more concerned about protecting their IP. Can't win the game if the other team has your playbook, and you can't steal theirs if they know which parts of you bite.

The whole *tech before people* thing used to bother me on some level, but hey, we *are* saving lives in the process, so I guess it comes out a wash.

Anyway, what's done is done. Risler is still alive and he'll be leaving with a devastating amount of data, which means that as far as *my* stats are concerned, I'm golden.

Assuming, of course, I get him out in one piece.

I take off running, snatching up the guard's gun on my sprint to the door. Half a clip to the glass does the job of any access chip, then the rest I spend clearing my path to the fence.

"An extraction team will be waiting at your scheduled rendezvous," I say once I'm safely through the hole Risler cut on his way in. "As long as you stay off the main roads, you shouldn't encounter any more problems."

That's the perk of infiltrating clandestine targets: they never want to admit they've been hit, which means they won't report him. It'll be days before they pull together a log of the files he stole, and weeks before they come clean to their superiors.

By sunrise, Risler will be a ghost.

I don't stick with him until the pickup. Melds fare better over short stints, so now that he's out of danger, a desk jockey will guide him back to the airstrip, five klicks away.

My part in his story is done.

Risler doesn't honor me with a thank you—they never do—but at least he doesn't curse me out of his head. I give Jarvis the command to terminate the neural link, and the next second I'm back in my room, soaked through with sweat.

Only then does the scale of my equipment failure truly sink in, sending me collapsing down to the bed, my body shaking to the bone. Not one, but both of my power systems failed tonight, even though I've barely just turned eighteen.

This isn't supposed to happen yet.

Not like this. Not this badly.

I'm supposed to have more time.

CHAPTER 2

"The good news is, it wasn't a catastrophic failure," Lin says, unhooking the scanners from around my temples.

Yeah, no kidding. I grind my teeth as the examination chair rises back into a sitting position. If my CIP had experienced a catastrophic failure, we wouldn't be having this conversation. Or any conversation, for that matter, seeing how I would be dead. Turns out, grafting electrical components to the human brain ends rather badly when those components implode. Whoever would've guessed?

"Then what was it?" I don't bother moderating my tone for the good doctor. I have been stuck in this infernal chair, cycling through diagnostics for almost three hours. My ass is numb. Every one of my muscles is stiff and screaming. And to top it all off, this *unforeseen malfunction*—as Lin so astutely called it—has left me with a headache that could level a city block. I am in no mood for her sunny disposition, or answers that tell me nothing I don't already know.

"An electromagnetic surge," she says. "It shorted out your power unit."

"So why didn't my backup kick in?" I hug my legs to my chest. Isn't that why Syntex gave me a backup to begin with?

"Because according to these scans, your reserve unit has been non-functional for a couple of days. A battery failure, it looks like." Lin glances down at the tablet in her hands. For a woman who works exclusively with the most tech-enhanced individuals in the world, Sandria Lin is surprisingly mod free. Almost entirely natural, actually, save for the implants in her eyes which allow her to read the data on the transparent screen—a real curiosity given that company freebies are a perk of the job.

I asked her about it once, why she didn't have so much as a basic wrist unit installed, or a keypad in her palm.

"Just because we *can* implant technology doesn't mean we *should*," she told me.

Like I said, a real curiosity.

"The hell did you miss a *battery failure*?" I hiss. Twice a week, I spend an entire afternoon in this sterile white room while my systems undergo maintenance. In all that time, how did she not notice an equipment failure this massive? Christ-that-was, maybe an extra mod or two would help her do a better job.

"Look, Sil, I know this feels like a big, scary thing"—Lin always talks to me like this. Like I'm still the doe-eyed eight-year-old Syntex recruited—"but batteries fail and the surge was minor. Nothing I'm seeing tells me we should be any more worried than usual at this stage."

At this stage. She knows exactly what's been gnawing at my mind, not just since losing Jarvis this morning, but ever since I turned eighteen last month. For everyone else, eighteen means freedom. The freedom to apply for travel permits and move between sectors, to pick whatever mods they want and access the age-restricted items in the vendos. But for Walkers, eighteen means the beginning of the end. Once Syntex puts the tech in our heads, there is no way to get it out again, or stop it degrading. By nineteen, I'll be lucky to experience only one *unforeseen malfunction* a day. If I reach my twentieth birthday, I'll be a walking miracle.

"I did notice your blood alcohol was quite high though," Lin continues, her gaze boring into mine. "You want to tell me about that?"

"I wasn't drunk when my mission came in if that's what you're—"

"I'm not your commanding officer, Sil." She sighs. "I'm not here to tell you off."

Then why does it feel like she's about to grace me with a Miles-worthy lecture?

"But I am concerned about how you're handling the transition into your twilight phase."

Twilight phase. The euphemism never fails to rub me the wrong way. I guess no one wanted to call it what it really is: a death sentence. Not that I get to complain. Syntex has never been anything but forthright about my life expectancy. They gave me all the facts before I chose to join the Mindwalking program. I wasn't forced into it.

"I'm handling it fine," I snap. Lin is one of those *when life gives you lemons, make lemonade* types. Well, sorry, Doc, but even before we irradiated the planet, lemons didn't grow on this side of the Demarcation Line, and the food synthesizers make anything of the citric variety taste like hand sanitizer, so excuse me if I don't rush out to drink some. "We were celebrating, that's all," I say. *Not drowning our sorrows.*

"Celebrating what?"

"Lena's six thousand nine hundred and seventy-ninth day." After nineteen, we start counting in days, not years. Otherwise the count ends too quickly.

"Sounds like the kind of celebration you might keep repeating."

Yes, for as long as possible. I jerk away from the hand Lin tries to put on my shoulder. "I don't need a shrink, okay? I need my systems to work."

With another sigh, she lets it go, though I can tell she doesn't want to. If Lin had her way, we'd spend half our lives in this office, dissecting our every thought and feeling. Which would be a huge waste of life, if you ask me. One day soon my tech *is* going to fail. Jondi's tech is going to fail. Lena's is already halfway there. Talking about it won't make it any less true.

"Well, we can jump-start your CIP for now," Lin says, "but replacing the reserve unit will have to wait until after tomorrow's gala; the Director wants you operational for the exhibition. In the meantime, I'll upgrade your surge protection, that way you shouldn't experience any more nasty surprises. Lie back for me."

The chair reclines flat again, two metal pads emerging on either side of the headrest to cup my temples. I flinch at the harsh, mechanical sound, my hands clenching tight against the leather as Lin presses a nanite injector to my neck.

Just think about something else. I start counting the ceiling tiles to distract myself. Lena finds my aversion to nanites hilarious, since—and I quote—*getting modded sucks so much worse*, and I've never had a problem with that.

But nanite shots are different.

Rationally, I know the tiny robots are too small to feel, but I've always maintained I can feel them just the same, skittering around my brain as they work to upgrade my systems. I still wake up in a cold sweat sometimes, convinced the wretched things are chewing their way out of my skin. Not as often as I did back when Syntex was prepping my body for the tech, and I had to be injected with a new batch of the creepy critters every day, but enough that the very sound of an injector sets my nerves alight, even a decade on. I guess there are some things you never get used to.

"This next part might sting a little," Lin says, slipping a rubber guard into my mouth.

So it's going to hurt then.

Super.

"Ready?"

I don't bother answering, and Lin doesn't wait for my reply. We both know this needs to happen. No matter how unpleasant.

The jolt she zaps me with almost arches me off the chair, searing a path from my skull right down to my toes. *Son of a . . .* you know what I want? Five minutes alone with the guy who decided *sting a little* was synonymous with *hurt like a motherbitch*. Seriously, just give me five minutes inside his head. I could do some real damage.

The electricity is still buzzing hard between my teeth when Lin reaches behind my ear to restart my CIP. I suck in a breath, silently willing the tech to work. Her favorable prognosis has done little to quell the worry festering in my mind, the voices whispering that this was bigger than a minor glitch and a faulty battery. It feels like the start of a downward spiral, and eight classes of Walkers have already shown me exactly where it ends. Once you hit twilight, there is no escaping the dusk.

But then a moment later, Jarvis boots back to life and the relief is so absolute it makes me forget the fear—and the pain. It was totally worth it to feel right again.

I don't bother going back to my room. Despite the hangover and the early morning, I'm too keyed up to sleep. Plus, I'm starving, so as soon as Lin releases me, I head over to the mess.

"You look like shit." Lena's tearing into a grilled cheese sandwich when I join her at our usual table. Comfort food is her thing of late. Then again, so are daily glitches, so I can't really blame her. I have half a mind to switch my perfectly balanced bowl of oats for something fried and salty myself, though I know I shouldn't. *Healthy body, healthy tech!* our nutritionist always says. But hey, maybe that's just an elaborate ploy to hoard all the good cheese.

"You don't look so hot either," I tell Lena, though it isn't even remotely true. She's always had a level of control over her aesthetic mods that I could never hope to achieve. It's not a vanity thing—Lena couldn't care less if people find her attractive, and she could sweet-talk a miser into leaving her his fortune with little more than a smile—it's just that she loves manipulating appearance tech in ways no one else would ever think to, making unnatural shapes and colors feel like the most natural thing in the world.

Her hair is gold today. And I don't mean bright blond, but *gold*, as if Midas himself reached out from the myths of old and touched it. The color perfectly complements the deep hue of her skin and the warmth of her honeyed irises. If she woke up sweating vodka like I did, then she's hiding it disgustingly well.

"It's been a long morning," I say, leaning over for a bite of her sandwich.

"Mission?"

"Yeah—holy crap, El, did you put mac 'n' cheese in this thing?"

"Sure did."

"I didn't know the synthesizers let you do that." I steal another mouthful. Man, that's good. And everything my hangover's craving.

"They're not supposed to." Lena flashes me a grin. "I guilted Lin into relaxing my dietary parameters after my last glitch. She's such a sucker for self-pity. How'd your mission go?"

"She got the idiot out. *During* a CIP failure." Jondi drops down next to me, a mammoth breakfast plate in hand. By virtue of being a thousand feet tall and 300% muscle, he gets to eat whatever he wants. And since he's both the best hacker and the biggest gossip in the building, he always knows everything worth knowing.

"You had a CIP failure?" Lena doesn't take the news quite so casually.

"A surge." I shrug, avoiding her eyes. "Lin says it was minor. Nothing to worry about."

Lena doesn't push it, and for that, I'm grateful. We never really talk about glitch stuff; we talk *around* it, as if by ignoring the inevitable we can somehow stave it off. A few years ago, we were still the young Walkers, and tech failures seemed so abstract and far away, a problem for the distant future. But two blinks and a heartbeat later, that future is hurtling towards us at full speed, ready and eager to relegate us to the past.

"Well, I can't believe you glitched and still kept your perfect record." Jondi fixes me a mock glare. "I think they're throwing you the easy ones."

"The hell they are." I pinch a piece of bacon off his plate. "You just need to spend a little less time in the gym and a little more in the Meld labs." *Like I do*, is what I stop myself adding. I study more than any Walker in the program, I run more drills and simulations, and I dissect my past missions for sport. My record is perfect because I'm fighting to keep it *perfect*. That way, the others won't forget me when I'm gone. How could they if they're out chasing my streak?

"Hard pass." Jondi snatches the bacon back from between my fingers with his teeth. "I'd rather have my abs than your stats."

"That's because you're all pretty and no bright." I roll my eyes in Lena's direction. "Was I this insufferable at his age?"

"Nah, you were a mature seventeen."

"I think the word you're looking for is grotesquely boring." Jondi tosses a stray piece of macaroni at her head.

"That's two words, genius." Lena's gaze flicks up for a moment, a sure sign that her CIP has pushed an alert to her ocular display. A mission, probably. Syntex has agents all over the world, and it's only breakfast time for a handful of them. Right now, it's close to midnight in the Pacific Federation and the Unified Chinese Continent, also known as happy hour for corporate espionage, when the bulk of our agents get themselves into trouble.

But if it were a mission, Lena would have already excused herself from the table. We don't drag our feet on this stuff.

"What is it, El?" I ask as the blood drains from her cheeks. "What's wrong?"

"It's the Director. He . . . he wants to see me."

"*Now?*"

She shakes her head, scrubbing both hands over her face. "Tomorrow. After the gala. I'm"—her voice cracks to a whisper, sending my stomach plummeting to my knees—"I think I'm being decommissioned."

"El, come on, let's not jump to—" Jondi starts but Lena silences him with a curt, "The hell else could it be?"

And this far into twilight, she's not wrong.

Ever since his son took over the program, Director Paxton has been what you'd call a *hands off* kind of boss; we rarely see him outside of the yearly galas and certain milestones in our career.

Most notably, the end of them, when he thanks us for our service and pays out our contracts.

"El . . ." I try—and fail—to come up with something comforting to say. We all knew this was coming, but it makes me want to put my fist through someone just the same. Decommissioning is designed to free up our time once the glitches grow too severe, so we can go back and visit our families before a catastrophic failure burns us out. But we're Lena's family; her parents died smuggling her across the border when she was three. The Republic of Canada doesn't take too kindly to its citizens trying to defect. Neither does the United American State, for that matter. Though we do stop short of shooting them.

I'm still looking for the right words to ease her heartbreak when Jarvis pushes me an alert of my own. Lin must have cleared me to go back in the rotation. "Shit, I'm so sorry, El, I have to—"

"Go." She rises from the table, shoving what's left of her breakfast towards Jondi. "Someone has to get the Reggies out of trouble."

By the time I'm done with my mission, Lena's nowhere to be found. She skips lunch and our afternoon training session, blows off dinner, and ignores my messages when I ping her CIP. So I leave her to it. This morning, I got a tiny taste of what she's been living with this past year. If space is what she needs, then I'm happy to give it.

My room is still the mess I left it in this morning, an oh-so-pleasant reminder of my first unforeseen malfunction.

Well, that's just perfect. I take my time tidying everything away, reorganizing my desk and neatly folding back my uniforms, the tension in my shoulders easing as, bit by bit, I impose order over the chaos. In my haste to find a hard line, I also sent a stack of family holoforms crashing to the floor, and their smiling faces stare up at me as I work.

I tuck the glass cube of Dad back in the closet without hesitation, because no matter how many years pass, his disapproval of me still stings. My siblings go next, but a rare flash of home-sickness compels me to keep the cube of Mom out on my bedside table. She always knows what to say when I'm feeling off-center, how to remind me that I'm doing the right thing. Or, at least, she used to. I don't make time to visit much anymore, and with five other kids to think about, neither does she.

Which is good, I guess. It means the nanites in the water are doing their job, keeping our citizens alive and healthy. *Fertile.* No small feat considering how close we came to wiping ourselves out a century ago. Our trigger-happy ancestors threw so many nukes at each other they turned the whole damn planet into a doomsday prepper's wet dream.

Radioactive storms, epidemics, tsunamis, droughts . . . every worst-case scenario in the book started killing us off. By the time Syntex developed reliable food synthesizers and the immunity boosters that allow our bodies to survive the resulting hotbed of contamination and disease, the global population had dwindled to less than a hundred million. Low enough to turn the race for arms into a race for bodies. Gone are the days of shooing people away at the border; governments are now doing everything in their power to tempt people in. And get them to *stay* in.

That's why I'll never understand Dad's refusal to back my decision. He's witnessed first-hand the crucial role Syntex plays in placating the population—hell, he lives in an apartment they pay for and enjoys access to all their best tech. He *knows* our products are the reason American citizens aren't defecting en masse in search of a better life elsewhere. No mass defections means fewer government measures designed to contain and control.

It means freedom.

And joining the program made me a part of that.

It made me important.

Once all my things are back in their rightful place, I can finally relax. I crash down to the bed, stripping off my clothes and boots as I go. I try reaching Lena one more time—if only to say goodnight—but when my ping goes unanswered, I give up the fight and curl under my sheets. I don't care that it's only gone eight, or that Miles will have my ass tomorrow if I don't turn in my mission logs; I'm long past ready to leave this cluster of a day behind.

It's the influx of light that wakes me, shattering what might have otherwise become an excellent dream.

"Jarvis, turn that off," I mutter, burying my face in my pillow. But the shock my body braces for doesn't come, and there's no alarm screeching either. This isn't an urgent alert. So Jarvis better have a damn good reason for waking me up at stupid o'clock for the second night in a row.

"My apologies, Captain, but it appears you have a visitor," he says.

I sit up in the bed, blinking the sleep from my eyes. There's a shadow lurking in my doorway, silhouetted by the brightness streaming in from the corridor.

"El, is that you—" The words catch in my throat as I flick on the main lights.

Lieutenant Cole Risler is even bigger in person than he felt when I commandeered his mind, though he seems shrunken somehow, and frazzled, his hair sticking up at odd angles, a grizzled layer of stubble marking his jaw. He's softer in the face than the picture in his file suggested, more boy next door than hard-boiled meathead.

But the gun he's brandishing looks every inch a real gun.

I freeze, pulling the sheets up to my chest, as if this thin piece of synthesized cotton might somehow stop a bullet. I've never had a gun pointed at me before. I mean, I have, plenty of times, just not in my own body, where it actually counts.

"Lieutenant—"

"You're still in my head," Risler growls, stepping into the room. "I can feel you . . . digging around in there." He's a much bigger mess up close. Dark circles under his eyes, a flush to his cheeks, sweat clinging to his skin. It looks as though he hasn't slept since I got him out of that server farm. Or washed, for that matter. How he broke into the barracks in this sorry state, I don't know, though breaking and entering *is* what our field ops are trained to do. Which makes *why hasn't security spotted him?* the better question.

"No, that's—" I try to swallow down the quiver in my voice. I'm not used to dealing with agents outside of their heads, where I'm in control. "That's not how this works, Lieutenant. I would never enter your mind without permission. I couldn't even if I wanted to."

"Don't lie to me!" The gun shakes in his hand.

"I'm not lying." I press myself against the headboard, the metal biting the skin at my back. "I'm here. In this room. With you."

"Liar!" Risler roars. "Did you think I wouldn't notice you in there? Did you think I'd let you get away with it?" He rubs his temple with the barrel of the gun, making me flinch. His other hand keeps clenching and unclenching at his side, his nails gouging bloody half-moons into his palm, as though trying to dig their way clean through.

"Lieutenant, I'm not in your head. I can't be in two minds at once," I say, edging towards my bedside table, where I keep my own gun. The models we're issued for personal safety have a setting that'll leave him incapacitated but not dead. Then he'll become a problem for psych to solve.

"Don't you move!" Risler lets off a shot, missing my fingers by an inch. I lurch back, my heart stuttering beneath my ribs. Pissed off agents I can handle—that's basically their default state—but unhinged is a whole different ballgame.

"Lieutenant, please, let's talk about this." I change tack, slowly raising my arms. No way am I letting this lunatic kill me over some insane delusion. If I can keep him distracted a few more seconds, security should arrive. Jarvis triggered an alarm the moment it became clear this visit was unwelcome, and even if he hadn't, you don't fire a gun in the Syntex building without drawing attention. "Whatever's happening to you, we can figure it out, okay? Just put the gun down."

"I should have never let you in." Risler's outright shaking now, his whole body vibrating like a plucked string. "You Junkers . . . you're not right. What you do . . . it's *not right*."

Footsteps echo behind him, racing up the hall towards us.

"I have to get you out of my head." Risler clocks them at the same time I do, a manic edge creeping into his words. "*I want you out of my head!*"

That's all the warning he gives me. I don't even have time to scream before he presses the gun to his chin and pulls the trigger, splattering his brain across the ceiling.

CHAPTER 3

Risler's final act follows me all the way to the gym, haunting my punches as I try to exorcise his ghost. *Thunk, thunk, thunk*. I show the leather bag no mercy, my bare feet dancing across the mats.

"Jarvis, give me some music," I growl. The gym is far too quiet at four in the morning. Unnervingly so. And my nerves have already had their fill of nerves today.

"Yes, Captain. What would you like to hear?"

"I don't care. Just make it loud." Loud enough to drown out the ringing in my ears and the memory of the gunshot. The sound Risler's skull made when it burst into a thousand pieces.

Mindjacking. That's what conspiracists call the rubbish he was ranting about. Or at least, that's what they used to call it, then someone had some fun changing that j-a to an f-u, because the trolls who frequent anti-tech sites are oh so original.

It's both illegal and impossible, by the way. Mindjacking. Syntex isn't some comic book villain; we're a corporation, and as such, we're bound by the law. And yes, I've tested it. We all try to game the system when we first learn to Meld. Jondi even lost a whole month's credits to me once, betting he could hack my CIP and take control. It doesn't work. There are too many protocols in place designed to prevent us forging neural links without consent. The government insists on it.

Thunk, thunk, thunk. The moment Jarvis starts blasting his preferred brand of electrock inside my head—volume cranked to an almost painful level—I attack the bag with renewed vigor, syncing my punches to the beat. Left, right, left. Right, left, right.

Over and over until the adrenaline pulsing through my veins is more sweat than grief.

Left, right, left. Right, left, right.

Until the weight eases off my chest.

Left, right, left. Right, left, right.

Until I can think again.

Left, right, left. Right, left, right.

Until a hand lands on my shoulder.

The hell . . . I move on instinct, hooking my assailant's arm and flipping him forward. "Jarvis, kill the music," I bark as he hits the mat with a resounding thud. As *Miles* hits the mat, I should say. Since that's my commanding officer I just assaulted.

"Shit . . . Miles . . . I'm sorry." Technically speaking, I'm supposed to address him as *Sir*, but he hates answering to that almost as much as he hates us using his full name and rank: Lieutenant General Milford Paxton, heir apparent to Syntex Technologies. Pretty sure the last Walker to call him *that* is still out running laps.

"Don't be sorry, that flip was textbook." With a groan, Miles climbs back to his feet. Despite the early hour, he's already dressed in his standard uniform of training slacks and a black tee—both crisp and freshly ironed—his blond curls hanging past his ears in that perfectly messy way they always do, as though they'd never graced his pillow.

"Did Lin send you?" I turn back towards the bag, my teeth grinding together.

Security forced me to see her even though Risler never touched me. She draped a blanket around my shoulders despite me telling her I wasn't cold. She kept saying things like, *You're in shock, Sil,* and, *This wasn't your fault.* And because I wanted out of her office, I just sat there and nodded, when in reality, every part of me wanted to scream: *I'm not in shock, Lin, and I'm definitely not feeling guilty.* Pissed off is what I am. I saved Risler's life, for fuck's sake, and then he came to my room to make me watch him end it.

"Lin may have nudged me in your direction." Miles plants himself behind the bag, holding it steady. "To make sure you get some rest."

Right. Like there's any chance of that happening.

"They're cleaning my room." I shrug, as though it's the most natural thing in the world. As though I'm waiting for house-keeping to change my sheets instead of a biohazard team to scrape a field agent off my ceiling.

"Plenty of bunks going spare in the barracks," Miles says.

"Yeah, well, I fancied a workout."

"And?" He cocks an eyebrow.

"And what?"

"Is it helping?" His gaze could strip the flesh off my bones. Sometimes, when Miles looks at me, his eyes are distant, as though his mind has wandered off elsewhere. But right now, they're clear and focused, studying me like I'm a broken toy that needs fixing.

"More than sleeping would." My fists continue terrorizing the leather. *Thunk, thunk, thunk. Thunk, thunk, thunk.* Until my anger bleeds red through the wrappings on my hands. I didn't bother gloving up for this impromptu session. I wanted to feel the violence.

"Tell me what happened, Sil." Miles drops the pretense, finally lending voice to the question he came here to ask.

"A lunatic with a gun happened, Miles. There's nothing else to tell."

"You sure about that?" He taps a quick command into the keypad in his palm and the bag lurches back on its rails. My next punch hits air instead of packed sand.

"Hey, I'm not done!"

"Those bloody knuckles say you are. So let's talk instead." A hint of authority creeps into his voice. A reminder, albeit a gentle one, to mind my insubordination. In the two years he's been my superior, I've never known Miles to pull rank on his Walkers—an impressive feat considering that he came to the job young and by way of his father. The words *pampered*, *green*, and *unqualified* got bandied around a lot during his first few months, often within earshot. But instead of chewing us out the way he should have, Miles chose to earn our respect the old-fashioned way: by not sucking at the job.

"Did the Lieutenant say anything to you?" he asks. "About why he attacked?"

"Does it matter?"

"I think it does," Miles says, and suddenly I do feel as though he's pulling rank.

"Are you . . . *ordering* me to talk about this?"

"I'm not ordering, Sil." He takes a step towards me, his face soft and open, filled with concern. "I'm asking. Because you witnessed something awful, and talking about it might help." The sincerity in his words—the worry—intensifies the pressure building beneath my ribs. I don't like it when Miles worries about me. I've always been the one he doesn't need to worry about.

"He accused me of breaking into his head." I give him an inch. But only one. "Then he blew it open with a forty-five."

"That's all he said?"

"Yep. End of story."

"Is it?" Miles reaches for my hands, a question in his eyes.

Well, it was certainly the end of Risler's story. I let him take them. *Damn near the end of mine too.*

"You know, Sil, it's okay to not be okay," Miles says, peeling back the bloodied wrappings. "No one would think less of you."

I'd think less of me. I hiss as the tape pulls away from my skin. It would make *me* feel less. Like I was letting the program down. Like I was letting *him* down.

"Can I please stay and train a little longer?" If Miles won't believe me when I say I'm fine, I'll just have to show him that it'll take more than one broken agent to throw me off balance. "I promise to leave the punching bag alone."

"Damn right, you'll leave it alone." Miles taps another command into his palm and a host of virtual attackers spring to life, surrounding us completely. "You're going to be far too busy dealing with *them.*"

Risler's blood has been scraped off the ceiling by the time Miles banishes me from the gym, but I swear I can still see it—and *smell* it—the bitter tang of metal hiding beneath the bleach. I edge into my room, scanning the walls for any piece of him the cleanup crew might have missed. They've done a good job; I'll give them that. They've even patched up the bullet hole by my bed, though the paint they used is a brighter shade of white and the bedside table remains dinged at the corner. I run my fingers along the dented metal, pretending it means nothing, that I didn't come within an inch of death today. This morning, another year of life felt as fleeting as a bolt of lightning; now it feels like an eternity I almost didn't get to have.

And suddenly, I can't breathe. And I sure as hell can't stay here. I *can't.*

<W914> ping <W807> Can I come over?

I'm halfway across the hall by the time I finish typing the message into my palm.

<W807> ping <W914> Like you're not already here.

Lena's reply comes instantly. I had a feeling she'd be awake, waiting up for an SOS like this one. News travels fast around this building and security weren't exactly quiet when they descended on the floor. I expect the whole compound has downloaded the footage of my run-in with Risler by now.

Hell of a way to be remembered.

"So I hear Syntex's favorite daughter leaves a lasting impression." Lena's teeth are a flash in the dark.

"Funny." I pick a path over to the bed. Lena may have an

unhealthy relationship with mess, but at least her room's not haunted by some field agent's brain matter.

"You okay?" she asks as I slide under the covers.

"Sure. Why wouldn't I be?" It's not my blood congealing in some bucket.

"Oh, no reason," she says, but the smile in her voice is gone. *You know, Sil, it's okay to not be okay.*

"I just need to sleep." I roll onto my side, putting my back between us. A wall to keep her out. Or maybe it's to keep this helpless feeling in, so it doesn't consume us both.

I want you out of my head. That's what Risler said to me a moment before putting a bullet through his. *Well, Lieutenant, I couldn't agree more.* I bite down hard on my lip, forcing in a ragged breath. Lena's pillow smells faintly of her strawberry-scented shampoo, but for some reason it's wet and slick with salt. I don't even realize I'm crying until she wraps her arms around my waist and buries her head in the crook of my neck.

"This wasn't your fault, Sil," she says. "You did nothing wrong."

When Lin told me that same thing, I didn't need it to be true.

Now, I'd give anything to believe it.

"I was supposed to save him, El."

"You did."

"But what if I did this too?" I could beat this fear into submission around Miles, but I've never been able to hide anything from Lena. "What if my glitch made him think—"

"It *didn't.*" The word is a whisper in my ear, quiet but assured.

"How can you know that?"

"Because I've lived through enough of them." Her whole body tenses. "Trust me, when you lose an agent to a glitch, you'll *know.*"

I pull her closer beneath the sheets and twine our legs together, drawing comfort from her strength. When Lena first started logging errors, she made us swear not to treat her any different. *No tears, no kid gloves, and no pity,* she said. And she meant it too. This past year, she's lost neural links, mod control, access to her drives . . . Last week, she even spent a day entirely blind when her CIP stopped communicating with the implants in her eyes. But no matter what twilight threw her way, or what the glitches did to her stats, Lena never let it break her.

Yet here I am, one bad day in, already falling apart.

"Please don't leave me, El," I breathe my fear into the dark. "I can't do this without you."

Lena doesn't make that promise; we both know she can't. Instead, she just grips me tighter.

"I know we're not supposed to say this," she whispers as a wave of silent sobs ripple through my chest, "but there are days when being a Walker sucks."

"Yeah." I can't help but agree. Because some days, it really does.

CHAPTER 4

By the following afternoon, I've trained out my mood and slapped on a smile. As the top-ranked Walker in the program, I don't get to hide in my room feeling sullen during the company's biggest event of the year. And quite frankly, I wouldn't want to, because Syntex's annual gala is the hottest ticket in town, and—to quote Jondi—I'm not just saying that because I'll be there. It's an evening filled with tech, booze, and security-cleared officials. You need code-word access to get into this party; the toys showcased here aren't for the children to play with.

As always, the gala is held at the top of the Syntex building, in a spinning observatory of steel and glass that offers a panoramic view of the city. The New York hub was the first to rise from the ashes of the Annihilation, proof that our technology could rebuild, restore, and resist the effects of the lingering radiation. We started by reclaiming Manhattan, then sector by sector, grew outward as we decontaminated more land, though the island remains the heart of both the city, and the United American State.

Where once lay a park, now lies the Tech District, a four-kilometer-wide block of prime real estate that houses the most impressive collection of skyscrapers built since the bombs fell. None quite as grand as the Syntex tower, with its unique form of twisted curves and soft angles, but a few of our competitors—Glindell, Cytron, Excelsis—come close. The rest of the city makes up for what it lacks in height with ads and color, disguising the sprawl beneath an ever-changing parade of vivid lights and VR displays.

Inside the observatory, no expense has been spared in decorating. We're talking sculptures that remake themselves on the hour; floor to ceiling projections that show the wonders of the world as they once were; bio-cognizant fairy lights that respond to each individual guest as they draw near.

At intervals across the room, Syntex's latest innovations stand proud on raised daises, drawing gasps and approving nods from the crowd. Our new line of cybernetic organs is proving to be a real showstopper, as is the holographic dream recorder, and the meal patches R&D perfected last month—though I'm personally more interested in the metabolic taste changers, which can imbue any meal with the user's flavor profile of choice. Definitely adding those to my wish list.

In a week's time, the buying teams will return to submit their bids for this wide array of medical, nutritional, and recreational tech, as well as the company's extensive catalogue of security offerings. It's called the Contracts Dinner, and it's the reason Jondi, Lena, and I have each been assigned our own station, complete with a six-foot-high display showcasing our image and stats. We are the crowning jewel of Syntex's collection. Eighteen years after the program first launched, the technology in our heads is still the only thing these Generals and politicians want to talk about. The one innovation no competitor has managed to replicate.

Per the Director's request, every Walker on display is at their most striking tonight. I've gone for a look that utilizes the aesthetic mods embedded in my skin, turning the alabaster dewy and metallic. My hair is arranged in a shoulder-length bob with side-swept bangs, set in a style called *hidden rainbow*, the top layer tinted a pale silver to match my eyes, and the rest programmed to look like, well . . . a rainbow, so that when I move or ruffle my hair the colors peek through. Lena talked me into it; apparently this style is all the rage in the sectors. The Reggies must have more free time than we do seeing how it took her an age to perfect the code.

For her exhibition look, Lena's opted to stick with yesterday's gold theme ramped up to eleven, adding a shimmery glow to every part of her body. It's unusual for her to sport the same coloring two days in a row, but her CIP glitched out hard this morning so she had to keep things simple.

Jondi, on the other hand, is rocking a tapestry of bright, full-body tattoos that pop against his light skin, winding up both sides of his neck and into his close-cropped hair. To better show them off, he's already ditched his jacket, rolled up his sleeves, and teased open a few buttons. That boy really is the biggest attention whore I've ever met.

<W807> ping <W914> Are you seeing this?

Lena winks at me through the crowd.

<W914> ping <W807> Kind of impossible to miss. Bet you ten credits his shirt comes off in the next hour.
<W807> ping <W914> Bet you twenty he's caught making out with a guest.
<W914> ping <W807> The blond in the red dress? Or that guy he's following to the bathroom?
<W807> ping <W914> Ooh. Tough call. But speaking of guys worth following to the bathroom . . . I found you a treat.
<W914> ping <W807> Uh-oh. Why does this feel like a trick?
<W807> ping <W914> Just open the file, Golden Girl.

So I do. And wow, the waiter she caught loitering behind the tech booth could definitely give Jondi a run for his money. Razor-sharp cheekbones, marble-cut jaw, a stare that's black-hole deep; he's even got a perfectly placed scar through his eyebrow that screams *dangerous*, but in a socially attractive way. *His very own ink, too . . .* I can't help but notice, peeking out from beneath the cuff of his sleeve. Pity he'll be getting fired in a minute or else I'd orchestrate a run-in for sure. Catering staff aren't allowed to use their keypads in the guest areas, and slacking off during the height of service is never a great look. He'll be gone before my next break.

<W807> ping <W914> So am I right, or am I right?
<W914> ping <W807> You're shameless.

I bite back a smirk, forcing my mind out of the gutter as Miles leads a fresh delegation of dignitaries over to my station.

"Captain Sarrah." He offers me a strained smile, the tedium of playing host cracking through his gracious mask. "I trust you remember the acquisitions team from the Chicago hub?" His eyes flick to my hands for the briefest of moments, the only remaining sign of this morning's concern.

Nothing left for him to worry about there; I rearrange them so he can see the unmarked skin at my knuckles. Lin treated my bruises earlier this afternoon. Physically speaking, I'm good as new.

"It's a pleasure to see you all again," I say, silently thanking him for the reminder. Of the five hubs we've rebuilt since the Annihilation, Chicago is second only to New York in terms of wealth, size, and military contracts, so it pays to keep their buyers sweet. *The charm and arm*, Miles calls it. And he hates it almost as much as he hates wearing a suit.

"I was hoping you'd do us the honor of a demonstration," he says, channeling his father perfectly. Then, while his charges are busy fawning over my stats, he leans in to add, "If you make it a *long* demonstration, I'll let you skip drills tomorrow. The small talk is killing me."

"Yes, *Sir*." I bury the laugh rising in my throat. What I'm supposed to do when asked for a demonstration is pick one of our guests at random, use my CIP to glean their identity, then read them their life story. Only the polite stuff, of course, nothing they'd be too ashamed to tell the kids.

But I don't do that.

Instead of focusing my efforts on some half-drunk corporate buyer, I focus them on Miles instead.

I don't know what possesses me to do it. Maybe it's because he's so obviously out of his element, and I can't help but watch him squirm. Or maybe it's because his gaze has already drifted off into the distance, and I want to tempt him back from wherever he goes when his mind wanders. Or hell, maybe I'm just trying to give him something to think about other than my violent meltdown in the gym.

Either way, I pull up *his* personnel file and say, "How about we let our guests really get to know you, General Milford—you never told me your middle name was *Eugene*—Paxton."

His attention snaps back to the present.

"Born and raised right here in Sector One, you're a certified genius by almost every metric we have," I continue, projecting the data streaming across my field of vision a few inches from my face, so that our audience can follow the work behind the information. It's a party trick, mostly. But it's effective.

"Graduated high school at thirteen. Undergrad at fifteen. Then a Masters in Advanced Engineering, where you passed every class with honors. Oh, except for Practical Ethics." That nugget of information I get by unlocking his university transcripts, which I'm not technically supposed to do, but the hack was too easy to pass up. "What happened, General, did you have an off day?"

Miles's lip quirks up in amusement and he cocks his head to the side, as though daring me to keep pushing my luck. I'll be paying for this stunt tomorrow for sure. He'll probably run me to the moon and back.

"You officially joined the corporation at seventeen and have since enjoyed a meteoric rise through the ranks. At your father's behest, you spent the first five years sequestered in Sector Four's Applied Science division, working to improve Walker technology, before finally returning to Sector One to claim your seat on the board and control of the Mindwalking program." I conclude my demonstration with a flourish, pushing his company portrait—the one he says makes him look like a pompous ass—to the display behind me.

"Impressive, isn't she?" Miles nods at his guests, affecting the perfect mix of embarrassment and pride. "She only missed *one* of the finer details."

"And what's that?" I ask.

"Eugene is less a middle name, and more my father's idea of a cruel joke," he says, eliciting a laugh from the gathered officials. "I'm also not a huge fan of my school records getting hacked."

"Oh, I'd barely call it a hack. Your alma mater has terrible firewalls."

"Then I'll be sure to inform them an upgrade is in order."

"I think we all know that wouldn't have kept me out." I flash the buyers a conspiratorial smile. With Jarvis in my head, few systems present a real challenge, and Syntex turns a blind eye to most of our casual hacking because it keeps our skills sharp. They trust us to stay invisible and out of places we *really* shouldn't be. I mean, hell, even Jondi knows better than to hack classified company files.

"We appreciate your time, Captain." Miles points the team towards the next attraction on their tour, though he hangs back as they mutter their thanks and shuffle away, lingering at my station.

"That was quite the demonstration, Sil. I'm going to enjoy repaying the favor." The humor in his eyes is making me brave.

"It was totally worth the extra laps."

"Let's hope you still believe that tomorrow," Miles says. "Though I am glad to see you're feeling better." He raises a hand to my hair, running a couple of multicolored strands between his fingers. "I like this new look. And that you didn't change your face."

My cheeks warm in reply, growing red at how well he knows me—and what I'm wont to do when things get tough. Truth is, I did think about changing it for tonight, so that I could be someone other than *the Walker who drove an agent to blow his brains out.* I decided against it in the end. Bone structure alterations are tedious at the best of times, and I wasn't exactly feeling my best today. Besides, I like this face. I've been wearing it for almost six months now. The longest I've worn a face since I had my aesthetic mods installed.

"Milford, you appear to have lost your guests." The Director's voice cuts between us, snapping my posture straight.

Paxton Senior is the perfect blueprint rendering of his son, like two product versions honed fine by a generation. But unlike Miles, he holds himself apart, emerging from his penthouse office only when the need requires. Events like this, for instance. Where his presence isn't just expected, it closes deals.

"Yes, I was about to head back and join them." Maybe it's my imagination, but a shadow crosses Miles's expression, as though tonight, his father's presence is also *unwelcome*. "Captain Sarrah, thank you again for the—"

An explosion of static swallows the rest of his words whole.

The hell . . . I scan the room for answers, every part of me tensing as the crackle gives way to a deep, mechanical laugh. In place of our demo reels, the screens in the hall are all glitching red, and judging by the frantic way Miles and his father are assaulting their keypads, this isn't a marketing stunt; it's a breach.

We're being hacked.

<W807> ping <W914> Unholy mother.
<W1021> ping <W914> Is this for real?

Both Lena and Jondi message me at the same time. But before I can shake off the shock and ping them back a *sure looks like it*, the glitch changes, rending another collective gasp.

Oh, this is really not good.

Sweat prickles my palms, a cold heat rising. The pattern tessellating across the screens is as unmistakable as it is damning. A honeycomb. Calling card of the Analog Army, an anti-corp faction that's been a major thorn in Syntex's side.

Power belongs to people, not companies.

Their manifesto bleeds to life in crisp crimson letters.

Do not let them rule you.

Do not let them own you.

Do not surrender control.

And now the hall really erupts, the scandal of such a brazen attack rippling through the crowd.

"How the hell did a bunch of back-alley hackers get past our firewalls?" Miles barks into his comm, lending voice to the only question that matters. A breach like this isn't supposed to be possible. Least of all by a fringe group of ideologues who—on a good day— are classed as a mild annoyance. They hijack an ad board here, sabotage a tech shipment there; nothing a little extra security can't fix. Whereas this screams organization. It screams resources, and planning, and drive. It screams *you'd better believe we're a threat.*

The kind that could only have come from *inside* the building.

"Jarvis, get me the camera feeds from the elevators." My fingers drum a terse symphony against my thigh. "Flag anyone who left this floor in the last few minutes."

A hack of this magnitude would require direct access, so if the Analog Army were smart, they'd have coded in a delay and hauled ass before it hit. But not too long of a delay, or else our malware detectors would have nixed the virus. That's a five-minute escape window at best.

Bingo. Jarvis pushes me a file that fits the bill. One of the catering staff made it out to the street with seconds to spare, though I can't pull his ID since he's expertly avoiding the cameras—and I do mean *expertly*, seeing how that's damn near impossible in a building this secure. He'd have gotten away clean, too, if not for the hint of a tattoo visible beneath his sleeve.

Son of a . . .

"Miles . . . I mean, Sir—" I whip towards him, the picture Lena sent me burning a hole through my drives. "I know how they—"

"Not now, Sil," he snaps, eyes fixed firmly on his father. While I was busy playing detective, cyber security managed to regain control of the screens, and now the Director is marching up to the main stage, all nonchalance, swagger, and teeth, as though the world's most embarrassing hack never happened.

"Ninety-three seconds." His words thunder starkly around the hall, amplified by his voice boosters. "That's how long it took our team to neutralize this surprise drill. I think we can all agree that's remarkable." He leads our guests in a hesitant round of applause, much to their bewilderment.

"What's more"—the Director forges on undeterred—"our logs are showing that *had* this been a real attack, we'd have experienced *no* data loss, *no* program compromise, and *no* damage to our underlying systems. Which in turn means *no* disruption to the first-rate products we sell to *you*." This time, when he pauses for effect, the applause rings louder. "I daresay our resident hacker, Steve, is rather disappointed." Hell, he even gets a laugh.

<W1021> ping <W914> Dia-fucking-bolical.

Jondi echoes my thoughts exactly.

<W807> ping <W914> I can't believe he's pulling this off.

But somehow, the Director *is* selling this lie, and as he continues to wax lyrical about the myriad of ways Syntex is working to safeguard its IP, the crowd slowly relaxes back into the party mood, mollified by his charisma and charm. If I wasn't sitting on evidence that proves otherwise, I might believe him myself.

"*Sir*." Now that the immediate threat is over, I try for Miles's attention again. Only for his father's next face-saving trick to immediately command mine.

"And to continue our demonstration, it is my honor to introduce our most accomplished Mindwalker, Captain Sil Sarrah," he says, lighting my station up like a neon sign. "In celebration of yet another record-breaking year for the program, she's kindly offered to showcase an operation."

The hell I did. A violent shiver races down my spine, all thought of pretty waiters forgotten. Even if I'm assigned the easiest of extractions, there's no such thing as a risk-free mission, or a happy Meld guarantee. That's exactly why we *don't* perform them live; it opens the door to embarrassment.

And we're barely just clear of one of those.

"What are you doing?" Miles grits a similar concern into his comm.

Which his father deftly ignores.

"Captain Sarrah, I trust you will provide our guests with an enlightening show?"

I force a nod despite the panic. Because what choice do I have? He's already told the entire room I volunteered.

"You cannot broadcast this operation," Miles hisses another protest through a painfully clenched jaw, examining the mission details streaming to his wrist. Details that—for some reason—the Director has not seen fit to share with me. "Please. Think how something this volatile will play in the press. I'm asking you nice—"

But it's no use. With every head in the hall turned our way, Miles can't fight his father's wishes any more than I can. Already, the screens behind me have synced to my ocular implants and Jarvis is pestering me to verify my voiceprint. This terrible idea is going ahead whether we like it or not.

"Walker designation W914," I say, swallowing down the nerves. The tightness in my chest has nothing to do with doubt. I know I'm good at this; I'm the best Syntex has ever seen. But I'd be lying if I said my *unforeseen malfunction* didn't rattle me, the memory clinging to my flesh like shrapnel, making it impossible to breathe without wondering, *what if it happens again? What if I fail?*

<W807> ping <W914> You've got this, Sil.

Lena shoots me a smile through the crowd.

<W807> ping <W914> Show these bureaucrats what a Walker can really do.

"Jarvis, open secure channel." I steel my shoulders and force the words out. Time to see these volatile mission stats for myself. "This is Captain Sil Sarrah of Walker Division Nine," I say as a woman's heavy breathing fills my mind, frantic and urgent. "You've been recommended for immediate extraction. Please speak your consent to authorize the Meld." I only pray that Lieutenant Neve Harper won't spend too long refusing my help in front of all these people. My operational skills are plenty honed enough to withstand public scrutiny—my bedside manner, on the other hand . . . not so much.

"I consent!" Harper screams so fast it takes me by surprise. "Please, just get me out of here."

Huh. I guess wishful thinking really does work.

"Initiate neural link," I tell Jarvis, and then a moment later, the sea of eyes observing me disappears. From this point on, they'll find the direct feed my CIP is broadcasting to the screens far more engaging. Our bodies move little when we work, though they will sometimes replicate the more urgent actions our hosts perform. Either way, our guests' *entertainment* is not my biggest concern right now, the firefight raging around Harper is.

My new arms fly up to cup my ears. As far as I can tell, I'm in some kind of underground parking structure, sandwiched between an armored truck and a rapidly disintegrating pillar, bullets screaming around me. I'd guess there are at least six or seven shooters, maybe more, but I can't get visual confirmation because according to Jarvis, no cameras exist here.

No cameras? That unnerves me far more than the chaos. What kind of installation—corporate, military, or otherwise—doesn't spring for cameras?

And the news only gets worse from there. Camera feeds are not the only thing I'm missing; I'm missing *everything*. We have zero information on this facility, bar the original blueprints, and those are twenty years out of date.

Christ-that-was, no wonder the Lieutenant let me in without a fuss. Her odds of getting out on her own had been calculated at 3.05%, but even with me in her head, Jarvis's projections are barely any better.

6.98%.

Shit.

My panic mixes with Harper's, sending her heart into a frenzied song. I'm beginning to understand why the Director kept these mission stats off the screens. Our rescue threshold is 7.5%.

Shit. Shit. Shit. Bullets continue to terrorize the concrete at my back as I pull up the recommended mission plan, which only serves to confirm my fears. This isn't an extraction at all, it's a termination.

"Command should have never sent me here." Harper sounds damn near hysterical, a lunatic raving in my mind. "We didn't have enough intel to infiltrate."

Or to escape, for that matter. I start taking stock of my options. Without security feeds to guide my aim, the gun at my hip will do little against so many, and I can't punch my way out of a firefight. What I need is a distraction so I can get to the stairwell marked on these blueprints. I'll figure out the rest once I'm not getting shot at.

Carefully, I edge towards the armored truck, jimmy open the door and climb inside. The mammoth vehicle vibrates as bullets ricochet off the metal, the windshield splintering as round upon round assaults the glass. Staying low, I rummage around the seats, tossing aside soiled clothes and empty protein packs until I happen across something useful. Drug inhalers. Four of them. Enough to get some Reggie pretty damn high or start a couple of small fires, depending on what you do with them. Looks like it's my lucky day, shitty luck notwithstanding; the driver of this truck's a stim junkie.

I gather up the cartridges and steal back out into the lot. It takes a pretty hot flame to set a medicinal inhaler alight—they're designed with safety in mind—but street dealers aren't quite so judicious when they pressurize their product. These days, an addict is more likely to blow themselves up than overdose. Bad for them, good for me. I swear to never complain about the country's drug problem again.

"How's their ammo holding?" I ask Jarvis.

"Based on my analysis, there is a 65% chance that 75% of the shooters will need to reload their weapons in approximately nine seconds," he says.

So terrible odds then.

I grip my own gun tighter, waiting for the lull. Then as soon as the worst of the shooting abates, I spring up, tossing three of the inhalers towards my attackers, each followed by a bullet. Screams erupt as the cartridges burst into flames, sending two of the guards crashing to their knees, faces clasped in their hands.

I run, weaving haphazardly between the cars. Naturally, Harper has decided that now would be a good time to start yelling and her voice clashes up against Jarvis.

"Twenty-nine yards to entry," he says. "Twenty-seven. Twenty-five."

The remaining guards give chase once my makeshift bombs lose their potency, shooting as they go. But they're no longer a united front, and that gives me a fighting chance. I duck behind a car and take aim. A man goes down on my first shot, and another on my second, though by my third, the rest have already sought cover. Damn. I fish out my remaining inhaler and send it up in flames at their feet, buying myself a few extra seconds.

"Sixteen yards to entry," Jarvis says as Harper's wails intensify. "Twelve."

A bullet hits the concrete an inch from my leg.

"Eight yards."

"Christ-that-was, Jarvis, shut up!" I snap. Unless he's figured out a way to make Harper run faster, the countdown isn't helping.

I tear into the stairwell, barricading the door with a loose piece of pipe I pry off the wall. The entire frame shudders as a hail of bullets batter the other side, but the lead-enforced steel holds firm. A century of radioactive storms has forced us to build solidly again. Never thought I'd find myself grateful for that.

"Captain, according to the mission plan, you should be taking the stairs *down* now," Jarvis says when I hesitate between floors, reminding me of my mandate. The very idea makes my— *Harper's*—stomach roil. Since Command has deemed this extraction untenable, they're instructing me to protect the tech in her body. *Only* the tech. My orders are to lead the Lieutenant to the onsite incinerator, ensuring she meets the kind of death that leaves nothing behind for our competitors to dissect.

I'm supposed to kill her.

While a room full of people watches on.

Think how something this volatile will play in the press . . . It's little wonder Miles tried to divert this mission off-screen. I don't know what the Director is thinking, quite frankly, running a termination live. But if this is some sick way of showing his investors that he'd do anything to protect their IP, then he's picked the wrong Walker for the job. Because I don't care how bad the odds are, I am not walking this woman to her death. Not when it's in my power to stop it.

"Push the building schematics to my ocular display," I tell Jarvis, taking the stairs *up*.

"Captain, the order is very clear—"

"Yeah, well, we're going off-script," I mutter. There are still three bullets left in Harper's gun, so if all else fails, I can spare her the *prisoner ever after*. As for the tech, well, *fuck* the tech. I signed up for a lot of things when I joined the program, but I never agreed to run terminations. And if the Director knowingly sprung this on me—in front of an audience, no less—well then, fuck him very much too.

"What were you sent here to do?" I bark at Harper, trying to keep her from melting down entirely. "Lieutenant, *answer me!*"

"Data retrieval," she finally manages between sobs. "They wanted me to clone the server then purge it."

"And did you?"

"I didn't even get close before security found me."

"Then I need you to tell me everything you know about this facility," I say.

If I'm going to publicly disobey my orders, it'll take more than one rescued field agent to shield me from the fallout. Which is why I intend to do more than just save Harper's life. I'm going to complete her mission.

CHAPTER 5

The good thing about a complete lack of cameras is that if I can't see security, then security can't see me. And that I can work with.

Two flights up from the parking lot, the sub-levels meet the ground, though the darkness rippling outside the windows tells me little about where—or *what*—this facility might be. Not that it much matters, since the wheres, whats, and whys of these missions are way above my pay grade. I don't usually ask, and my hosts know better than to tell. That's how Syntex likes it. Tightly controlled, compartmentalized information. So they'll be pleased to know this place is giving me jack.

The whole compound is decorated in such a way as to be instantly forgotten, but given the distinct lack of insignia on the walls, my credits are on *black site*. That would certainly excuse the deafening number of alarms. Whatever's being developed here, someone really doesn't want it getting out.

Which makes securing it doubly important.

I kick open an emergency door, adding yet another pitch to the chorus of wails echoing through the building. Good. If security thinks I've made a run for it, they won't look for me inside.

Doubling back into the stairwell, I start climbing, each step a battle against the growing fatigue in Harper's muscles. Her body isn't holding up as well as I expect it to, and neither is her mind. To be quite honest, she strikes me as too old for a mission like this, an inch away from being retired and settling down with a nice desk.

Can't retire if she's dead . . . I grit her teeth and push through the pain. Some small part of me realizes how stupid this plan is, that if I fail, I'll be in for a world of trouble. Gross insubordination, the Director will call it. Syntex might not be a military outfit, but he does like to run it as such. He likes discipline and order, and for his Walkers to follow their mandates and get the job done.

You are getting the job done. Two jobs, in fact. I silence the doubts with a large dose of logic. I've made the decision now and I'm going all in on it. I won't let this homicide of a mission taint my perfect record.

It takes every trick in my arsenal to avoid capture once I reach the right floor. I might not have camera feeds to work with, but Harper's ocular scanners come equipped with heat map capabilities, and her cochlear implants make echolocation possible. Jarvis can work wonders with those two things alone, building me a rough picture of the building and the people inside it.

Just as I'd hoped, security is clustering around the lower levels, looking for a phantom that has long since disappeared. So I do the opposite of what feels natural: I slow down. If I'm monitoring heat maps, it's safe to assume that they are too, and there's nothing more suspicious than a thermal signature running up and down the halls like it's on fire.

My biggest advantage is Jarvis, and how quickly he keeps me updated with information. That's how I know when to stop and take cover, when to fight. When I do fight, I leave security slumped peacefully in chairs rather than sprawled out on the floor where they'll draw attention. Once they're down, stealing their access chips is easy, though it's gruesome work seeing how I have to cut them out of their palms. I would have personally stopped after *one* maiming, but Harper insists I harvest the chips from all three guards I encounter, in case they don't share the same clearance level. It's a good tip, and not something I'd have thought of myself. Getting agents *out* of places they shouldn't be is my usual line of work, getting into them is hers. Glad to see she's finally pulling her weight.

"The server room should be on the left," Harper says as I approach the end of a long corridor. A low hum steadily builds around me, vibrating the carpeted tiles beneath my feet. Yep, this is it, alright. Little else would call for this much power.

The first two security chips do nothing but elicit a very loud, conspicuous sound, but when I press the third to the scanner, the display turns green and the door slides open with a whoosh. A welcome rush of chilled air spills out, making me shiver. It's hard to describe what it's like being in someone else's body. I don't feel everything Harper does, but I do experience heightened sensations. Temperature, fatigue, nausea, *pain*, those types of signals pass freely down the neural link. Right now, Harper is hot and tired therefore I'm hot and tired, even though all *I've* done today is make small talk and program my hair.

The server room is modestly sized and dimly lit, ringed by the industrial-grade coolers required to keep the hard disks nice and frosty. A single access terminal sits beside the main stack, though of course, it's password protected. I get to work coding the hack. I'm no Jondi with computers, but I do okay when it comes to snooping through things I'm not supposed to see. It takes me a few minutes to design a worm that will bring these firewalls down, then once I'm in, I start the data transferring onto the nanodots Harper brought along for the task. Then there's nothing to do but wait and hope that the copy completes before security figures out what I'm up to.

I honestly don't know how our field ops do this; wait on a tiny bar to creep across the screen while their lives hang in the balance. So instead of twiddling Harper's thumbs, I decide to buy myself an insurance policy, for the event that I don't get her out in one piece. In that scenario, any data I bring home will go a long way to minimizing the fallout from this . . . lapse in judgment.

"Jarvis, set up for a quick read," I say, highlighting the main file directory.

"Yes, Captain. Ready for capture."

I hit open on all the documents at once. Jarvis will take a snapshot of each for analysis later. It's not as good as having physical copies of the files complete with their metadata, but it's better than nothing. Little of what flashes before my eyes lingers long enough to leave an impression; then again, that's not my department. My department is knowing when it's time to call it quits, and based on the new alarm going off on this floor, I'd say my time is up.

"We need to get out of here!" Harper hisses.

Yes, thank you for that perceptive assessment. I shove the nanodots back in her pocket and quickly run a delete script through the terminal. Then, to ensure a data retrieval specialist won't be able to work their magic, I put a bullet through two of the cooling units in the room. The rest I go at with Harper's knife, severing the cables that feed the power-hungry beasts and destroying the controls. A server array like this gives off so much heat that it'll only take an hour for the rise in temperature to corrupt the drives beyond repair. Security isn't likely to get replacements here in time. Not with me keeping them busy.

"Captain, I'm showing hostiles moving in your direction," Jarvis says.

They've found me then. Damn. I jab the knife into the final cooler, then make for the door. There's a whole armada headed my way, and they're only a couple of corridors over, which closes off all my escape routes bar one. And it's far from my first choice.

Crap. I run towards the stairwell, throwing harried glances at the wall of bodies at my back. I should have gotten out sooner. I don't have the firepower to take this many guards on.

"Stop where you are!" the nearest man shouts, his command followed by a bullet. It misses, though his next one wreaks vengeance through fabric and flesh. Pain races down my leg, sending me to my knees. Unholy mother . . . gunshots *burn.*

With a growl, I drag myself up and keep running. It's a graze, I think, though with the adrenaline coursing through Harper's body, it could very well be more than that. I don't stop to check.

That's the most important rule of extractions. Don't stop. Don't turn back. There'll be plenty of time to hurt once Harper's out.

I skid into the stairwell, security hot on my heels, their bullets slamming into walls and ricocheting off the handrails.

"Why the hell are you going *up?*" Harper yells, having finally graduated to the *questioning my decisions* stage of our relationship.

Super.

"The blueprints indicate a crane on the roof," I say, pushing her body harder. This facility must be somewhere off-island. Sector Three or Four, maybe, where the bulk of our industrial districts lie. Hopefully, the owner never saw fit to get rid of it when he diversified into the black site business.

"*And?*" Harper screeches.

"And that's why I'm going up." I don't bother sharing the rest of my plan with her, mostly because it's not a plan: it's a Hail Mary—though one could argue the point of hailing *anything* now that religion is just a novel way to swear.

My good leg is groaning by the time I burst out into the cold night air; its injured friend is screaming bloody murder. I turn in place, examining my surroundings. The perimeter lights throw the compound into sharp relief, though it's as unremarkable on the outside as it was in. Generic industrial complex through and through, complete with its own security gate for access.

When I don't spot the crane immediately, my hand tightens on Harper's gun, considering the single round I saved for this eventuality. The final kindness I can offer her. But then I spot the metal structure overhanging the far side of the building and I'm running again, dodging gunshots as they dance around my feet.

I don't slow down as I approach the steel goliath, and I sure as hell don't ask Jarvis to calculate my odds of success. The bullet I've been saving ends up hurtling towards the winch instead of Harper's brain, shooting the line free, and then I launch myself at the hook, praying to a god I don't believe in that the cable will run out before her body shatters against the pavement.

And then I'm falling.

And falling.

With the wind whistling in my ears and Harper shrieking like a banshee in my mind.

I squeeze my eyes shut, tensing for the impact that will surely kill her. But then with a snap that rips through my shoulders, the cable pulls tight, lurching Harper to a halt mere inches from the ground.

Holy. Shit. Something between a retch and a giggle escapes my throat. I can't believe that actually worked.

"Jarvis—"

"The gate is twenty meters to your left, Captain," he says, anticipating my question. He's good like that.

"And security?"

"I'm only showing one guard."

A smile tugs at my lips as I take off running. One security guard is a walk in the park compared to the horde I've just escaped, and though his friends are still shooting at me from the roof, the distance between us makes their aim optimistic at best. When I steal a look at my stats, the numbers are now showing a 76% chance of successful extraction. They'd be higher but my encounter with the crane left at least one of Harper's shoulders dislocated. She'll be spending some time in a med-bay once this mission's done. But I'm willing to bet she'd take a med-bay over an incinerator any day.

I'm almost to the gate when a shadow passes overhead, near invisible against the inky darkness. If it weren't for the alert it's triggered on my radar, I might not have noticed it at all.

"Jarvis, can you get a read on that for me?" I turn my head skywards.

That's when the pain hits.

CHAPTER 6

I'm screaming and screaming and screaming. The pain in my head is the kind I'd swallow a bullet to be rid of. Hell, I'd devour the entire clip. I feel it in my brain, my bones, bubbling beneath my skin, a hundred thousand knives hacking at the nerves inside my skull. I drop to my knees, cradling my face in my hands. I don't know what this is. I don't know why it's happening. But I'd gladly sell my soul to make it stop.

"Sil—" Someone is calling my name, though they sound small and far away, a whisper compared to the roar of blood pounding in my ears.

"Sil—"

I recognize the voice now. It's Lin.

"Sil, open your eyes for me." It's her *everything is going to be okay* voice, which definitely means something bad just happened. Maybe I experienced another glitch then, though they shouldn't hurt this much unless . . . crap. Am I burning out? Already?

No. I shake my head stubbornly, sending another flash of pain streaking through my temples. *I can't be. It's too soon.*

"Sil, the neural link terminated when your host died," Lin continues. "You're back in your own body. You're safe."

If anything, those words make me feel worse.

"But I got Harper out," I mumble. We were out; I *remember* it, running across the compound grounds, a single guard standing between me and a successful extraction. There's no way he gained the upper hand so quickly. He hadn't even started shooting yet.

"It was a drone strike," Miles cuts in. "There's nothing you could have done."

"A drone strike?" I look up to find him crouched in front of me. Lin is hovering protectively beside him and behind her . . . *oh no.* My whole body begins to shake. *No, no, no, no, no.* We're still in the exhibition hall, though the festivities have very much lost their mirth. Instead, the crowd gathered around us exchanges disapproving mutters and pointed slights.

Because I failed.

I let Harper die right in front of them.

The second agent in as many days to have died because of me.

"I don't understand." An acrid mix of fear and shame pools in my stomach, threatening to send the glut of canapés I ate earlier spilling out over my shoes. "Why would they blow up their own facility? Their own *people*?"

"Whatever you took, they obviously didn't want you to have it," Miles says. Gone is the humor in his eyes and the playful air he exuded earlier. He's all business now; my commanding officer, not my friend, anger darkening his features.

He should be angry. I disobeyed my orders. I did it publicly and I didn't do it well.

I embarrassed him. I embarrassed the entire program.

On a night when we desperately needed a win.

I'd venture that's why the Director is nowhere to be found right now. No doubt he has more than a few nervous investors to placate.

My muscles tense, waiting for Miles to deliver the dressing-down I deserve, but instead, he drapes his jacket around my shoulders and says, "Come on, let's get you somewhere quiet."

I hiss as the fabric touches my skin and a sharp pain ripples across my back. When he helps me to my feet, my left leg gives out from under me, trembling as if I got shot alongside Harper.

"Take it slow." Lin wraps an arm around my waist for support. "The neural link severed incorrectly, so you're experiencing some residual side effects from your host's injuries. They'll pass in an hour or two."

I suppose that serves me right for treating Harper's body with such disregard. Not that I care about the pain. All I can think about as they lead me from the hall are the two words flashing across every screen. *Mission failed.* I've run six hundred and fifty-nine missions for Syntex and until today my stat bar has always read 100%.

Now it reads 99.85%.

The shame lingers long after the pain passes. Long after Miles schedules a disciplinary hearing for the morning, and long after I exhaust myself in the Meld lab trying to pinpoint where I went wrong.

Hubris is the conclusion I come to. Had I stuck to doing my job instead of showing off and trying to do Harper's, she'd still be alive. I could have gotten her out before they scrambled that drone—the sims confirm it. If I had, then maybe they wouldn't have bothered scrambling the drone at all, because it wasn't Harper they cared about; it was the data she stole.

The data *I* stole.

My mouth fills with bile and metal, my insides knotting tight. With one bad decision, I sentenced a woman to death today. And I didn't even make that decision for her; I made it for me.

"Captain, shall I reload the program?" Jarvis prompts as the screens in the lab dim to a faint glow, fading black with inactivity.

"No. Shut it down," I say, un-pairing from the console. No matter how many times I beat the simulator, my new stats remain the same: one field agent short of perfect. What I need to do now is look forward, not back. Give the disciplinary board a reason to let this terrible mistake slide.

"And Jarvis, get me an ID on this guy." I bring up the file Lena sent me, of the oh-so-pretty waiter who ruined my night. If he was as careful in the room as he was in the elevator, this might be the only good picture we have of his face. Which makes it my only lead. "Hack the city's facial recognition grid if you have

to," I say. "I want to know who he is and where I can find him."
So that I can offer up his neck in an effort to save mine.

Do not let them rule you. Do not let them own you. Do not surrender control. His army's misguided rhetoric grinds my teeth to a dust. Syntex doesn't *rule* anyone. The government takes our lead on legislation because we've proven time and time again that our technology saves lives. I'd say that earns us the right to ensure no bureaucrat can interfere with that mission by passing some asinine law. Or worse, by blocking a necessary one.

By the time I return to my room, I'm running on fumes and a grudge, craving sleep the way an addict would a fix. I toe off my boots, chewing on a dental strip as I tie back my hair and shrug out of my clothes, my sights set firmly on the bed. But before I can climb in and leave this wretched day behind, Jarvis pushes me an alert.

\<W1021\> ping \<W914\> We need to talk.

Jondi's message immediately sets me on edge.
Nothing good has ever come from that phrase.
And I've about reached my limit for bad.

\<W914\> ping \<W1021\> It's three in the morning. Can it wait?
\<W1021\> ping \<W914\> Let me in.

I guess that's a *no* then. A sigh and an oversized shirt later, I'm waving him through the door—though if he's here to check up on me then I'll be waving him right out again. I'm not some delicate flower who can't handle failure. No matter how public, or how hard I've worked to avoid it.

"I don't need a babysitter, J," I say as he sweeps into the room. "But a little sleep would be nice."

Jondi doesn't reply. He simply closes the space between us and kisses me.

"*The hell*—" I shove him back. "What do you think you're doing?" I doubt there's ever been a worse time to assume I'm in the mood for a hook-up, and even if I was, I'm perfectly capable of initiating it myself.

"I told you, we need to talk." He pulls me close again, as if this is some deranged mating game we're playing.

"That word doesn't mean what you think it means."

"Privately." He makes a show of kissing my neck, though his lips barely graze the skin. "Now kiss me back. This has to look convincing." There's an urgency to his voice that tells me he's serious. So I do as he asked, and as soon as I press my mouth to his he lifts me clean off the floor and walks us over to the bed.

This show we're putting on is not a difficult one to fake; Jondi's a good kisser, though it's hard to enjoy when my mind is spinning at a thousand miles an hour, wondering what we could possibly need privacy for at this time of night—other than what we're already doing.

"Okay, I think that's convincing enough." I reach for the privacy button beside my headboard. The lights on the cameras respond immediately, flashing twice before falling idle. For the next hour, security won't run surveillance on this room. While most of us are used to being watched by now, there are still some things we'd rather Syntex didn't commit to video, and our . . . *extra-curricular activities* pretty much top that list.

"You better have a damn good explanation for this." The second the cameras are off, I twist free of Jondi's arms. "Because I'm really not in the—"

"You're being decommissioned, Sil." His declaration stops me cold.

"*What*?"

"That's not even the worst part." He projects his ocular display forward. Seems Jondi indulged in a little rule-breaking himself tonight, seeing how I'm looking at a classified memo that's definitely not meant for our eyes. I'd scold him for being reckless enough to hack security, but the words I see sitting alongside *recommended for immediate decommissioning* instantly eclipse the urge.

"They're having me *arrested*?" I choke out. "For *failing a mission*?" That's not just overkill, it's downright nuclear. Missions fail all the time. And as much as publicly disobeying my orders wasn't a great look, I'm hardly the first Walker to gamble against their mandate and lose.

"That's not why," Jondi says. "Keep reading."

I follow the data down until I find it, trying to keep the letters from blurring as anger prickles my eyes. *Stealing proprietary IP.* The accusation crashes against something deep beneath my ribcage. Syntex thinks I've turned spy.

"J, I would never—"

"Please, you think I don't know that?" He brushes off my protest. "This has to be about those files you stole tonight. Nothing else fits."

"But I stole the files for *them*," I say. "They were my host's original mission; I only took screenshots in case I couldn't get her out. This is a mistake, it has to be."

"It's not a mistake." Jondi pulls up another document.

My official arrest warrant. Complete with the Director's sworn affidavit of my crime. And Christ-that-was, he's not just accusing me of stealing, but of orchestrating tonight's cyber-attack as well.

Miss Sarrah colluded with a hostile faction in order to distract from her true goal. If not for the swift actions of our security team, her theft of classified files from Lieutenant Neve Harper (deceased) would have likely gone unnoticed.

"No . . . that's not . . . it can't—" My hands fist in my hair, scraping angry trails into my scalp. "He *assigned* me that mission. You were there, you *saw* it." Hell, the entire room saw it. Miles even tried to—that's it! "Miles!" I lurch off the bed, the obvious solution forming. "He tried to stop the mission. If I just go and give him everything, he can fix this, J. *He'll fix it.*"

"I don't think he can, Sil." Jondi grabs my shoulders. "This order came straight from the Director. So either Miles didn't try to intervene, or he did and his father signed this warrant anyway. You have to run."

"*Run?*" Okay, now I'm sure he's lost it. "I can't *run*. Whatever this is, I'll get it straightened out."

"And if you can't?" Jondi's fingers bite deeper into my flesh. "You've got a year left on the clock, Sil, two if you're lucky. Do you really want to spend that time in a cage?" His face darkens, the ghost of his childhood looming near. Jondi didn't grow up in the hubs like I did; he had the distinct misfortune of being born on the wrong side of the Demarcation Line, where work camps are still legal and human rights aren't law. For him, death by catastrophic failure isn't the nightmare, bars on the windows and doors is.

"Jondi, I didn't do this," I say. "At worst, they'll make me sit a lie detector—which I'll pass with flying colors."

"But that's exactly the point." His voice climbs an octave. "Syntex has a dozen ways to tell if you're lying, so why would the Director jump straight to decommissioning? When has he ever done that?"

It's a good question, and one I have no answer for. Because Jondi's right: this is flat-out unprecedented. Even our field ops get the benefit of the doubt when they're suspected of turning double. But what bothers me more is that it doesn't make *sense*. I'm a multi-million-credit asset with a stellar record and at least another year of operational viability. The Director shouldn't be so willing to lock me away.

"You should have seen his face when you made a play for that server, Sil," Jondi continues. "He's hiding something, I'm sure of it, and now he's scapegoating you to cover it up. Think about it," he says as I begin to pace the room. "We both know that lie he spun won't hold past tomorrow. Once the Analog Army claims credit for their attack, it's game over, he's stuck fielding angry calls from investors unless—"

"He finds a patsy." I drop back down to the bed, the reality of my predicament ringing clear. An inside job may be embarrassing, but an outside hack is a major breach. And by disobeying orders so brazenly, I gave him the perfect excuse to pin this PR nightmare on me.

Fuck, this is bad. My plan to sway the disciplinary board suddenly feels laughably naïve. I don't think a picture and a hunch is going to cut it anymore. Not when the Director is hell-bent on turning my hearing into a trial. But if I'm here, at least I can defend myself; out in the sectors, I'd be on my own.

"No one you care about would blame you for running," Jondi says, as though sensing the objection bubbling in my throat: *won't running make me look guilty?* "And to hell with the rest, Sil. Your freedom is worth more than your reputation."

Is it, though? The thought is faint but persistent. Since I became a Walker, my reputation—my record—has defined me. It determines my pay, my perks, the bonus my family will get when I burn out. I've been Syntex's golden girl for so long now, I'm not sure I know how to be anything else.

"Where would I go?" The words are a betrayal on my tongue, every bit as damning and absolute as a confession. "I'm a human homing beacon, J. No matter how far I run, they'll find me."

Syntex doesn't take risks when it comes to protecting its assets. There's one GPS tracker in my arm, and another hardwired into my CIP. About the only place I could hide is a shielded bunker buried beneath ten feet of concrete, and even then, security would track me all the way there.

"Not necessarily." Jondi springs to his feet, dragging me up with him. "Is your backup still offline?"

"Yeah, why—?" I balk as I realize what he's suggesting.

It'll work, that's for sure. But it'll also mean going it alone. Without Jarvis.

CHAPTER 7

Jondi's escape plan is less a plan and more a colossally bad idea. Not only does it require us to cross the building unseen, it also involves breaking pretty much every law counter-espionage has a name for.

"Don't worry about the cameras, Lena's got us covered," he says, helping me stuff a handful of clothes into my bag. "As soon as we're ready, she'll use a virus to take them out. Lights and heat maps too. That should give us three minutes of dead air before the system reboots."

Three minutes. Just long enough to reach Lin's office if we run. Fast.

"And if Lena's *caught*?" I swat him with a sweatshirt. Jondi and I have already committed enough infractions to land ourselves in matching cells. The last thing I want is for Lena to join us there.

"No one is getting caught tonight." He flashes me his cockiest grin. "Trust me, security won't suspect a thing by the time I'm done with their servers."

I suppose that's as much reassurance as I can hope for. I don't love the idea of either of them risking their freedom for mine, but in the absence of good options, a bad one will have to do.

Once my bag is packed, I change into the most nondescript clothes I own: ribbed black leggings, black tank, and a form-fitting hoodie. It's training gear, but the neoplex fabric is engineered for maximum durability and to regulate my body temperature. My eyes I dull from their silver to a less conspicuous gray, though I

60

keep the ridiculous *hidden rainbow* hair seeing how it's *the* style of the moment. Unless I want to end up dead in some competitor's lab, I'm going to have to blend in with the Reggies, because if anyone discovers what I am . . . my stomach gives a painful lurch. There's a reason the Walker barracks are among the most secure in the building, and why we never leave this skyscraper without a protective detail attached: money. Specifically, the absurd amount a CIP would fetch on the black market. Out in the sectors, the only thing a Walker is good for is a king's ransom.

Which is why the final thing I grab is my gun. My box of family holoforms I leave tucked away in the closet. I tell myself I don't need to bring them since I won't be gone all that long. Only until I figure this mess out. And I *will* figure it out. I have to.

"You ready?" Jondi asks.

"Not even a little."

"Then here we go." He types one final command into his palm, a go signal for Lena, I assume, since a moment later, the lights around us flicker and die.

"Now!" Jondi grabs hold of my hand and we take off running.

With the virus live, the building lapses into silence, the hum from the cameras and the tungsten strips overhead fizzling down to naught. Had we attempted this lunacy during the day, the halls would be lined with a dozen curious faces, poking their heads out to see what's going on. But since everyone's asleep, our treachery goes unnoticed.

We barrel down the corridors, our boots hammering the tiles. The medical wing sits three floors above the barracks and we jump the stairs together, making short work of the climb. By the time we reach Lin's office, my breaths are coming hard and fast, my heart pounding its dismay against my ribcage. But we make it, stealing into the room a whisper before the lights bloom back into full blaze.

"Sil!" Lena throws her arms around me the instant I collapse into the door. "Christ-that-was, I can't believe this is happening."

She's squeezing me so tight I feel the pulse racing beneath her skin.

"I know. I really screwed things up, huh?" I hug her back just as tightly. I don't want to leave Lena. Not on day 6982, when she's so close to burning out.

"Like hell you did." Lena's voice roughens to a growl. "The Director should have never put you in that position—especially not in front of a crowd." She pulls back to look at me. Her short hair is still mussed and disheveled from sleep, her dimpled smile turned sour, the gold in her eyes rimmed with red. "I mean . . . *fuck*, Sil. You're not even opted in!" Lena's never been one for tears but her anger is thick with them now, made righteous with indignation.

No, I'm not. My own rage swells to match. Terminations aren't a prerequisite for joining the program; we get to decide if they're something we're willing to stomach for a—not insignificant—bump in pay.

But I've opted out every single time.

The Director had *no right* to assign this one to me.

"El, did you loop the camera feed in here?" Jondi's already tapping away at Lin's console, bringing the screens and the examination chair roaring to life.

"Yeah, we're set."

"Good." He looks back at me. "Then now we shut down your CIP." He says it so simply, like he's not about to fry the better part of my brain. Shorting my circuits won't just cost me Jarvis; I'll lose access to everything. My archives, my credits, my knowledge database, my mods, the files I stole from the black site; Jarvis controls it all. Without him, I won't even be able to use my palm pad since I don't have a wrist unit installed. I never saw the point of getting one.

"Sil, there's no other way," Jondi says when I hesitate. Running seemed like my only option when it was just the two of us in my room, an arrest warrant sitting heavy between us. Now, I'm not so sure. Or maybe I'm losing my nerve. It's easy to be brave when it's someone else's life hanging in the balance. Harder when you stand to lose more than just your stats.

"Do *you* think I should run?" I turn to ask Lena.

I want her to tell me no, that running is a mistake, that this nightmare will work itself out come morning. I want her to tell me to stay.

But of course, she doesn't.

I'm not that kind of lucky.

"We're going to fix this, Sil," she says, leading me over to the chair. "It won't be forever."

Well, none of us have forever, so it better not be. I lie back as the leather reclines into place, the metal paddles emerging from the headrest. I set my shoulders, trying to ignore the dread working through my body. There are no words to describe how much I hate this plan. This is a terrible, terrible plan.

"Ready?" Jondi asks.

I'm about to nod when a flash of panic grips me. "No, wait—" I lurch away from the sickening crackle of electricity.

"Sil—"

"Just . . . give me a second." We've been so preoccupied with getting me out of Syntex, we haven't spared a thought for what comes next, how I'll survive in the sectors. I've lived in this fully serviced building for so long, I've all but forgotten what it's like to get by without Syntex tending to my every need.

Food banks, public clinics, hygiene stations . . . I vaguely remember my family's trips to them all, a timeworn collection of sights and smells I can't quite shake no matter how blurred their outlines become. The storm bunkers are the only memory that's weathered the years intact, and that's because I *hated* them. Hated the mad dash to safety when the radiation alarms sounded. Hated being cooped up for hours inside an airtight box. Even now, the very thought of it makes my skin itch. If a storm hits before I figure this mess out, I don't know what I'd do; entry to the bunkers would require a scan of my ID chip, then I'd be well and truly made. What I do know is that for everything else, I'll need the credits I'm about to lose access to. And that's preventable.

"Jarvis, transfer half my savings to a burner account—something untraceable—then link it to my payment chip," I say. "The rest goes to Captain Jondi Garrett."

"Commencing transfer," Jarvis replies in his usual, helpful tone.

Damn, I'm going to miss him. And no, I don't care how pathetic that sounds. Jarvis is as much a part of me as Lena and Jondi.

"If anything happens to me, you get those credits to my family," I say, placing my head back between the paddles. The whole point of signing away my future was to ensure I could provide for theirs. I won't let one mistake rob them of that.

"Sil—"

"Just do it, J." *Do it before I change my mind.*

"I wouldn't. Not unless you mean to kill her." The shock of Lin's voice sends Jondi reeling back from the console. The three of us whip towards the door, staring slack-jawed at the doctor who has suddenly appeared, as if by magic.

"I receive an alert any time this room is in use," she tells us. "But I suppose you weren't to know that."

No, we weren't.

Obviously.

"May I ask what the three of you are doing?"

"We're not—" Lena starts.

"This isn't what it—" As does Jondi.

"Shorting out my CIP," I say, cutting them both off. Something tells me no lie will come close to matching the truth here, and I'd rather keep Lin asking questions in place of raising the alarm.

"For any particular reason?" She crosses her arms, fixing us a shrewd look.

So she doesn't know what the Director has planned for me then, or else she probably would have guessed.

Okay, good. I can work with that.

"To deactivate the tracker." I forward her the memos Jondi sent me, hoping they'll hold her attention while I edge towards my gun. Could I actually bring myself to shoot Lin? I'm not altogether sure. I've never killed anyone in my own body before. And I know that sounds like an arbitrary line, but somehow, it's not. When I'm on a mission, I do everything in my power to get my host out. That's my job.

This would be murder.

A necessary murder. I close in on my bag. If Lin alerts security, it won't just be me rotting in a cell.

"I see." Lin glances up from her tablet, freezing my hand mid-reach. "Jondi, Lena, you'd best get back to your rooms before arrest warrants are issued for you too," she says, pointing them towards the door. "In five minutes' time, I'll ask that you arrange for another blackout. I trust you can manage that?"

Their mouths drop open in unison, their legs staying glued to the spot.

"I assure you, Sil will be well taken care of." It's not a threat, but the way Lin says it hardly fills me with confidence, either. Still, I nod for them to do as she asked. No point security catching up with all three of us.

Jondi gives my hand a squeeze on his way out and Lena hugs me. I try to tell her something as she does, to make her swear she won't burn out before I'm back. But the words stick on my tongue, too fraught and loaded to say out loud. When she breaks away, her absence stings like an open wound.

And then they're gone, and I find myself alone with Lin, fingers inching towards my gun again.

"Relax, Sil. If I was going to report you, I'd have done it already," she says, unhooking a small device from its place on the wall. "Give me your arm."

I move as though on autopilot, so used to doing as she asks in this room.

Lin presses the device to the crease of my elbow and hits the button on the side.

"What are you—*ow!*" I hiss as something rips out of my skin, leaving behind a cut that reaches down to the bone.

"That solves the problem of your first tracker." She injects a batch of nanites into the wound. I flinch as the tiny critters get to work, breathing through the sickening sensation of my flesh knitting closed.

"I don't have time to extract the other, I'm afraid," Lin continues, "but there's a mod parlor in the Pleasure District you could try." She scribbles a name on the back of my hand. "Ask for Zell. If he can get it out, you'll be able to restart your CIP. Until then, get yourself a Personal Ear-In Aid from the kiosk across the street. It won't come close to the real thing, but it'll help you navigate the city. I assume you have a plan for leaving the building?"

"Erm . . . yeah, I—" The question cracks my voice in surprise. "I'll take the service elevator down to maintenance, then the fire exit out," I say, mentally running the route. "It's the only way to beat the cameras." And even at full pelt, it'll be a close race.

"I was afraid you'd say that." Lin sighs, reaching back into her drawers. "Tonight's attack triggered an internal lockdown. Access to the entry floors is currently limited to senior staff, so you'll be needing this." Without a flicker of hesitation, she places a scalpel down on the desk. "Your gun, too. Set to incapacitate instead of kill. Do you understand what I'm saying?" She holds her right palm up for me to see.

Oh.

My whole body shudders with the realization.

"Yes, I"—so very desperately want to say no—"yes."

"Good. Housekeeping won't check this room until dawn. That buys you a few hours. Now lie back and I'll take care of your CIP."

I hesitate, searching for the trick, the lie, the *distraction*. Maybe security is already on their way. Maybe this is just a ploy to keep me from doing something rash or violent. Maybe Lin'll stick a sedative in my neck the second I let my guard down and buy into the charade.

"Why are you helping me?" I ask, meeting her inexplicable

kindness with a glare. Lin's worked for Syntex since the Walker program first began—that's *eighteen years* of loyal service she's risking. It can't be for no reason.

"Because I know you didn't do this, Sil." She gives my arms a squeeze. "I've known you since the day you were recruited. You're no spy."

More than anything else tonight, those words make my throat burn. I couldn't say why her opinion of me matters so much, only that it does. Lin's the closest thing I've had to a parent since I joined Syntex—a sentiment that's entirely unfair to my actual parents, but true nonetheless. Once the tech is installed, they don't look at you the same anymore. Something changes deep behind their eyes.

"So you think I should run too?"

"I think you deserve better. You all do," Lin says with a sadness I don't expect. "Now lie back." She guides my shoulders down to the chair.

"I thought you said this would kill me."

"The way Jondi had it configured would have." She repositions the metal rods to sit lower on my temples and adjusts the settings on the console. "Go live what's left of your life, Sil," she says, slipping a rubber guard between my teeth. "With any luck, I'll never see you here again."

CHAPTER 8

The bustle of the Pleasure District almost distracts me from the deafening silence raging in my head, the cacophony of synthesized beats escaping the bars and mod parlors almost drowning out the memory of what it took to get here.

Almost.

Oh, who am I kidding? The ghost of Lin's blood clings to my hands no matter how hard I scrub at them, stubborn as a stain that refuses to dull. Her permission did little to ease the reality of my escape—even though she did the hard part for me, seizing hold of the gun when I couldn't press the trigger myself.

I'll be fine, Sil. Worry about you, she said.

So I did.

Once she was unconscious, I picked up the scalpel and cut the access chip from her palm, grateful that no one could see the shake in my fingers or the stomach acid soiling the tiles. I never appreciated how much the neural link dampens the more unpleasant parts of my job. How it insulates the horror.

How I'd miss the safety that comes with being a body away.

I never got to thank Lin, either, I realize as I approach the end of another neon-clad street. Not the way she deserved for taking such a massive risk.

"Turn left." My new Ear-In Aid pulls me back to the present. The vendor must have sold me the obnoxious kind because it's both too chipper and too chatty, following each instruction with what—I assume—some marketing exec deemed a 'fun fact'.

"Did you know that Sector One is home to six notable

districts?" it chirps at me now. "Among them, the Pleasure District boasts the largest number of bars, flesh workers, and body modification specialists in the United American State, all working to ensure you have a wonderful night!"

Fascinating. I roll my eyes, wanting nothing more than to rip the blasted thing out and silence it with my boot. But exiled to this maze of crowded alleyways and holographic signs, I can't really spare the help.

I don't know this city. Other than to visit my family, I rarely come out here at all. Few of us do. Leaving Syntex means having to pre-clear our destinations, and getting lumbered with a security team, and if you try to give that security team the slip so you can flirt your way through the bar in peace, it means a lecture from Miles and extra drills. Which kind of takes the fun out of a joyride around the island.

And Manhattan wasn't exactly a *joy* to ride in the first place.

It's smoggy, it's claustrophobic, it's loud, cursed with more lights and drug dens than open spaces or trees. It stinks too. Not just of garbage or grease-laden food, but of the decontamination spray the city releases after a radioactive storm, a sour blue mist that coats the sidewalks and never quite fades away.

"Did you know that the New York hub is the most densely populated of the five American cities?" the Ear-In offers.

Yes, I've noticed. I pull my hood down lower, dodging drunks and tweakers as I snake a path through the crowd. Ad boards scream at me as I walk, trying to convince me to install their apps, or buy their mods, or come drink away my problems while I gamble with their line of interest-free credit. And though the buildings in this part of the sector are squat, and brutish, and gray, they're disguised behind augmented facades that do a pretty convincing job from afar. The Annihilation may have turned the world ugly, but with the right veneer, even a slum can resemble an upper-class neighborhood. Albeit one that pixelates in a strong wind.

"Did you know that body modifications are more affordable in the United American State than anywhere else in the world?"

the Ear-In asks. "Thanks to the government's *Tech Forward* initiative, every citizen now qualifies for a free base unit and yearly upgrades! Why not visit a parlor today?"

That's the plan. I finally glimpse the right sign down an alley that manages to cram twice as many glowing LEDs per square inch as those around it, a feat I didn't think was possible, but there you go.

Sinsinnati. My whole body sighs at the name. Puns and alliteration appear to be the Pleasure District's MO. Cyber City, ModDen Paradise, TechTopia, Devil's Drill; the more reputable establishments hailing their practical products while their seedier counterparts emphasize their sins.

"Did you know that tech hesitancy rates are at an all-time low?" the Ear-In continues its spiel. "Over 60% of the population now has at least one sub-skin unit installed!"

"More like seventy-five," I mutter, making for Sinsinnati's door. Syntex has been working hard to raise that number, chipping away at the culture of myth and conspiracy that has always plagued the tech sector, one outreach program at a time. Before the Annihilation, the world was divided into two groups: the haves and the have-nots. Those who could afford the latest implants, and those left behind. Now we're the wants and the want-nots. Those who worship technology, and those who thoroughly distrust it.

In this sector, everyone I've passed has sported no less than three of the more common enhancements. Glow strips, hair changers, programmable tattoos, palm pads, wrist units . . . I've even seen a few gearheads donning them all.

But move away from the inner sectors and this insatiable appetite for technology wanes. I'm not only talking about the technophobic here, or anti-corporate factions like the Analog Army. I'm talking about cults dedicated to the eradication of technology *altogether*. And no, that's not hyperbolic.

Do these sects realize that without the tech, they'd die of every type of cancer in about five seconds flat . . . probably, but they seem to think a tech-free death is better than a tech-enhanced life. Only a few months ago, the military raided an apartment complex littered with charred corpses. The geniuses had tried to cleanse the nanites out of their blood using fire and, quite predictably, died in the process. I believe that's called Darwinism.

"You have arrived at your destination!" The Ear-In blasts my eardrums with a celebratory ring.

Son of a . . . I switch the infernal device off.

With a little luck, I won't have to switch it on again.

It's definitely no Jarvis.

Sinsinnati might resemble a hole from the outside, but once I step through the curtain of cascading lights—not at all tacky, by the way—the place transforms into a visual feast. It's truly an assault on the senses, a rainbow gone supernova inside an electrical sub-station then dosed with a bucket of psychedelic stims. Flashing displays crowd every inch of wall space, screaming about the latest mods the parlor has to offer, as well as the multitude of fantasies available for play in the holodeck levels—which include an impressive selection of barely clothed, not entirely human holoforms, and a new line of anthropomorphic sex bots as well.

Okay. I think I'm starting to understand the name.

I walk straight up to the front desk, checking to ensure my hair is hiding the power button behind my ear and the port at the nape of my neck. Lin may rate this . . . *establishment*, but I've never been one for blind trust. Whoever this Zell is, I want to size him up first. Though let's be honest, I'd probably throw my lot in with Syntex's biggest competitor if it meant getting Jarvis back. He's barely been gone an hour and I already *miss* him. Jondi and Lena too. They're the reason I have to take this risk.

I *have* to take it.

"I'm looking for Zell," I tell the man sitting behind the desk, a muscled brute dressed in tight leather and high-gloss PVC.

"And you are?" he asks, his voice as gruff and uninterested as his demeanor.

"A friend of Sandria Lin's," I say, unwilling to part with my own name. Not that it'd do him much good; Zell doesn't know me from Eve. Though if *Lin* means anything to this desk-warmer, he doesn't show it, he only taps out a message into the keypad in his palm.

"Go through." He waves me inside without specifying *where* I should go, and since I get the impression he wouldn't elaborate no matter how sweetly I ask, I don't bother.

So much for customer service.

Turns out, the neon floor lighting is far more helpful than some underpaid grunt, guiding me through the labyrinth of unmarked doors. The sickening buzz of bone drills leaks out of a few of them, moans of pain—and pleasure—escape from others, along with the bitter smell of cauterized flesh. It makes me appreciate Lin's ordered, *private* office all the more. I can't imagine subjecting myself to such invasive procedures in a place like this by choice. Though I suppose that's exactly what I'm about to do.

I follow the pulsing lights to a door that automatically slides open as I approach, the gentle pound of tech-metal floating out to greet me. *Guess this one's mine then.* I force my feet across the threshold. If only the Director could see his golden girl now. He'd try to have me arrested all over again.

"You're early, Diet-Mod," the man inside—Zell, I presume—says, keeping his back to me. "I wasn't expecting you for another hou—" The word cuts off abruptly as he turns around, jumping so far out of his skin his head almost hits the ceiling.

"Who the devil are you?" Zell is so painfully thin it's a wonder he doesn't slip through the cracks in the floor. His features bug out of his face as though spring-loaded, oversized in a way that lends him a gaunt, hollow look. He could be twenty or fifty, I honestly couldn't say. But the one thing that's blindingly obvious is that he's at least a part-time junkie. The eyes are a dead giveaway, his pupils blown wide, only a sliver of his irises rimming the edge. Nice to know the citizens of Sinsinnati are living up to the sin.

"Who were you expecting?" I hedge. Someone lighter on the tech than me, I'd venture, if the name *Diet-Mod* is anything to go by.

"No one." Zell scrubs a hand over his neck. "A friend."

Right, sure. A friend he happens to share with Syntex's in-house physician. That's not at all suspicious.

"Then that's who I am," I say. Whatever Lin and this guy are into is a question for another day. I can't risk spooking the one hope I have for getting Jarvis back.

"So what can I do for you, *friend*?" Zell's sizing me up too, searching for my connection to Lin even as I resolve to ignore his.

"I need help with a tracker," I say. Might as well get straight to the point.

"Ah." The tension leaves his shoulders in a rush, like air escaping a balloon. "Let me guess, overprotective boyfriend?"

"Actually, no." Why do men always assume everything revolves around them? "I need one removed."

"Ex-boyfriend then." Zell smirks. "Well, roll up your sleeve, I'll have that sucker out in no time."

He's already rooting around his drawers for an extractor when I break the bad news.

"It's not in my arm."

"Christ-that-was." Zell lets out a comedy-level sigh. "Don't tell me he talked you into getting it somewhere kinky, 'cause then removal becomes a pain and it'll cost you extra."

"What? *No.*" Gross. "And there is no *boyfriend.*"

"Where the devil is your tracker then?" Zell looks me up and down, as though trying to locate it through sheer force of will.

I take a breath, mentally weighing my options. I could still walk away from him, no harm, no foul, no heinous betrayal of company secrets. I don't have to cross this line.

Yes, you do.

Jarvis is the key to everything. Without him, I'll never figure out what the Director is hiding, or prove to Miles I haven't turned spy. I won't be able to mend my reputation, or make it back home to my friends. Hell, without Jarvis, I'm not sure I'll survive the sector. This tracker has to come out. Now. And besides, Zell's a junkie. No one would believe him if he decided to mouth off about the Walker who strolled into his parlor.

"Tracker's in my head." I take the leap, sweeping my hair to the side.

"Your *head*?" Zell's eyes bug out even further. "The hell possessed you to put it there? It's wicked painful, not to mention danger—" The protest dies on his tongue as he clocks the tech I've revealed. "Holy motherboard. You're a—no, you can't be," Zell says, but he's already crossed the room to examine the port at my neck. "By my mods. You are, aren't you? Bugger me purple, I have to tell—"

"No, no. We won't be telling anyone." I block his way to the door, flashing him the butt of my gun. I'd rather not hold a pistol to his head while he's busy poking around in mine, but I will if I have to. "There's a GPS tracker somewhere in my Cerebral Intelligence Processor. I can't reboot it until it's removed. Can you help me or not?"

Zell studies me for a long moment, unbridled hunger burning in his eyes. I'm every tech fanatic's wet dream and he's about as zealous as they come; I can tell by the sheer number of mods he's sporting. His irises change color with every blink, his hair cycling through animal prints like a digital safari. He's got *multiple* screens implanted in not one, but both wrists, as well as some heavy-duty ports that mark him as a bot racer. To a guy like this, a new toy is worth more than a few credits. Which isn't to say he wouldn't sell me out in a heartbeat, just that he wouldn't do it *yet*. He'd want to play with the hardware first.

"I don't suppose you know where they put it?" he finally asks.

I shake my head. If I did, then this would be easy.

"Do you at least have the unit schematics?"

Another firm no. Though I give him top marks for trying to get his hands on those.

"Then I'll need to take a scan."

Damn. I was so hoping he wouldn't say that. A scan of my brain would fetch millions, and give our competitors real insight into the miniaturization technology that makes our CIPs possible. That's the bit no one else has been able to crack.

"*One* scan," I say. "And you destroy it before I leave."

"*Destroy* it? Are you out of your—"

"Sorry, but I have to insist." I flash him the gun again. Classified IP is not leaving this parlor on my watch. My freedom is only worth so much.

"Will you at least let me look at it?" Zell sulks, puffing out his cheeks.

"I'll give you ten minutes. But with your ocular implants turned *off*. And, in return, there are a couple of extra mods I'll need your help with."

"Deal." Despite my ground rules, Zell's downright giddy as he guides me over to the chair in the center of the room. It's a similar model to the one in Lin's office, though the leather is worn and cracked in places, the metal teeming with rust. I don't want to think about the caliber of person who occupied it before me, or how thoroughly Zell might have cleaned up after them. *Assuming he cleaned up at all.* I shiver. Given the disordered state of this room, I wouldn't bet my life on it.

"But I have to warn you," Zell continues, placing a scanner at each of my temples, "if this tracker of yours is buried deep, I might do some damage getting it out. Without the schematics, can't guarantee I won't."

"Fine." Boy, this bright idea of mine sure gets better and better.

"Oh, and seeing as this sucker's probably beneath the bone, this is gonna hurt like the devil's screwing you himself."

"I don't care," I spit the words through my teeth. Because hell, doesn't it always?

CHAPTER 9

```
<Cerebral Intelligence Processor W914//ONLINE>
<. . .>
<W914__Request system diagnostic>
<. . .>
<Commencing system diagnostic>
<. . .>
<. . .>
<. . .>
<392 Errors logged>
<. . .>
<View main system log? Y/N>
<W914__Y>
<. . .>
<Data processors//ONLINE//Reporting damage>
<Working drives//ONLINE//Reporting damage>
<Archive drives//ONLINE//Reporting damage>
<Aesthetics suite//ONLINE//Reporting damage>
<Secondary power unit//OFFLINE>
<. . .>
<Overall system performance//68%>
<. . .>
<View full system log? Y/N>
<W914__N>
<W914__Exit diagnostic>
```

68% efficiency. Christ-that-was, Zell didn't just damage my CIP, he butchered it. And left me with the mother of all migraines to boot. I knock back my drink, holding the payment chip in my palm to the reader so that the automated bar-bot—which boasts a whopping choice of two liquors and chastises you for not ordering them fast enough—will pour me another.

The place I've dragged myself to is a graffiti-riddled dive with sticky floors and holo-hostesses that flicker in and out of existence as often as they smile, but it's a necessary evil since I'm feeling more than a little sorry for myself. Failed mission, dead agent, an almost arrest . . . I think it's fair to say I'm having a pretty bad night.

"Captain, your blood alcohol has risen above acceptable levels," Jarvis tells me.

At least I have him back now, and he does sound like his usual self—though he has informed me that some of my systems no longer work as well as they should. Naturally, that includes the processors he needs to analyze the documents I stole from the black site. He can still do it, but instead of taking hours, the exercise will take days. Days out here, alone. Away from Lena and Jondi and a proper repair to a CIP already nearing its end of life.

"Stop killing my buzz, Jarvis." I swallow another mouthful of vodka, wincing as the clear liquid burns down my throat. "You're my AI, not my dad." *Or my commanding officer.* And thank fuck for that, too. I shudder. The last thing I want is for Miles to see how far I've fallen. Barely three hours on the run and I've already let a junkie fiddle with my tech, then gotten drunk in some third-rate bar.

Talk about overachieving.

"No, Captain. Our being related is a biological impossibility," Jarvis confirms.

"Yes, quite."

"You say something, sweetheart?" the guy sitting two seats up from me asks.

Not to you, asshole. I reach for the knife I swiped off Zell's desk and scrape the blade across the metal bar top, flashing him my resting stab face until he turns back to his drink. I'll have to be more careful talking to Jarvis out here. Reggies aren't supposed to have invisible friends living inside their heads. First-gen CIPs were actually designed with this problem in mind; Syntex programmed them to follow thought commands as well as typed and verbal ones. A good idea in theory, but downright disastrous in real life. Turns out, computers aren't great at differentiating between true thoughts and thought spirals. Three accidental deaths later, that unpredictable function was scrubbed.

I'm halfway through my . . . fourth? Hell, maybe it's my fifth drink when Jarvis pushes me an alert.

"I'm too drunk for a mission, remember?" I mutter, downing the rest of the glass. *And definitely too on the run.*

"Yes, Captain, but my search of the facial recognition grid has yielded a match."

"Super." It takes me a second to fully process the words. "Wait, what search?"

"The search you requested on this image." A familiar face fills my display, all razor-sharp cheeks and mathematically perfect angles.

Christ-that-was. I snap straight in my seat, blinking away the stupor.

The pretty waiter.

With everything that's happened since a drone blew my record sky-high, I forgot about the Analog asshole who set this cluster of events in motion.

Ryder Stone.

Even his name annoys me.

As does the fact that it's the *only* thing about him Jarvis was able to find.

"Where did the hit come from?" I ask, the makings of an idea stirring beneath the drink. Ryder Stone is part of the Analog Army, a group that, despite its best efforts, Syntex has never managed to crack. This could be my way back into the company's good graces. A chance to prove I'm no traitor.

"The Low-Tech Lounge," Jarvis says, pushing me a map.

Unbelievable. I can't help but marvel at the glowing pin. After a night of apocalyptically bad luck, my ticket home just strolled into a bar across the street.

"Stay on him," I growl, already beelining for the door. I don't have much of a plan beyond: *find an angle to exploit*, but on my feet is where I do my best thinking and Ryder presents an opportunity I can't afford to miss. Now that the Analog Army has publicly declared itself a threat, any information I can glean about them will go a long way to demonstrating my loyalty. And if I happen to deliver the hacker responsible for tonight's attack at the same time, well, that should give the Director all the excuse he needs to rescind my arrest. An undercover operation, he could call it. Another top-line initiative for keeping the company's investments safe.

True to the map, the Low-Tech Lounge is only a short walk away, and like everything else in this district, it more than lives up to its name. No holo-hostesses, no bar-bots, no frills, just a scuffed stretch of bar and a lot of unsavory-looking people. Exactly the type of place I'd expect to find an anti-corporate stooge.

A generic techno beat pumps through the speakers, drowning out the sound of self-pity and despair.

But not the jeers.

I bristle at the flurry of crude epithets the drunks hurl my way, my hands itching for my gun. *Ignore them.* I keep my head up and tune out all talk of my . . . *assets* as I scan the room for my prey. And damn, the picture Lena snapped didn't do him justice.

In the flesh, Ryder Stone is the perfect mix of smooth lines and hard angles, bow-shaped lips and artfully tousled hair.

He's almost too *pretty.* As I slide onto the seat beside him, I catch a proper glimpse of the tattoo beneath his rolled-up sleeve. It's old school, not the programmable kind you can get in any mod parlor, but the type that's punched into the skin with a needle. It's also larger and more impressive than I first thought, the honeycomb pattern tessellating up past his elbow. Not the kind of ink you bleed for unless you're deep into the cause.

"I'm not interested in company." Ryder assumes the worst of me, his eyes staying glued to his drink.

"That's a shame." I drop my bag to the floor and make myself obnoxiously comfortable. "Because I can think of one company that would be very interested in you, *Ryder Stone*." I play my ace as my opening gambit, projecting the image of him out from the new screen Zell installed at my wrist. Charm offensives are Lena's forte, whereas I prefer to keep things mean. The harder the push, the bigger the win. And judging by the violent twitch in Ryder's jaw, the button I pushed won big.

He's wondering how he missed a camera.

Because if he missed one, then what else did he miss?

"Catering pays the bills." Ryder buries the panic behind a long sip of drink, his fingers drumming their displeasure against the sticky bar.

"Not when you bail out early." I pull up the footage of his escape. "Care to change your answer?"

"That depends who's asking." He finally turns to look at me.

Moment of truth. I stiffen. If Ryder saw me in the exhibition hall, it's game over. Not only will this drunken plan of mine fail, but I'll have outed myself to a bona fide hater of all things Junker.

Do not surrender control. Hardly takes a scientist to riddle out *that* part of the Analogs' manifesto. I guess they don't much care that the work we do ensures our citizens get the best life-enhancing tech—even when foreign governments don't feel like sharing it. Or maybe they're just afraid of us. No one wants to think they could wake up one day with someone else in control of their mind. A senseless fear, yes, but it's persistent. And it's made us the villains of the Syntex story. Poster children for tech-nology gone too far.

It doesn't help that we die young and come from predominantly poor backgrounds. To our families, our recruitment is a boon; they're offered credits, superior housing and education, a better life for their other children. Though from the outside it must look like a horror. Like selling your kid for a handful of silver. What the naysayers always overlook is that our parents don't make this decision. We do. And right now, I've decided to go all in on the hope that Ryder was too busy orchestrating his hack to peruse the merchandise.

"Consider me an ally," I say, getting ready to fight or fly.

But instead of recognition, his eyes flash with amusement, his head tilting curiously to one side. "My allies don't usually open with blackmail."

"These aren't for blackmail." I make a show of deleting the files from my wrist unit—though the originals stay safely stored on my CIP. "They're to prove a point."

"Which is?"

"You screwed up tonight."

"Is that so?" When Ryder smiles, his left cheek dimples, but not the right, a quirk that only adds to his impish charm. "And you know this how?" he asks, glancing down at some alert on his screen.

Rude.

I ignore the message light flashing on my own unit, choosing my next words carefully, to best command his attention. "You're not the only one who gate-crashed that party," I say. "But unlike you, I did my job *right*."

Bingo. His head snaps back up. Except this time, it feels as though he's looking at me through bionic eyes, seeing all the way down to my bones.

"Are you sure about that?" He smirks. Like he knows something I don't.

"I'm sure your poor excuse for a stunt didn't make the news boards."

"That's because they're a little . . . *preoccupied*." Ryder skulls the rest of his drink before leaning in to whisper, "So tell me, what exactly did you do to warrant a city-wide manhunt, Fugitive-at-Large Sil Sarrah?"

The shock of my name stops me cold.

"How did you—?"

"You should really check your alerts." His smirk widens to a grin. "Could be important."

And sure enough, the bulletin flashing on my screen proves critical with a giant red C.

My face. Sitting under the headline: *Wanted by Syntex Technologies.*

Shit. Shit. Shit. Housekeeping must have found Lin. My pulse quickens, the air in my lungs growing thick. The Director was kind enough not to betray much more than my name, but he's offering a reward for my capture. A pretty big one. Which is probably why my back is suddenly pressed flush against Ryder's chest, his knife digging into my throat.

"Motherf—"

His other hand clamps over my mouth, silencing the curse mid-stream. I guess even anti-corp anarchists will sell out their principles for a price. Well, sorry, but I'm not letting this opportunistic prick score a win without a fight. So I do the only thing I can with my gun out of reach and his blade kissing my neck: I bite down viciously hard on his fingers.

"Christ-that-was, would you cool it?" Ryder clutches me tighter. "I'm trying to help you. *Look.*"

I follow his gaze across the floor, where every drunk in the bar is staring daggers in our direction, having received the same alert. If they were looking at me with hunger before, they now look downright ravenous. But this time, it's not my *assets* they're lusting after; it's the bounty on my head.

"Play along, okay?" Ryder starts edging us towards the door, turning his knife on the mob. "Stay back. She's mine to bring in."

"Or maybe you're both *ours* to bring in." The closest man readies the bottle in his hand. "We all saw you getting cozy at the bar; I bet Syntex pays a few credits for you too." His lip quirks with greed and malice, the words drawing a fresh wave of taunts from the crowd.

"You'd best step off, kid." A second voice cleaves the air. "Leave the bitch to the grown-ups."

"Yeah, so . . . I don't think they're letting us go easy," Ryder mutters as the horde presses in around us.

"No kidding." I could have told him one knife would do nothing to dissuade two dozen bloodthirsty drunks armed with makeshift weapons. They don't see us as a threat; they see us as a payday. So if we want out of this mess, we're going to have to fight. "Just please tell me you're not a pacifist."

"Not tonight." Ryder loosens his grip.

"Then on my mark, you go left, I'll go right." My muscles coil in anticipation. "Wait for it . . . wait for it . . . *Now!*" I break free of his arms and throw a fist to the nearest thug's nose. A sharp jolt of pain shoots through my hand as it meets cartilage and bone. It's been a while since I fought anyone in my own body and I must admit, I've forgotten how hard faces are.

The guy I punched regains his balance and charges at me. I lurch to the side, sending him crashing into a table instead. A glass to the back of the head ensures he stays there.

"We need to get out of here!" I yell at Ryder, barely ducking the new set of knuckles hurtling towards my chin.

"Hey, if you have a plan, I'm all ears." A lucky kick brings the guy he's fighting to his knees. And I do mean *lucky*, seeing how he's one hundred percent brawn and no technique, already bleeding and short the knife he started with.

Amateur.

The obvious plan would be to leave him to the drunks while I battle my way free. But if I do that, I'm right back to square one: on the run and alone, with no clear path to proving my loyalty. So instead of giving Ryder the finger and pounding flesh to the door, I decide to use the brawl as an opportunity to impress. To show the Analog Army my value.

"Here's a plan"—I pummel another thug then tap out a command for Jarvis to hack the cameras and push the feeds to my ocular display—"try not to die 'til I get back." Before Ryder has the chance to argue, I throw myself into the tide of bodies, using the security feeds to guide my punches and carve a teeth-strewn trail back to my bag, where I foolishly left my gun. Turns out, copious amounts of vodka don't make for great decision-making. Shocker.

The moment I fire two rounds into the ceiling, the rabid mob hits the ground, all save for a few misguided heroes with more liquor in their blood than sense.

"Awfully big gun for such a little girl," hero number one—the bruiser I hit with a glass—says, wobbling a step towards me. "You even know how to aim that thing?" That's the true beauty of alcohol, I suppose. It makes you forget that you got your ass handed to you by the very person you're threatening all of two minutes ago.

"Let's find out." I put a round in his knee and he goes down screaming. "Now, would anyone else like to test my aim?" I train the gun on each of his friends in turn, sending them cowering to the ground, hands held in surrender.

"You ready to run?" I ask Ryder, pulling up my hood.

"No time like the present." He nods, sticking close as we hightail our way out of the bar and into a sprint, leaving our attackers to deal with the fallout of my trigger-happy finger.

"Holy shit." Ryder slows to a stop once we're a few streets clear of danger, safely hidden down an empty alley. "I can't believe you shot him."

"No point having a gun if you're too afraid to use it." I double over to catch my breath. I learned that lesson the hard way on my first mission out. A mission I damn near failed on account of my aversion to collateral damage. *The security guard is just doing his job*, a small voice in my mind had whispered. *He doesn't deserve to die*. Well, that security guard shook off the stun round early and raised the alarm while my host was still seventeen floors from freedom. She took two bullets to the side by the time I got her out. Almost died on the transport home.

You make that mistake exactly once.

"How'd you get that thing, anyway?" Ryder asks. "Live ammo weapons are impossible to buy."

"Not if you know the right people." I play it coy, leaving him to draw his own conclusions. Hopefully, his mind will jump to *has excellent criminal connections* rather than *grabbed it off her bedside table before fleeing the tech goliath she works for.*

"These 'right people' teach you how to fight, too?" He appraises my lack of injuries, having barely made it out of the bar with his face intact. His lip is split on one side, his hair matted with blood from a deep cut to his temple. Come morning, he'll be sporting at least one black eye, if not two. Yet, somehow— annoyingly—he utterly owns the look.

"Maybe." I shrug.

"But you're not planning to tell me who *they* are?"

"Nope." That's definitely a hard pass.

"Okay, then you at least have to tell me what you did to piss Syntex off," Ryder says, leaning into the wall. There's an air of nonchalance to his movements, a languid fluidity to the way he slouches against the soot-covered bricks and tucks his hands into his pockets, like he's already forgotten our violent game of evade the drunks.

"I stole something from them," I say. Because a pinch of truth will make the rest of my lies easier to swallow.

"Did you now?"

"You don't believe me?"

"I don't know you well enough to believe you. What I do know is that anyone smart enough to steal from Syntex wouldn't go bragging about it to strangers in bars."

So that's what this is then; he's testing me.

Good. That means he's interested.

"First of all, I wasn't *bragging*," I say, narrowing my eyes in threat. "And secondly, I knew exactly who I was *not* bragging to. I tracked you down because I think we both want the same thing."

That earns me another lazy smile. "And what would that be, Fugitive-at-Large Sil Sarrah?"

"Companies to stop commanding the kind of power Syntex has."

"You're quite the concerned citizen." The look Ryder fixes me could sublimate steel. He's not buying what I'm selling. Yet.

"Aren't you?" I hurl the question right back. "They're not military, but they act like it. They're not government, but they get to decide our laws all the same." I parrot some of his army's rhetoric for good measure. "Well, sorry, but that doesn't sit well with me. So I took something from them. Something I can use to bring them down."

"And exactly how are you planning to do that?" A trace of hunger creeps into his voice.

Time to lay the final piece of my trap.

"No idea." I shrug, leaving the *please won't you help me* door wide open for him to step through. Nothing guys like more than coming to the rescue of a damsel in distress.

And sure enough, Ryder takes the bait, hook, line, and sinker, pushing off the wall to say, "Then maybe we *can* help each other. I know a few people who feel the same way." He flashes me his tattoo, his offer ringing loud and clear. "So how about it, Fugitive-at-Large Sil Sarrah? Wanna make some new friends?"

Not really, no. But since Ryder's friends represent the best chance I have for getting back to *my* friends, I slip my gun back into my bag and say, "Let's go."

Ten years ago, Syntex recruited me. Today, I'm going to let the enemy do the same thing.

CHAPTER 10

I should have changed my face while I still had the chance, I think as we pass yet another building-sized rendering of it. Ryder was right; Syntex really has plastered my picture across every news board in the sector. The Director's up there too, urging anyone with information about my whereabouts to come forward. *Sil Sarrah is both armed and dangerous,* he declares, staring directly down the lens. *Our security team is doing everything it can to apprehend her before anyone else is hurt.*

Before anyone else is hurt. Guilt churns my stomach, clawing acid at my insides. I never meant for anyone to get hurt on my way out of the building, least of all Lin. But if not for her help— and her inexplicable connections—I'd be in a cell right now. Held at the mercy of a lie.

Whatever's in my head, the Director must want it *bad* to break with company protocol like this. As a rule, we don't air our dirty laundry in public. Though given how odd it was for him to issue an arrest warrant for me in the first place, I should have banked on something like this happening. I should have taken precautions. But instead of carving myself a new face the moment I got Jarvis back, I chose to go drink away my troubles. And now that I've gone all in on this Analog Army plan, it's too late. Bone changers are military-grade tech, not available to the Reggies. Using them in front of Ryder is a non-starter.

What I *can* do is change my hair to something less conspicuous than this *hidden rainbow,* seeing how the style just became too infamous to help me blend in. Except, when I type in the command, Jarvis informs me that my hair changers aren't responding. Because of course they're not. Why would this one tiny thing go my way?

So I keep the hair. And when Ryder suggests I might consider dulling it down, I tell him to mind his own business. To be perfectly honest, I half wish he'd keep pressing me so that I'd have good reason to snap and release this pressure building inside my chest.

It's not actually the hair I'm mad about; it's what the hair represents. I don't know if this malfunction is yet another twilight glitch, or a side effect of Zell's tinkering. I don't know how many days his butchery might have cost me, or how many I have left. In the space of one night, I've managed to set fire to everything important in my life: my reputation, my record, my *friends*, with no real hope for getting them back except a half-baked plan fuelled entirely by desperation. Now I'm about to walk into an organization that hates the very idea of me, and a growing part of my brain is screaming *why bother?* If after ten years of exemplary service, the Director can throw me to the bounty hunters on a whim, then why am I still twisting myself in knots to please him? Why keep risking my neck and my freedom when I could go spend my remaining days in a holopark, drowning my sorrows in stims?

And maybe I would do that if Jondi and Lena were here. If all three of us had run instead of just me. Lena would find us the best places to drink, game, and party, and Jondi would keep our exploits off the grid. And I'd—

You'd what, Sil? Even in fantasy the thought fails to complete.

Mindwalking is the only thing I've ever been good at—the only thing I'll ever *be* good at since the job came with an early retirement guarantee. I can't let this last mission end my career, and I sure as hell won't let it define my legacy. This plan might be reckless and ill-conceived but it is going to work.

It has to.

"So where exactly is this super-secret lair of yours?" I ask as we cross out of the Pleasure District and into the slums. The

Annihilation—and the war that followed—left our major capitals in pieces, and we've only managed to repair a fraction of the damage in the hundred years since. The result is a city that feels like a contradiction.

Outside the augmented districts, condemned buildings sit alongside rows of brutalist apartment blocks, built from brown brick and reinforced concrete, for function over style. A stark contrast to the monoliths of steel and glass that loom heavy in the distance.

As a kid, I used to run through the neighborhood in search of them. Funny how even a skyscraper can disappear at certain angles. From where my family lived, we couldn't see the Syntex building at all; the tenements around us were crammed in too close and too high. But then a few streets over, it would suddenly appear, standing proud and ominous, like an alien spaceship come to claim the land.

Every time I fall into a mood and wonder whether I made the right choice, joining the program, I need only look at how some of the city still lives to know that I did.

I did right by my family. Even if they'll now associate me with the word *traitor*.

"We're almost there," Ryder says, making another seemingly random left turn.

I realized he was taking evasive measures about twenty minutes ago, when Jarvis informed me we'd doubled back on ourselves for a second time. My guess is Ryder's trying to confuse me, so I won't remember the way to his army's hideout. Which is too bad, really, since I'm mapping our route.

Better luck next time, AA-hole.

While we walk, I have Jarvis push me everything Syntex has about the group, which, admittedly, is next to nothing. What little we do have doesn't tell me much beyond they're not really an *army* at all. They have no centralized leadership, no headquarters, no known hierarchy or initiation rights . . . just small cells acting in the name of the cause. Which strikes me as horribly inefficient.

"So can I ask you something?" I cinch my hood tighter, hugging my arms to my chest. This time of year, the morning chill borders on cruel.

"No one ever died trying." Ryder flashes me his teeth. Thanks to a couple of first-aid injectors, the bruises on his face are next to healed, though the smugness isn't something even nanites can fix.

Dick.

"Why keep the army fragmented?" I force my voice to stay pleasant. "Couldn't you make more of a splash if the cells came together?"

"Maybe we could." Ryder shrugs, veering us down a dark alley. "Or maybe we'd become everything we're fighting against. Size corrupts, Fugitive-at-Large Sil Sarrah," he says, as though it's the most obvious thing in the world. "Once you start naming leaders, you start assigning power, and before you know it, it's only the loudest voices in the room getting heard, or the most violent. And *those* voices tend to garner the wrong kind of attention. The kind that gets you arrested, dead, or blown the hell up."

"Okay . . ." I suppose that makes sense—if you're drunk and you squint a little. "But if you're trying to avoid attention, then why go so big now?" I ask. "Why hack their flagship gala?"

"Because, sometimes, big is what it takes to get the job done." The self-assured smile tells me that line has worked for him before.

Arrogant dick.

"Alright, this is it. Home sweet home." Before I can assault him with another question, Ryder pulls us to a stop outside what appears to be an abandoned building. Or at least a *properly* abandoned building, unlike the two neighboring concrete wrecks, which show clear signs of habitation. I run a quick scan of the interior. Nothing. No heat signatures, human or electric. So either it's shielded, or Ryder's leading me into a trap.

I'm desperate enough to follow him in either way.

The building proves an equally depressing dump on the inside. Peeling paint, water-damaged floors, semi-collapsed ceilings . . .

the whole place is one big health and safety violation. In a past life, it might have been a suite of offices, what with the ugly carpet tiles and the obnoxious strip lighting. Now it's a sad shell.

But not an empty shell, judging by the number of cables taped to the walls. They must be running some serious equipment in here, though how they're shielding this much power, I don't know. Better yet, how are they paying for it?

The room Ryder makes for is a tangled mess of screens, servers, and computer terminals, all arranged around a master console that dominates the center of the floor. It's an impressive set-up; best tech on the market plus a few extras the average consumer would be hard-pressed to find—including several Syntex ones. Not the kind of gear I expected the Analog Army to be running. I always pictured them as zealots, bootstrapping their hacks off second-rate tech while they plot to bring down the *Man*. Though I guess if they did that, they'd never get anything done.

Discreetly, I tap out a command for Jarvis to run another scan. Only two bodies hiding among the hardware. Not so many that I couldn't shoot my way free if things go bad. A small mercy, yes, but I'll take what I can get.

I keep to the shadows as Ryder heads towards heat signature number one, a petite, pixie-esque girl hunched over the central monitor. She's got a slim, delicate face, rich brown skin, and black hair with neon accents. Green ones, as though she cracked open a glow stick and dipped the ends inside.

"Good, you're back, we need a deciding vote." The pixie hurries him over with a snap.

"What are we voting on?" Ryder asks, hopping up to sit cross-legged on her desk.

"Whether to leak the hack." A second head pokes out from between the server stacks, belonging to a girl who can only be described as the very model of a modern anarchist. Blue hair, kohl-lined eyes, piercings wherever she could think to shove a needle, and a honeycomb tattoo to rival Ryder's, though hers is of the Fluid Ink variety, so it slowly builds and fades across her chest. "You know, since Syntex has gone and buried it—*like I told you they would.*" Blue Hair grins, as though amused by the prospect of losing credit for their attack. "So are you pro or con?" She asks the world's most redundant question.

Because, obviously, Ryder's pro.

"Con." His vote strikes me dumb. "I know we planned for it to hit the news boards, but it's better this way. All the payoff, none of the heat," he says. Which doesn't make a lick of sense since there is no *payoff* if no one ever hears about the breach. They'll have put a target on their backs for nothing.

"You're both cowards." The pixie's scowl grows teeth. "Some of my best work and no one will see it. Just because some idiot spy pulled focus."

"Speaking of that idiot spy." Ryder beckons me forward. "Fugitive-at-Large Sil Sarrah, meet Brin and Aja." He points first to Blue Hair, then to the neon-tipped pixie.

Their jaws drop in unison.

Seems they recognize my face too.

"Are you out of your mind?" Aja hisses. "What were you thinking, bringing her here?" She taps a command into her palm and every screen in the room goes blank.

I have to say, for self-proclaimed haters of consumer tech, their bodies are sporting a fair bit of it between them. Ryder's mods are sparse: a keypad in one hand and a small screen on his wrist. No aesthetic mods though. His eyes and hair don't have that tell-tale sheen that screams color changers. Both are a plain, dark brown. Not ochre, or honey, or any of those metallic shades we favor now. Just . . . brown. The kind the rest of us decided was too boring. But there's something nice about the simplicity of it, and the way it complements his bronzed skin. Something . . . *compelling.*

Aja and Brin, on the other hand, are the full-fat soda of mods to his diet. I daresay they've got more than I do; hell, Brin's even had defensive strips embedded in her arms and neck. It's been a while since I've seen shielding mods on someone outside the military. Running a live current an inch above your skin seems like a good idea in theory, but the civilian models weren't powerful enough to deter a determined mugger, nor were they insulated enough to protect their owner from getting zapped. Only masochists and paranoid freaks ended up not getting them removed, so this girl's either fifty shades of suspicious, or really into pain.

"I was thinking that if we have her, then Syntex doesn't," Ryder says. "And they obviously want her. *Bad.*"

"How do we even know she's good for anything but trouble?" Aja's eyes flash red. So she's got mood announcers too. Those were all the rage back when they first hit the market, though I've never understood why anyone would want to broadcast their every fleeting emotion to the world.

"Besides the ridiculous reward, you mean?" Ryder raises an eyebrow. "Come on, A, you know they wouldn't offer up that much unless she really pissed them off. She could be useful."

"How useful could she be if she got *caught*?"

I bite back a response, though it takes a herculean effort. The way they're talking about me like I'm not standing *right here* is beginning to grate on my nerves. And sure, it's petty, but I'm in a petty sort of mood, so using my new wrist unit, I hack into Aja's terminal. The firewall she's using is state of the art—for Reggies. She probably thinks it's bulletproof, but with Jarvis's help, the hack is so damn easy I have to slow myself down to avoid suspicion.

Once I'm in, I have him plant a hundred of the documents I stole on the hard drive. Innocuous ones, of course, duds he's already analyzed and discounted as fluff. Since the files came from a black site, nothing's stamped with a Syntex logo—or a logo of any kind—so I redact a few lines at random to give them the feel of company secrets. It should be enough to convince them I have something valuable to trade.

"The hell—" Aja whips around as I reactivate her screens. She starts frantically tapping at her keypad, which does her no good seeing how I've time-locked her out. The look on her face is the most satisfying thing I've seen all year.

"Shit, the network's under attack, someone's—"

To her credit, Aja works it out faster than I thought she would.

"You hacked my system?" The glare she gifts me spells violence.

"You wanted proof I was useful. Consider this a taste." I offer her my sweetest smile.

But what do you know; Aja doesn't have a sweet tooth.

"Oh, I'm so gonna enjoy beating the crap out of—"

"A—*stop*." Ryder grabs her arm before she can take a swing at me. "You need to see this." He directs her attention back to the screens.

"Holy crap." Her eyes widen as they study the files I planted. "Are these—"

"Classified company records." Brin lets out a long whistle. "No wonder they plastered your face across the sector. How many of these did you steal?"

"Around twelve million." I shrug. Like it's nothing. Then for good measure I add, "I'd have gotten more but your little stunt set cyber security on my tail."

"Then where's the rest of it?" Aja's mood announcers turn a hungry green.

"Somewhere safe." I stay deliberately vague. Not claiming credit for the gala attack can only mean one thing: the hack was a distraction, not the goal. A precursor to something bigger. Until I figure out what that is, I'm keeping my leverage to myself.

"Then what's to stop us turning you in and never hurting for credits again?" Aja asks, venom dripping off each word.

"Nothing, I suppose." The threat packs about as much bite as a kitten. I extract agents from the most secure places on earth for a living; I'm not afraid of some back-alley hacker with more attitude than sense. "Other than the fact that I just indexed the contents of your system and sent the directory to an off-site server."

"Bullshit, you did."

"Check if you don't believe me."

Aja's face pales as she does.

"So do what you want." I lean back against the wall and cross my ankles, affecting Ryder's air of nonchalance. "But if they get me, they get you too."

"Christ-that-was, Syntex isn't *getting* anyone." Ryder steps between us, arms held up like a shield. "Never learned to play well with others, did you?" He shakes his head at me. Hard to tell if he's actually pissed off or not. I get the sense that arrogant smile doesn't leave his face no matter what he's feeling.

"A, why don't you see about securing our systems a little better. Make sure we're untraceable." He fixes her a meaningful look, as though worried someone might suddenly try to glean their location. "As for you, Fugitive-at-Large Sil Sarrah, come with me, I'll give you the grand tour—before you wind up shooting someone else today."

"You *shot* someone?" both girls exclaim as he leads me over to the stairwell.

"He deserved it." I'm taking their shock as a personal win, though to their irritating toy-boy I say, "You know, just *Sil* is both easier *and* makes you sound like less of an ass."

"Sorry, but you don't get to pick your own nickname."

Not a nickname, asshole, just my name, I stifle the response, following him down the stairs. Arguing with his level of obnoxious probably works about as well as shouting into the wind.

Ryder's grand tour turns out to be a grand disappointment. The floor where the three of them sleep has been cleared of refuse, but that's about the kindest thing I can say for it. Graffiti covers every inch of cracked plaster; some new—like the giant honeycomb mural—but there are older tags too, ominous predictions from before the Annihilation. *The rapture is coming,* and *the end is nigh* are the more uplifting of the bunch. Back then, no one truly expected to survive the fallout.

Along the far wall, a row of offices act as bedrooms, with cardboard covering what remains of the glass doors, offering a modicum of privacy. The rest of the space is littered with much cruder, makeshift cubicles. Pretty sure I can guess which type of accommodation Ryder's about to offer me.

"This'll be you, for now." He points to the cubicle at the very center of the room, where they'll be able to watch my every move. "Bathrooms are off to the right. We're tapped into the water main, but not freezing is as good as it gets, I'm afraid. The nearest hygiene station is right down the block though, and I can find you a spare sleeping bag. Other than that, we're a no-frills operation."

"It's just the three of you here?" I ask, glancing around the floor. The offices are all visibly spoken for, but none of the other cubicles appear to be in use.

"It varies." Ryder shrugs. "We're loosely affiliated with a few other cells, so people come and go, but right now, it's just us."

So the cells *do* work together then; I file that piece of information away. Though it still doesn't make for much of an army. "And you really think three hackers stand a chance against the world's biggest tech company?"

"I mean . . . it only took *one* man to start the Annihilation . . ." Ryder flashes me another self-assured smile. He really does elevate smugness to an art form.

"That's a bit of a stretch," I say, though I suppose he's *technically* right. It may have taken all seven governments to burn the world to ash, but it was one man who dismantled the failsafes that kept our ancestors from blowing themselves to pieces. Never underestimate the power a single man can wield when the rest of us quit paying attention.

"Which is exactly why we need those documents you stole." Ryder leads me over to my new home, such as it is. "The more we have on them, the harder we can hit."

"Then you'd better find a way to convince me I can trust you," I say, tossing my bag inside.

"Hey, I brought you to my super-secret lair . . . I'd say that's deserving of a little trust."

"Sorry, but I risked my life getting these out. You want what I have, prove to me you're good for more than just a pointless stunt." I let the challenge hang between us, hinting after their endgame. If I can get him to betray that, then the Director will have to welcome me home with open arms. I could be back at Syntex by week's end. I might not even miss the Contracts Dinner.

"And what will you offer me in return, Fugitive-at-Large Sil Sarrah?" Ryder closes the space between us, locking his eyes with mine. That's when I see it. The full extent of his desperation. How far he'll go to destroy the company that saved the human race from extinction. It makes my next lie come so easily, I almost believe it myself.

"Everything you need to take them down."

CHAPTER 11

<W914> ping <W807> Happy 6983rd birthday! You better not be having too much fun without me—

<Delete message? Y/N>
<W914__Y>

<W914> ping <W807> You wouldn't believe where I am right now, El, or the dumb-ass thing I'm doing—

<Delete message? Y/N>
<W914__Y>

<W914> ping <W807> I miss your face.

<Delete message? Y/N>
<W914__Y>

I draft a hundred messages for Lena.

A hundred more for Jondi.

I delete them without pressing send.

Our communications are monitored at the best of times, and if Syntex is this desperate to get me back, I have to assume they're watching the two people who matter to me most. For all I know, my escape could have landed them in a heap of trouble—questioned for sure, or worse if the Director caught wind of Jondi's hack. I wish I had some way to see them, to know that they're

98

okay, but I can't risk implicating them any more than I already have. I can't even risk a message to Miles, though I've written a hundred of those as well. Apologies, mostly, replies to the dozen-odd messages he's sent me. *Come back to the barracks, Sil. I know you're scared, but I can protect you.*

Except, I don't think he can.

Not when his father is the one calling for my head.

Not until I have something better to offer him.

Though a day in, I'm still no closer to learning the Analog Army's endgame, their timeline, or much of anything, really, other than that the ceilings in this dump leak, and—that of the half-dozen empty cubicles he could have assigned me—Ryder's picked the one under the worst of it. I'm going to go ahead and say he did it on purpose.

Ass.

Another ice-cold droplet splatters against my forehead, bringing a curse to my lips. Even if I was waterproof enough to sleep through this indoor rain, the moans coming from Aja's room would have woken me up ten times over. Funny, I wouldn't have taken her for the night terrors type, but wherever her mind goes in sleep definitely sounds less than pleasant.

"No . . . please don't . . ." The pitch of her terror rises, her screams growing too loud to ignore. "Please . . . *don't kill—*"

"Jay-Jay?" The door to the neighboring office swings open, a bleary-eyed Brin emerging from inside. Judging by the practiced way she skips rooms and snaps Aja out of the dream, I'm guessing this has happened before.

So the angry pixie isn't made of steel then. As their voices drop to a whisper, I sneak out of my cubicle and tiptoe across the floor, activating the speech enhancers in my cochleas.

"It's okay," Brin mutters, more gently than I'd have imagined possible for a girl covered in defensive strips. "It's over. You're safe."

I press my face to the glass, peering through the gaps in the cardboard. Both girls look softer in sleep, the intimate way they're tangled hinting at a relationship that runs deeper than friendship.

Huh.

That only surprises me since neither seems the sort to let others in. Then again, Aja didn't strike me as a holo-sports fan, either, yet the walls to her office are lined with projections of those.

"They'll pay for what they took from us," Brin breathes into her hair. "I promise you, Jay-Jay, we will make them pay."

A sour taste fills my mouth, my heart stuttering out of rhythm. *Make them pay* screams *personal vendetta*, not *generalized grudge*. It screams of pain, and hate, and resolve. The kind that makes people dangerous.

"Hasn't anyone told you it's rude to spy?" Ryder's voice sends me reeling back from the glass. He's leaned against the door to his office, dressed in nothing but a pair of loose pants that sit low on his hips, showing off a perfectly cut stomach—to match his perfectly smug smirk.

"I wasn't *spying*." My cheeks flame red as I hightail it back to my cubicle. "I went to see what all the screaming was about."

"And did you learn anything interesting, Sil Sarrah?" he asks, strolling over to join me.

Yes, to be more careful next time. I bury the embarrassment behind a scowl. At least he's finally dropped the whole *Fugitive-at-Large* thing. That might make him more tolerable. Just.

"Only that Syntex stars in Aja's nightmares," I say, trying my luck. "I don't suppose you fancy telling me why?"

"Trust is earned, remember?" Ryder rests his elbows on the cubicle wall. "You ready to share those documents yet?" The honeycomb tattoo on his left arm extends all the way up to his shoulder, giving it a mechanical look. Shame the pattern stands for something so stupid, because wow, does it suit him. I've always liked tattoos—and the people they're usually attached to.

He's also got a series of dots and lines etched across his heart. Morse code, I think, though it's not so much a message as a name, and a date. Four years ago, Ryder lost someone important enough to immortalize in ink. Someone called Aiden.

"Nope," I say, more on principle than because I've found anything his merry band of hackers could abuse. So far, Jarvis has uncovered shipping manifests, personnel logs, financial records . . . nothing that would explain the Director's extreme reaction. Though whatever *was* being developed at that black site required an exorbitant amount of funding, enough that I'm starting to understand why the owner chose to blow the joint sky-high instead of letting Harper escape with their files. That much money either means technology that's life-changing, or life-ending. Either way, it's not the kind of research anyone wants to share.

"Then I guess we both like keeping secrets." With a lazy smile— and an amused glance at the puddle growing beside my pillow—Ryder wanders back to his office.

Argh. Infuriating ass.

I'm still very much awake when he creeps out again an hour later, easing the door shut behind him so as not to attract attention. Mine, I'm guessing, since I'm the only one here lacking in *trust.* Sadly for him, not only am I up, I'm dying for a distraction. I've been absently staring at the ceiling, asking myself the same questions over and over. *Whose life was Aja begging for in that nightmare? Why does she believe Syntex took it? And how did the company wrong Brin?* But with no obvious answers springing to mind—and my database search coming up empty—I'm glad for the interruption.

I feign sleep as Ryder steals across the floor, staying still and silent until he disappears into the stairwell. Only then do I inch out of my sleeping bag.

"Jarvis, give me eyes on the street," I whisper, lacing up my boots. "I want to see where he goes." The whole point of throwing my lot in with the Analog Army was to find out what this cell is up to. And if Ryder's deliberately trying to stop me knowing something, then I'd venture it's worth knowing.

By having Jarvis hop security feeds, I'm able to trail him at a safe distance. Ryder's careful as he crosses the sector; he sticks to shadowy streets and narrow lanes, keeping his head down and his tread long. Which suits me just fine seeing how I'm not looking to draw attention either. Problem is, that's about to become impossible, because if Jarvis's route projections hold true, then Ryder's headed straight for a checkpoint.

The hell are you doing, AA? I mentally weigh my options as he joins the crowd of shift workers shuffling towards the gate. Following him through the streets was one thing; the cameras in the slums are passive, they record without analyzing. But checkpoints are crawling with the expensive, active kind. Strolling through one would be like flashing Syntex a neon sign that says: *Here I am. Come and get me.*

"Jarvis, how long before I'm in range of facial recognition?" I ask.

"Approximately forty-five seconds, Captain."

Damn. Panic slows my stride as the spiked fences loom closer, the high-pitched whine of ID chips clearing the scanners setting my nerves alight. I'm about to turn back and call this game of follow-the-anarchist a bust when Ryder edges out of the crowd, ducking into the alleyway that runs alongside the complex. I'd call it a stroke of luck but the timing feels too convenient.

He knows he's got a tail.

"Are there eyes down there?" I ask Jarvis.

"Yes, Captain. Two cameras monitoring the staff entrance, though the feeds appear to be looped."

Impressive.

My estimation of Ryder rises an inch. He did that surprisingly quick.

"Can you access the original streams?"

"Yes, Captain."

"Then push them to my ocular display," I say, leaving nothing to chance. I can't have Ryder getting the upper hand.

I spot the moment he decides to confront his shadow, both on the camera feeds and in the way his body tenses, coiling for the fight. He eases to a stop, discreetly fishing a knife out of his pocket.

Sorry, AA, but that won't do you much good.

Not when I can see it coming.

Ryder waits until I'm right behind him to make his move, spinning around with all the grace of a drunk ballerina. I duck clear of the attack, snatching the blade from between his fingers as I shove him up against the blackened bricks and pin him there with an artfully placed knee.

"Christ-that-was." His eyes widen at the sight of me. "How fast are your reflexes?"

"Faster than yours," I say. Which, let's face it, is all that matters.

"You followed me?"

"You weren't kind enough to extend me an invitation."

"I can't imagine why." Ryder glances down at the knife I'm holding to his throat, trying to play it off with a smile, though there's no hiding the way his Adam's apple quivers beneath the metal. "Mind if we continue this as friends?"

"Friends don't let friends illegally cross checkpoints." I push away from him, handing the weapon back by the hilt.

"What makes you think I don't have a sector pass?"

That honeycomb tattoo. The brazen attack on the gala. His willingness to harbor the most wanted fugitive in the city. No way this guy's record is clean enough to score a sector pass.

"Call it an educated guess."

"Why do I get the feeling you make a lot of those?"

"Why do I get the feeling you'd rather I didn't?"

That earns me another smile, though Ryder's heart isn't in this one. His eyes flick up to the cameras then back towards the screen at his wrist, his brow furrowing. Whatever hack he used to loop the feeds must be about to expire.

Good. I can work with that.

"I want in," I tell him.

"You don't even know where I'm going."

I know he's willing to break the law to get there. That's reason enough.

"Well, consider this your chance to impress me," I say. Then when he hesitates, I add, "Trust is earned, remember? So *earn* some."

"Okay, fine." With another harried glance at the cameras, Ryder relents. "But put this on—" He unhooks the projection chip he'd stuck at his hairline. "You're more likely to get recognized than I am. And you have to play nice, Sil Sarrah." He fixes me a sharp look. "I'd rather not end up in a cell today."

"I can manage that." I place the chip below my bangs and activate it. "But you do realize facial filters won't beat a scan, right?" I say as a light mist sprays across my skin, applying a thin layer of holographic film to my nose, chin, and cheeks. Street-level appearance tech isn't sophisticated enough to game the facial recognition matrix, though it does a pretty decent job of tricking the naked eye, making you look more like your chosen holo-soap character than yourself.

"Then it's a good thing we don't need them to." Ryder types something into his palm and a moment later, the door labeled *Authorized personnel only* swings open.

Well, I'll be.

This Analog cell has a sector guard in their pocket.

They're proving even more resourceful than I first thought.

"Get inside, quickly." The man—Jimmy, according to his security tag—waves us into the locker room. Judging by the size of his pupils and the dull tinge to his skin, he's either hungover, or coming down off something. His hair is thinning and peppered with gray, his chin covered in a gruff layer of stubble. Not gonna lie, he's precisely the kind of guard I'd picture taking bribes from unsavory factions, right down to the stale scent of whiskey wafting off his skin.

"The deal was for one crossing." Jimmy looks me up and down. It's dark enough in the room, and my face is hidden enough, that I doubt he'll recognize me—especially through the facial filters—but I drop my eyes to the floor just the same. No point pushing my luck until it breaks.

"Deal's changed," Ryder tells him, slipping a nanodot out of his pocket. "If you want the app, it has to be both of us. In and out."

And it seems Jimmy wants it real bad because instead of arguing, he snatches the dot from Ryder's hand and says, "This had better fucking work."

"It will—once I send you the decryption key. But you don't get that until we cross back safely."

"That is *not* what we agreed."

"Take it or leave it." Ryder holds his ground like a pro. "I can't have you getting cold feet while we're still on the wrong side of that gate."

Jimmy's face puckers, the angry vein in his forehead growing fit to burst. But then with a huff that sends spittle spewing from between his lips, he whips open a locker and tosses Ryder a uniform. "Put this on. Then put these on her." He slams a pair of electric cuffs down to the bench.

"Like hell he will," I say.

"He will if you want to make it out of here. This isn't your pimp's basement, sweetheart, you can't just waltz on through."

I'm about to tell Jimmy exactly where he can shove his cuffs when Ryder pulls me aside and whispers, "You promised to play nice, remember? *Please.* I don't have a plan B here."

"Fine." Against my better judgment, I hold out my wrists. I do owe him this, I suppose. He never meant to bring me along on this little adventure, and he's taking a massive risk in an effort to win my trust. "But if these don't come off on the other side, I will kill you," I say.

"I'd expect nothing less." The tension eases from his shoulders as the cuffs click shut with a sickening snap.

"Hurry it up," Jimmy barks, then as soon as Ryder's dressed, he leads us out of the locker room. To anyone monitoring the cameras, nothing about this picture would look wrong. Just two guards escorting a prisoner through the complex. A decent ploy so long as no one decides to look too close.

And much to my relief, no one does.

"My shift ends in six hours." Jimmy pries open the fire escape at the opposite end of the building. "If you're not back by then, you're on your own." He spares us one final glance before slamming the door shut in our faces.

Real nice guy, that Jimmy.

"You feel like telling me what's on that dot?" I ask as we steal away from the checkpoint. Whatever it is must be all kinds of valuable, seeing how smuggling us across sector lines isn't just a sackable offense, it could land Jimmy in real trouble.

"Would you actually stop asking if I didn't?" Now that the danger is behind us, Ryder's smile has returned to its full strength.

"Probably not." I offer him one back. *Guys prefer a smile to a beat-down, Sil,* Lena once told me; back when I decided to get good at something other than Mindwalking. And while I've personally always preferred the ones who don't, I should try to put some points on the board.

"It's code," Ryder starts, consulting the map on his screen. "See, Jimmy's got himself into a bit of a hole, gambling with credits he doesn't have. So we made a deal. He gets me into Sector Two in exchange for an app which pilfers credits from nearby payment chips. Tiny amounts, mind you, nothing noticeable." He steers us off the main strip, to a quieter street with fewer cameras. "But given the kind of traffic that moves through this complex, he should have enough to pay off the sharks within a week."

Well, that answers a question I didn't ask: where this AA cell gets its funding. No way they develop an app this useful without exploiting it themselves.

"So you're helping him steal."

"Steal is such an ugly word." Ryder's teeth flash brighter than the dawn. "I prefer to think of it as enabling a small evil in order to prevent a larger one." Another turn leads us past a long line of densely packed apartment blocks, towards the MagTrain station looming overhead.

"Aja's the one who wrote the app, I take it?"

"Best programmer this side of the corporate sphere," Ryder says.

Yeah, no kidding; she'd have to be to pull off this kind of scam. We're talking multiple hacks of the payment chip system, not to mention some pretty inventive siphoning code. If Aja's capable of that, then she's definitely someone Syntex would want to keep an eye on. Hell, they'd probably offer her a job.

"And Brin?" I ask as we slip through the turnstiles. Might as well get as much as I can from him while he's still feeling chatty. "Is she a hacker too?"

"When she needs to be." Ryder takes the stairs to the platform at a lazy run. "But Brin's real specialty is getting into places."

"Then why didn't you send *her* to hack the gala?" I risk the more pointed question.

"Because even Brin can't be in two places at once," is all Ryder says to that, and since I get the impression that's all he will say, I let it go.

"Are you at least planning to tell me where we're headed?" I ask, moving the conversation back to safer ground.

"Where would the fun in that be, Sil Sarrah?" He pulls me into a half-empty carriage. "You wanted on this train, so sit back and enjoy the ride."

CHAPTER 12

The fucking Games District.

That's why we risked our necks crossing a checkpoint, so that Ryder could play . . . Christ-that-was, I don't even know what this idiot's playing at, but the only evil he can *prevent* from here is keeping some twelve-year-old from breaking his high scores.

With a screech and a gust of air, the MagTrain speeds away from the platform, leaving us stranded among the LEDs and life-sized VR displays. There are more ad boards in the Games District than the rest of the city combined, and they're all currently trying to tempt us in with a different offering. Light cycles, war simulators, relationship packages, kill fantasies, pre-Annihilation tours . . . you name it, they've monetized it, then rendered it out in dazzling 3D.

"Plenty of perfectly good holoparks in our sector, you know," I say as Ryder makes for the most decrepit arcade in a line of twenty, a place called Valholo that's definitely seen better days. A virtual Viking ship teeters precariously over the entrance, filling the air with the sound of oars gliding through pixelated water. The illusion would have been state of the art ten years ago; now it just looks like the cheap knock-off the neighboring parks cast aside.

"Not like this one," Ryder says, walking through the holo-horde of Vikings that rush us as we near the door.

Exactly like this one, actually. I bite back the response. *Only cleaner and with newer games.*

Like most holoparks, the inside of Valholo resembles a black sheet of graph paper. The games floor is segmented like a grid, neon strips marking the boundaries of each individual station. One person per meter-wide square, an immersion chip stuck to their temple and a second-sight visor covering their eyes. The more upmarket establishments have long since gone wireless, but this place still relies on cables that snake down from the ceiling, hardwiring the players into the park's central illusion matrix.

"So I'm guessing you like the . . . shooters?" Ryder asks as we approach the sales screen. "Something with a nice gun?"

"Funny." I resist the urge to cock him with mine. "And no. I prefer puzzles," I say, saving myself a lie. Jondi's the one who likes shooters, since he's got an exceptional knack for trash-talk and better aim in VR than real life. But I already do enough shooting on the job. When I make time to play, I like the peace of something quiet. Something with a problem I can solve.

Unless I'm playing with Lena. A sharp ache of longing pierces through my chest. Then it's always a street racer because *it's the only time I ever beat you, Golden Girl.* And since it makes her happy, I don't mind getting beat.

"Then maybe you can help me finish Minesweeper," Ryder says, flicking through Valholo's vast selection of games. "I've been blowing myself up on the last level for weeks."

"You play *Minesweeper*?" The ache fast turns to surprise. Not because it's some niche game—I've played it myself, and the last level is most definitely rigged—but because the information doesn't quite fit. Everything about Ryder feels as though it's set to overdrive, constantly spinning at full speed. I can't imagine him slowing down to enjoy a brainteaser. Or at all, to be honest. It's kind of hard to see beyond the manifesto and the ink.

"Don't look so shocked, Sil Sarrah." Of course he has to go and ruin it with a grin.

"Just please tell me we're not actually here to play *videogames*," I hiss as he pays for a joint session—a landscape tour, of all things. He doesn't even pick something good.

"What else would we do at a holopark?" Ryder asks, a

challenge in his eyes, as though daring me to turn back now, before I learn the true answer. And there has to be a different answer here. There *has* to be. I mean, sure, Ryder's got some pretty inane tendencies, but he doesn't strike me as the kind of stupid who'd skip sectors for a mediocre high.

We make our way to our assigned squares, weaving through the ordered lines of holo-heads already getting their fix. They all stand stock-still, the game taking place entirely inside their minds. Without the second-sight visors, it looks like something out of a horrorform. Like a bunch of brain-dead zombies being sucked dry by the grid. But once I slip my visor on, the whole room bursts into fits of light and color, offering me a glimpse of the races they're running, or the alien scourge they're fighting at the galaxy's edge.

"Don't bother customizing an avatar," Ryder says as he sticks the immersion chip to his temple. "Where we're going, it's true-skins only."

"Since when are landscape tours *true-skin only*?" I flash him my favorite scowl. That function is reserved for virtual meet-ups. So that average Joe with the bad teeth and the hygiene problem can't trick you into thinking he's pretty.

"Call it a one-time special." Ryder activates the illusion, instantly becoming lost to some faraway dream.

I sure do know how to pick them. With a sigh, I plug my own chip into the matrix then press it against my skin. "Jarvis, record this colossal waste of time for me, would you?" I say, just in case I trip and stumble into something useful. Then as soon as he confirms that he's piggybacking the feed, I hit *immerse* and join Ryder in the game.

Much like initiating a neural link, phasing into VR is a seamless experience. One second, I'm standing with my fellow pixel junkies in Valholo, then the next, I'm with Ryder at Niagara Falls, at one of the observation decks tourists used to frequent before the bombs reduced the seventh wonder of the world to a crater.

The roar of the waves hits me first, closely followed by the spray coming off the water, and the sharp bite of the wind. I crane my neck for a better look, marveling at the rainbow rising out of the swirling mists. It might not be the genuine article, but it's pretty damn close. Landscape tours are such tried and tested technology, even a second-rate establishment like this can't screw them up.

"Let's go, Sil Sarrah. We're not here to enjoy the view." Ryder hops the guardrail.

"The hell are you doing?" My breath catches as he lands in the overgrown grass on the other side. The bank is maybe half a foot wide. Tops. A couple of steps in the wrong direction will send him tumbling over the edge.

Not that it would kill him—VR-induced deaths are beyond rare—at worst, he'll jolt out of the game with enough adrenaline in his blood to floor an elephant. But since these experiences are designed to mimic real life in every possible way, falling into a rock-filled whirlpool as powerful as this one wouldn't just suck, it would Suck with a capital S.

"It's called taking a leap of faith," Ryder says. "You coming?"

"Into the waterfall?" I raise an eyebrow. "No. Not until you tell me why." I'm not putting my mind through hell unless I'm sure there's a prize at the end.

"Because we're learning to trust each other, remember?" He meets me glare for glare. "So trust I have a good reason for doing this."

"Other than just hazing me, you mean?" I—grudgingly—accept the hand he offers. The stubborn part of my brain wants to slap it away, because I'm perfectly capable of scaling a guard-rail on my own, thank you very much. But the reasonable part decides to take it, letting Ryder help me over to the grass. I'm supposed to be playing nice, after all.

"I would never dream of *just* hazing you, Sil Sarrah." His eyes dance with amusement. "Now come on, we can't be late."

Yes, we wouldn't want to keep those rocks at the bottom waiting.

"I'm not gonna chicken out, you know," I say when his fingers seek mine again, pulling me close to his side as we turn to face the ledge.

"I'm not doubting your resolve." Even staring down a dizzying drop, Ryder's smiling. "But we need to clear the door together."

Then before I get the chance to ask, *what door?* he launches us into the void.

It only takes 3.2 seconds for two people to fall 167 feet.

Barely enough time to scream.

We hit the water with enough force to drive the air clean from my lungs, plunging into the frosty depths like a speeding bullet. And though the rocks I'm expecting to smash against are nowhere to be found, the current is punishing, pounding us from all sides. Ryder's hand tightens on mine, keeping me from trying to kick my way back to the surface. *Trust I have a good reason for doing this.* I will myself to relax. To remember that the pain screaming through my body only *feels* real. That if Ryder's messing with me, I can break his nose the moment our brains recognize it's game over and spit us out of VR.

But instead of landing back in Valholo with my heart bursting through my chest, he drags me into a dark spot in the game, and then I land on top of him, in some kind of . . . underground bunker? I think . . . coughing up the contents of Lake Ontario.

"That never gets any more pleasant." Ryder groans beneath me, his pulse racing every bit as fast as mine. "You alright?" He reaches up to sweep the wet hair off my face.

"Fine." I'm quick to push away from him, climbing back to my feet. The room we've landed in looks as though it was crudely carved right into the rock, yet, somehow, it's entirely devoid of texture; lit, despite having no light source. Like it was coded in a hurry. When I run my fingers along the stone, they meet nothing but solid air. No sensory feedback.

Son of a . . . I suddenly know exactly where we are. "This is the dark web."

The holy grail of the digital world. A series of underground chat rooms and bazaars so secret, they can only be accessed through purpose-built—and damn near untraceable—portals. That's what Ryder meant by *door.*

Christ-that-was, I've hit the espionage jackpot with this guy. The Analog Army's way into the criminal underworld is the kind of information Syntex would kill for.

"Not bad, Sil Sarrah. You worked that out faster than most," Ryder says, and it warms me to hear a note of admiration in his voice. It shouldn't, but it does. I can't help it. The urge to excel is coded in my DNA.

"Well, now that I have, will you finally tell me what we're here for?" I ask.

"It's not a what, it's a *who*." He motions for me to follow him out of the room, into an equally textureless corridor that stretches endlessly in both directions. "A few weeks ago, one of our sister cells arranged sanctuary for a woman they think can confirm a theory of mine. It's taken me this long to convince her to talk." We cast no shadow as he leads me past door after nondescript door.

"So we're off to meet a what . . . criminal mastermind? Fugitive? Hacker?" *Conspiracist, terrorist, paranoid wackjob . . .* I keep those less polite guesses in my head. But who else would go to such lengths to avoid meeting in the open? Or insist on true-skin technology?

"Actually, she's a cognitive engineer." Ryder pulls to a stop in front of a door marked MLS-DDT—the same serial flashing on his wrist. "Or, at least, she used to be. At Glindell Technologies."

That instantly piques my attention.

Since the Annihilation, only three other companies have come close to matching Syntex's innovation and clout: Glindell, Cytron, and Excelsis. Of those, Glindell is the most frequent target for our domestic raids. As the only other name in neural interfaces, beating their products to market is how we stay ahead.

"She's also got admin privileges over this chat room, so no antagonizing her, please," Ryder adds, giving me a dark look. "If we get booted out, there's no way back in."

"Don't worry, I'll behave," I assure him. At this point, it's in my best interest to. Ryder's lips have finally loosened and Jarvis is recording every word he says—and *will* say to one of our corporate rivals. I don't want to cut this excursion short any more than he does.

"Marlea?" He raps his knuckles against the metal. "Marlea, it's Ryder. Open up."

Footsteps echo from inside, and the unmistakable sound of a shotgun being cocked. The virtual manifestation of Marlea's admin privileges, I assume. Seems the goal of this game is much like any other: try not to get shot.

"Move away from the door." Her command packs far more authority than your average scientist.

We both step back, raising our arms as the viewing panel slides open.

"Who's that with you?" A pair of narrowed eyes fix on me through the gap.

"A friend," Ryder says. "I don't visit the dark web alone." The lie rolls off his tongue so smoothly I almost believe him myself.

Marlea, on the other hand, is having none of his crap.

"Please." He catches the edge of the panel before she can slam it shut. "What you know could change everything—it could bring Syntex down."

For a long moment, it appears his plea will go unanswered. Marlea stands firm inside her encrypted coffin, tapping her shotgun nervously against the wall. But then with a sharp release of air, her scowl softens and she beckons us into the chat.

"You stay on that side or I'll blow you out of the session, understand?" The barrel finds each of us in turn, tracing our movements as we fold down to the ground.

"Thank you for agreeing to meet me," Ryder says once Marlea's followed suit. "I know it wasn't an easy decision."

"Just ask your questions." She balances the shotgun across her knees. "I don't like being online."

"Of course. I'm sorry. We just want to hear what happened to you."

And it's beyond clear that *something* happened to this woman. She's entirely free of tech, though she didn't use to be. There are scars on her wrists and palms from where units once lived. Nasty ones. As though the hardware was removed in a hurry, by someone lacking in skill. They look a couple of months old, tops, so whatever drove Marlea to this happened recently enough that the wounds have not yet healed, which means she never sought treatment for them. I'd also bet my life she hasn't eaten a proper meal in weeks and hasn't slept in longer still. Her eyes have the same haunted look I've seen on Walkers nearing their nineteenth birthday. As though she already knows she's dead. As though she's just waiting for the reaper to come calling.

"Why are you so interested in this?" Marlea's voice fills with anger, the type you cloak yourself with when you're afraid. "No one else believes me, let alone cares."

"Because you're not the first person I've met who's been mindjacked," Ryder says.

Well, now we're both staring at him.

Mindjacking? That's what we illegally crossed a checkpoint for? A paranoid myth?

"But you're the first solid lead I've found in almost two years," Ryder continues. "I need to know what you remember."

Something behind Marlea's expression cracks, her tough mask crumbling with relief. Whether it's Ryder's heartfelt sincerity that swayed her or just feeling heard, I don't know, but little by little, the makings of a smile tug at her lips and she says, "Then it's lucky for you I remember everything."

CHAPTER 13

"I couldn't sleep that night."

Marlea's story starts exactly the way I expect. Though Syntex has tried to keep the logistics of Mindwalking quiet, over time, details got out, as details are wont to do. And *this* particular detail is pretty common knowledge: it's a thousand times easier to Meld with a conscious mind than it is to coax your way into a sleeping one. Ever tried talking a non-lucid brain into taking your request for control seriously? Well, I have, and trust me, it's no picnic.

But even if this *mindjacker* did find a way around the consent laws, they'd still have to get their host *up*. REM sleep runs deeper than you think, and shaking someone awake from the inside is like trying to catch a bullet with your teeth. So it's little wonder Marlea is claiming to have been awake; otherwise, her story would hold no weight at all.

"I had a big concept demo the next day," she continues, "for a new type of neural processor that was going to put my name on the map. That's why I was still awake at 3 a.m. That's what made it so easy for him."

"You're sure it was a *him*?" Ryder's voice is as soft as I've ever heard it.

"Yes, I'm sure," Marlea snaps. "I won't forget his voice as long as I live, or how it felt when he—" She forces in a ragged breath, the wetness in her eyes spilling over. "I could feel him in there . . . digging around. He had total control, like he'd trapped me behind an invisible wall and no matter how hard I clawed at it, I couldn't break free."

Though I *know* what she's describing is impossible, something about the words splinters my resolve. *I can feel you . . . digging around in there.* Cole Risler said that exact same thing to me the night he came to my room nursing a grudge and a gun, long after I'd left him to his own mind.

"What did he have you do?" Ryder asks. "Once he seized control?"

"Steal something, of course," Marlea says, picking at a mangled scab on her arm. "Isn't that what Junkers were designed to do?"

Yes, so engineers like you can breathe the air and drink the water. I bristle. Not a one of these conspiracy nuts would have lived to see their first birthday without Syntex technology, and if they think foreign governments—or less charitable corporations, for that matter—would just *share* as many life-prolonging advances as we do, on their own, for *free*, then they're really not paying attention.

"And do you know what he—"

"Wanted me to steal?" Marlea finishes Ryder's question. "Your guess is as good as mine; he wasn't exactly liberal with the details when he took my body for a joyride. But since he dragged me back to the office, I'd say we were headed for my prototype." She sighs, not a small release of air, but with her whole body, like even her bones are tired. "All I know for sure is that we never got there. One minute he was in my head and then *poof*, he was gone."

"*Gone?*" Ryder's eating up her story as though he's every bit as starved as she is.

"Asshole never even said goodbye. Don't get me wrong; I don't think he meant to cut out. In fact, I know he didn't. He meant to use me, then dispose of me. He kept saying it would be over soon, that if I stopped fighting him, he'd make it quick. Can you believe that?" Her voice turns savage. "Bastard had the nerve to think he was doing me a *favor*. But I don't know, maybe something glitched with his tech."

We're all quiet for a moment after that. As much as I want to call this woman out on her bullshit, I can't bring myself to do it. Marlea may not have been mindjacked, but something did break her, and the last thing she needs is some insensitive bitch pouring salt on those wounds.

Ryder, on the other hand, keeps right on pushing. "Marlea, I need you to think back on one last thing for me." His body tenses with anticipation, as though this is the true question he came to ask. "When this Walker first tried to get in your head, did he say anything odd, or that you didn't understand . . . a sequence of numbers maybe? Or a phrase that felt out of place, like it might have been a command for his Cerebral Intelligence Processor?"

The words turn my blood cold.

Our CIPs are common knowledge, but only in the abstract. The way we interact with them during missions is something only an insider would know—something only an insider *should* know. So then how did a member of the Analog Army get wind of that information?

"No, I don't—actually, yes." Marlea jerks upright. "Yes, there *was* something. The whole time he was in my head, I was fighting him, and even before he disappeared for good, there were moments when I thought I'd managed to push him out. But then I'd feel him trying to get back in again, and I'd hear . . . no, I didn't hear it exactly, it was more like an echo, but before he came crashing back in, he'd say: *I'm asking you nicely.*"

I'm asking you nicely? I gawk at her. Is that supposed to be a joke? Some twisted version of consent? This is all so far-fetched I can't hold my tongue any longer. "I don't understand. If he could get into your mind without permission, why didn't he just fix his tech and try again? Finish the job?" I ignore the sharp nudge Ryder gives me. Sorry, AA, but it's a fair question, especially since she's suggesting something so ludicrous.

"Because the first thing I did once he vanished was make sure he'd never be able to do it again." Marlea sweeps up her hair to reveal another ugly scar at the nape of her neck.

Christ-that-was, she didn't just get rid of her tech; she ripped out her ID chip. She must truly believe this happened to have resorted to such measures. Without that chip she can't do anything: go to work, move between sectors, use the storm shelters or the health clinics. She's cut herself off completely. All to escape some imaginary voice in her head.

We don't linger in the dark web much longer. Whatever Ryder was after, Marlea's tale must have given it to him in spades, because he doesn't protest when she terminates the chat, eager to resume her digital exile.

He's distant as we return our immersion kits and leave Valholo behind, thinking hard on the conspiracy she spun for him.

"You wanna tell me what that was about?" I ask once the silence grows thick between us, hovering like a dense, radioactive cloud. Ryder may be a part of the most fundamentally misguided organization to have sprung up since the Annihilation, but he's obviously not a total idiot. He's got an agenda, and friends in some pretty interesting places if this trip is anything to go by. There has to be a reason he's buying the fiction Marlea's selling.

"That was the first real proof I've found in almost two years," he says, steering us clear of the crowd and the VR displays, to walk beneath the MagTrain.

"Proof of what, exactly?" I grit as we trace a path along the tracks. *That some disgruntled, ex-Glindell employee is out there spreading lies?*

"Weren't you paying attention?" Ryder's tongue clicks against his teeth. "Syntex has been playing fast and loose with consent laws. And thanks to Marlea, I can finally prove it."

Okay, so maybe he is an idiot then.

"You call that proof?"

"You don't?"

"No, I don't. The only thing I saw in there was a broken woman talking about something impossible."

Even if Marlea's words did tug at a memory, I have to discount them as nonsense. Because I've tried it myself. A hundred times over. Every which way. Hell, even Jondi couldn't crack the system. And if Jondi and the *supercomputer in his head* can't crack it, that means it can't be cracked.

"Well, what can I say"—Ryder's steps quicken with his mood— "Syntex has a habit of leaving broken people in its wake."

Oh good, we're back to cryptic remarks that tell me nothing. I should have known our brief bout of cooperation wouldn't last—noncommittal answers are basically this guy's MO—and I'm getting pretty sick of pulling teeth. "Are you the least bit capable of answering a question properly?" I snap. *Or does everything have to be an extraction?*

"Maybe you should phrase your questions better," is how he chooses to reply to that.

Ass.

"Fine, what makes you think she's not some lunatic who's making it all up? State the *full* reason," I spell it out nice and clear.

"I told you, she's not the first person I've met who's been mindjacked," Ryder says. Then before I can berate him some more for giving me absolutely nothing—*again*—he adds, "But she is different. The others were all attacked a couple of years ago, and only for incredibly short stints. My guess is they were still testing the tech back then, ironing out the kinks. Then suddenly, the mindjackings stopped. No more rumors, no more survivors."

"Maybe that's because it's not true."

"Or maybe Syntex got better at covering its crimes." His voice rises as a steel bullet rumbles past overhead. "Maybe it no longer lets its victims go."

"That's a little paranoid, don't you think?"

"No, I don't. I've been tracking missing persons data for two years, and there are over a dozen cases that fit the pattern."

Oh, give me a break.

"It's a city, Ryder." I motion around the sprawl. "Sometimes, people just disappear."

"No, Sil, *people* don't just disappear. *Vagrants* disappear.

Junkies disappear. But cognitive engineers from Glindell Technologies don't *just* disappear. Neither do lab technicians from Cytron, or data analysts from Excelsis. All working on classified projects one day, gone the next. Vanished without a trace." The words ring too loud in the wake of the MagTrain, blunt and brimming with accusation.

"Are you actually suggesting that Syntex is mindjacking civilians for their *access*?" I gape at him.

"That's exactly what I'm suggesting," Ryder spits. "Why risk an agent when you can mindjack your competition, get them to do your dirty work, then kill them when you're done?"

"Christ-that-was, would you listen to yourself? That's beyond far-fetched."

"Do you have a better explanation?"

Only, like, a million.

"Let's pretend for a minute you're right," I say. "How would it even work? You really think all these people just *forgot* they had Meld structures installed?"

Our agents undergo an intensive nanite regime to prepare their minds for the Meld. Without those fundamental changes in brain morphology, the neural link wouldn't be possible.

"No"—Ryder kicks at the dirt—"I think Syntex found a way to force those structures on them."

"Okay, *how*? And *why*?" I'm more than willing to keep pushing him for answers, just as he pushed Marlea. Because what he's suggesting isn't just impossible, it doesn't make any sense. Corporate espionage is, at worst, a misdemeanor crime. Bad for our agents, yes, since spies caught in the act have basically no rights. Not to their lives or any propriety tech in their bodies. But if traced back to Syntex, the company would walk away with a slap on the wrist and a fine.

Mindjacking civilians, on the other hand, would amount to a gross breach of the Cybernetics Control Act, and that's no small thing. The news would trigger a global panic. We'd lose all public trust. There's no way Syntex would ever be so short-sighted.

Except, this time, Ryder doesn't reply. He jerks to a stop and turns to look at me head-on, suspicion blooming across his face.

"Here's what I don't understand," he says. "You steal from these guys; the company director is on every news board in the city, personally calling for your arrest; why are you defending them?"

"I am not *defending* them."

"It sure sounds like you are."

Damn. Maybe I shouldn't have pushed so hard.

"Think what you want." I shrug as nonchalantly as the rising fear allows. "But you're not going to bring Syntex down with some paranoid ramblings, so excuse me for wanting to focus my efforts on more credible avenues."

"And what would those avenues be, exactly? Because so far, you've given me next to nothing." The muscles in Ryder's jaw twitch in agitation. Marlea was his olive branch, his way of proving he's more than just honeycomb ink and senseless stunts. But then I went and failed his test. I didn't react the way he expected, and now he's worried I won't hold up my end of the deal. If I want to keep watching this cell, I'm going to have to return the favor.

"What's your handle?" I ask as another MagTrain thunders past overhead.

"What?" The question catches him off-guard.

"Your user handle. So I can ping you."

The smallest trace of his annoyance fades. "Why? Can't you hack my unit the way you did Aja's?"

"I've been told that's impolite. Apparently, I don't play well with others." I offer him a look that says, *ball's in your court.*

"Okay, I'll bite." He leans in to type the details directly into my palm. I shiver as his fingers dance across my skin, tapping the sub-dermal keys with unnatural gentleness. Lena's the only one I usually let play with my tech, and that's only because it's impossible to keep a wave from crashing. But from a stranger, this kind of touch feels too familiar. Too . . . *presumptuous.*

Which is why he's doing it. I shake the feeling off. Ryder's been playing his own games since the moment I met him; the handle he gives me is proof of that. RESISTANCE_RYDER. A dummy account if I've ever seen one. For all his talk of trust, he's not willing to betray his secrets any more than I am.

Maybe this'll change his mind. As Ryder resumes our march towards the station, I have Jarvis package up the financial records from the black site, then scramble my ping through my own dummy account, picking a user handle I think will make him smile.

<FUGITIVE_AT_LARGE_SS> Download the attachment.

And smile Ryder does. In a way that makes him look like something other than an arrogant dick.

"Clever," he says. "You think that up all by yourself?"

Well, that didn't last.

"Just read it, would you?" I roll my eyes. "Syntex is up to something off book, and the financials suggest it's—"

"Something big." He lets out a long whistle. "This kind of money usually means tech that comes with a body count."

That's one thing we agree on. Hell, maybe I've been playing this whole spy thing wrong by keeping my cards so close to my chest. Maybe I should be using Ryder to help me figure this mess out, using his hate for Syntex to fuel my search for answers. He doesn't need to know I'm not being entirely honest about *who* I'm investigating, or that I plan to use anything I find on him and this black site to buy my way *back* to the company instead of taking it down. So long as I control the flow of information, then I control the narrative. Ryder will stay none the wiser.

"My thoughts exactly," I say, following him up to the platform. "Which is why we should be focusing on *this* instead of some far-fetched conspiracy."

"Oh, I don't know about that." The remaining suspicion melts away from Ryder's face, his eyes regaining their ever-present humor. "In my experience, it's the most far-fetched stories that turn out to be true. And besides, there's no rule that says we can't hit Syntex with both."

It's almost midday by the time we make it back to the checkpoint, less than ten minutes shy of the end of Jimmy's shift.

"I don't know about you, Sil Sarrah, but I could really go for something other than a protein cube," Ryder says as we approach the gate. "You hungry?"

"That depends." My stomach gives a painful growl. "You know a place that does a good grilled cheese?" If I'm going to be stuck out in the sectors, I might as well make the most of it. And that definitely includes ditching my dietary parameters in favor of something that would make Jondi jealous and Lena proud.

"I think we can manage that." Ryder nods in approval—hell, I daresay he even looks pleased. "Does that mean I can trust you to play nice this one last time?" He tugs my hood up, covering my hair.

"Hey, I'm as eager as you are to get on the right side of those scanners," I say. Especially now that real food's on the table—and now that my facial filters have begun to itch. Appearance changers are only designed to last a few hours at a time—after that, the projection chip loses its charge and the holographic film starts to peel away. I give these another thirty minutes. Tops. They're already glitching at the sides.

"Even more, I'd venture." Ryder runs his fingers over an errant edge along my cheek, gently sticking it back down. "You're going to look like your most wanted self again soon."

"Then let's do this." The ghost of his touch lingers against my skin. One more crossing then I'll be safe again. Or at least as safe as a fugitive can be in a city full of eyes.

The sour stench of whiskey hits me the moment Jimmy opens the door, a wave potent enough to sting my nostrils. Christ-that-was, the man's in worse shape than he was this morning.

"Cutting it a little close, aren't you?" He hurries us into the empty corridor, shooting harried glances over his shoulder as we shuffle inside. "Hold out your hands." He pulls the electric cuffs out of his belt. "Quickly. New rotation will be clocking on any minute."

The metal has already snapped shut around my wrists by the time I realize my mistake.

Jimmy's not carrying the extra uniform for Ryder.

We just walked into a trap.

CHAPTER 14

"Son of a—"

Jimmy fires a jolt of electricity through the cuffs that sends me to my knees. The current is powerful enough to floor a man twice my size, but it's my CIP that makes me doubly vulnerable. Pain shoots between my temples, a sharp and furious buzz that quickly consumes my skull, bringing with it a deluge of error messages.

Shit, shit, shit. I drop my head into my hands. This is not good.

"Jimmy, what are you—"

A wild swing of his baton cuts Ryder off and he joins me on the ground, spitting blood.

"Didn't think I'd figure out who your girlfriend is, did you?" Jimmy aims a kick to his ribs before slapping a pair of cuffs on him too.

Oh, this is really not good.

"I'm not who you think I am." I force the words out, trying to pull the world back into focus. Jarvis is flashing me a giant *surge detected* warning, but thankfully—*fuck, thankfully*—the activity log scrolling in my periphery is showing that he's intact. The shock didn't fry my remaining power cell.

"Do I look like I was born yesterday?" Jimmy yanks my head back by the hair. "I thought you seemed familiar this morning, even through those facial filters of yours. So I checked the bulletins and what do you know, *Sil Sarrah*, you're worth a lot more than some app."

Bad. This is very, very bad.

"Jimmy, think this through." Ryder peels himself off the floor. "Why would I bring the subject of a citywide manhunt here?"

It really does sound stupid when he says it out loud.

Which is probably why he didn't invite me in the first place.

Think, damn it, I will myself. *This is what you do.* I've been extracting agents from situations far worse than this one for *years.* So what if I'm running this mission in my own body? I still have my tech; I can figure this out.

And the truth is, I do see a way—though it's pretty much guaranteed to turn my Jimmy problem into a Ryder problem. Pulling this trigger means burning all the goodwill I've built with him today, losing his help and any chance of learning his army's endgame.

"You're making a big mistake here, Jimmy." I pull it anyway, since a cage would prove equally problematic. "I am *not* Sil Sarrah."

"Save it for the authorities, sweetheart."

"Jimmy—"

"And you, Romeo." He hauls us both back to our feet. "I'm sure the law would love to get its hands on you too."

This is your chance, I realize as Ryder continues to try and reason with him. Electric cuffs are designed to render palm pads inactive, so if I want to get an order to Jarvis unheard, this might be my only shot.

"Initiate bone changers," I whisper as quietly as I can. "Minor facial reconstruction. Generate alias to match. Ear out for indirect commands."

"Yes, Captain." Jarvis acknowledges my instructions and I get to work on my part of the plan while he gets to work on his.

"Jimmy, listen to me. My name isn't Sil Sarrah, it's Myleen May—you can scan my face if you don't believe me. Please, just scan my face."

Out of the corner of my eye, I see Ryder looking at me as though I've lost my mind, which, let's be honest, I might well have. But this bad idea of mine is the only play we've got left.

"Don't worry, sweetheart, you'll get your scan." Jimmy pushes us forward. "I'm taking you to the gate right now."

The exact opposite of what I need him to do. There's no way we're leaving this place through the front door, where there are other, more sober guards. This needs to stay between us and Jimmy. And it needs to stay off the main scanner.

"I wouldn't do that if I were you."

"And why's that?" The sneer in his voice curls my fingers into tight fists.

"Because"—I bite back a scream as the bone changers kick into high gear beneath my skin. *Unholy mother*; I forgot how much that stings—"an ID scan is going to show I have a record, just not the one you think." I fight to keep my voice level. "I'm wanted for a bunch of petty thefts. Stupid stuff you won't get a reward for. But if you turn me over to the cops, you better believe I'm telling them how you let us pass through this morning."

That stops him for a moment.

But only one.

"They'll never believe you." Jimmy gives us another none-too-gentle shove, continuing our steady march towards the gate.

"You sure about that?" I ask. "'Cause judging by the stench of booze on your breath, I doubt you'll make a credible witness."

"I'll be backing her up, too." Ryder quickly catches up to my plan. At least the part he can see. "If we go down, you'll go down with us."

"Nice try, but you can't talk your way out of this."

"Just do a—" I almost double over as the bone changers attack my cheekbones. "Do a facial scan first. Keep it off the record. If you're right, all it costs you is a few minutes. But if you're wrong, then we get to go home and you get your app. Everybody wins."

With that, Jimmy finally jerks us to a stop.

Then promptly sends another jolt coursing through our cuffs.

"Have it your way," he says as we both curse into the floor. "Just remember, I'm in control here."

"Captain, a power surge has interrupted the bone changers at 32% completion," Jarvis tells me. "Shall I resume the reconstruction?"

"*Yes*—" I take a pause so he'll recognize the command before continuing for Jimmy's benefit. "We get it, you're in charge."

A needle-like pain shoots through my skull as Jarvis reactivates the nanites. Indirect commands are more an art than a science, for when a Walker can't openly communicate with their CIP. I rarely have cause to use them, but Syntex trains us for every eventuality. And I've never been more grateful.

"Whatever, bitch. It's your funeral." Jimmy turns us about, heading towards one of the back rooms instead.

Good. This is good. Now I just need the bone changers to finish their work.

"Bone alterations 40% complete," Jarvis says as we cross into the next corridor. The surge from the cuffs must have slowed my systems down since this is taking far longer than it should. And hurting more.

"Ryder—" I whisper when Jimmy stops to address another guard. "I need you to buy me some time."

"What?"

"Time, genius. Stall for time."

"How exactly am I supposed to do that?" He shakes his cuffs at me.

"*Figure it out*," I hiss. He helped get us into this mess; the least he can do is help get us out.

For a long moment, Ryder only glares at me, as though trying to uncover the missing part of my plan—the one currently hidden by the facial filters—or maybe weighing up his odds of getting out of here alone. We both know they're pretty bad.

"Oh, you so owe me," he finally says, then as soon as the second guard disappears, he rears back and slams his head into Jimmy's nose.

"What the f—"

Ryder's rewarded with a flash of electricity that buckles his knees.

Do more, I implore him with my eyes. *Drag this out.*

"Bone alterations 50% complete."

Jimmy tugs him up by the ear. "You're gonna pay for—"

Ryder spits in his face.

And for that he gets a blow to the gut that swiftly doubles him over. Jimmy's too wasted to do much real damage with his fists, so it shouldn't be enough to drive him back to the scuffed linoleum, but Ryder goes down anyway. Because I asked him to buy me more time.

"Bone alterations 60% complete."

If it's any consolation, I'd venture I'm in just as much pain as he is.

"On your feet, you little shit," Jimmy barks until Ryder stumbles back up, trailing blood on the wall he uses for support. He fires me a look that says, *your turn.*

"Bone alterations 70% complete."

I'm not quite ready for my turn yet, but that doesn't stop Jimmy from frog-marching us towards the door marked *Control Center.*

Come on, come on, come on. I drag my feet as much as I dare, begging the nanites to work faster.

We're barely ten paces away now.

Five.

"Bone alterations 80% complete."

"Please tell me there's a plan here, *Myleen*," Ryder mutters as Jimmy shoves us into the room, making a beeline for the hand-held scanner on the desk.

"Wait! Disable my facial filters first," I say. "That way, you'll be sure the scans are right."

Which they would be even with the filters on, but Jimmy's sauced enough to buy my desperate logic. He puts the scanner aside and grabs me roughly by the chin.

"Bone alterations 85% complete."

With clumsy fingers, Jimmy unhooks the projection chip from my hairline and tears the holographic film off my skin. Ryder's eyes widen as my face is revealed. It shouldn't be drastically different, just different enough for the guy I spent the last day and a half with to notice the change.

But one problem at a time.

I'll deal with Ryder later. Assuming I'm not in a cell.

"Bone alterations 90% complete."

Jimmy forces me down into a chair and activates the scanner.

"Bone alterations 95% complete."

My heart is pounding a tattoo beneath my ribs, my fear permeating the air in pungent clouds. I squirm in Jimmy's grasp, looking at the floor, the wall, anywhere but him.

"Hold still—"

The infrared beam hits me right as Jarvis pushes a picture of my new face to my ocular display. I let out the breath I'm holding, the relief whistling out from between my teeth. The changes really are subtle. My jaw is a touch more rounded, my nose a smidge narrower, and my cheekbones sharper and more pronounced.

"Shit," Jimmy curses as a visual ID pops up on the monitors. *Myleen May*, the name reads. Wanted for several counts of petty theft.

"Satisfied?" I ask, batting the scanner away. Across the room, I can feel Ryder staring daggers at me, but he's smart enough to swallow his anger. For now.

"You can still get what you want here, Jimmy," he says. "Just let us go. You'll get your app, we keep our freedom. It's a good deal all round."

The walk back to the locker room is the single longest of my life. Jarvis can build aliases to fool every system known to man, but not in two minutes flat. It won't take much for Myleen May to betray me if Jimmy chooses to check into her a little more. And if she doesn't, Ryder just might. If looks could kill, the ones he keeps sneaking me would spark a genocide.

When the outside door finally swings open, the air has never tasted sweeter, the scent of smoke and burning rubber washing over me like an expensive perfume.

Ryder's cuffs come off first and he jumps into the alley, rubbing his wrists and the broken skin the electricity left behind. For a second, I fear he might bolt and leave me to Jimmy's mercy, but then with a sigh and a crack of his knuckles, he turns back to my captor and says, "I'll send you the code as soon as hers come off too."

My hands are released, though the grip on my shirt remains firm.

"*Code*," Jimmy growls.

Ryder taps a command into his keypad and a moment later, the unit in Jimmy's palm beeps. Then as soon as the app kicks up on his screen, he pushes me into the street, straight into Ryder's chest, slamming the door shut behind us.

Out of the lion's den and into a viper's pit.

This really isn't my day.

I make to pull away from him, but before I can properly find my feet, Ryder shoves me up against the wall and pins my arms to my sides.

"Oh no, you're not going anywhere, *Myleen*. We need to talk."

"Get your hands off me." I throw a knee to his stomach—harder than is strictly necessary—sending him lurching back, a curse on his tongue. *Never pick a fight you can't win, AA-hole*. I haul ass down the alley, looking to put as much space between us as I can.

A day and a half. I only lasted a day and a half before blowing my cover.

"How'd you change your face, Sil?" Ryder trails me into the shadows. The anger rolling off him is so thick and dense it feels as though it's whipping at my skin, like an easterly wind on a cold winter's morning.

"How do you think I changed my face?" I speed up, wrapping my arms tight around me. My skull is still throbbing from the reconstruction and the nanites have left me hankering for that grilled cheese. I am in no mood for this conversation.

"I think that outside of a bone sculptor, the only way to do what you did was with military-grade tech."

"Then you have your answer, don't you?" Why is this clown even following me? We both know this ill-fated alliance of ours is over.

"Where'd you get the tech, Sil?" Or perhaps Ryder didn't get that memo.

"Oh, for the love of everything unholy"—I explode—"would you please stop playing it dumb? I got the tech the same place I got the documents: from *them*. Because I worked for them. And if you haven't figured that out yet, then maybe you're not as smart as you think you are."

"You worked for *Syntex*?" Ryder spins me around.

"Welcome to the conversation."

"As what?"

I can practically see the cogs whirring in his mind, trying to puzzle the pieces together. My mods, my fighting skills, my gun . . . he's not going to believe I was some low-level analyst.

"An agent, what else?" I say. No other explanation would make sense. Except, *Walker*. But there's no chance in hell I'm telling him *that*.

"Bullshit. You're too young to be an agent."

"Well, if you say so. I'm sure you're an expert on Syntex's hiring practices." I don't know why I'm keeping this charade going. It's not Ryder I'm mad at, it's myself, but boy, fighting him feels good. "In case you're not, though, let me put this in terms you'll understand: there are people in this virtuous city of ours who are less suspicious around teenage girls than they are around women. They talk more. They reveal more. Would you like me to draw you a picture?" The lie leaves a bitter taste in my mouth, mostly because it's not a lie, only a lie for me.

"Then what's an *agent* doing trying to burn Syntex?" he asks.

"They burned me first." I lace my voice with anger, so that he'll think me a disgruntled employee.

"So that's why you're doing this? Revenge?"

"Why do you care why I'm doing this?" We're both panting

now, standing face to face in the alley, barely an inch of space between us.

"Because I trusted you!"

"Well, that's—" Ryder's words stop me cold. It's not so much what he said, but how he said it. Like he'd swallowed a fistful of glass. Like he's hurt. Like *I've* hurt him.

Christ-that-was, I really should have just walked away.

Now, it's too late. Because all around us, the storm sirens start blaring.

CHAPTER 15

There are three kinds of storm alarms: storm incoming, storm nearing, and *get to a shelter right freaking now because the storm is here.*

Today we've hit the jackpot with siren number three.

"I don't understand; there were no projected alerts." I quickly bring up the forecast. When Jarvis checked it for me this morning, there was nothing of note showing on the radars—not moving inland, anyway—and I've long since stopped asking him to stay on top of the hourly updates. The Syntex building is one big bunker, basically, designed to withstand the next Annihilation. These past ten years, radioactive storms have been little more than a minor inconvenience. If I saw one coming, I'd just stay inside.

"The winds must have changed," Ryder says, studying the alert on his own screen.

"Well, what do we do?" A note of panic breaks through my voice. Everyone on the street is speeding back towards the checkpoint complex, but taking refuge in the bunker there seems riskier than scanning into a regular shelter and hoping the law isn't planning a raid.

"Christ-that-was, you really are a pampered Syntex agent, aren't you?" Ryder rolls his eyes. "Come on, there's a place that doesn't check chips a few minutes away. We might make it if we run."

So we run, with the storm sirens wailing around us and the wind picking up speed at our backs. Each block we cross is emptier than the last, the hub lapsing into silence as the remaining stragglers disappear into the closer shelters. There are hundreds of them scattered all over the city, enough for every man, woman, and child to seek refuge while our past surges through the streets in deadly, radioactive clouds. In theory, they're supposed to act as safe havens, a place where the righteous and unsavory alike can escape the fallout without fear. But even a *pampered Syntex agent* like me knows that's not how it works in practice. Sector guards are not the only corruptible force in town.

The shelter Ryder leads me to is in the basement of a food bank, a steel-reinforced bunker purpose-built to protect against the storms. We make it there right as the sirens turn from a wail to a high-pitched screech, collapsing into the airlock seconds before the radiation hits. On a good day, the air we breathe is lethal to anyone whose blood isn't teeming with nanites; during the storms, the toxicity spikes to bone-melting levels.

True to Ryder's word, security don't scan our chips when we clear containment; they barely even spare us a glance as we join the crowd gathered in the main space.

Walking into the shelter is like walking into a memory, the kind that instantly reignites the hate I had for the storms as a child. There's nothing worse than being forced to spend hours cooped up underground, and something about the way these bunkers smell—the potent mix of antiseptic and recycled air—has always made me feel as though I'm drowning in bleach.

That feeling certainly hasn't gone away. My skin begins to itch as we head towards a couple of empty mats. This shelter looks exactly like the one my parents used to take me to: clean but cramped, stuffed full of sleeping bags and blankets for when the storms run late into the night.

My fight with Ryder follows us all the way down to the floor, though we both know this isn't the time or place to unleash that can of worms. At least my face is no longer a neon sign that would have every one of our bunkmates racing to ping the tip line. That's something, I suppose. Though according to the updates Jarvis is now diligently flashing me, Ryder and I are going to be stuck here for a while, the ghost of my revelations hanging over us like a shroud.

Super.

To be perfectly honest, I have no idea why he hasn't cut me loose yet. His grudge against Syntex must run deeper than oil if he's willing to overlook my . . . *colorful* employment history just to get his hands on the documents I stole.

Maybe I'm not quite as burned as I first thought.

The silence between us has barely grown uncomfortable when a wave of gasps rends through the crowd, all heads turning towards the entrance.

"What's going on?" I crane my neck for a better look. *Oh no.* Bile rises in my throat as I spot the source of the commotion. There are people streaming into the airlock through the outside door, screaming to be let inside, their voices muffled by the reinforced glass.

"Damn, that's a lot of stragglers." Ryder's face falls. "There are always a few that don't make it in time . . . but this—"

"Is more than a few," I finish for him. There must be thirty-odd people in there, both children and adults, and though they've only been exposed for a few minutes, they're already showing advanced signs of radiation poisoning. The one thing that might save them now is an armload of prescription-grade nanites.

So then why is no one hauling ass to give them some?

"Erm . . . Myleen . . . Where are you going?" Ryder asks as I start pushing my way to the front. With the last straggler sealed safely inside the airlock, the containment signals turn green and the glass box opens up, allowing them to spill into the bunker.

The head of the group—a clean-shaven man with bushy brows and a small boy clinging to his arm—is outright yelling by the time I cross the room, something about a faulty MagTrain getting stuck between platforms. Sounds like they had to pry open the carriage and climb down from the tracks. How they managed that with all the kids, I don't know; those rails run thirty feet above ground.

As he collapses to his knees, the man keeps begging for doses of the nanites that could spare them, pushing his son forward so the staff will see the jaundiced tinge to his skin and the way his eyes are bleeding at the corners. The rest of the group isn't faring much better. Those who can stand are being guided to cots by security, while others are throwing their guts up against the wall. And still, no one is doing a damn thing to actually try and save them.

"What's the problem?" I give voice to the question they're too sick to ask. The manager—a Dr. Jean Essa, according to the nametag—doesn't strike me as a power-hungry sadist, or else she'd be scanning ID chips for sure. She's a harassed-looking woman in her fifties, with salt-peppered hair and deep lines around her eyes and mouth.

"Please, miss, go back to your mat. There's nothing you can do here." Jean sounds about ready to snap, a wire stretched to the point of breaking.

"But they need treatment."

"And I want to help them, I really do, but I've got no radiation blockers left."

"What? How is that possible?" That's literally the one thing— the *only* thing—these shelters are supposed to keep on hand.

"You'll have to ask the gang that raided us last week." She sighs, pulling nervously at her fingers. "They took all our prescriptives and the next delivery isn't due for another three days. Until then, I've only got prophylactics."

"Then give them those and stick them in an accelerator!" Why are we still debating this? That's precisely what accelerators are designed to do: enhance the nanites, make them more efficient. And if this woman tries to tell me a gang ran off with that too, I am seriously going to lose it.

"Even if our accelerator could fit more than two people at a time, prophylactics won't do anything for this level of exposure," Jean says. "I'm sorry, but it's too late. Keeping them comfortable is the only thing we can do."

No. Not good enough. I have Jarvis send a map of the sector to my ocular display. My job—everything I've done since the day I was recruited—has been about ensuring life-saving tech gets to the people who need it most. Now there are thirty people dying right in front of me; I won't stand here and do nothing.

"Where's the nearest place that would have them?" I ask.

"Erm . . . the Eastside Clinic might," Jean says. "But I don't see how that's—"

"Get me a nano-pen," I cut her off.

"Excuse me?"

"The prophylactics. Go get me some!" I half yell at Doctor Useless. I don't need her to understand my request, just to follow basic instructions.

A quick hack of the clinic's manifest shows they've got plenty of doses in stock, and based on the map I'm looking at, it's only eight minutes from here on foot. Given the current radiation levels, and the radioactive load these prophylactics are designed to combat, I'll have ample time to get there once they're swimming through my veins.

"Sorry, but I need to borrow my friend for a quick second . . ." Ryder drags me away by the elbow. "The hell do you think you're doing?" he hisses.

"What does it look like I'm doing?"

"Killing yourself. In an unnecessarily gruesome fashion."

"Oh, please. I can make it to that clinic long before the prophylactics wear off."

"And what good is that if you can't make it *back*?"

"I'll have the radiation blockers for the trip back. Where's the problem?"

"You've never actually seen radiation blockers at work, have you?" Ryder gives me that look again, the *you really are a pampered Syntex agent* look. "We're talking sub-cellular regenerating nanites here, Sil. They'll put you on your ass for hours."

Oh. That is a problem; I look at the route Jarvis has calculated. With a few . . . *risky* . . . adjustments, I can still make it. I think.

Thirteen minutes forty-four seconds for the round trip. The prophylactics should protect me for fifteen.

"Then I'll just have to run faster," I say, turning back to Jean who's returned with the nano-pens I asked for. I snatch one from the box and press it to the crease of my arm. Once I step outside, the nanites will start absorbing the excess radiation, working to protect my cells until they're overwhelmed by the storm.

"Christ-that-was, why are the interesting ones always out of their damn minds," Ryder swears before grabbing a second pen.

"What are you doing?"

"Coming with you." He grins, shooting the nanites into his blood.

"Like hell you are."

"Thirty people will die if you fall and break your ankle. Is bringing backup such a terrible idea?"

No, I guess it's not.

"Fine. But you better not slow me down," I say. Then before either of us can rethink this terrible idea, I punch the button on the side of the airlock and we both step inside.

"Keep those people alive until we get back," I tell Jean as the glass slides shut behind us. Under less deadly circumstances, the expression on the good doctor's face would be funny. She's staring at us slack-jawed, her mouth opening and closing but making no sound, as though she's lost the ability to speak.

"You sure about this?" A nervous edge creeps into Ryder's voice as we wait for the outside door to engage.

"Would you believe me if I said yes?" I try to play off the doubts. Since this isn't a sanctioned mission, Jarvis isn't calculating my odds of success, but I'm well aware they're far from rosy. If I had to guess, I'd put them around 65%. Hardly the worst I've ever faced, but I'd be lying if I said I didn't wish for better.

"Not even a little," Ryder tells me.

But then it's too late to change our minds because the containment signals turn green and the airlock spits us out into the unprotected air.

The heat hits me like a tidal wave, a wall so thick and dense I almost double over. And we're not even outside yet. It'll only get worse once we leave the building.

"Let's go." I grit my teeth and plunge headfirst into the stairwell.

"I assume there's a reason we're heading up instead of out?" Ryder asks when we barrel past the first-floor landing.

"We're taking a shortcut," I say. Based on Jarvis's projections, a street-level route will take too long if we attempt it both ways, so instead, we'll be cutting across the rooftops.

"Of course we are." Ryder doesn't balk when he realizes what I have planned—and he doesn't have a supercomputer in his head mapping trajectories. So if I'm *out of my damn mind*, what does that make him?

Reckless.

There really is no other word to describe him. Taking on the drunks in that bar . . . agreeing to smuggle a fugitive across sector lines . . . trusting me with his door to the dark web . . . all for the chance to wage war against a tech goliath. Ryder is reckless through and through, and I can't help but wonder *why*. What possesses someone to play games with their life this way? Especially when they're not living on borrowed time?

The strangest thing about radioactive storms is that you can't *see* them. They're not physical things, like dust storms—though the wind is blowing something fierce all the same, a convection oven set to high. But the radiation itself is invisible. Which doesn't stop me thinking I can feel it as we burst onto the roof, soaking into my skin, my bones, my cells, the nanites in my blood feeding on it like gluttons at a feast.

I choke the feeling down, sprinting towards the nearest ledge. In this part of the sector, the buildings are packed close and tight, with thick bundles of cables running between them. Perfect for those looking to get somewhere *fast*.

Jarvis has already analyzed the angle and force I'd need to clear this first jump and it's well within my ability, so I leap off the edge without fear, landing hard atop the neighboring roof.

A moment later, Ryder skids to a halt beside me.

"So this is how you like to get around," he says, as though it's the most natural thing in the world, as though he didn't just follow me off a building.

"No better way to travel."

Though crossing this next chasm is going to take more than nonchalance and a good leap. There's a main thoroughfare cutting between this block and the next. Two lanes of traffic as well as a MagTrain track. I don't need a supercomputer to tell me there's no way we're jumping *that*.

"I hope you're not afraid of heights." I strip off my jacket, making for the cable bundle connecting the two buildings. The lines are shielded, so they won't fry me, and the neoplex fabric should be strong enough to take my weight. This is not a risky move; I've pulled it a dozen times on missions. Though I must admit, the fall looks scarier through my own eyes.

Be afraid when you're not being cooked alive. I throw the jacket over the cables and wrap the sleeves around my palms. Jarvis estimates it'll take me 8.5 seconds to zip across to the other side. I can easily hold on that long. No problem. But that doesn't stop my heart from objecting loudly beneath my ribcage, or sweat from beading at my temples.

"You really are out of your mind." Ryder's disbelief does little to quell my nerves. It's oddly satisfying though, knowing I've impressed him. And maybe the exposure is starting to rot my brain because—for some reason—I want to do it again. Which is why I flash him a smile and say, "I'll see you on the other side." When in doubt, act more confident than you feel. Like Lena does after every glitch. Fighting fear is like walking a tightrope. Anything short of total commitment and they'll be pressure-washing me off the pavement.

So I close my eyes and take the leap. The fabric pulls taut beneath my fingers, groaning with the strain as I fly into the wind. I scream without meaning to, the sound fast turning from fear to exhilaration.

See, that's the problem with Mindwalking; you never really *feel* the danger. Risk is an abstract; beyond worrying about your stats, you never really taste it. No lows but no highs, either. And this is a high in more ways than distance from the ground.

I'm almost to the other side when the neoplex begins to tear, the seams fraying apart one overburdened thread at a time. *Just a few more seconds . . .* I will the jacket to hold firm, my stomach lurching into my throat. But as it turns out, the structural integrity of my clothing is not my biggest concern, the cable holding me is.

I feel the drop before my mind truly registers it, the wire going slack as the far end rips loose of its moorings. On instinct, I claw for the wire, grabbing hold as it swings into the front of the building.

I hit the bricks side on. Hard.

"Sil!" Ryder's yell is barely audible over the crash of blood pounding in my ears. Pain races down my arms in vicious waves, my shoulders protesting the impact. I drag in a breath, then another, and another, fighting the wild surge of vertigo-induced panic. *Find a foothold and climb.* I run my toes along the wall until they snag a perch. I'm only a few meters shy of the rooftop. I can do this.

With a grunt, I start shimmying up the wire, dragging my body up one agonizing inch at a time. When I finally pull myself over the edge, all I want to do is lie there, staring at the sky until my pulse stops echoing through my skull. But that little stunt cost me almost a minute; if I don't get moving, this risk will have been for nothing.

I spring back to my feet, scanning the pings Ryder's sending me.

<RESISTANCE_RYDER> Christ-that-was.
<RESISTANCE_RYDER> You okay?
<RESISTANCE_RYDER> Can you still make it?
<FUGITIVE_AT_LARGE_SS> I'm fine. Go back to the shelter.

He might as well get out of the radiation seeing how there's no way he can catch up to me now. Which is a relief, actually. My spur of the moment ride-along almost cost him his freedom earlier; I'd hate for this new excursion to cost him his life.

The heat—already a blistering inferno—only intensifies as I race from roof to roof, taunting the nanites in my blood.

"Jarvis, is it supposed to be this hot?" I have him sample the radiation again.

"Levels holding steady at 25,000 Sieverts per hour," he tells me. "Twelve minutes and twenty-two seconds to critical cell damage."

"That's comforting, thanks."

"You're welcome, Captain," he says. Jarvis never did do well with sarcasm.

A street away from the clinic, I scale a fire escape down to the road, descending the rickety ladders as fast as I dare. From here, it'll take another thirty-odd seconds to reach the building, twenty more to get inside, another minute or so to find the radiation blockers . . . damn, this is going to be tight.

I burst into the clinic, hopping the security stiles in one leap. The layout of these places is always the same: a waiting room filled with benches, a reception area enclosed behind shatterproof glass, and row upon row of diagnostic scanners and dispensaries. Almost everything these days—bar catastrophic or genetic conditions—can be treated with a standard dose of nanites so long as they're programmed correctly. But there's always a room in the back where clinics keep their heavy-duty bots. Nanites may have saved the human race from extinction, but they can just as soon eat you alive if you're not careful, which is why the prescription-grade ones are kept under lock and key. And while I don't have a key, I've been cracking locks since before Syntex put a super-computer in my head. With Jarvis in there, the hack takes about five seconds.

The radiation blockers are clearly labeled with the black and yellow trefoil symbol that has come to define the world, and I can tell by the size of the auto-injector that these critters are no joke. I supposed they'd have to be, given the kind of damage they're designed to repair. The kind of damage I'm destined for if I don't get a move on.

I stuff an entire case in my bag then double back towards the door. I'll be taking the ground route this time—roughly eight minutes at full sprint—which will get me back to the shelter with seconds to spare. *If* I can keep that pace up. I'm tired; I'm covered in sweat; my throat is parched and my shoulders are screaming. And somehow—*impossibly*—the air has grown hotter, so hot I swear it's singeing the hair on my arms. There's a smell in the air too, the bitter scent of dying flesh, decaying rubbish, and despair. The taste of it on my tongue is making me queasy.

I'm running full pelt down the street when the countdown in my ocular display flickers for a moment, filling my periphery with static. When the feed restores, the *time remaining to critical cell damage* has changed. It's no longer reading four minutes; it's reading thirteen seconds.

"Erm . . . Jarvis? What just happened?"

"My apologies, Captain. My original radiation scans appear to have been incorrect. New readings indicate that your viability period has reduced by three minutes and forty-seven seconds."

"The hell do you mean they were *incorrect*?"

Not once has Jarvis made a mistake before. *Not once.* If he's screwed up this badly it can only mean . . .

"The error appears to have been caused by a glitch on server core five."

The words stop my heart cold. This was a glitch. A glitch told me I had time to make a medicine run during a radioactive storm. A glitch just killed me.

"Well, are there any closer shelters?" I bark.

"I'm sorry, Captain, but the nearest shelter is your intended destination, approximately three minutes away." Which, given these new readings, is three minutes too far.

"Damn it!" I yell, doubling over. My skin feels as though it's on fire, my lungs as though they're filled with nails. And the sensation only worsens as the countdown hits zero and the nanites in my blood give up the ghost, allowing the radiation to attack my cells unopposed.

I don't know what possesses me to do it. Maybe it's the idea of leaving thirty people to wonder if I up and left them to die, or maybe I just want someone to know what happened to me. Either way, I type out a message.

<FUGITIVE_AT_LARGE_SS> ping <RESISTANCE_RYDER> My math
    was off. I'm not gonna make it.
<RESISTANCE_RYDER> Where are you?

His reply comes almost instantly.

<FUGITIVE_AT_LARGE_SS> Five blocks away.
<RESISTANCE_RYDER> Send me a tracking pin.
<FUGITIVE_AT_LARGE_SS> Why?
<RESISTANCE_RYDER> Because I'm coming for you.
<FUGITIVE_AT_LARGE_SS> Don't be ridiculous. That's suicide.
<RESISTANCE_RYDER> Shut up and keep running.

So I do. Though every step feels harder than the last, my muscles trembling with the effort.

I'm still two streets shy of the shelter when my vision turns red at the corners, my eyes filling with blood, not tears. I fall to my knees and retch, hacking up the protein cubes Ryder and I ate on our way back from the Games District.

You don't have time for this, Sil, Miles's voice rings through my mind. *I didn't train you to quit when things get hard. So get up. Drag yourself there if you have to.*

But my legs aren't responding anymore, and even my hate for disappointing him can't trump the effects of ionizing radiation.

I collapse to the ground, my shoulders sizzling against the scorched asphalt. I guess this is where my life will end. Lying helpless on the sidewalk, the storm boiling the blood in my veins. *Burning from the outside in, instead of burning out,* the thought is like a bad cosmic joke. For years, my biggest fear was falling prey to the ticking time bomb in my head. I told myself any alternative would be better.

Except, this doesn't feel better, and I don't want to die today. I want the months or weeks or days still owed to me.

With a growl, I reach for one of the radiation blockers. It takes me three tries to unscrew the cap, and two more to hit the activator with enough force to shoot the nanites into my arm, but when I do, my vision instantly glazes over, my whole body bowing with the pain.

Ryder was right about these things. I let loose a scream, glancing towards the top of the street.

Maybe he really will come for me, or maybe he won't. Maybe he's only interested in saving the doses in my bag and the documents he thinks I'm hiding. It's hard to care when the world is already slipping away.

The sun is the last thing I see, which is strange because the sky is blanketed with clouds. But I see it all the same. Orange and bright and hurtling towards me. It's such a beautiful sight I wish I could stare at it forever. If only I'd bothered to look at it more while I still had the chance.

CHAPTER 16

I don't think I'm dead. At least, I hope I'm not, because if this is death, then death *sucks*. Every single one of my nerves is screaming out an SOS, though they might as well be screaming into a black hole, for all the good it's doing.

I blink away the light torturing my eyes, groaning as I sit up in the . . . bed? No, it can't be a bed. It's too hard for that, too . . . leathery, like the padded chair in Lin's office. There's also a deep hum buzzing all around me, a bassy sound that resonates through my bones.

An accelerator. I think I'm in an accelerator. That would explain why the walls in this tiny room are lined with thick steel plates, and why the churning sensation coursing through my veins feels so familiar. I spent a full week in one of these after my CIP was implanted, to ensure my brain wouldn't reject the hardware. And though Syntex's accelerator is more rec room than utilitarian broom-closet, I'd still rate my stay there as less pleasant than the surgeries.

I press both hands to my stomach, trying to dull the ache throbbing beneath my ribs. My clothes are gone, though someone was kind enough to leave me a fresh set so I could change out of this paper gown, as well as a dental strip to chew on, and a washcloth with which to wipe my face. Probably the same someone who decontaminated my bag and left it at the foot of the table. The moment I'm dressed and clean, I lean over to grab it, ignoring the pain lancing through my skull. Looks like everything is still inside: my training gear, my cables, my gun. The only thing missing is the box of radiation blockers.

Well, I'll be.

This must be the shelter's accelerator.

Ryder came through for me after all.

He ran into a radioactive storm to save my life.

"Welcome back, Sil Sarrah."

I look up to find him standing in the doorway. The hum vibrating between the walls dissipates as he steps inside, quieting the storm raging in my blood. Guess that means I'm fully cooked.

"How's it feel to not be dead?" he asks.

"Kinda crappy." I drop my head to the metal, fighting off a fresh wave of nausea. "Pretty sure I can *taste* my cells. You think that's normal?"

"Seeing as you've just regenerated half of them . . . probably." He hops up beside me, so that we're sat shoulder to shoulder. "That was a really stupid thing you did, Sil," he says. "Brave, but stupid."

Yeah, tell me about it. "Did it work?"

"Last of the stragglers walked out of here a couple of hours ago." This might be the first genuine smile Ryder's ever offered me. No derision, no bite, no arrogance. Just a real smile. "Then the bulk of the staff left too," he continues. "They got tired of watching you sleep. I offered to stay and make sure you didn't accidentally irradiate yourself again."

And there's that missing arrogance . . . I'd roll my eyes if they didn't hurt so much. "How long have I been out?"

"Close to a day and a half. You were in bad shape by the time I got you inside. If you hadn't pumped yourself full of RBs, I doubt you'd have made it."

"How did *you* make it?" I ask. Given the radiation levels, the prophylactics he took would have worked themselves to the grave after his first exposure, and popping those things isn't like popping candy; another dose so soon after the first would have wreaked havoc with his immune system.

"Lead-lined fashion." Ryder points to an orange hazmat suit hanging outside the door. "The clinic keeps one on hand. They might have even let you borrow it had you actually stopped to *ask* before charging out of here so fast."

This time, I do roll my eyes at him, pain be damned. We both know those things will protect you for all of five minutes. They're designed for conducting emergency repairs to the airlocks, not sprinting across the city. Running in one would work about as well as running in cement shoes.

"So what is it, Sil Sarrah, you got a death wish or something?" he asks.

Not a death wish, no, an expiration date.

"It was the right thing to do." I shrug. Because it was. Because I had the power to help.

"Huh." Ryder turns to study me head-on, his brow pulling down in the middle, as though trying to decipher a complex bit of code. "You really are quite impressive, you know that?" he finally says. And then he does about the last thing I expect: he lifts a hand to my cheek and leans his face into mine, a question in his eyes. Seems the reckless boy who likes to play with fire has a thing for prickly girls with suicidal tendencies. Why am I not surprised?

I should pull away from him, let him know in no uncertain terms that *that* is off the table. He's a means to an end, not some Reggie I'm lusting after; our relationship is based on need and a lie.

Except, I don't.

With a tiny nod, I let him kiss me.

Hell, I kiss him *back*.

I've often wondered how our agents do this, how they can fake attraction to get the job done. But this is almost too easy. It doesn't hurt that Ryder's good-looking, and risking his neck to save mine scored him a couple of points as well. I can play this part if it means buying my way back to the Analog Army. Kissing—or even sex, for that matter—has never been a sacred act for me. Flings are a Walker rite of passage. We don't have time to fall in love or save ourselves for some mythical soul mate. We only get a few years to do as much living as we can manage.

And kissing Ryder is exactly my kind of living.

His lips are soft but they're not shy, and he tastes of something rich and sweet, sugar drops mixed with mint and coffee. His hands aren't shy either, skimming over my shoulders and sides, leaving my skin—still sensitive from the radiation—tingling in their wake.

Not bad for a Reggie.

I almost feel bad for faking it.

I almost *forget* I'm faking it.

So much so that I don't realize what's about to happen until a split second before it does. Ryder's fingers slide through my hair, moving towards the nape of my neck—and the port I've worked to keep hidden. Far too deliberately to have stumbled across it by accident. Here I was, congratulating myself on playing him so well, when all this time, he's been playing me.

In an instant, my gun is out of my bag and in my hand, the barrel pressed tight against his temple. "How long have you known?"

"Whoa, easy . . ." Ryder raises his arms. "I'm not that bad a kisser."

"*How long?*" I drive the metal deeper into his flesh.

"Known? About three seconds," he says, sounding all too calm for a guy about to get his head blown open. "But I suspected it the moment you changed your face."

Which probably means a hundred agents are already headed my way.

"Who did you tell?"

"Don't worry, *Captain* Sil Sarrah. I didn't tell anyone. I just want to talk."

Right, like that's going to happen. *Argh.* I can't believe I got taken in by this poor excuse for an anarchist. I doubt there's ever been a worse double agent in the history of the world.

"Seriously, would you please put the gun down?" Ryder says. "You're not going to shoot me."

"Funny, that's what the last guy thought too," I remind him, rising to my feet. My whole body rails against the decision to stay vertical, but I force myself up nonetheless. I need to get out of here.

"Yeah, but that asshole wasn't half as charming as I am."

"And you're not half as charming as you think you are." I steady my weight against the wall, keeping the gun pointed at Ryder's chest. The dizziness will abate in a minute and then I can split. Disappearing shouldn't be hard once I'm clear of this bunker; Ryder may have puzzled out my secret, but he won't be able to track me through the sprawl. Not if I lock him in this room, anyhow.

"Jarvis, get me control of the accelerator panel," I say as the world pulls back into focus.

"Jarvis?" Ryder cocks his head. "You named it?"

"I named *him*," I snap, edging towards the door. "And I'd play nice, if I were you. He's about to decide how high to set this microwave."

In truth, I'm only planning to leave him to sweat in here for a few minutes, on a setting so low it'll barely make his skin itch. Ryder doesn't know that though, and for the first time, a hint of fear crosses his expression.

"Sil, wait—" he says as I command the accelerator shut.

But I don't.

I tear out of the shelter as fast as my legs will carry me, hugging the wall for support until I hit the street and the cold air lifts the remaining fog from my head.

My ill-advised dalliance with the Analog Army is officially over.

CHAPTER 17

<Cerebral Intelligence Processor W914//ONLINE>

<. . .>

<W914__Request system diagnostic>

<. . .>

<Commencing system diagnostic>

<. . .>

<. . .>

<. . .>

<684 Errors logged>

<. . .>

<View main system log? Y/N>

<W914__Y>

<. . .>

<Data processors//ONLINE//Reporting damage>

<Working drives//ONLINE//Reporting damage>

<Archive drives//OFFLINE>

<Ocular transmitters//ONLINE//Reporting damage>

<Cochlear transmitters//ONLINE//Reporting damage>

<Aesthetics suite//ONLINE//Reporting damage>

<Main power unit//ONLINE//Reporting damage>

<Secondary power unit//OFFLINE>

<. . .>

<Overall system performance//52%>

<. . .>

<View full system log? Y/N>

<W914__N>
<W914__Exit diagnostic>

A neon-clad bar and three drinks later, I'm starting to feel human again. Since they're non-alcoholic, the surly tech-head manning the bar is giving me the stink eye, but my preferred choice of liquor only served to anger the pain communing between my temples, so I switched to something sugary and filled with caffeine.

Maybe I should switch to a quieter place too—the pounding beats in this one are giving my headache a headache—but I like the anonymity here. It's packed full of mod-happy trendsetters sporting ridiculous programmed hair like mine, and the UV lights make it impossible to tell one face from another, especially as we're all wearing the novelty, glow-in-the-dark sunglasses they hand out at the door. It's the perfect place to hide while I wallow in the fact that in just three days, I've run my CIP down by almost half.

Half.

The reality ties a noose around my neck. No wonder my processors glitched out so badly I damn near nuked myself in a storm. It took Lena six months of twilight to reach 52%. At this rate, I'll be beating her to the grave.

Which is why I should be using this time to send everything I've gathered on the Analog Army to Miles. I may have blown my cover before exposing their endgame, but I didn't come away with nothing. I have the names of the hackers responsible for the gala attack. I have their faces. I have the location of their headquarters and footage of their exploits in the dark web. With the cell saving Syntex some embarrassment by not claiming credit for the breach, that should be enough to convince the Director to lift the bounty off my head and bring me home. To my friends. And Lin. And the world's most thorough diagnostic and CIP repair.

Instead, I've spent the last hour thinking about the look on Ryder's face when I locked him in that accelerator, the fear breaking through the bravado. I'm not sure what's worse, the fact I so casually threatened to screw with the nanites in his blood, or him believing I'd do it. I'm also not sure why I care. He was a means to an end. A way to slide back into Syntex's good graces. That's *all*.

So then why can't I bring myself to hit send? Why is the voice that should be saying, *this is your best chance of seeing Lena and Jondi again* suddenly screaming, *if you give Miles that information, Ryder will never taste daylight again*?

Christ-that-was, that Analog idiot is like a virus. He's infected me. Gotten under my skin.

He also saved your life. That thought is more uncomfortable than the wobbly metal stool I'm occupying. He didn't have to do that. He could have grabbed the box of radiation blockers and left me to burn in the street, or dumped me back in the shelter and never looked back. He didn't have to stay. He didn't have to kiss me.

"Tell me something happy, Jarvis," I mutter around my drink. *Give me something to think about other than the Syntex-hating Reggie I shouldn't be thinking about.*

"Yes, Captain. I have successfully analyzed another 834,567 documents," Jarvis says. "Does that satisfy your criteria?"

Seeing how at full health he would have been able to analyze *millions* by now, no, it doesn't.

"Did you find anything good?" I take another sip of my synthetic-tasting soda.

"Most of the documents appear to be low-level memos," Jarvis tells me. "But there is one file I think might interest you." He pushes an image to my ocular display.

The hell . . . The drink turns sour in my mouth.

"You're sure this came from the black site?" I ask. My processors haven't exactly been reliable today; maybe he pulled a document from a different directory by mistake.

"The timestamp and geo-location data confirm it," Jarvis says. Well . . . shit.

I don't need him to explain the image to me; I've seen diagrams like it a thousand times before, this same cross-section of a skull showing a tiny computer grafted to the brain, with fiber-optic cables connecting it to the eyes, ears, and spine.

A Cerebral Intelligence Processor.

That's what was being developed at the black site.

Someone else has finally cracked the secret of Mindwalking technology.

And they're trying to cover it up.

My first instinct is to take this file and march it right into the Syntex building, because this is holier than a few hackers and some dark web Grail; it's the Ark of the freaking Covenant.

I'm already on my feet by the time my second instinct stops me cold. *He knows.* No other explanation makes sense. The Director wouldn't have tried to lock me up unless he realized I'd stumbled across something explosive. So either he's afraid our investors will get wind of this, or he's complicit. Until I figure out which, I can't hand myself in.

I sink back to my chair, my foot tapping a nervous rhythm against the bar. There's no way for me to dig into the Director's motives from here. He's too private, too . . . *insulated.* But I also can't do it from a cell. What I need is inside help. Which means doing the one thing I promised myself I wouldn't do.

Damn. I order something strong and expensive so that Stink Eye behind the bar will stop staring daggers at me. Then the moment he turns his attention to the next seat-warmer on his hit list, I drop my chin into my hands and say, "Jarvis, get an encrypted message to Lena and Jondi. Tell them we need to meet. How and when of their choosing. But it's got to be soon."

"Yes, Captain."

"And Jarvis, I need you to be invisible. Bounce the message off the moon if you have to, I don't want them getting in troub—"

"Talking to your imaginary friend again?" The voice sends my train of thought careening off the tracks.

Son of a . . . I lurch to my feet. *The hell did he find me?*

"Whoa . . . easy," Ryder says. "If I wanted to sell you out, you'd already be in cuffs."

"Then why haven't you?" Oh, how I wish my gun were in my hand. In this crowded mess of a bar, it would take an hour for anyone to notice I'd shot him.

"Don't need the credits." Ryder shrugs.

No. Given the type of code Aja can write for him, I don't imagine he does.

"How'd you find me?"

"Check the back of your shirt." He points to my left shoulder. "I figured you'd leave in a hurry once I confirmed my theory."

Unbelievable.

"You *bugged* me?" I feel around the fabric until my fingers find the tracking dot he'd stuck there. Suppose I should have seen that coming, this clown's been bugging me for days.

"And you locked me in a live accelerator," Ryder says. "I think that makes us square."

I can hardly argue with that. "Then what do you want?"

"I told you, I just want to talk." He orders himself a drink. Grain spirits, no ice. Not sure if I should be revolted or impressed.

"Fine. But not here," I say, pushing away from the bar. This isn't the type of conversation I want to have within earshot of other people. So instead, I lead Ryder over to one of the booths in the corner and call up the privacy screen, engulfing us inside our own secluded bubble.

"Want anything?" he asks, scrolling through the offers dancing across the table.

"For you to get on with it." I minimize the menus. I've already wasted time enough on him.

"Alright." Ryder projects a 3D image out from his wrist. "You recognize this guy?"

"No. Should I?" I ask. The face staring out at me belongs to his brother, I assume—or some other close relation—same strong jaw and piercing eyes, though this guy looks several years older, and infinitely more serious.

"How about this one?" Ryder taps a few keys and the face takes on a new aspect, growing chiseled and unusual, with a host of visible mods and a power button behind the left ear.

Well . . . crap. My stomach pulls into a tight knot. No wonder Ryder knows things he shouldn't about the Walker program; he's related to a dead one.

"That first holo is what my brother looks—*might* have looked like if Syntex hadn't stuck a bomb in his head," he corrects the wishful slip of tense. "This is what he looked like when he burned out. I take it you recognize him now?"

Yeah, I recognize him. That's a picture of Aiden Stone. He was a few classes ahead of me in the program. Fifth generation Walker, I think, and one of Syntex's finest recruits until he suffered a catastrophic failure at eighteen to the day. Totally out of the blue. No twilight phase, no build-up of glitches. The family— *Ryder*—would have never gotten the chance to say goodbye.

"Why are you telling me this?" I ask as the image of Aiden flickers and dies.

"Because I know what Syntex agents tend to think about my . . . *loyalties.*" He rolls up his sleeve to the elbow, exposing the honeycomb tattoo underneath. "Believe me, Aiden wasn't shy about expressing those views." Ryder knocks back the rest of his drink. "But see, here's the thing, Sil Sarrah, I'm not an idiot. I like being able to breathe the air and drink the water. I like that food synthesizers have kept what's left of us from starving, and hey, if you want to cover every inch of your body with mods, I'm cool with that too. I don't *hate* tech corporations, and I'm certainly not looking to put them out of business. That's not what the Analog Army is about."

"Then what *is* it about?" I ask. Because he and his honey-combed friends have some brand of anti-corp agenda, of that I'm sure. Even if it's not the one I originally imagined.

"For most of the cells—those we work with, anyway—it's about limiting corporate power and reach," Ryder says, locking his eyes on mine. "But for me, it's about righting a wrong." His shoulders harden, the muscles in his neck pulling tight. "The Walker program's been active for what . . . eighteen years now?"

"Yeah . . . and?"

"And they still haven't found a way to keep you alive past nineteen. Don't you find that suspicious?"

Once a conspiracy nut, always a conspiracy nut.

"No, I don't." I meet his question with a glare. "The CIPs fuse with our brainstems; there is no way to get them out without killing us. It's not Syntex's fault our brains erode the units. That's just the cost of—"

"Doing business, yes, I know." Ryder drops his head to the screen. "Christ-that-was, don't you ever get tired, thinking of yourself as a piece of hardware they can simply . . . replace?"

"Sure, all the time." I choke down another mouthful of liquor. "But that's what I signed up for."

"Oh, spare me the official party line," he spits. "We're talking about *the company that saved the human race from extinction,* or whatever other bullshit their marketing likes to claim. You honestly think they couldn't R&D up a fix if they applied themselves?" A simmering note of rage colors his voice, as though his loss stings as fresh today as it did four years ago.

"I think if there was a fix, they'd have found it by now." My temper is fast rising to match. Syntex might not care about our lives, but it does care about its bottom line, and keeping us operational makes fiscal sense. I'm not naïve. I've always known their altruistic arm was self-serving; they donate tech to keep our citizens happy and alive so they can sell them stuff. It's about money. It's always been about money—and about preventing the labor market from running dry. And while that's not a pretty reality, it's the only reality we've got.

"Oh really?" Ryder's eyes narrow at the corners, the fire in them growing wild. "Then why has your director refused to fund a single one of the trials your own doctors have proposed? Why would he actively stonewall research unless he saw you as disposable?"

Christ-that-was, where is he getting this crap? Because even if it were true—and I'd bet my tech it's not—there's no way Lin, or anyone else on the medical staff, leaked this kind of information.

Is there? The worst thing about doubt is how it pops up unbidden, squirming your insides raw. Lin did help me escape the building. She did send me to a mod artist who asked far fewer questions than he should. And she did it without a moment's hesitation. Is leaking classified information truly such a stretch?

"You're reaching," I say, dismissing the thought quick smart. Helping me—helping *one of her Walkers*—makes sense in a way that betraying the program doesn't. What reason would Lin possibly have for turning traitor or breaking bad?

"You sure?" Ryder pulls up the Director's latest news broadcast, where he calls me something much worse than *armed and dangerous*. "Because from where I'm sitting, it looks like he's more than happy to throw you away."

Yes, the view must be spectacular from that high horse of his.

"Look, I'm sorry about your brother," I say. "I really am, and I get why you're pissed—"

"No, I don't think you do." The neon glass in Ryder's hand shatters to pieces. "Syntex is so busy trying to control the rest of us, they're not bothering to protect their own people."

And we're back to his obsession with mindjacking.

I swear, talking to Ryder is like watching a holoform stuck on loop. Though given the document Jarvis uncovered earlier, the charge no longer strikes me as quite so far-fetched. Because if another company has developed a working CIP prototype, then it stands to reason they could have also found a way to circumvent consent laws. And because no one knows about it, no one's taking them to task.

"What if I told you it's not Syntex?" I ask, sounding the idea out. "That someone else is behind the breach?"

It's what makes sense. I mean . . . Ryder finds proof of mindjacking right around the time a black site cracks the secret to Walker tech . . . that doesn't feel like a coincidence to me.

"Nice try, but this has Syntex written all over it," he says. "No one else has the clout to pull it off. No one."

"So that's it? You've already made up your mind?"

"Haven't you?" Ryder pulls down my neon sunglasses. "Or are you willing to put your master to the test?"

"The hell's that supposed to mean?" I slap his hand away.

"It means let me prove it to you." His tone is as serious as a nanite-resistant epidemic. "Marlea gave me the missing piece of the puzzle, but without you—"

"You can't put it together." Gravity vanishes out from under me. That's why he's here then, why he didn't ditch me at the checkpoint, or leave me to die in that storm. Why he was so desperate to cop a feel of my port, he kissed me.

"You need a Walker to test your theory." The words taste heavy on my tongue. So much for thinking it was my life he cared about.

"And you need someone to open your eyes," Ryder says, leaning sharply across the table. "Unless you'd rather stay loyal to the wicked stepmother trying to put you in a cage?"

The words hit a nerve deep inside my gut. Because he's not wrong. I was the Director's best asset and he never even offered me the chance to surrender the documents I stole—which I would have done in a heartbeat.

Still, giving the Analog Army access to my tech . . .

"Yeah, sorry, but that's a hard pass." I refuse to be the first to blink.

"Why? You afraid I might be right?"

"No"—my jaw twitches—"I'm just not in the habit of wasting time chasing ghosts."

"Then do it to prove me wrong," Ryder says. "I think we both know you'd enjoy that."

Oh I really, *really* would. "The answer's still no."

"Then how about this, Sil Sarrah." He snakes my drink and finishes it off in one. "Do it for the satisfaction of knowing Syntex didn't betray you *after* they put a ticking time bomb in your head."

CHAPTER 18

This is the stupidest thing I've ever done. By quite some margin. The Director is already accusing me of espionage; I can only imagine what he'd call this. Letting Ryder play with the computer in my head . . . he'd have to invent some new, more pointed word. Something with teeth.

Christ-that-was. My hands fist at my sides. The hell was I thinking, agreeing to this madness? Miles would quite literally yell at me for a straight week. I should have said no and walked away, left Ryder behind once and for good. Yet here I am, following him through the streets like a lost puppy. Because he didn't just hit a nerve, he strung it up and beat it to a pulp. I need to make certain he's wrong; that Syntex isn't risking everything I've worked for by circumventing consent laws.

We've long since left the Pleasure District behind, cutting through back alleys and quiet lanes towards what used to be the Meatpacking District. The roads are wider here, the buildings larger and more derelict, echoes of the Annihilation visible despite years of regeneration. This part of the sector used to house the food deliveries that graced Manhattan Island every day. Now, only a fraction of the warehouses remain functional. We don't ship food in anymore, we synthesize it. There's nowhere left to ship it in from.

"So how far along are you?" Ryder asks as we weave between the steel goliaths.

"*Excuse me?*"

"Into your twilight phase. You're past the threshold, right?"

I lurch to a stop. "How the—"

"I have a brain, Sil Sarrah," he says. "And you have a super-computer grafted to yours. Your *math* hasn't been off in ten years. You got stuck in that storm because you're glitching."

He's not wrong, even if he is being an ass about it.

"How bad have they gotten?"

The question brings my fear rushing to the surface, a giant 52% *bad* flashing through my mind. I'm three days, a hack butcher, two electric shocks, and a boatload of radioactivity into my exile, with no access to a proper diagnostic or a CIP repair. Nothing is working quite as well as I'd like it to.

"Not so bad I'll burn out while we do this, if that's what you're asking," I snap. I don't talk about this stuff with my closest friends; why would I do it with him?

"It wasn't," Ryder says. Then when I shrug and push past him, he reaches for my arm, his fingers gently circling my wrist. "Sil— it wasn't."

This time, I believe him, if only because he's finally used my name in a way that feels sincere, as though I'm a person instead of a curiosity. Funny, most Reggies turn cold when they realize what I am, whereas the brown in Ryder's eyes has grown warmer.

"Tell me your theory." I change the subject, reminding myself that he doesn't care about *me*; he only cares about what I can do for him.

"My theory?"

"For how Syntex forced Meld structures on the general popu-lation. I assume you have one that's not too stupid to say out loud?"

"Tough call given my present company." Ryder's lip quirks into a smile. "I hear she's not into conspiracy theories."

"Not much into stalling, either."

His smile only grows wider. "Did you know that by the twenty-second century, every man, woman, and child on the planet had access to fluoridated water?"

"Yes, I've read the history books too." I daresay I've read more of them than he has, seeing how it only takes me a few minutes to read a book cover to cover. "But you can't add Meld structures to the water supply."

"True," Ryder concedes. "But you can add nanites."

"Oh, come on, prescriptives in the water? No one is footing that bill." Or taking that big a risk. With a 0.2% rate of rejection, nanites that powerful would never go unnoticed.

"Who said anything about prescriptives?" Ryder cocks an eyebrow. "I'm talking about run-of-the-mill immunity boosters. The kind already in there."

"That's ridiculous," I say. "Regular nanites aren't powerful enough to forge Meld structures."

"Sure they are. They're just slower than your bosses would like. Think about it for a second. Test your assumptions." He shoots me a self-satisfied look, knowing full well I'd recognize the phrase.

Test your assumptions. It's a problem-solving technique from our training his brother must have told him about. The theory is simple: take each variable of the equation in turn and ask yourself, *if this wasn't true, would the situation still be impossible?*

Well, Syntex injects us with military-grade prescriptives because it's the fastest way to prep our minds for the tech; a few intensive weeks and then we're ready to start running sims. Beyond efficiency though, there's no real reason the process couldn't happen slower, over months or even years. The only thing stopping Syntex from doing that is the government's regulatory oversight of the bots. But if I remove that factor from the equation . . . if what Ryder claims is true, and they've decided to brazenly disregard one law, then what's to say they haven't broken another?

Syntex could *theoretically* have weaponized the water supply. If it wanted to.

Which it doesn't. I honestly don't know why I'm still entertaining Ryder's paranoia. The company has plenty of *legal* ways to keep an eye on its competitors. It would never compromise a lucrative public health contract—not to mention all its hard-won public trust—just to gain access to a handful of employees.

"Don't worry, I don't expect you to believe me," Ryder says. "Hell, no one else does. Most of the other cells only tolerate my theories because Aja does, and they're looking to stay on her good side."

Well, that's hardly reassuring. Knowing I'm headed to some abandoned warehouse with the guy even the anarchists think is cracked. "And Brin?"

"Also looking to stay on Aja's good side," Ryder admits. "That's why I need your help, so I can finally prove it."

"And how exactly are you gonna do that?" I ask. This is the part of his plan he hasn't divulged yet, and—I'm guessing—the reason we're stealing between warehouses at dawn, though I'm not altogether sure what he hopes to achieve here. He must realize I can't access any Meld-specific protocols without alerting Syntex to the breach. His brother would have told him that much. He seems to have told him everything else.

"The answer is right behind this door." Ryder pulls to a stop in front of an old meatpacking depot. I expect the rusted metal to squeal as he wrenches it open, but it slides back on its hinges smoothly, as though recently oiled.

"Welcome to my Fortress of Solitude," he says, waving me inside.

"Fortress of Solitude, huh?" I step into the pitch-black space. "You're a fan of old movies."

"Aiden's doing." A self-conscious edge creeps into Ryder's voice. "He got deep into the archives during implantation. I'm assuming you did too, since you named your CIP *Jarvis*. Or is that the world's strangest coincidence?"

"It's not," I say. Syntex's library of pre-Annihilation content is what got me through hours spent holed up in accelerators and diagnostic chairs. Movies were simpler back then. Less in your face, less immersive, less likely to trigger a headache. Once I lost myself in one, hours would fly by without me noticing. I doubt I'd have survived the boredom without them. "But even before Syntex, my dad was a fan," I add, for no other reason than it feels important.

"Was?" Ryder's smile sours at the corners, as though he's stepped in something private. Something he understands.

"*Is*, I guess." I fend off his misplaced concern. *He just no longer watches them with me.* "So, I take it there's a reason we're standing in an empty warehouse?" I ask, eager to relegate this thorny subject to the past. Where I should have left it.

"Not entirely empty." For once, Ryder takes the hint. He flicks a switch and a series of lights spring to life, throwing the space into sharp relief. The cavernous building is as run-down as I expect, though true to his word, it's not empty. There's a small room squatting in the center of the floor, a crude construction of concrete blocks and wire mesh.

Well, I'll be.

Ryder's built himself a Faraday cage, a shielded hideaway safe from electrical interference and prying eyes. That's how he means for us to fly under Syntex's radar.

"You planned ahead." Every part of my body tightens. I thought Ryder brought me here on a whim, that he saw an opportunity and decided to take it. But he has a freaking *Faraday cage* squirreled away, waiting for the day he got his hands on a Walker. That level of commitment usually means one of two things: he's either more delusional than I first thought, or he's right.

"I like to be prepared," Ryder says, beckoning me towards the metal prison. "In here, it'll just be you, me, and a private connectivity hub."

Insulated from everything but the crime we're committing.

I force my feet across the threshold, reminding myself that the only reason I'm doing this is to put his mindjacking nonsense to bed. Then we can both move on.

"You don't mind if we sit for this, do you?" he asks. "I think I'd rather sit." Ryder folds to the ground. More than anything else, it's his fear that scares me. He's trying to hide it; he's almost doing a good job, but I can see it lurking behind his eyes, feel it in the way he looks at me as I drop down in front of him.

Like I'm dangerous.

Like I'm about to break into his mind.

"This is my ID number, for the uplink." Ryder pings me his details. His *real* details.

"Why are you doing this?" I stare at the ten-digit code.

"Because the man holding all the keys shouldn't also get a map to the city," he says, squaring his shoulders and setting his jaw, as though bracing for pain. "Let's get this over with."

"Fine by me." I'm as eager to prove his theory wrong as he is to prove it right. "Jarvis, prepare to Meld with user ID 6453734348."

"I'm sorry, Captain, but I'm not showing an active mission request."

"That's because we're going rogue," I say, tapping in my override code. "Open secure channel."

"Yes, Captain."

This is it, the moment of truth. If Ryder's brain isn't Meld-ready, Jarvis won't be able to connect us.

A second goes by, and then two, and then—right as I'm about to let out the breath I'm holding—a familiar click sounds in my ear and Ryder's breathing fills my mind. Steady but shallow. Baited.

"I guess that confirms my theory." He scrubs both hands through his hair, as though trying to tug the connection loose.

"I thought you already knew?" It takes every ounce of control I have to keep my voice level. Syntex really did it. They weaponized the water supply, and no amount of telling myself there could be a hundred perfectly good reasons for *why* would help quell the dread bubbling beneath my skin.

"Suspecting and knowing aren't the same thing," Ryder says, peering at me through his lashes. "Do the rest, would you? Before I lose my nerve."

"It won't work," I whisper, though I'm not entirely sure who I'm trying to convince anymore.

"Then what have you got to worry about?"

You know what? Nothing. I sit up straighter, meeting Ryder's challenge with a glare. I have absolutely nothing to worry about. Meld structures alone do not a crime make. They don't hurt anyone. They don't cost them anything. And just because I'm not privy to Syntex's reasons for installing them in the general population, doesn't mean they don't exist.

"Jarvis, initiate neural link," I say, and this time, my voice is solid.

"Yes, Captain, standing by for verbal consent."

"Assume we won't get it."

"I'm sorry, Captain, I cannot engage Meld protocols without verbal consent from the host," Jarvis tells me. Because he's a computer, he doesn't add a sarcastic, *as you well know*, but I swear I hear it in his tone.

"This isn't a request, Jarvis, it's an order."

"Pursuant to section eighteen of the Cybernetics Control Act, I cannot comply with that order."

"Just do it, please."

"I cannot comply with that order."

"Damn it, Jarvis, initiate the fucking link."

"I'm sorry, Captain, but I cannot comply with that order."

Relief washes over me, sharp and potent. Three direct orders, three outright refusals. Exactly as it should be.

"See? I told you this was a waste of time." I make to stand but Ryder reaches out to stop me.

"Remember what Marlea said." His grip on my arm is feather-light, urgent but not threatening. "Ask him nicely."

And just like when he kissed me, I suddenly *know* what's about to happen, and I'm scared, not because I think it won't work, but because, somehow, I'm sure it will.

"Jarvis, initiate neural link. I'm"—I have to force the words out—"asking you nicely."

That's all it takes.

One second I'm in my body, safe in my conviction that Syntex would never break this law, then the next, I'm sat across from it, looking at myself through Ryder's eyes, every bit a party to their crime.

I suck in a breath through his teeth, then another, and another, trying to find my feet in his mind. It's a strange sensation to explain, but hosts don't all feel the same. When they fight me, their minds take on a viscous quality, like sinking through quicksand. Some are more solid than others; some are squishy and malleable; some are quiet and some are loud. Ryder's mind is an ocean, endless and deceptively calm, with powerful currents lurking beneath the surface, waiting to drag me under.

"Well, this is disconcerting," he says as I command his arms to move. "I'd love to say it's not as bad as I thought it would be, but that would be a lie."

And suddenly I—*he*—can't breathe.

"Terminate the neural link." I gasp at the air. "Now, Jarvis, do it now." I snap back to my own body and instantly double over, the neon drinks in my stomach spilling out over the floor.

Christ-that-was, the hell did I just do? My nails dig into my temples, trying to claw the memory out. There's a hurricane gathering speed inside my chest, too much anger and disgust to make sense of. I've done some truly awful things during my missions. I've killed, I've maimed, I've tortured, I've left law-abiding citizens to bleed to death from wounds I inflicted. But there's always been a code to it. Rules. It wasn't random, or malicious. It wasn't a violation. But if Syntex is mindjacking people then I'm no more than a thug for hire. And my wicked stepmother is exactly as wicked as Ryder said.

"Well, go on, tell me how right you were." I press my forehead to the cinderblocks, blinking back the burn in my eyes. "I know you're dying to."

"Not really, no." The hitch in Ryder's voice takes me by surprise. I figured he'd be halfway through his victory lap by now, but when I turn to look at him, I find he's shaking worse than I am, his face drawn and pale as a sheet.

"Ryder?" The storm fast turns from rage to worry. I'm not usually around to witness the aftermath of my . . . *skills*. My job is to extract our field ops, then set them loose; the rest I leave to the shrinks. Assuming they need a shrink, that is—which most of them *don't*. 90% suffer no lasting consequences from the Meld, with only a handful choosing to revoke their consent for future melded extractions.

Except, this wasn't a regular Meld.

This was what drove Risler to swallow a bullet and Marlea to go to ground.

This was the nightmare.

I was the nightmare.

"Give me a minute, please." Ryder puts up a hand to stop me getting too close. "I just need a minute."

I nod, shuffling back towards the opposite wall. "Jarvis, take my neural bridge offline," I say. It's not much, but it's the only way I can think to make him feel safe. Or saf*er*, at least. No one's mind is truly safe anymore. Not when we can—

The hand wrapped around my heart squeezes tighter, the chill from the concrete seeping into my bones.

"Why did you make me do that?" I ask once the feeling grows too tight to ignore.

"Because I had to see the truth for myself." Ryder finally opens his eyes. "And so did you. You never would have believed it otherwise."

Right. The words reignite the anger my guilt had pushed aside, a cruel reminder of the lengths he went to in order to prove his theory.

To use me.

"Then I hope the truth was worth almost dying for." I climb back to my feet, suddenly desperate to be done with him, and his *truth*, and his hollow attempts to pretend he did any of this for *my* benefit.

"What's that supposed to mean?" Ryder staggers up after me.

"It means congratulations, you kept me alive long enough to get what you wanted."

"Hold on—" He's unsteady as he moves to block my way. "You think I saved your life because you were *convenient*?"

"I have a gun, Ryder, and I won't ask you again. Move."

"No. Not until you answer the question." Even close to collapse, this clown's as stubborn as a wall and about ten shades denser.

"Fine. You know what, yes," I explode. "That's exactly what I think."

"Then maybe you're not as bright as you think you are."

"Oh, spare me. You needed a Walker."

"You're right. I did. But I'm a pretty resourceful guy; I could have found one without exposing myself to enough radiation to glow in the dark."

"Why bother running into that storm then?"

"Because *you* were out there, you unbelievably frustrating idiot!" Ryder falls back against the cinderblocks. "Don't you get it, Sil? I should have walked away from you the moment you cornered me in that bar. Nothing about your story added up. Your behavior would have made a dead man suspicious. But here I am anyway." He bats aside a tangle of protruding wires. "Christ-that-was, is it just me, or have we been fighting all day for no reason?"

"We have plenty of reasons to fight," I say. And few reasons not to. Not least of which being he just set my life on fire.

"Well, this isn't one of them." Ryder sighs, and for the first time, his mask is entirely gone. No arrogance, no swagger, no hint of a smile. "I didn't save your life because you're convenient, Sil—you're actually the least convenient person I've ever met—and believe it or not, there were a hundred ways to confirm you were a Walker without kissing you."

"Then why'd you do it?" I ask instead of leaving. I want to leave. Or at least, I *want* to want to. I'm plenty pissed enough to. At him, at Syntex, at myself, at the hardware slowly burning a hole through my brain. But no matter how hard I will them to, my legs refuse to budge.

"Honestly?" Ryder takes a hesitant step towards me. "I figured it would be my only chance."

Well, I certainly didn't expect him to say *that*.

"You hate everything about me."

"I hate everything about the company you work for." Another step brings him close enough to touch. Or hit. I could still go either way. "And after what we just did, you should too."

Reality rushes back between us, cold and sobering. Today I did the one thing I thought I would never do, the one thing Syntex vowed it would never allow *anyone* to do. I broke into a civilian mind without consent, and now that civilian is looking at me as though the world has tilted off its axis. As though everything's changed.

And it has.

I know that.

I just don't know how I could ever set it right.

"I'm sorry, Ryder." That seems as good a place as any to start. Especially since I've never said that word to a host before. Never felt the need.

"Don't be sorry, Sil. Just be honest with me for once."

"About what?" I ask. Because right at this moment, the question in his eyes is the one thing I can deal with.

"The games you've been playing," he says. "Where you really got those documents. Why *you* haven't walked away from *me* yet."

It appears Ryder's nowhere near as oblivious as I first thought.

"You're no double agent, Sil," he continues, "or if you are, you're the worst I've ever seen. It's time you told me the real reason Syntex wants to put you in a cage."

CHAPTER 19

The truth is liberating. Like letting loose the butterflies gnawing on your insides.

Shame there are a hundred more lurking in my future, but since I'm returning to the Analog Army with Ryder, lies are a necessity—as are the bone changes required to put my face back the way it was before our stand-off with Jimmy. Because if there's one thing we both agree on, it's that the truth of *what* I am should remain squarely between us. And that means not drawing the girls' attention to any of those things I *shouldn't* be able to do.

"They each have their own reason for hating the program," is all Ryder offers in explanation, staying infuriatingly vague. "They won't understand . . . *this*." His motion between us brings a flush to my cheeks, though the memory of Brin's words brings a shudder. *They'll pay for what they took from us. We will make them pay.*

If the Mindwalking program took a brother from Ryder, then who did it take from Aja and Brin?

"How much do they know? About you, I mean. About Aiden?" I ask as we approach his cell's run-down lair. I swear, the place looks even more decrepit now than when we left it two days ago. There's a fresh layer of graffiti glistening in the morning light, and a new sign that reads *Contamination area: keep out.* These guys have hiding in plain sight down to an art.

"Brin . . . only as much as my ink suggests," Ryder says, prying open the door.

So no specifics then, just his general disdain for tech giants.

"And Aja?" I slip in after him.

"Aja knows. What Aiden used to be." He seems to choose his words carefully, like there's more to the story. To *their* story.

"She does, huh?" The question escapes before I can stop it. Brin or no Brin, I get the impression these two share a connection that runs deeper than a common goal. And I'm not usually wrong about this stuff.

"It's not like that. We've just known each other a very long time," Ryder says.

I wait for him to add something more, to fill in the blanks like a normal person might. But of course, he doesn't, and I pretend not to care. These past few days have really done a number on my brain if I'm getting jealous over some pretty Reggie. That's always been Jondi's MO, not mine.

To be perfectly honest, letting Ryder talk me into coming back here probably wasn't the best idea, but a smart Walker uses any and all resources at their disposal. Syntex taught me that. And right now, Ryder's the best I've got. We might not be aligned on everything, but we're aligned enough to use each other. Our experiment made it clear that the Director isn't just trying to keep a lid on competitor tech. He's in this. He weaponized the water supply and dismantled the protocols keeping the program legal. For all I know, he's the one who founded that black site so he could deploy Walker tech off book and use it with impunity.

Well, sorry, but I won't allow one greedy man with a God complex to undo all the good Syntex has ever done. Our tech is in the water, in the food, in every citizen's blood. If news of the Director's crimes gets out, it'll be anarchy. Public trust would be irreparably damaged. The cults would have a field day. People will die.

I can't let that happen. I won't.

And if that means playing nice with the other side while I figure out how to oust him—quietly and without scandal—then so be it.

"The hell have you been?" Aja's voice greets us as we step into the computer lab. She's currently occupying not one, but two of the central workstations, studying the monitors with enough intensity to set the glass alight. Her neon tips are pink today, her fingers flying between keyboards with unparalleled speed. Brin, on the other hand, is sitting idle at the terminal beside her, looking orders of magnitude more relaxed with her boots on the desk and her hands buried in her hair, absently weaving the blue strands into a braid.

"Yeah, Rye, what gives?" She leans her head back and fixes him an upside-down glare. "You were only supposed to be gone a few hours."

"We decided to take the scenic route home," he says, strolling over to the console.

"There is no *scenic* route home from Sector Two." Aja's gaze remains glued to her screens. "Wait—*we?*" Her fingers quit their dance, her eyes flicking up to find mine. "So you haven't ditched the stray yet."

And she hasn't forgiven it for the hack on her system. Good to know.

"Be nice, A. That stray saved my skin crossing back into the sector." Ryder artfully leaves out the part where I got him into trouble in the first place, and the part where I almost got him killed in a radioactive storm.

Smart.

"Well, you picked a hell of a day to go AWOL." Aja's scowl deserves its own zip code. "You missed the big reveal."

"Don't tell me we're in?" Ryder's face lights up.

"Damn right, we are. Worked through the night, but the uplink is solid." With a few taps she sends an image to every screen in the room.

Holy. Shit. The air catches in my lungs.

I'd recognize that spinning logo even if it wasn't stamped on all my mods. A double helix forged of bone and metal, rendered in black in place of the consumer-facing silver.

"Is that—?"

"Syntex's internal server?" The steel in Brin's lips quirks into a smile. "You know it, Sarrah. Full, unrestricted access to the most secure network in the world."

At a higher root directory than I was ever privy to, no less. That black logo is reserved for the company's upper echelons; I've only ever glimpsed it in passing on Miles's unit.

Unbelievable. I can't quit gaping at the screens. I knew this cell had an endgame cooking, but I never dreamed they'd be capable of such an impressive hack. Hell, forget impressive, a hack like this should be *impossible*.

"Took us two years, five cells, and more bribes than you can imagine to worm our way in, but it was worth every credit." Brin's downright bursting with glee. "Wanna know how we did it?"

"Bee—" Aja warns, her mood announcers flashing red.

"Oh, come on, Jay-Jay, let me show off a little. It's not like Sarrah can run over there and tattle; she's higher on their shit list than we are." Brin spins around in her chair. "See, tech conglomerates are all the same," she tells me. "They think short-term—and they assume we do too. So we played a long game.

"We started by pinging their radar with months of low-key attacks, making noise to get them worried. Which prompted them to bring on a ton of new security personnel. More guys on site, more chance of finding one willing to take a bribe. That's how we were able to credential Rye onto the catering staff for their gala," she says, absently tracing the defensive strips embedded in her neck. "Then once he was in the room, all he had to do was give them a bit of a scare and *bam*!" Brin slams a hand to the table. "Suddenly, cyber security is preoccupied, and their servers are less protected than they've ever been." With a wink, she provides me the final piece of the puzzle.

Getting into places might be Brin's specialty, but they needed Ryder to create the distraction because *even Brin can't be in two places at once*. And hers was by far the harder job: to steal into the server room.

Christ-that-was. No wonder they didn't care about losing credit for the attack. By leveraging their reputation as a disorganized, short-sighted collection of cells, the Analog Army was able to do what none of our competitors have managed. They broke into Syntex's deepest levels and snagged themselves an active node.

They played the company perfectly.

"How long do you think we'll go unnoticed?" Ryder leans into Aja's screen for a better look.

"Another six hours maybe," she says. "Twelve if we're lucky."

"Is that gonna be enough?"

"To get it all? Not even close. But don't worry, I'm prioritizing the grab." She highlights a directory that immediately commands both his—and my—attention. *SYN_MWP*.

Syntex's Mindwalking program.

The folders she's already copied populate the screen too fast to read, but my oculars catch a few of the names as they blur past. One name, in particular, screams out at me from among the rush of scrolling data.

"We look with our eyes, Sarrah." Aja slaps my hand away as it gravitates towards the keys. There's a prickle of dread stirring inside my gut. Barely there, but there enough to raise the hairs on my arms and strip my throat dry. There enough that I have to make sure I imagined it.

"Here, use this one." Ryder grants me access to a terminal on the opposite side of the desk.

"Thanks." I quickly scan the directory for the folder that piqued my interest.

SYN_MWP_DECEASED_ASSETS.

My greatest fear reduced to a few crisp letters.

"What is it?" he asks as I click my way inside, his voice dropping to a whisper. "What's wrong?"

"Probably nothing," I say.

It doesn't surprise me that Syntex keeps a record of its dead Walkers—hell, it doesn't even bother me that much. Not really.

Given the meticulous records the company keeps of our lives, I assumed it would document our deaths, too. That's just what companies do with expensive IP.

What bothers me is the timestamp sitting alongside the files.

This folder was last updated yesterday morning.

On Lena's 6984th day.

Please don't be in here. My hands begin to shake as I scroll through the list of retired designations. *Christ-that-was, please don't be—*

Everything stops, not least of which the beating of my heart. And despite the ever-present hum coming from the servers, the air seems to fall silent, empty save for me and this one file.

CATASTROPHIC_INCIDENT_W807.

I don't mean to click on the video.

I truly don't.

But my fingers move without volition, filling the screen with a scene so familiar, it cleaves my chest wide open. Beside me, Ryder stiffens, but I only have eyes for the boy tucking into a plateful of bacon, still sweaty from his morning run, and the girl sat opposite him, picking at her French toast, her hair glitching in and out of the loose waves she set it in.

They both look tired. Jondi like he's been up all night hacking things he shouldn't; Lena as though she's spent the morning crying, which she only ever does when she's so mad her body can't contain the anger. Judging by the visible glitches, I can guess what she was crying about.

"Sil—" Ryder makes to kill the feed but I deliberately block his way.

"Leave it, please," I say. I don't want to watch what happens next any more than he does, but I have to watch it. I *have* to.

"I'm not sure that's a good—"

"I said *leave it*." Though my growl is whisper-quiet, it stays his hand just the same. He, of all people, should understand why I can't turn away from this. Why I have to see it through to the end. Because Ryder's brother is somewhere in this folder too.

Filed away behind a number, like an obsolete piece of hardware Syntex can just . . . *replace.*

A full minute goes by before it happens. A full minute of Lena and Jondi just goofing around, pretending—as always—that everything's okay.

And then the screaming starts.

Lena's arms fly up to cup her head, sending her breakfast tumbling off the table. She tries to stand, once, twice, again, until finally, she collapses down to the floor, her shoulders shaking with the pain.

It's times like these I wish security cameras were still the black and white relics of old, where the image was so bad it made facial recognition impossible. Where you couldn't see a play-by-play of your best friend burning out in glorious fucking Technicolor. But of course, Syntex's cameras are top of the line, so I see everything. The blood leaking from her nose and eyes. The way her cheeks blister and peel from the heat. The smoke escaping her ears as the computer inside her skull catches fire.

There are two ways to burn out; if you're lucky, the failing component severs your brainstem as it implodes, ending things quickly.

Lena isn't lucky.

The catastrophic failure she's experiencing is taking her out agonizingly slow.

A crowd gathers as she thrashes against the tiles, her whole body seizing, her face ashen and slick with blood. Jondi races to her side, screaming for someone—for anyone—to get help, and it takes every ounce of strength I have to stop myself doing the same.

Ryder puts a hand to the small of my back, to keep me calm, or keep me up, or maybe it's to keep himself from smashing the screen to pieces.

They still haven't found a way to keep you alive past nineteen. Don't you find that suspicious? His words echo through my mind, and in that moment, I hate him. For being right. For being honest about it. For saying something I should have been saying all along. If the lot of us had banded together, we could've forced Syntex to find a solution. That is their mandate: see a problem, fix it. It's what they've been doing day in, day out since the Annihilation. It's what they could have done for us. For Lena.

It takes her five whole minutes to die, by which time, both Lin and Miles have arrived. Lin injects her with a painkiller and Miles barks a command to disperse the audience, but there's little else either of them can do. I know that. I've known that since I was eight years old. But that doesn't stop me wanting to beat my fists against Lin's chest and scream at her to try something. Anything. Whatever it takes to change the ending.

Except, Lin can't change it. And neither can I. I'm staring at my past and future all at once and I can't save Lena any more than I can save myself.

"The hell are you two watching over there?" The dying sounds escaping our terminal draw Aja away from hers. "Christ-that-was, Sarrah. Morbid much?" Her mood announcers turn an orange-ringed black as she clocks the image. Anger tinged with concern. For Ryder, not for me. Because as far as she's aware, I'm just the callous bitch who made him watch a Walker burn out. Like his brother.

"Sorry—" I try—and fail—to force out some excuse, almost choking on the bile in my mouth. "I have to go."

I couldn't give a damn what Aja thinks of me right now, or if I'm about to betray my secret and torch this last remaining bridge. I need to get out of here before the heat sparking in my veins catches fire. Before it razes this whole damn building to the ground.

I don't know how I make it out of that room, but the grief simmering behind my eyes has brimmed over by the time I reach the stairwell. I'm still three floors shy of freedom when the pain grows too debilitating to ignore, sending me stumbling through the first door I see, into an oversized closet filled with boxes, computer terminals, and screens.

A dumping ground for things used then replaced.

Like Lena.

I shove the nearest monitor off the shelves, letting loose a scream. I need to hit something, just to feel it break. I need to burn this wretched world to ash.

"Sil—" Of course—*of fucking course*—Ryder followed me in here.

"Go away." Glass splinters at my feet as I send another monitor crashing to the ground.

"No. Not until you talk to me."

"I wouldn't hold your breath," I mutter, though I probably do owe him an explanation, or an apology, or . . . *something*. I did just make him relive the horror of his brother's death, all so I could pretend I didn't abandon my best friend to hers.

"You knew her, didn't you?" he says. "That's why you looked up her designation. To check if she'd—"

"No—we are not—" My voice cracks as I whip towards him. "You don't get to talk about her. *Don't you dare talk about her!*" The punch I aim at his jaw swings wide and my fist crashes into the wall. Pain shoots up my arm, momentarily easing the ache pounding beneath my ribs. So I do it again, and again, and again, until my grief runs in red rivulets down the plaster.

"Sil—" Ryder catches my hand before I can pulverize my bones to dust.

"Christ-that-was. Why won't you leave me alone?"

"Because I know what this feels like, remember? How unfair it is." He fishes a cloth out from one of the boxes and wraps it around my knuckles. "But if you let it destroy you then they win, Sil. They win, and nothing changes. Unless *we* change it." His fingers linger on mine, his eyes so full of sincerity they drain the fight right out of me.

I don't have the strength to rail at him anymore. And I'm tired of feeling alone.

So I kiss him. Not gently, either; I kiss him as though my life depends on it. Like he's the sole source of oxygen in a room filling with water. Lena always said there were only three ways to deal with your feelings: eat them, pound them into submission, or fuck until they disappear. Well, the idea of food is making my stomach roil and my hand's already lost its run-in with the wall. I need a distraction. To feel anything but this black hole swirling inside my chest. Anything that might silence the voices screaming, *you'll be joining her real soon.*

"Sil—" Ryder shudders as I press him up against the shelves. "Is this the best idea?"

"Why wouldn't it be?" I know he wants me. I can tell by the hitch in his voice and his vice-like grip on my arms. Too tight, painful almost, as though he can't bear the thought of letting go.

"You just lost a friend," he whispers. "You're upset."

"So make me feel better." I pull his mouth back to mine. It's not like this darkness will disappear anytime soon. Lena wasn't just a friend, she was *the* Friend. Capital F. She was the first person to offer me a smile when I joined the program, and the first to visit me after the implantation. The first to show me how to *really* use my CIP, and the first to tell me the hardware wasn't what made me special.

Lena was the first girl I ever loved.

My soul mate.

My sister.

Not by blood, but in every other way that mattered.

If we wait for this hole in my heart to heal, we'll be waiting forever.

And I don't have forever.

My shirt falls to the ground, closely followed by his. A moan escapes Ryder's throat as I trace the ink along his arm, but there's a cautious edge to his hunger, and the way his fingers stutter and stall against my spine.

I tease our bodies closer, urging him to keep going, to keep kissing me, to stop overthinking this. He's not my first, and given the short work he makes of my bra, I very much doubt I'm his. This doesn't have to be some big thing.

And maybe Ryder finally gets that, because with a groan he leaves hesitation behind, running his hands over my waist, my shoulders, my sides, and everywhere he touches me a thousand candles spark to life, an inferno so intense it wrenches a sob from between my lips.

"Sil—" Ryder stills, tilting my face up to look at him. "Are you sure this is what you want?" He's all shadows and hard angles in the dim light, a holoform stripped of color.

Yes. It suddenly occurs to me that I do want this. I do want him, and not only to distract from the pain. I want him because he's the first guy to ever look at me like this. Like it might kill him to look away.

"I'm sure," I breathe. "I don't want you to stop." Then since I don't trust myself to say any more without shattering, I kiss him, again and again and again, until the tension leaves his muscles and his body molds back into mine. Ryder whispers my name, drawing it out as if in prayer, and for a second, at least, the sound of it on his tongue makes me forget the storm raging inside. Because his touch is proof that I was here and real and cared for, that once I join Lena and the rest of the *deceased assets* on the scrap heap, someone might remember me.

CHAPTER 20

Stillness is the greatest enemy of pain; the second you stop moving, it catches up to you.

My distraction worked, for a little while, but now that the moment's faded, the pain's come crashing back, washing over me in violent waves. Drowning me. I feel Lena's ghost in every ragged breath I take, see her blood-streaked face every time I close my eyes. I swear, I even smell the burning lump of metal that killed her, taste smoke in the back of my throat.

It tastes like inevitability.

A senseless and *pointless* inevitability given what the Director is doing.

If his decision to weaponize the water supply goes public, it'll negate all the good any of us have ever done.

Lena will have died for nothing.

Ryder's body is still tangled with mine between the stacks, his fingers tracing lazy circles around the port at my neck, a sensation so alien it feels far more intimate than what we just did.

I don't think I can stand it.

Sex has always been easier for me than intimacy; that's kind of how it goes when all your friends have an expedited shelf life. So this . . . *after* part . . . the cuddling . . . it's safe to say I've never been good at it.

Which is why I'm relieved when Jarvis pushes a message to my ocular display.

<UNKNOWN_USER> 4075167397550000.

The sender is anonymous, but seeing how it came through to my personal account—the one only a select few have the handle to—I know exactly who it's from.

Jondi.

Just thinking his name sends an ache of longing through my chest.

Last night I had Jarvis message him and Lena both, thinking the three of us could figure out this mess together.

But Lena was already gone.

At least the string of numbers Jondi's sent me proves easy enough to decipher. Coordinates to some place mid-sector, followed by a time. Hours away yet, but it gives me the perfect excuse to break out of Ryder's embrace and reach for my clothes.

"Somewhere you need to be?" He props himself up on one elbow.

Actually, yes. Though truth be told, I'd have found a reason to escape his arms and this storeroom even if I didn't. Because he wants to talk. I can tell by the feigned nonchalance of the question and the way he studies me as I shimmy into my pants. But I can't talk about this. Not about what we saw. Or how I feel. Or what horrible memories it might have dredged up for him. I just *can't.* I won't survive the words.

"Away," I say, avoiding his eyes.

"Away from here, or from me?"

"Just away. Let's not make a big deal of it, okay?"

"Okay." Ryder's quick to dress as he springs to his feet. "Then how about we talk, instead?"

Reggies really are as predictable as the dawn.

"It was sex, Ryder. What more is there to say?"

"I didn't mean about the sex. I meant about your friend."

"*Lena,*" I snap. "Her name is *Lena.*" *Was* Lena, I correct in my head. While I was out breaking laws with him, she slipped into the past tense.

"Lena." His hands slide up my ribs, making me shiver. "I've been where you are, Sil. Talk to me. Maybe I can help."

No, he can't. Because no, he hasn't. Not really.

His brother's unexpected burnout may have robbed him of the chance to say goodbye, but Ryder was never supposed to be there when it happened. Whereas *I* should have been there. I should have been there for Lena at the end.

"What's the point?" I shrug him off. "That's my future on that video." And no amount of talking will change that.

"Hey—" Ryder spins me around. "I'm not gonna let that happen," he says, as though there's a damn thing he can do to stop it.

This isn't some pre-Annihilation fairy tale where love and a can-do spirit is enough to win the day. His misguided fascination with me is not a magic balm that will keep my hardware from imploding. I am going to die. Like Lena. And it's going to happen soon.

"I really need to go," I say, rescuing my bag. I have to get some air and pull myself together, clear this smoke from my head before it settles there as ash. And I can't do that while Ryder's waltzing around a storeroom all disheveled, making eyes and promises he can't possibly keep. I mean . . . honestly, he should know better than to ask a Junker to go steady.

"Would you give up the tech, Sil?" His question freezes me halfway to the door. "If there was a way?"

"There is no way."

"I know that. But would you?"

I don't do hypotheticals. Or wishful thinking, for that matter. "You can't change the weather, Ryder. No use trying."

"But if we found a solution, could you live without it?"

Oh, I see where this is going. Ryder's a fixer. He wants to fix me. Or save me. Or, Christ-that-was, I don't even know what he wants. I do know the tech is part of who I am. Not just what I do, but why I *matter*. Everything good about me—everything valuable—was engineered in a lab, and that's been true long enough I'm not sure there'd be anything left worth saving without it. So no. I wouldn't give up my CIP. And if he cared about *me* instead of his grudge against Syntex, he'd be searching for a way to patch the tech, not rid me of it entirely.

"Look, I'm sorry you're having some kind of buyer's remorse here," I say, "but I made this choice a long time ago, and I'm not interested in a do-over."

"Oh please, this was never a *choice*." Ryder's face darkens at the word.

"The hell is that supposed to mean?"

"It means Syntex *stole* your life, Sil."

"Syntex *gave* me a life," I growl at him. "You have no idea how bad things were before I joined the prog—"

"I think I have a pretty good idea, actually." He cuts me off mid-word. "You were dirt poor, right? Born to parents who couldn't afford kids, but had them anyway because they wanted to do their part in growing the population. So they had you, and they loved you, but things were hard. You weren't starving, but you were never full. You weren't sick, but you were never healthy. Government services helped you enough to survive, but not live. How am I doing so far?" Ryder doesn't give me a chance to respond.

"Then when you were eight years old, a Syntex rep knocked on your door," he continues, "and hell if they weren't the most impressive person you'd ever met. Mods from head to toe—all top of the line—they even let you play with them. Just you, not your brothers and sisters. *You're special*, they said. *Your genes are special. Only a handful of people have genes as special as yours.* Then they told you about the special computer your special genes meant you could have, and because you were *eight years old,* you never stopped to wonder how Syntex knew so much about your genes in the first place, or how star-spangled awful it is that the clinic your family visited sold your medical records to the highest bidder. All you could think about was what they were offering."

I'm not sure if it's my recruitment he's describing now, or his brother's. Hard to tell seeing how familiar this story sounds.

"So when the rep turned to you and asked if you wanted to help your family—to help your *country*—you said yes without giving it a second thought. Your parents cried; they begged you not to trade your future for some hardware and a few credits. But you did it anyway, because you didn't just want nice things for yourself, you wanted nice things for them, too. And thanks to those handy child-autonomy laws Syntex helped pass, your consent was the only *yes* that rep needed. So no, Sil, you didn't make a *choice*," Ryder spits. "You were manipulated. By a company that's spent billions making sure they never hear the word *no*."

The silence that follows *that* assertion is so dense I could reach out and snap it in half. Which, coincidentally, is what I'd like to do to Ryder's neck. A dead brother doesn't give him the right to take the most important decision I've ever made and twist it into something sinister. I did this. Me. And he doesn't get to say otherwise.

"Is that what you have to tell yourself?" I lace my voice with venom. "That your brother didn't *choose* to leave, he was *manipulated* into doing it? Because guess what, Ryder, if he was anything like me, he probably wanted to go. Anything to get away from you." The words hit exactly as I mean them to, blowing Ryder's pupils wide. I'm being deliberately cruel; I know that. But I won't stand here silently while he strips all meaning from the last ten years of my life.

"You know what, Sil? You can push me away as much as you like," Ryder yells as I barrel out of the storeroom. "It won't make what I said any less true."

I don't bother dignifying that with an answer.

I no longer answer to Ryder Stone.

The buildings on the north side of the sector are grander than they have any right to be. Here, glass and metal dominate the sky, endowing the high-rises with an ever-present shimmer. The roads are flat and free of potholes, the sidewalks wide and clear of trash. There are gated parks too, and large enclosures filled with *real* trees, not the holographic kind that flicker in and out of existence. I never even saw a real tree until Syntex recruited me. In the slums, the mere illusion of life has to do.

But this is the Diamond District, where tech companies house their shareholders, upper-level employees, and the families of those who sell their future.

It's where they house my family.

Christ-that-was. My throat grows tight as I approach the top of their street. I shouldn't have come here. I don't remember deciding to, but with hours to go before my meeting with Jondi— and Ryder's words weighing heavy on my mind—I walked and I walked and I walked and before I knew it, I was sneaking across a manicured courtyard towards a building I've never called home.

The home they made without me.

Ten floors of radiation-resistant glass gleam purple in the evening light, beckoning me forward. This place is everything I dreamed of as a child. It has its own rooftop garden, and a holopark, and a shelter, and these apartments come furnished with their own private food synthesizers and body cleansers as well. No more lukewarm rations or queuing up to wash with the masses. The residents of the Diamond District are living the all-new American dream.

You didn't make a choice. You were manipulated. I try to shake the echo of Ryder's voice as I stake out the entrance. This is what I wanted for them. Then . . . now . . . this is what they deserve.

Though the very fact I was able to get this close without setting off a dozen alarms adds another crack to my already splintered heart. Syntex didn't bother putting my family under surveillance. Because why would they? Ten years of dwindling visitation requests tell them this is the last place I'd ever come.

I don't go up to the apartment. With the Director calling for my head on every news board in the city, I figure it best not to announce myself to the entire Sarrah clan. And besides, I don't think I could handle seeing my dad or siblings right now. Truth is, I don't know how to talk to them anymore, and I stopped coming around because I hate the way they look at me. Like I'm not entirely human. Like the hardware is all they can see.

Which is why instead of heading to the residential floors, I steal up to the building's business center. My mom may not need to work, but she's never been one for sitting still, so while my dad stays home with the kids, she makes a tidy living programming food synthesizers for some of the best restaurants in town.

The smell of her efforts assaults me as I hack my way into her workshop, a cloud of mouth-watering aromas that set my stomach growling.

"Mom?" I call out from the doorway.

"Lyra, is that you?"

Of course she'd assume I'm my sister. That's far more plausible than her fugitive daughter dropping by for a visit unprompted and unannounced.

"What have we said about hacking locks, young lady? You know you're not supposed—"

"No, Mom, it's me." I follow her voice through the deep stacks of synthesizers awaiting her expertise. "Sil."

"Sil?" Her head pops up from behind an industrial-grade unit, her eyes widening with panic and surprise. More panic than surprise, really. They dart wildly between me, the door, and the cameras, her whole body tensing in anticipation of the alarms.

"You don't have to worry, I looped the feed." I'm suddenly struck by just how stupid it was to come here. For all I know, my entire family has bought into the Director's narrative, and her next words will serve to summon the law. But my mom doesn't do that. Instead, she rushes over to hug me and says, "My stars, honey, we've been worried sick."

"I'm sorry." Shame claws at my insides. Four days I've been on the run, the best part of a week. And in all that time, it never occurred to me to let them know I was okay. That's how adept

I've become at suppressing this part of my life.

"Are you sure it's safe for you to be here?" She only hugs me tighter, as though it would pain her to send me away. But I suspect she would if she had to. I'm not the only daughter she has to protect.

"I swear I took precautions, Mom." I don't think I could handle her telling me to go. Not when everyone else I have left is so desperately out of reach. "Syntex will never know I was here."

"My sweet girl, I don't care about that. I'm just happy you're alright."

Her words shatter me, causing my guilt and grief to bubble over.

"Oh honey, what's wrong?" My mother hasn't seen me cry in years. Not since I was eight and about to undergo implantation. Back then, it wasn't the future that scared me—glitches, decommissioning, burning out . . . none of it even registered. Back then, it was the pain I was afraid of, and the endless nanite regimes, and I was missing home so badly I felt my family's absence in every breath and heartbeat. Back then, my mom would still visit me at the barracks; sit with me for hours while the nanites did their work. I can't remember when she stopped visiting, or when I started feeling more alone here than at the Syntex building. I wish I could though. I wish I could go back and change it.

"I'm in trouble, Mom"—the words hiccup out between sobs—"and I don't know what to do."

"Nonsense." Her hands clamp around my shoulders. "You always know what to do. You were a problem solver long before Syntex came along, and whatever's going on, you'll figure it out. I trust that." There's no hitch to her voice, no doubt in her face as she wipes the tears off my cheeks with the edge of her sleeve. Only total belief. Despite the wealth of evidence to suggest I don't deserve it. "Now come on, I've just put the finishing touches on a new pie. You can be my guinea pig." She leads me over to a table that's groaning under the weight of her experiments.

Aside from the mountains of food and hastily scribbled recipes, my mother's filled her workshop with dozens upon dozens of holoforms of the kids. And not to sound like some old nana, but damn they've gotten big.

Last time I was here, the twins were barely even crawling, not running around with sheets draped across their shoulders, terrorizing the robodog. Lyra and Rani were still hovering in that clumsy space between childhood and teen—though they both appear to have grown out of it now, coming into their features and the world of mods my parents promised they could explore once they were *older*. And Amanzi . . . shy, quiet Amanzi, is what . . . ten . . . eleven? And she looks so much like I did at that age, it's startling. I guess one day my parents will know what I'd have grown up to look like.

"They miss you," my mom says, passing me a plate of pie. "Your father does too."

"You don't have to say that." I tear my eyes away from the glass cubes. We both know my siblings barely remember me at this point, and my dad is unlikely to have said anything about me at all. Maybe if he'd never been an emotions kind of dad, this chasm he's forged between us would be easier to bear—but the truth is, he turned cold the day I had my CIP installed. He hasn't looked at me the same since.

"It's true. The only thing they've talked about these last few days is how—"

"The entire city's looking for me?" I finish for her. It is what we're both thinking.

"You want to tell me what happened?" My mother's brow is furrowed, her hands knotted with concern. I used to take after her, back before the mods. Same green eyes and dark hair, same rounded chin and high cheekbones. Now, you'd never guess we were related.

"I disobeyed an order and things sort of . . . spiraled from there." I shrug. "It's not important."

"Then what's on your mind?" she asks. "You didn't risk the trip here for my pie."

No, but that's only because I'd forgotten how good it is. My mother programs a synthesizer better than any three-star technician. She is right though. I didn't come here for pie; I came to quell this feeling simmering inside my gut, the one screaming, *Ryder's right, you know. You sold your future for nothing.*

"Did you want me to do it?" I choke the words out. "Become a Walker, I mean?"

"Oh, honey." My mom looks at me as though she always suspected I'd ask her this question. Like this conversation was inevitable. "What's brought this on?"

"Nothing, it's just—" *I watched my best friend die today. In agony. Clawing at the hardware Syntex put in her head. The hardware I let them put in my head.* "I need to know if—" *I did the right thing. If it was worth it. If you'd have still loved me had I turned them down and all of this disappeared.* "You know what, it doesn't matter." I can't give voice to this fear, because honestly, I'm not sure what would be worse: hearing her say yes, they were happy to trade my future for an upgrade, or no, that ten years ago, I made the biggest mistake of my life.

My drastically shortened life.

"I'm sorry, Mom, I should go," I say, wishing I'd never come here in the first place. My visits only ever end one way: with me leaving, and the gulf between us growing ever more pronounced. And it seems today will be no different.

"Sil Sierra Sarrah—" My mother's eyes narrow down to danger, pinning me in place. "Don't you dare think for *one* second we'd have chosen this for you," she says. "But that doesn't mean you haven't made us so, *so* proud."

Proud. The word grows heavier the longer I carry it, like a ship taking on water. I used to be proud of what I do. I used to think the good outweighed the bad. That it made leaving them necessary. Now, I'm not so sure anymore.

I'm not sure why they allowed it.

"You didn't stop me," I whisper, speaking my fear at the ground. If they truly didn't want this for me, wouldn't they have objected louder? Shouldn't they have *fought* harder?

"We tried, honey. Believe me, we tried." My mom runs a hand through my hair, smiling at the ridiculous colors. "When your father realized what Syntex had planned for you, he threw their rep out of the house, forbid him from ever contacting you again. But by then, it was too late; he'd already filled your head with promises and offered you a place in the program. Once you accepted, we had no choice but to support your decision. The law was on their side."

"Oh."

Her answer shakes loose a memory.

Of her and Dad, begging me to reconsider. Telling me over and over that I could still change my mind. That the credits don't matter. That I have to be *certain* because once the hardware is installed, there will be no going back.

Of me, signing the contract anyway. Thinking I knew best.

Thanks to those handy child-autonomy laws Syntex helped pass, your consent was the only yes *that rep needed.* Ryder's words assault me on loop. I always assumed that law was passed to *protect* kids. So that children from the anti-tech cults couldn't be denied life-saving treatment by their parents. So that orphans and runaways could make their own medical decisions at any age, no questions asked. I never stopped to think how it might be applied the other way around: to keep loving parents from talking sense into their kids.

"Your father has never forgiven himself for letting it happen," my mom continues, skimming a thumb over my cheek. "He feels responsible."

My chest tightens, my own weight of responsibility growing thick. Because suddenly, my dad's cold indifference makes all the sense in the world. Not disgust or disapproval as I had come to believe, but regret and shame. Grief.

"It's not his fault," I say, pulling my mother into another bone-crushing hug. "Please, tell him that for me. Tell him I'm okay."

I can't change the past or undo what's been done—and to be

quite honest, I'm not sure I'd want to. When I think about the life I could have had outside the program, the only thing I see is a never-ending slum and a hole where Lena and Jondi should be. For better or worse, I'm living the final act of the future I chose.

The *legacy* I chose.

Now I just have to make it count for something.

CHAPTER 21

```
<Cerebral Intelligence Processor W914__System alert>
<. . .>
<Bone changers not responding>
<. . .>
<Offline? Y/N>
<W914__N>
<W914__Reset bone changers>
<. . .>
<Bone changers not responding>
<. . .>
<Offline? Y/N>
<W914__Y>
<W914__Exit alert>
```

Strolling up to Jondi's coordinates come midnight, I can't help but wonder whether Jarvis has glitched out again and sent me to the wrong place. I'm at the seedy end of the Credit District, Sector One's heart for all things money, where the government banks sit alongside less . . . *reputable* institutions. Shark tanks, we call them. Run by monsters with sharper teeth and a deadlier bite.

Around me, the Bounty Boards are working overtime, cycling through this week's list of most wanted degenerates—and those most successful at bringing them to heel. The hunters flashing across these screens are every bit as famous as the holo-stars I grew up watching, with some even boasting their own digi-streams and merchandising lines. They dress like the demented offspring of superheroes and law enforcement bots, with sports-branded armor, and obnoxiously overpowered weapons given that they spend their days chasing gamblers and drunks. Rarely do they go after anyone who'd present a real challenge.

Like me, for instance. My face has pride of place up on those boards tonight. With the Contracts Dinner fast approaching, the Director seems doubly desperate to track me down, so that he can enjoy his company's most lucrative night in peace. But I'm pretty sure I could take any one of these showboaters in a fight, and that's assuming they'd ever find me in the first place. The average bounty hunter makes trailing gamers to a holopark look like hard work.

Jondi's instructions lead me straight to the most dilapidated building on the street, a squat, weathered structure with bars on the windows and barbed wire lining the roof. The sign above the door reads *Workhouse Surrender Bureau,* which is a polite way of saying *dumping ground for the desperate and the damned.*

The actual workhouses aren't here—they're out in Sector Five, where there's more space and the ethical violations go un-noticed—this is just the transfer point, where the hunters bring those who have saddled themselves with so much debt, they'll never be able to pay it back.

There's no way Jondi picked this place by choice. The work-houses this side of the Demarcation Line may not be as notorious as the work camps beyond it, but they're bad enough that he gets uncomfortable at the mere mention of the word. No one—not even Ryder—could claim that Jondi was *manipulated* into joining the program. If my life was hard before I was recruited, then his was made of impenetrable steel. No rights, no tech, no freedom. Nothing to look forward to but impossible quotas and an unscalable mountain of debt.

That's why he chose to meet here. The realization dawns clear as a smogless sky.

This building is the last place Syntex would ever look for him.

The Workhouse Surrender Bureau is the dictionary definition of depressing on the inside. The walls are drab, the gray paint cracked and peeling, partially masked by LED displays warning that security is watching. That the hunters always get their man. That a debt repaid is the highest form of fulfillment.

"Sil!" Jondi barrels out from one of the offices and sweeps me into his arms. "Christ-that-was, it's good to see you."

"You too." My throat burns at the sight of him. Though I've only been gone a few days, it feels like months, so I expect him to appear changed, to have altered his face or eyes, reprogrammed his ink maybe. But Jondi is exactly as I left him the night of the gala. Close-cropped hair, raven black against his light skin, a stark contrast to the bright tattoos creeping up the sides of his neck.

"I can't believe you kept your face—and this hair," he says, appraising me in much the same way.

"Stupid, I know." I tuck the multicolored strands behind my ear. My decision to stick with the Analog Army may have forced my hand at first, but I had ample time to remake myself once I left that bad decision behind. Except, when I tried, Jarvis informed me my bone changers had stopped responding, so a new face was out of the question. But the hair I wouldn't have changed even if my aesthetic mods weren't on the fritz. It was the last thing Lena did for me. One final piece of her I'm not yet ready to give up.

"Sil, there's something I need to tell you." Perhaps Jondi's guessed at the reason, because he presses his forehead to mine, his hand moving to cup my neck.

"Lena," I say, so he doesn't have to, so neither of us has to hear the words aloud.

"It was quick," he breathes, clutching me tighter. "She never even felt it."

A lie, but a kind lie, meant to give comfort and spare me the truth. He doesn't know about the Analog Army's hack into Syntex's servers, or the directory full of snuff films our employer keeps squirreled away. He doesn't know that I *heard* the desperate pitch of Lena's scream as the pain consumed her, or that I *saw* the way she curled in on herself, like a sheet of plastic exposed to a flame.

"I should have been there," I confess the feeling that's settled between my bones. Not only for Lena, but for him, too. For after.

"No." Jondi shakes his head. "She wouldn't have wanted that."

Just as I wouldn't have wanted her to watch me.

But that doesn't ease the guilt gnawing at my insides. Friendship means being there even when it's hard. It means being there to the end.

"Argh, enough of this nonsense." Jondi sniffs. "If she saw us blubbering like this she'd slap us both into next Sunday."

I laugh—though the sound is more pained than joyful—because she absolutely would, too. Then she'd throw in a few choice digs at how we're getting soft in our old age.

"So, listen." Jondi turns serious, leading me towards the office from which he'd emerged. "I don't want you to freak out, okay? But there's someone else here to see you."

"The hell—" I lurch back as the door swings open, reaching for my gun. "*You told someone about this?*"

Unbelievable.

The one person in the world I thought I could trust and he goes and does—

"Hello, Sil." Miles's greeting stays my hand mid-draw.

I freeze in the doorway, torn between the urge to run away from my commanding officer and the need to run towards him. Miles may have become more friend than boss to me these past two years, but he's also a Paxton, and a high-ranking Syntex employee. Directly accountable—not to mention *related*—to the man looking to put me in a cage.

"Please don't be afraid. I'm not here to bring you in," Miles says, pushing off the battered desk.

"He's not, Sil, I swear." Jondi places himself between us. "He knows why the Director went nuclear after your mission. Just let him explain."

199

"I'll happily talk at gunpoint," Miles adds. "If it'll make you feel safer."

Not really. I leave the weapon in my waistband. We both know bullets won't get me far if he decides to call in the cavalry. Staying out of Syntex's crosshairs is one thing, but once you're in them, things only ever end one way.

"You're sure about this, J?" I drop my voice to a whisper. I want so badly to believe that Miles is on our side; that his loyalties lie with his Walkers and not his father. But if the last few days have taught me anything, it's that trust is hard to build and easy to betray.

"I wouldn't be here if I wasn't." Jondi gives my fingers a squeeze. "Please, Sil, hear him out."

"Okay." I step into the room proper. "I'm listening."

"Just answer me one thing first." Miles takes a step towards me, his face drawn ragged with worry, like the night he found me beating my anger into a leather bag. I tense all over, waiting for him to hit me with any one of a hundred questions. About where I've been. What I've been doing. *Who* I've been doing it with. But instead he asks, "Are you alright?"

Christ-that-was, how to even begin answering that question?

"I'm fine," I say, casting my eyes to the floor. Because if I try to say much else I'll fall apart. And I can't do that in front of Miles again. I won't. No matter how bad things have gotten. "Now tell me what's going on." I lean my weight into the wall, not yet comfortable enough to join Jondi in one of the uncomfortable-looking chairs.

"Okay." Miles nods, perching back atop the desk. "A couple of years ago—when I was still working for the Applied Science division—my research subjects started exhibiting subtle changes in brain morphology," he says, "not unlike the Meld structures our agents have installed. Which should have been impossible." His fingers drum across the splintering wood. "So we called in some more volunteers—and what do you know, they also showed signs of neural manipulation.

"That's why I chose to leave the lab. I knew my father was the only one with the means to implement this kind of change in the population, and that he'd never keep evidence of such a massive breach on the company server. If any existed, it'd be on his private one. So I came home and began working to hack his files. That's how I learned he was circumventing consent laws—though I still don't know the ins and outs of how he's doing it. How he's getting around the Cybernetics Control Act."

I do.

I have the how-to guide sitting pretty on my drives.

In full sound and color.

Marlea's tale, Ryder's investigation, the Analog Army's gateway to the dark web . . . I could solve this mystery for him—prove I'm good for more than just disobeying orders and a bounty—with the press of a button.

If I could bring myself to press it.

Which you can't. The very thought ties my stomach in knots. Even despite the way we left things, I can't bring myself to sell Ryder out today any more than I could in that bar, before I knew he was interested in something other than my CIP, or how it felt to have him run his hands over my body.

"Why not go to the board?" I ask Miles instead. "Force your father out?"

"Because all I have so far are a few unbranded files with no provenance," he says. "I've been trying to get hold of something more concrete for months, but you beat me to it."

It takes me a second to put together what he means. To put it all together. The unmitigated cluster of events that led the three of us to the Workhouse Surrender Bureau in the middle of the night.

"*You* sent Harper to that black site." Heat sears through my veins, turning the world red at the edges.

"To *his* black site, yes," Miles says. "Though granted, the mission was less than ideal. I had to use a retired agent in order to stay off my father's radar, and I had virtually no intel on the facility for her to work with. But I thought sending her in during the gala—while he was distracted—would give her a fighting chance."

"Well, you thought *wrong*." I hurl the charge at him, too keyed up to mind my insubordination. Miles should know better than anyone that there's a method to when Syntex retires its agents, a finely honed cost-benefit analysis. If Harper was pulled from the rotation, then every metric at his disposal would have been screaming *she isn't up to the job*. And he sent her in anyway. He sent her in to die.

"I made a mistake." At least Miles has the grace to look sorry about it. "My father wasn't as distracted as I'd hoped, and she wasn't as discreet. The second she tripped an alarm, he was alerted to the breach, and once he knew she was in there, he had to make sure she wouldn't get out."

So that's why he ordered the termination. It was his data Harper was trying to steal.

But then . . .

"Why would he assign that mission to me?" I ask. "In front of everyone?"

"Isn't it obvious?" Miles cocks an eyebrow, as though surprised I haven't yet figured it out. "What better way to deflect a security breach than a demonstration of what he'd do to protect company IP? You were his best and brightest, Sil. Until that night you'd never disobeyed an order. He trusted you'd do it."

That's because he didn't take into account a different record of mine: my perfect extraction record, the one I was so worried about losing.

"Look, I know I've handled this all wrong," Miles continues, "and I can't tell you how sorry I am my father dragged you into this mess. I wanted to stop him quietly, without involving anyone else, or miring the program in scandal. But I wouldn't be here—risking everything I've worked for—if I didn't want to put an end to what he's doing. The files you took are the only way to do that."

"They won't help." I suddenly feel bone-tired, as though the weight of the last few days is bearing down on my spine. "They're also unbranded, and I only have screenshots so there's no metadata. You'll never prove they belong to him."

"That only matters if he's alive to challenge them."

"Wait—" Jondi's head snaps up. "You can't mean—you never said anything about *killing* anyone."

"I know how it sounds, and trust me, I've spent months trying to come up with a different solution. But what else can I do?" Miles claws at the back of his neck. "My father is too powerful to challenge, too careful to leave a paper trail, and he'll never step down on his own. If I come at him with those documents, he'll deny all knowledge of them. If I try to seize his private server, he'll erase the drives. That black site I sent Harper to?" Miles shoots us both a pained look. "I spent *two years* working to find it, and he barely hesitated before razing the place to the ground. What does that tell you?"

Son of a . . . It only takes me a second to follow the logic to its natural end.

"He has more than one," I say, and I can tell by the shift in Jondi's expression that he's reached the same conclusion.

"Exactly." Miles lets out a deep sigh, as though relieved to find we understand. That we don't think him a monster. "We have no way of knowing how many other sites he's hiding, or how many illegal Walkers he's got at his command, what he's doing with them now that he's installed Meld structures in every mind in the city."

I could offer him a few answers for that, too.

Because Ryder took me to see a woman who knows precisely what he's doing with them. He's mindjacking our competitors' employees for their access, then disposing of them when he's done. And why wouldn't he? They're completely expendable, have none of his proprietary tech in their bodies, and won't ever trace back to him. It's the perfect crime.

"Just think what he could do with this power." Miles starts to pace the room. "Any security guard in the city, any police officer, or board member, or judge . . . there's nothing to stop him seizing control of anyone he needs. Even if I did manage to put him in a cell, he'd only get himself out again. That's why I *have* to do this." The steel in his expression is no match for the heartbreak. "Then once he's . . . *gone*"—Miles can't quite seem to say *dead*—"I can use those documents to bully the board into letting me put this right. It's the only way to save the company, and then maybe . . . one day"—he takes a breath before adding—"all of you."

Okay, well, now we're both staring at him, struck silent by the words.

"I'm sorry for not telling you this before; I didn't want to get your hopes up until the research was yielding results," Miles says, glancing between us. "But this is the reason I fought for the Program Director job when I returned—so I'd have access to your medical scans." He taps a command into his palm and a moment later, Jarvis informs me that a nearby user would like to share a directory called *Project Defuse* with me. Jondi's CIP must have pushed him the same message because we both bark "commence transfer" at the same time.

"I've already begun running trials," Miles says as a hundred-odd files populate my ocular display. Hypotheses, proposed surgical techniques, simulation stats detailing months of hardware erosion studies.

"Sil, are you seeing this?" Jondi's face lights up at the promise these documents hold.

"Yeah, I see it." A lump forms in my throat. It's the real deal, too. Hard, clinical data. Proof that Miles is searching for a way to get the tech out of our heads clean. That's where he goes when his mind wanders off. To *this*.

"My father is happy to watch you die young because it's cheaper in the short run than outlaying the credits to save you," he tells us. "So he schedules every minute of your day, makes a game of your performance stats, keeps you too damn occupied to question *why* the company isn't maximizing its return on investment by keeping you alive." The derision in Miles's voice makes it clear how he feels about his father's myopic business practices.

"His aversion to spending money means I've had to conduct this work off book, so progress is slow, but once he's gone, I'll make it my top priority. I swear to you both, I will stop the burnouts." His eyes turn sad as he says it, and I don't need the supercomputer in my head to know why. Every piece of data on these pages is telling me the same thing: he won't find it in time to stop *my* burnout. The research isn't far enough along.

But it might bear fruit in time to save Jondi, or failing that, the classes of Walkers recruited after us.

One day, this research will save lives.

If Miles is in a position to complete it.

Which is why I square my shoulders and say, "I should be the one to kill him."

"What?" Miles and Jondi exclaim in unison.

"No. Absolutely not."

"Miles, just—"

"I said, *no*, Sil."

Yes, and I'm choosing to exercise my right not to listen.

"Just . . . *think* about it for a second." I put up a hand to temper his protests. "If you do this and something goes wrong— or the board so much as suspects you were involved—you'll either spend the rest of your life in jail, or they won't let you assume control of the company. But if *I* publicly take the blame, then we can make sure it never traces back to you." Hell, it won't even be a hard story to sell, seeing how the entire city already thinks I've turned double.

This is what I can do to help him save the program. To ensure that what happened to Lena never happens to another of my friends.

"Sil, you don't understand . . . even with my access, you'll never get within a hundred feet of him," Miles says. "He knows what's in your head. He knows you'll put the information together eventually. He'll be expecting you to try something."

"Which is exactly why he'll come to me." The solution forms quickly, and when it does, I don't question it. This whole *not having a future thing* may have ruined my ability to plan ahead, but I've always been good at thinking on my feet, working the problem. "He'll want to know if I betrayed his secrets before he kills me. If I turn myself in, I bet he's the first to visit my cell."

"And then what?" Miles pinches the bridge of his nose with two fingers. "What good would letting him torture you to death do?"

"It won't get to that." The finer details start resolving in my mind, a deadly mosaic taking shape piece by piece. "Because you'll make sure I'm ready for him when he comes."

"Okay, you know what—we need to stop." Jondi jerks to his feet. "Can you please just *stop* and think about what you're saying?" He grabs my shoulders and gives them a hard shake. "Turning yourself in . . . getting locked up . . . *killing* the Director. It's cracked, Sil. *Cracked.*"

"It's the cleanest way, J. You know it is," I breathe, placing my hands over his. If I do this, then we have a real shot at burying the damage the Director's done.

"No, Jondi's right." Miles exhales through his teeth, as though resigning back to his senses. "My father is not your responsibility. He's mine. I won't let you throw your life away."

"My life is already over." I ping them both the results of my last diagnostic. Maybe not physically—not yet—but it's through; I see that now. And they will too once that less-than-rosy 52% sinks in.

"Please, Miles, let me do this," I say, watching the play of indecision in his eyes.

My best friend is dead, my tech is fast degrading, and the Director's smear campaign has made damn sure no agent—desperate, dying, or otherwise—will ever grant me access to their head again. This might be my last chance to do something good. Something important.

"I won't be able to protect you." Miles fixes me a penetrating look. "If you do this, there's a good chance you won't leave that building alive."

"I know," I say, refusing to betray fear.

This story needs a villain. Someone he can blame when all hell breaks loose and the rumors begin to fly. That'll be my role. A Walker gone bad. An anomaly. A problem with an obvious solution. That's how we'll ensure Syntex survives this, so that one day, Jondi and the rest of the Walkers will survive it too.

CHAPTER 22

The full weight of what I've volunteered to do is only just beginning to settle, churning my stomach as I approach the Analog Army's graffiti-clad lair. Again. Though I promised myself I was done with Ryder and his merry band of hackers.

I'm only here because I have to be, I think the words over and over. *I'm only here because we need their help.*

For my plan to work, Miles has to walk away clean, so there's only so much he can do from the inside. And since I won't allow Jondi to get caught with his hand in the cookie jar either, we'll need an outside force to keep security distracted and ensure no one ever points the finger in.

So then why does being here feel so . . . wrong? Why has a raging pit of dread cracked open beneath my ribs?

You know why, a tiny voice whispers in my mind.

Because I've never gone in looking to kill before.

Until today, killing wasn't the point.

Stop lying to yourself, the voice grows louder, reminding me that deep down, it's not the mission I'm afraid of. It's seeing *him* again. It's how much I *want* to see him again. How afraid I am he won't want to see me. And that's terrifying because wanting him is incompatible with what I have to do.

It's incompatible with who I am.

Christ-that-was, maybe this is a bad idea. I sag against the wall, massaging the ache shooting between my temples, five days' worth of fatigue pulling at my bones. What I wouldn't give for a few hours in a real bed or a meal that isn't cube-shaped. Hell,

I'd sell my soul for the mind-numbing monotony of a diagnostic chair and Lin's assurance that the glitches I'm experiencing are normal for this stage of twilight.

But I'm long past that.

I accelerated my timeline the moment I let Zell tinker with my CIP.

I knew the risks and I took them anyway.

All I can do now is see that decision through to the end.

<FUGITIVE_AT_LARGE_SS> ping <RESISTANCE_RYDER> Let me up?

The sun's already on the rise by the time I find the nerve to hit send, threading the sky with streaks of gold that do nothing to combat the chill in the air. I hug my arms to my chest, trying to stave off the cold as I wait for him to wake and see my message. Yet despite the early hour, only a few minutes pass before the door inches open.

"I didn't think you'd be coming back." Draped as he is in shadow, I can't read Ryder's expression, but there's no anger to his voice—though there's hardly much warmth to it.

"That makes two of us," I say. "Can we talk?"

He nods, allowing me to slip inside.

Neither of us speaks as he leads the way to the second floor, past the damp cubicle I spent half a night in, and into the boarded-up office he's claimed as his own.

To my surprise, the room's not barren. I always pictured Ryder living like a field agent. No frills, no comforts, ready to close shop and leave at a moment's notice. Instead, the room feels homey. There are stacks of family holoforms—not just of him and Aiden, but of an older couple who fade from the cubes a year or two before Ryder hits his teens. Another premature loss documented in crisp 3D.

Scavenged VR posters cover the walls, announcing his taste in games and music. Some I recognize, some intrigue me through the art. And though the piles of clothes strewn over the floor should be setting my teeth on edge, somehow, the mess feels right, like a map to who he is beneath the armor.

"Why are you here, Sil?" Ryder asks once the silence between us grows painfully loud, drowning out the hum from the overhead fluorescents and the row of monitors in the corner.

I draw in a breath, my nails digging into my thighs. *Argh.* Why is this so hard?

"I need to ask you something," I finally manage.

"So ask." There's a sharp edge to his words, a terse reminder that our last conversation wasn't exactly . . . cordial. *If he was anything like me, he probably wanted to go. Anything to get away from you.* Ryder was trying to comfort me and in return, I insulted the memory of his dead brother. Classy. No wonder he's less than thrilled to see me.

Well, fine. I'll keep this about business.

I *should* keep it about business.

"Would ending the mindjackings be enough for you?" The question spills out in a single, unintelligible breath.

"What?"

"I have a source inside Syntex who's sure Director Paxton is responsible for the breach in consent laws," I say, slower this time. "It was his black site I infiltrated. His documents. His illegal tech. And I'm going to put an end to it. To him, I mean. But I have friends in that building, Ryder, and they don't deserve to take the fall for this. So I need to know . . . will that be enough?"

"Sil—"

"Please, just . . . answer the question."

"You're shaking." He grabs a sweatshirt off the floor and wraps it around my shoulders.

"Yes or no, Ryder?" I bat him away. My problem isn't that I'm cold, it's that I no longer fit inside my skin. That my whole body is rejecting me. And what I'm planning to do.

"I don't want to talk about Syntex." Ryder tilts my chin up. "Tell me what's wrong."

Everything's wrong.

This—his touch, the way his eyes are studying me, filled with soft sincerity and concern—is *wrong*.

A whip and a crack later, Ryder's cheek is red and my palm is stinging. I came here with a plan. To do a job. I can't afford to fall apart. But when he looks at me like that, I can't seem to hold myself together.

"Why are you here, Sil?" Ryder doesn't flinch.

"Because I'm scared, okay?" The truth explodes out of me in a violent wave. "I'm scared, and I wanted to see you, and I'm not ready to die." Those words are easier to admit than the ones I long to say: *I'm not ready to die like* this. Even if it's the right thing. Even if I'm going to die anyway. I don't want *this* to be what I die for. What I'm remembered for. What *he'll* remember me for.

Damn you, Ryder Stone. I fist my hands in my shirt, if only to stop them slapping him bloody. I was fine with my reality before I met him. I'd accepted it. I was resigned to it. Now, I feel like a wind-up toy taking on its maker, fighting a war I lost any hope of winning ten years ago.

He schedules every minute of your day, makes a game of your performance stats, keeps you too damn occupied to question. Miles was right; everything about my life was designed to keep me from living. Whereas everything about Ryder makes me not want to die.

"What if it didn't have to be this way?" he whispers, pulling me into him. "What if we knew someone who could—" Ryder's words cease to register as the double helix playing on his screens commands my attention.

"You're still in Syntex's server?" I break out of his embrace.

"What? Oh, that." He follows me over to the desk. "Unbelievable, huh? Aja was sure they'd have detected the breach by now, but we're still pulling data."

"That's more than unbelievable . . ." I mutter, squinting at the screen. There's a fresh flavor of dread rising in my throat, something sour that tastes suspiciously like fear. I don't care how good Aja's hacks are; there's no way Syntex hasn't spotted this leak.

I punch up the brightness, pushing the display's color settings to their limit. And as I suspected, every few seconds, the image buckles. Not noticeably—it's the kind of glitch you have to *know* to look for—but it's there.

"How long has it been doing this?" I point the bug out to Ryder.

"You mean that artifacting?" He leans in closer. "Can't say I've noticed it before. But the connection's been a little temperamental since last night."

Shit.

"That's because it's not private anymore. Grab whatever you can't live without. We have to get out of here," I say, already heading for the door. "Jarvis, run a scan for eyes on this building."

"Eyes on this building?" Ryder catches up to me as I speed past the line of cubicles. "The hell's going on, Sil? Hey . . . slow down—"

"We don't have time to slow down. There are two security drones parked above our heads," I relay Jarvis's findings.

"*Security drones?*" Ryder jerks me to a stop. "Christ-that-was, were you followed here?"

"Of course I wasn't *followed*." I bristle. "It's the hack, Ryder. Syntex traced your hack."

"No, that's not—" He drags a hand through his hair. "That's not possible. If they had, they'd have plugged the leak."

"You don't understand: they've *co-opted* the leak. They're feeding you junk files while they clone the contents of your server. Then once they're done, those drones they've got babysitting you are going to wipe this place off the map. We *need* to go."

I spot the moment my words sink in, reality paling Ryder to the bone.

"We have to warn Aja and Brin." He races into the stairwell, shooting *up* the stairs instead of down. Away from safety instead of towards it.

Son of a stubborn . . . "Ryder—wait!"

"Is there a way to corrupt the files?" he calls over his shoulder. "Because we can't let them have that data, Sil. Everything is on those drives. *Everything.*" The pitch of his panic tells me exactly what kind of information we're talking about.

Argh, this is bad. This is really, *really* bad.

"I'd need direct access," I say.

"You'll get it. Just please, help me fix this."

I nod as we barrel into the computer lab, ignoring every instinct screaming at me to turn and run the other way.

In spite of the early hour, Aja and Brin are both hunched over their terminals, watching their hack like a pair of hungry hawks, blissfully unaware that they're no longer the apex predator in this equation.

"Off the computers!" Ryder bellows.

"And a good morning to you too." Aja gives him the finger. She looks tired, deep shadows rimming her eyes, her copper skin bleached of its warmth by the harsh lighting. I'd bet my life she hasn't left her console for the best part of a day. I sure as hell wouldn't waste time on sleep if I were sitting on the greatest feat of hacking this side of the Annihilation.

"Yeah, Rye. You wanna try that again?" Brin cocks the metal in her brow. "Maybe add a *please* to the end. Or an explanation."

"Syntex is onto your hack," I answer in his stead, too impatient to dance around this disaster. "They've uploaded a program that's leaching data off your servers."

"Like hell they have." Aja's mood announcers flash red. "I've been monitoring the uplink all night; the hack is clean."

"No, it's not. They're just using code you've never seen before." I make for the nearest terminal. Something tells me this girl won't believe there's a problem until it's staring her in the eye.

"Rye, would you please control your pet?" she says. "It's touching things again."

I ignore the jibe, sending a log of the last day's data flow to her screen. "It's called a parasite, and it's classified tech." I throw her a snippet of the code for good measure. "It's hard to spot because it doesn't eat bandwidth the way a normal transfer does, it hides inside background processes, bloating them." A comparative usage chart serves to prove my point. The kind a twelve-year-old wouldn't have trouble deciphering, so a certified computer genius shouldn't struggle with it.

"Oh fuck." Aja clocks the issue immediately. "I've got to shut this down."

"No!" I lurch forward to stop her doing something stupid. "You need to let me cover your tracks first, otherwise they'll—"

Too late.

This girl's fingers are quicker than her bite, and she's already triggered a kill-switch to sever the connection. With just a few keys, Aja gave Syntex all the excuse they need to put an end to this AA cell for good. I only have enough time to send Jarvis one last, pre-emptive command and yell, "Everybody down!"

And then the world explodes.

CHAPTER 23

The force from the blast hits me first, throwing me into the wall with the wrath of a vengeful god. My body slams against the concrete, hard, pain howling down my sides like a banshee. Heat licks at my skin, my clothes, my eyes, smoke filling my lungs as the building rains down around me. Between the high-pitched ring thundering in my ears and the effort it takes to avoid getting crushed, I lose track of how many times the drones hit us. Three, maybe? Four? It's impossible to tell where one blast ends and another begins. But when the dust finally settles, I'm still breathing. Which means Jarvis was able to action my last-ditch command. By hacking the drones and flat-lining our biometric data, he tricked the bots into believing us dead and their mandate complete, sending them on their way.

I drag in a mouthful of air, then another, and another, pulling the world back to focus. An eerie silence settles across the room, broken only by the crash of rubble and the ominous buzz of exposed wires.

Strange.

I've never been this side of an explosion before, but I'd have expected there to be more noise. More . . . screaming.

Oh no . . . I shake the remaining fog from my mind. Why is no one screaming?

Pain shoots through my arm as I force myself up, a wave so sharp and potent I grunt and double over. Something is definitely broken. Not just bone, either; the agonizing crunch of metal and glass tells me my palm pad and screen are broken too, along with a couple of fingers.

"Jarvis, run a scan for vitals," I croak, spitting out the blood in my mouth.

"Yes, Captain." He pushes a viability survey to my ocular display.

All four of us are currently showing as *alive*, though one of these readings has been designated critical.

Shit. Shit. Shit.

"Ryder?" I shout his name as loud as I can manage, carving a path towards the nearest beating heart—no easy feat considering the number the drones did on this place. Inner-city security bots may be tamer than their tactical counterparts, but the explosive loads they carry are still plenty destructive. Most of the ceiling's gone, as well as large swathes of the floor. The rest is a deadly mess of concrete, rebar, and pipes, with split cables hanging menacingly from the ruins, coiled and ready to strike.

"Ryder!" I try him again and again, my panic rising with each second that meets silence. More terrifying than the thought that his is the heartbeat I'm losing is just how terrified I am of that thought. How deeply it paralyzes me. "*Ryder!*"

"Sil?" he rasps from behind the wall of rock blocking the stairs.

I clamber over to him as fast as my injuries allow, broken hand cradled to my chest, groaning at the effort. "Are you okay?"

"Yeah, we're both okay. Bruised, but okay."

Both?

"Sil, can you see Aja?" Brin's voice cuts through the wreckage, a full three octaves higher than usual. "She's not responding to my pings."

I turn to survey the rubble, bile rising in my throat as I spot an arm peeking out from beneath an Everest of debris.

No, no, no, no . . . I rush over and start clawing at the rocks, each one an agony on my ruined fingers. Only once I've cleared the topmost layer do I discover what saved Aja's life. The casing that used to house their server has collapsed in around her, shielding her body from the worst of the blast.

Unfortunately, it's also what's going to kill her.

"Sil, talk to us, what's happening in there?" Ryder asks.

"It's Aja, she's—" There's no easy way to describe Aja's condition, how close she is to slipping into the black. Her eyes are open but they're glassy, staring up without seeing me at all. A twisted rod of metal protrudes from her chest, blood pooling around it at an alarming rate. "She's hurt."

"How bad?" he and Brin ask in unison.

"Bad."

The crash of rocks behind me intensifies as they double their efforts to clear a path through.

"Please, Sil, you have to help her." The plea in Ryder's voice spears through my chest as cleanly as the metal speared through Aja's. I won't pretend to understand the relationship these two have, but I understand enough to know that letting Aja bleed to death is not something Ryder will forgive me for.

It's not something *I* would forgive me for.

"Jarvis, I need a full internal scan," I whisper.

"Yes, Captain." An exploded render of Aja's body materializes on my display, offering me a detailed view of her injuries. Looks like the rod has penetrated down into her lung, nicking a major artery on its way there. Jarvis puts her odds of survival at 45% if treated with nanites in the next eight to ten minutes. After that, her stats plummet faster than the spy planes Syntex blows out of the sky.

"Brin, can you reach the door from where you are?" I ask.

"Yes."

"Then run to a clinic and grab the strongest grade nanites they have. Blood sticks too. As many as you can carry. Ryder will clear the rocks by the time you're back," I say, as though it's a given. Because it has to be.

"I'm on it," she says. "Just please . . . keep her alive."

And I want to, I really do. Problem is, there's no way Brin gets those nanites in time. I need to slow the bleeding.

"Any ideas, Jarvis? I'm open to suggestions here . . ."

In response, he plays me a detailed simulation of how to clamp the artery. It's a simple procedure, but I'd need both hands for the job, and as it is, the dull ache in my arm has grown into a violent throb, bloodied splinters of my tech sprinkling out whenever I move my fingers. If I try to save Aja like this, I'll kill her faster. But with Brin gone and Ryder trapped behind an avalanche of concrete, the only person who can save Aja now is Aja.

Except Aja's too deep into shock and blood loss to do much of anything. Even if I manage to tease her awake, keeping her calm long enough to perform amateur surgery on herself, *without* losing consciousness again . . . Aja might be tough, but no one is that tough. No one.

Unless someone forces them to be.

No. I banish the image that flicks through my mind. Of Ryder, sitting slumped against a cinderblock wall, shaken and pale, his head cradled in his hands. I can't inflict that on another person. I won't.

"Jarvis, please tell me there's a different way." I rock back on my heels, willing him to find something—*anything*—that would spare me having to cross this line. I don't even care that launching an unauthorized Meld will give the Director another breach to add to my growing list of crimes; I care that this breach would be an *actual* crime. A violation. But instead of offering me a better solution, Jarvis only confirms what I already know.

"I'm sorry, Captain, but stemming the bleed presents the best chance for increasing the subject's odds of survival."

Damn. I squeeze my eyes shut and bite down hard on my lip. "Ryder, I need you to send me Aja's ID number." I don't make a conscious decision to say the words, but I say them all the same; I hear them leave my mouth, though they're a betrayal of everything I swore I would never do.

But it's either this or watch Aja die.

"What? Why?" The sound of shifting rocks quiets, Ryder's question rending pieces from my soul.

"It's the only way to save her," I say, and in that moment, I finally understand why the Director risked everything for this power. How many doors it opens. Good and bad.

"You can't mean—"

"My hand's broken, Ryder, Aja's unconscious, and I have to make her do something she really"—*really*—"won't want to do. I need that ID."

Though I can't see Ryder's face, I can *feel* the shock and disgust creep across it.

This thing I'm asking him to do—helping me mindjack Aja—it's not the same thing I did with him. Sure, I *technically* broke into his mind, but I did it with his consent. We were both in on the plan. We both agreed to it.

This is different.

Maybe I'd feel better if Aja was one of our agents. If I was imposing my will on someone who'd agreed to have Meld structures installed and *knew* this was a possibility. But the Director forced those on her too. He took away her options, and now I'm about to do the same. That's why I asked Ryder for Aja's ID instead of having Jarvis hack it. I want his permission. Otherwise, he'll never look at me the same again.

"Please, Ryder . . . she's running out of time."

And for better or worse, Ryder must really love this girl because with a pained curse and a thud that sounds suspiciously like he's put his fist to the wall, he pings me her details.

Which leaves me little reason not to say, "Jarvis, initiate neural link with user ID 6453747223. I'm asking you nicely."

I meet no resistance as the Meld propels me into Aja's head, though her being out cold presents its own challenge. When I seize control of a lucid mind, I pick up exactly where my host left off; what they're doing, what they're seeing, what they're hearing. But unconscious minds are trickier. Since they're not *in* control I can't just swoop in and take over; I have to wake them up first. From whatever state of slumber they're in.

And right now, Aja's in the midst of a nightmare.

She's five years old, a skinny-ass kid hiding beneath a desk in a security office, the kind you'd find in any high-end company building. Voices float in from the corridor, raised and urgent. A man desperately pleading for his life. Another, yelling at him to get on the ground. Then gunshots, and the heavy tread of footsteps sprinting away. Blood crying a river under the door.

The explosion must have triggered some deep-seated trauma from Aja's past, because the moment plays over and over, like a holoform stuck on loop, though each time, it plays out a little differently. Sometimes, Aja cowers in the corner; sometimes, she crawls behind the monitor array, hands cradling her ears; and sometimes, she works up the courage to cross the room and peek through the keyhole.

My stomach sinks as the scene unfolds through the tiny gap. The man with the gun is definitely a Syntex agent—I recognize the standard-issue neoplex clothing—and if I had to guess, I'd say the security guard begging for his life is Aja's father. The two share a nose, and the same deep brown hue to the skin.

Don't watch, I will her. *You don't want to watch this.* But of course, she does; otherwise, this version of the memory wouldn't exist. Two shots and a heart-wrenching scream later, Aja's cheeks are wet, her father's dead, and the agent is gone.

Christ-that-was, no wonder Syntex plays a starring role in this girl's nightmares.

We murdered her dad.

The easiest way to rouse an unconscious host is to kill their subconscious, like falling in a dream only to wake the moment you hit the ground. So as soon as the memory resets, I coax Aja out of the office by whispering, "*Go save your daddy. He needs your help.*" And like the good little girl she was, Aja follows my directions to a tee.

I've done a lot of questionable things during my time in the program, but leading a terrified child into the path of a bullet pretty much tops the list.

But it works.

The instant the shot ripples through her, Aja jolts awake,

swearing, the nightmare melting back into the dark recesses of her mind.

Only to be replaced by a wholly different one.

"Who are you? How'd you get in my head?" She figures out what's happening a split second before the true scale of her predicament hits.

The crimson stain spreading through her shirt.

The twisted shard of metal buried in her chest.

The smoking wreckage strewn all around her.

Then comes the pain. Lighting up her synapses like a wildfire spreading unchecked, near blinding, even down the neural link.

"The hell did you do to me?" Aja grits each syllable through a scream. She may not be in control of her body right now, but she's still in there, feeling everything, unable to slip back into oblivion while I'm compelling her mind to stay present. "*The hell did you do?*"

Nothing, yet. I drag a breath through her teeth, bracing for the horrors I'm about to inflict. "I'm sorry, Aja. I wish I could have done this a different way."

"*Sarrah?*" She recognizes my voice immediately. "Christ-that-was, you're a fucking *Junker?*" And takes the news about as well as I expect.

"This rod has to come out, okay?" I force her hands around the metal, gentle as I can manage. "I'll make it quick."

"What?" Her pulse stutters as she realizes what I mean to do. "*No.* Don't you dare—!"

With one smooth tug I pull the rod free, turning her protest into another scream. My own grunt of pain escapes her lips as I toss the bloodied metal aside, a wave of dizziness blurring my vision.

"Aja—?" Ryder's fear echoes from behind the rubble. "Sil? What's going on? Is she okay?" He sounds louder now that he's almost punched a hole through, though I shudder to think how much work there's left to be done. Both on his end, and mine.

"Just focus on clearing those rocks," I have her tell him, steeling myself for the rest. The pain may have struck Aja silent for a spell, but the moment it recedes, her efforts to cast me out double. Her mind takes on a spiked, hostile quality, pressing in around me like an iron maiden snapping shut.

"Aja, please listen—" I'm not too proud to beg if it'll move the needle. "That rod tore a hole in your artery. Brin's on her way with some nanites, but if I don't clamp it shut to slow the bleeding, you'll die before she gets here. Understand?"

"*Clamp it shut*? No . . . you can't . . ." Her protests take a hard left into terror, her hands breaking free of my control, clenching into tight fists at her sides. Clench, unclench. Clench, unclench. Destroying any hope I have of saving her life.

"Please, you have to stop fighting me."

I thought knowing what I intend to do—and *why*—might help ease Aja's panic. That's what used to work with me as a child; I've always found my fear of the unknown far greater than my fear of pain. Then again, I've never been held hostage inside my own mind, or forced to reach inside my own chest. But since I can't spare any more time convincing her it's this or dying, I need to just hurry up and get the job done.

"Please don't do this." Aja's voice cracks as I throw my entire weight behind the link, forcing her fists to open. "Please, Sil." Seems she's not above begging, either. Few are when it comes to avoiding pain.

"I'm sorry"—I sure am using that word a lot lately—"but it's your only chance." With another push, I lift Aja's hands to her chest, desperately wishing I could offer her the respite of unconsciousness, not least of all because I don't like pain any more than she does. But more than the pain, what I'm afraid of is watching the light leech out of her eyes—and the warmth leech out of Ryder's—if I sit by and do nothing.

I can't stop the scream that rips from Aja's throat as I dig down into the wound, and I don't even try. It feels good to scream when everything is breaking. It feels like a release.

"Captain, my readings are showing a dangerous amount of pressure on the Meld. Would you like to terminate?"

"Don't even think about it, Jarvis." Another guttural cry escapes my lips.

"Christ-that-was, Sil—what's happening?"

What needs to happen. I burrow down deeper, choking back the bile. It's a stomach-churning job, and even the sensory dampening offered by the neural link can't shield me from the nerve-shattering agony, or the warm squelch of blood, or the wet, springy texture of the artery when I finally locate the tear and squeeze it shut between Aja's fingers.

"Got it." I let out the breath I'm holding as the torture of movement fades to a more bearable throb, relieving the strain on my systems.

"Then get the hell out of my head, Sarrah," Aja croaks amid labored gasps, her voice thick with sweat, and tears, and venom.

"I will as soon as Brin gets back," I promise. "Until then, I'm the only thing keeping you conscious."

"I'm gonna kill you for this." Even with one foot in the grave, this viper's pissed and spoiling for a fight.

"Hey, so long as you don't die on me, I swear to let you try."

"Damn it, Sil—what's going on in there?" Ryder's panic finally grows too loud to ignore, demanding my attention.

"Bleeding's under control," I say as a gap draws open between the rocks and his face appears on the other side. He was downplaying his injuries when he told me he was just *bruised.* He's covered in dust, cuts marking his skin, blood smeared across his cheeks like war paint. And he's clearly in pain, flinching with every breath, hands clutched to his side as though trying to hold himself together.

Brin needs to hurry up and get here.

For all our sakes.

We're still a couple of feet short of a doorway when Aja's voice begins to quiet, the obscenities she's spitting growing faint and distant in my mind, as though she's hurling them from afar. When she blinks, I catch a glimpse of the scene from the opposite side of our stalemate.

"Erm . . . Jarvis, what's going on with my link?"

"Sensors are indicating a second build-up of pressure, Captain," he says. "Would you like to terminate?"

"Pressure from *where*?" A fresh torrent of dread needles my nerves. Aja's long since stopped trying to cast me out. Hell, she's barely even lucid anymore, let alone strong enough to—

Oh shit.

The realization hits deep inside my gut.

The strain isn't coming from Aja; it's coming from me. I'm not supposed to cling to dying minds this way—neural links are specifically designed to snap when a host loses viability, so as to spare our CIPs from sustaining damage during the break. What I'm experiencing right now is the same thing I experienced when a drone blew the Director's black site sky-high, except this time, it's happening in slow motion, the connection fraying one thread at a time as Aja inches closer to the black.

"No, no, no, no, no . . ." I try to jolt her awake from the inside. "Come on, Aja, you have to fight."

"Sil—" The crash of rocks cuts off abruptly. "Are you okay? Is Aja okay?"

"No, she's not *okay*," I growl. I can will a body to do almost anything while I'm in control, but I can't force a heart to keep beating. And I can't stay melded to a corpse. "Where the hell is Brin?"

"Here! I'm here!" Her voice echoes up the stairs, her breaths wheezing out a short staccato. "Please tell me I'm not too late . . . that she's alive."

"She is. But you need to get in here *fast*." My words, coming out of Aja's mouth, are Brin's first clue that something is amiss on this side of the wall.

"Jay-Jay?" She pokes her head through Ryder's unfinished doorway, her eyes widening with shock and fury as they take in the grisly scene.

Aja lying prone among the rubble, her own hand stuck inside her chest.

My body standing frozen and listless a few feet away, doing nothing to help.

"Brin, I can explain—" I hear Ryder start, but the rest of his words are lost as my ill-fated Meld triggers an alarm and Jarvis pushes me a dozen alerts. *System overload . . . Host signal below accepted threshold . . . Neural break imminent . . .* a veritable doomsday book of errors.

"Buy me some more time here, Jarvis. I don't care what it takes; you do not terminate this link. That's an order."

"Yes, Captain. Diverting power from other systems."

"The hell do you mean she's a *Junker*?" Brin's outrage cuts through the wails.

Oh for the love of everything unholy . . . "Would the two of you quit arguing and get in here?" I bark as a white-hot pain lances through my skull. My skull, not Aja's. "I can't hold her much longer!"

The frantic scramble of rocks intensifies, shaking the ground beneath my feet.

"Captain, I'm now logging errors on four out of five processors," Jarvis says. "Protocol mandates I shut the unit down to avoid catastrophic failure."

"Negative. Do not shut down." I claw at the connection with every last ounce of strength I have. "Damn it, Aja, you promised to kill me for this, remember?" A scream rends out from both our throats. "Don't give up that dream now." My vision bleeds black at the edges, my display flickering in and out of color. All except for the one vibrant shade of blue racing towards me. Towards Aja, I mean, because with a final slew of critical errors, my CIP crashes and the neural link breaks, propelling me back to my body. To the storm of pain and silence raging inside my mind.

CHAPTER 24

From the rubble, we head straight to one of the safe havens the Analogs know, a clinic staffed by security who look the other way and doctors who don't scan chips. Even after a mammoth dose of nanites and her bodyweight in blood sticks, Aja's injuries remain such that she's immediately whisked to a surgical bay, though the rest of us aren't deemed critical enough to jump the line. It takes most of the morning—the wait is long, and my keypad and screen so far past recovery, a nurse spends an hour picking metal fragments out of my flesh—but they fix my shattered fingers and Ryder's broken ribs.

In all that time, Brin only spares us one word.

Go.

Though she says it to Ryder, the sentiment is meant for me. I don't know exactly what transpired between these two while I was busy staving off the neural break, but something about the way Brin's eyes narrow in my presence suggests that she wasn't thrilled to learn *how* I kept her girlfriend alive.

"You should stay. For Aja," I tell Ryder once her glares turn downright threatening.

Instead, he follows me out and says, "Aja has Brin." Though I can see what that decision costs him in the slump of his shoulders and the drop of his chin. Feel it in the way he keeps glancing back towards the clinic.

Our next stop is the hygiene station, where I spend so long scrubbing the blood and dirt from my skin, the surly tech manning the cleansers shuts off the lukewarm mist and berates me for holding up the line.

Wrapped only in the threadbare towel I was issued on entry, I emerge into the locker room to find that Ryder has acquired us some new clothes from the vendos. A simple white tee and gray slacks for him, black leggings and a tank for me. The rest we pick up on our way to the food bank.

We're tucking into bowls of stew when my CIP *finally* comes back online, and that, together with the first proper meal I've had in days, is what makes me feel human again.

At least until Jarvis pushes me my latest diagnostic.

<Cerebral Intelligence Processor W914//ONLINE>
<. . .>
<W914__Request system diagnostic>
<. . .>
<Commencing system diagnostic>
<. . .>
<. . .>
<. . .>
<1082 Errors logged>
<. . .>
<View main system log? Y/N>
<W914__Y>
<. . .>
<Data processors//ONLINE//Reporting damage>
<Working drives//ONLINE//Critical damage//Service>
<Archive drives//OFFLINE>
<Ocular transmitters//ONLINE//Reporting damage>
<Cochlear transmitters//ONLINE//Critical damage//Service>
<Aesthetic suite//OFFLINE>
<Satellite uplink//ONLINE//Reporting damage>
<Neural bridge//ONLINE//Reporting damage>
<Main power unit//ONLINE//Reporting damage>
<Secondary power unit//OFFLINE>

```
<. . .>
<Overall system performance//34%>
<. . .>
<View full system log? Y/N>
<W914__N>
<W914__Exit diagnostic>
```

34%. The number curbs my appetite.

That's another 18% drop in *one* day.

Barely a month into twilight, and I've run my tech into the death throes of its end-of-life cycle.

"You okay?" Ryder asks when I bin my remaining food uneaten.

"Yeah, just not hungry," I lie, ignoring the way his eyes slide right over me. He's been like this since we left the clinic, spare with his looks and his smiles. I guess the reality of who he's left behind is starting to hit home. Or maybe it's the memory of what he watched me do. It's one thing to claim you're not afraid of the monster when it's trapped safe and tight in the closet; it's quite another when you're forced to look at it under the harsh light of day.

And though I know we need to talk about what happened, I can't bring myself to break the silence either. Because what would I even say? *Sorry I mindjacked your closest friend. Sorry Brin won't ping you back to tell you how she's doing. PS I'll be dead in a week or two, so you should go make up with your army . . .* doesn't exactly roll off the tongue.

So instead, we both keep to ourselves as we steal across the sector, heading to another of Ryder's secret hideaways, a safe house the cells use when their stunts draw a little too much attention. Well, *house* is overstating it—unless we're talking about the music vibrating through the walls. The Analogs have convinced the owner of a bot-fighting bar to let them requisition the back room, where the dulcet sounds of synth meet the heady crash of metal. It wouldn't be so bad if my head weren't already in fifty different kinds of pain.

"Sorry about the mess." Ryder picks a path through the empty liquor crates and the mangled shells of ruined androids. "I try not to spend too much time here."

Yeah, no kidding. I follow him over to the beat-up mattress in the corner. The faces on these battle-worn, eerily human machines are just plain creepy.

"I'm sorry too. About . . . Aja." I force out an apology of my own. Avoiding this conversation was all good and well when we were surrounded by prying eyes, but now that we're stuck in this robot graveyard, with nothing but a few feet of stale air between us, I'd rather just rip the Band-Aid off. Hear the words I fear are coming.

"Not your fault." Ryder pulls his knees to his chest, his whole body sagging against the wall, like an avatar whose host has phased out of VR. "The hack was our decision. Our mistake."

I've never seen him look this despondent before. Ryder's always been annoyingly upbeat. Even when he was pissed at me, or getting his ass handed to him by drunks, he radiated hope and light. Like some deranged bastion of optimism. Now, there's not an ounce of humor left in his eyes, no warmth, no hint of a smile.

And it absolutely breaks me.

"Jarvis, set up for a database search."

"Yes, Captain. Awaiting parameters," he says. The errors I'm logging have stripped him of his custom voiceprint, so instead of pre-Annihilation actor, he sounds like every other piece of AI in this city. Cold and clinical. Inhuman.

"What are you doing?" Ryder asks as I fold down next to him.

"The only thing I know how." And the last thing I should be. Jarvis has barely finished wrestling my systems back online; he's holding my drives together with patch code and sheer force of will; a database search is a power drain he doesn't need.

But Ryder needs it. And I need him to be able to look at me.

"Get me the medical file for Aria Ajax." I give Jarvis the fake name we used on Aja's intake information. Since my processors are still glitching, the hack takes him longer than it should, but eventually, a handful of documents pop up on my ocular display.

"She's doing better," I say. "They've transferred her out of the surgical bay. A couple more doses of nanites and she'll be good to go."

Every part of Ryder relaxes, the tension leaving his body like a river flowing towards the sea. "Thank you." He finally turns to look at me—to really *look* at me—for the first time since two security drones razed his clubhouse to the ground.

But for some reason, holding his attention only makes it harder to breathe.

"Yeah. No problem." I go to stand, to put some distance between us, but Ryder reaches out to stop me.

"I don't do well when people I care about get hurt," he says, and it feels like an explanation. "But I mean it, Sil. What you did—"

"I don't want to talk about what I did." Or how readily I did it. Lena, Jondi, and I used to joke about mindjacking; we tried to crack the system, made a game of it even. But only because we truly believed it was impossible. Because we were safe in our conviction that we'd never, *ever* illegally commandeer another person's mind. And I'm not sure doing it for a good reason makes it okay.

"I'm not sorry you did it," Ryder says, taking my hand in his.

"You're not?"

"I should be. I should be disgusted you even thought to suggest it—let alone that I agreed. But I'm not." He says it simply. Like it isn't a betrayal of everything he believes. "You saved her life, Sil. You knew how much it stood to hurt you, and you did it anyway."

Warmth spreads through my body, a fire that sparks in my toes and sears its way to my cheeks. "I couldn't just let her die," I say. Not when it was in my power to stop it.

"I know." His face sours. "That's what scares me."

I jerk back from him as though electrocuted.

"You asked if ending the mindjackings would be enough. This is why it can't be." A note of steel breaks through Ryder's voice.

"Because this is how it starts, Sil. A good deed here, another there. Walkers making a bad choice to do the right thing. People letting them because they're desperate and afraid. That's how Syntex will sell the country on this."

"I won't let that happen," I say. "I told you, I know who's behind it and I'm gonna put a stop—"

"And then what?" He cuts me off. "What happens when the next guy tries it? Or the next? And what about all the other terrible crap they make you do?"

"What are you talking about?" A rush of anger flares beneath my skin, but true to irritating form, Ryder ignores my question.

"Do you want to know why Brin reacted the way she did?" he asks.

Christ-that-was, I really am going to throttle him one day.

"Not particularly, Ryder. Is it somehow relevant?" Because in my experience, people are happy to hate me on principle alone.

"Brin was fourteen when she learned how far Syntex will go to protect its IP," he forges on undeterred. "And what they're willing to sacrifice. Her mom was an agent."

Was. The tiny word speaks volumes, announcing exactly where this story is about to go. "She died on a mission?"

"That was the official party line," Ryder mutters. "The op was classified, of course, so Brin had to bribe an analyst for the details. Turns out, her mom didn't just *die* on that mission; she was *killed*. By the Walker she let into her mind."

Well . . . damn. My heart sinks through the floor. Brin's mom was terminated.

"And Aja's father—"

I drop my head to the wall as Ryder continues working through his list of shitty things my employer did. I don't need him to tell me how Aja's father died. I saw it for myself.

"—was killed by a Syntex agent. During a *melded* extraction," he adds in a detail I don't expect, supplying me Aja's grudge against the program as well. The cause of both girls' nightmares.

"There's a human cost to what you do, Sil. And it goes beyond just your life," he says. "I want Syntex to stop building fail-safes into their people. I want them to stop sending their agents on missions so impossible, they're left with no choice but to give up control. I want what happened to Brin's mom to never happen again, and what happened to your friend on that video to never happen again." Ryder closes the space between us, his hand moving to cup my cheek. "I want what they did to you to *never* happen again."

My breath catches as his thumb skims over the power button behind my ear. "You want to end the Walker program." Not just the mindjackings, or the terminations, or the burnouts; Ryder wants to end it all.

"It's the only way, Sil," he whispers. "This kind of technology is too seductive. It only ever leads to one thing."

The words should terrify me.

They should confirm everything I've long suspected; Ryder and I want fundamentally different things.

We are fundamentally at odds.

Fundamentally incompatible.

But right at this moment, I can't bring myself to care. I'm bone-tired, everything hurts, and my skull feels as though it's getting sucked into a black hole. All I want to do is curl up and sleep until this nightmare passes. And judging by the deep shadows under Ryder's eyes and the tremble of his fingers against my skin, my guess is that's what he wants as well.

So without another word, I pull him down to the mattress, wrapping his body around mine—for warmth and comfort, not anything more—ignoring the voices screaming at me to walk away from him and make sure that this time, it sticks.

Because the truth is, I'm starting to think he might be right.

"Well, isn't this cozy?"

The voice jerks us both awake. Violently. For a split second, I'm stuck somewhere between reality and sleep, unsure if the faces scowling at me from the doorway are real or the dying remnant of a dream. Then I remember that Ryder's favorite hacker and her surly girlfriend are the last two people I'd ever choose to dream about—and they're definitely the last two people I feel like getting ambushed by at 3 a.m in the morning.

"Aja!" Ryder springs to his feet.

"Easy—" Brin puts up a hand to stop him getting too close. "She's supposed to be taking things slow."

"Yeah, Rye." Aja slinks forward and presses herself against him. "You'd know that if you'd bothered to stick around."

She looks pretty good for a girl who almost bled to death twenty-odd hours ago. A little unsteady maybe, and stripped bare of the dark make-up she usually wears, but otherwise, the clinic did one hell of a job patching her up.

"Sticking around wasn't an option." Ryder exchanges a meaningful look with Brin, whose muscles are coiled so tight I worry she'll burst a ligament. I'm going to go ahead and say that seeking us out wasn't her idea, though Aja doesn't appear thrilled to see me, either. Her mood announcers turn a stormy purple whenever she glances my way, as though she's trying to decide whether to thank me, or dig me a nice grave.

"Seriously, Rye, I knew you had shitty taste in girls . . . but a *Junker*? Really?"

I'm gifted another scathing glare.

"You do know I can hear you?"

"It's not half as satisfying when you can't."

"Christ-that-was, will you two ever play nice?" Ryder places himself between us. "Happy as I am to see you, A, what are you doing here?" He finally asks the question that matters. The one that's seen me inch closer and closer to a sharp piece of pipe, in case I need to threaten my way free.

Every person in this room knows what I am now, but only Ryder's proven he doesn't care. Brin's already made her opinion of me very clear, and the jury's still out on Aja. I may have saved her life, but given *how* I did it . . . well . . . I wouldn't be surprised if she dragged herself out of that clinic just to make good on her promise.

"Tell your girlfriend to chill, Rye. We're not here to spoil your honeymoon." When Aja rolls her eyes, her whole body rolls with them, elevating contempt to a new level. "We came to talk about our server problem."

"Shit." Ryder grits out a curse. Amid the carnage the Syntex drones left in their wake, neither of us has had much time to think on the bigger picture. His or mine.

"Do the other cells know yet?" he asks.

"About the crater-shaped hole where our building used to be? Yeah. The *gas explosion* made the news," Aja tells him. "And they're pissed, Rye. That hack was as much theirs as it was ours, and now it's gone."

"Two years' work down the drain." Brin hurls the charge at me as if it's somehow *my* fault. I bite my tongue, burying the urge to remind her that *they're* the ones who decided to overstay their welcome in the world's most secure server. Something tells me that would do nothing to ease the tension building in the air. Between Brin's black mood, Aja's scorn, and my dwindling patience, it's only going to take one spark to send this ill-advised gathering up in flames.

"Please tell me they're not thinking about doing something stupid," Ryder says.

"They're more than just *thinking* about it, Rye. They're already making plans to go postal."

"No . . . they can't." He begins pacing the room, tracing frantic circles around the remnants of ruined androids. "Damn it, we talked about this . . . if we start blowing things up, *terrorist* is the only word the public will associate with the Analog Army for the next decade. We'll have no credibility left to expose them."

"We have nothing left to expose them *with*," Brin reminds him. "We lost everything in that blast. Everything."

"But I haven't." I suddenly know exactly how to win the help I came for—even now that these girls are less than inclined to do me any favors.

"Does this really feel like the right time to be gloating, Sarrah?" Aja clicks her tongue against her teeth.

"I'm not *gloating*, it's just . . . what if I can offer them something better?" I ask. "Could you talk them off the ledge?"

"Let me guess, you're going to offer them those documents you stole." Brin's tone makes it plenty clear that if that's my idea, I should just shut up and butt the hell out.

So it's a good thing it's not.

"Actually, I'll do them one better," I say. "I'm going to kill the Director."

CHAPTER 25

Needless to say, I get their attention. Killing the Director of Syntex may not have been the Analog Army's original plan, but the girls seem to think it will please them just the same, especially after I share what I learned from Jondi and Miles. Hell, by the time Ryder and I finish catching them up on everything we've discovered these past few days, they even quit staring at me like I'm an overpriced piece of hardware they'd like to stick in a blender. For about five seconds, anyhow. But hey, baby steps. I've long since stopped believing in miracles.

"You got a timeframe in mind for this murder?" Brin asks once I've laid my cards on the table. "'Cause they won't wait another two years."

"They won't have to," I say. "I'm going in tomorrow night."

"*Tomorrow night?*" Ryder's head whips towards me. "Where's the rush, Sil?"

34%. That's the rush.

"Use that idiot brain of yours, Rye." Aja's the first to puzzle out my *other* reason for wanting to charge full speed ahead. "Tomorrow night's the—"

"Contracts Dinner. *Right*," he finishes for her.

The night Syntex wines and dines its corporate buyers while they submit their bids for tech showcased at the gala. It ticks all the boxes. Security will be tight, but they'll also have their hands full with the dignitaries; the Analog Army will get to avenge their loss by disrupting yet another flagship event; and I'll get to prevent them doing something worse to a building filled with my friends. If I go in tomorrow, everybody wins.

"This plan of yours better not involve screwing with anyone else's mind, Sarrah." Aja's voice burns with contempt, as though I took a stroll through her gray matter for fun. Her lack of gratitude would piss me off if not for my lingering sense of guilt—and shame. I don't get to demand a *thank you* for this violation.

"It doesn't," I say. "Though I will need your help to make it look good. Control the narrative."

"You Junkers like *controlling the narrative*, don't you?"

"A, come on." Ryder sighs.

"What? I don't have to be nice. You're the one sleeping with her."

"A—"

"*Seriously?*" My restraint is fast reaching its limit. Aja can be as pissed as she likes about the way I saved her life, but I'll be damned if I let myself get slut-shamed by a presumptuous pixie.

"Christ-that-was, *enough.*" It falls to Brin to be the voice of reason. Which really doesn't bode well for our chances of keeping this alliance afloat. "Now, I'm down with helping you pull this off, Sarrah, but in return, you have to destroy the data Syntex took from us. We walk away from this clean. Our sister cells, too. That's my price."

"I can live with that." I nod.

"Jay-Jay?"

"Yeah, yeah, whatever. I'm in."

"Good. Then it's settled."

"Not quite," I say, before I can talk myself out of it. "If we're gonna do this, I need to speak to Aja first. Alone."

"Why?" the three of them ask together, like a multi-pitched echo.

"It'll only take a minute." I don't elaborate and I don't back down, hoping Ryder will trust me and convince Brin to do the same. This is not a request I'm comfortable sharing with the group yet. Not until I'm truly ready to see it through.

"Jay-Jay?" Brin's hand tightens on Aja's shoulder.

"I'll bite," she tells her, appraising me with narrowed eyes.

"You sure?"

"It's fine, Bee. I can handle the Junker," she says, then with one final—albeit reluctant—glance, Brin and Ryder leave us to it.

"Well?" Aja snaps a prompt once they're gone. "You waiting for a written invitation?" She leans her weight into the wall. She tries to do it casually, but there's no hiding the way her shoulders cling to the cracked plaster, or the heavy timbre of her breaths. Given the beating her body took today, it's a miracle she's standing at all, let alone without help.

"You can sit, you know." I point to the dingy mattress.

But Aja doesn't budge an inch. "What do you want, Sarrah?"

I guess *nice* isn't my color.

"A favor," I say.

"Figures." The curious glint to her irises turns a suspicious green. "Is that why you saved me? Because you needed something?"

Christ-that-was . . . I knot both hands behind my back to keep from wringing her neck. I can't win with this girl. "No"—*you vindictive viper*—"I didn't need anything when I saved you. And just for the record, that all-expense trip around your head wasn't fun for me either. I did it for Ryder. Happy?"

"The honesty's a good start." Aja crosses her arms. "Now what do you want?"

"Code," I say through my teeth. "I'd write it myself but—"

"Are you actually about to blame a lack of tools?" She raises an eyebrow, appraising my naked palm with a sneer. "Because last I checked, you had a *supercomputer* in your head. You gave it a dorky name and everything."

"That's not—" I force in a breath, then force the words out. "You're better. The *supercomputer* in my head can hack into most places, but infiltrating Syntex . . . that was art." And art is what I'll need to pull this off. I'd ask Jondi to do it, but he'll have enough on his plate tracking down the data Syntex leeched off their servers. Besides, this is one play I'd rather keep close to my chest and away from him and Miles. Something tells me they won't like it.

"So can I have my dorky computer ping you the details?"

"You're asking for permission?" The corner of Aja's lip quirks into a sardonic smile.

At some point, Ryder is going to have to explain what drew him to this girl, because so far, her only setting seems to be *ball-breaking b*— "I'm trying here, okay?" I stop that thought in its tracks, before it can escape and screw me. "And that doesn't come naturally, so cut me a break, okay?"

"Fine." She flashes me her user handle. "Christ-that-was, Sarrah, are you this whiny around Ryder?"

"No, I save it all for you," I mutter, watching Aja's body straighten as she reads through the wish list Jarvis sends her.

"You're serious about this?"

Serious, yes. Certain, no.

"Can you do it?"

"You're damn right I can."

"Good." I have him ping her an address. "Then meet me here at midnight."

"So . . . does Ryder realize this is your idea of a good time?" Aja asks, eyeing Sinsinnati's dilapidated sign with enough disdain to blow out a couple more letters. As it stands, the logo reads *Sin-in-ati's*; it's lost a pair of consonants since I was last here, but the pulsating beats vibrating through the door are exactly as I remember. So is the bruiser manning the front desk, watching us from behind the glass with a pinched expression. It's happy hour in the Pleasure District and the mod parlors are gearing up for the rush. Maybe that's why he's giving us his most welcoming *come inside or get gone* frown. Real charmer, that one. No wonder he chose a career in customer service.

"Oh please, are we really gonna pretend you don't spend half your life in these places?" I point to Aja's wealth of visible mods, which repay the favor by flashing an irritated yellow.

"I have standards, Sarrah."

"Good for you. Now come on, I know one of their guys."

Okay . . . *know* might be overstating our relationship, but Zell's helped me before, and since he's the closest thing I have to a Lin outside the Syntex building, he'll just have to do.

"I don't do couples," Zell says the moment we step into his studio. "So if you want matching units, or you get off watching each other get modded, you'll have to take it next—" His words turn into a high-pitched yelp as I lower my hood and deactivate my facial filters. "You!" He stumbles back into the counter, sending half his tools clattering to the floor.

"Now I believe he knows you," Aja mutters under her breath. "What'd you do to this one, Sarrah? Mindjack him too?"

"Don't be ridiculous. I threatened to shoot him."

"Friendly."

"What can I say, I like to be liked." I bolt the door shut behind us.

"No, no, no, no, no . . . *you* can't be here." Zell jabs a finger at me. "You're . . . you're *wanted*."

"Not by most people," Aja assures him. And since elbowing her will likely sink this tenuous truce of ours, I settle for a nice, long roll of my eyes.

"Look, I'm not here to make your life harder," I say, holding my naked palm up for him to see. "My keypad broke and I'm in the market for a new one. Best you got. And I'm willing to pay double."

"Double?" Zell's reluctance ebbs at the thought of such a massive sale. Few people spring for top-of-the-line units—the extra features simply aren't *extra* enough to warrant the extra credits. But I prefer the feel of high-grade silicon beneath my skin, and I don't have time to adjust to an inferior system.

"Double," I confirm, hopping up onto the battered leather chair. "I need a couple of other implants too, and . . . a favor," I say. Best push my luck while he's still greed struck. "You've seen the inside of my head; do you have anything we can use to upload code to my system?"

"I could probably rig something up." Zell rubs his chin in a way—I assume—is meant to appear thoughtful. "What's in it for me?"

"You get to watch me jailbreak the Junker." Aja flashes him her teeth.

And that's all the persuasion it takes. The moment he's done installing my new tech, Zell starts tinkering with his terminal until it agrees to play ball with my CIP.

"That should do it," he says once the unit's ready, snapping a cable into the port at my neck.

"Good. Then it's my turn to play." Aja fishes a nanodot out of her pocket and sticks it to the underside of the console. Data floods the screen, line after line of code so intricate my jaw drops at the complexity—the *elegance*—of it.

"The hell did you pull this together so fast?" I can't help but ask. Work this involved . . . this girl's a damn prodigy.

"It's a Frankenstein." Aja bristles, as though ashamed of the world's most impressive bit of programming. "I didn't have time to design the code from scratch so I modified a couple of old viruses, then spliced in a rotating cypher and bits of that parasite you sent me. It's not pretty, but it'll do the job. It just needs a little adjusting to account for this bizarro operating system of yours," she says, fingers flying across the keys. "Get comfy, Junker. This'll take a few minutes."

A few minutes to write a patch that will interface with proprietary hardware . . . I almost laugh at the audacity of it. If not for Brin—and Aja's general dislike for CIP-enhanced individuals—I'd introduce her to Jondi. They'd definitely get along.

"Hey, Mod Minion—" Aja turns to Zell when she's done fiddling with the code. "Fancy doing me too? My oculars are older than I am."

"Enhanced vision, mood, or aesthetics?" He forces his eyes away from the detailed, grudgingly agreed-to scan of my brain.

"Since Sarrah's paying, let's go for the hat trick."

"That's a custom fit." Zell huffs with all the indignation of a man being asked to do his job. "I'll have to modify the install."

"So get modifying." Aja waves him off. Then with a curse and another overblown huff, Zell shuffles out.

"What was *that* about?" I ask once the door slides shut behind him. Aja strikes me as the type to upgrade her mods every release cycle. Even the incremental ones most people consider a rip-off.

"Figured you wouldn't want him around for this." She spins the screen towards me. "I ran a diagnostic on your CIP."

"Took the liberty, did you?" I bury the more colorful response simmering on my tongue.

"I'm sorry, was that rude? I slept through Junker 101." She taps a command into the console, highlighting the worst of what she's found. "You're logging errors on a bunch of major systems, Sarrah. Not small ones, either."

"I'm aware." How could I not be, with Robot Jarvis squatting in my head?

Though I was able to recover a backup of his voiceprint, I couldn't get the file to load, so every time he speaks, I'm reminded just how badly my CIP has degraded.

"Are you also aware that this code is insanely process heavy?" Aja asks. "You run it, there's no turning back."

"So what, you're having second thoughts now?" I raise an eyebrow. I'm about to hand her—and this Analog cell—everything they've been working for on a silver platter. Because Ryder was right: this tech is too seductive. The fact that Aja's still here is proof of that. Proof that once you open Pandora's box, there's no stopping the darkness that comes spilling out. And as much as I trust Miles to steer the program straight, I don't trust that no one else will think to break bad like his father. Not unless I run this code and make damn sure they can't.

"About the end result? No. I'm not having second thoughts," Aja says.

"So what's the problem?"

"Code's gonna kill you is the problem."

"Then congratulations, you get to make good on your promise," I snap. Because snapping is far easier than admitting the truth. I knew this program had the potential to trigger a catastrophic failure, knew it the moment I sent Aja my long list of requirements and Syntex's encryption protocols. But knowing something and hearing it aloud are two very different things.

"Don't get cute with me, Sarrah," Aja says. "I don't find you charming, and I couldn't care less how you choose to punch your ticket. Are you gonna tell Ryder, though?"

"What makes you think I haven't told him already?"

"Oh please. First you ask me for a piece of code that ticks every box on his wish list, but send him out of the room to do it. Then you drag me to the mod parlor self-respect forgot, in the middle of the night, and he's nowhere to be found . . . hardly takes a genius to notice you're keeping secrets."

"It's not like he doesn't know how my story ends." I turn to stare at the ceiling.

"He doesn't know it's going to end today."

"Neither do you," I say. Burnouts are unpredictable. Look at Ryder's brother; his tech imploded day one of twilight, no warning, no explanation, whereas Lena kept her CIP going another 408 days. So yeah, running this code might kill me, or it might not. It makes no difference either way; once I walk into that building, I'm not walking out again.

Since Miles can't be suspected of working with the Analog Army, he won't be able to help me; he'll have to play the dutiful son and demand justice for his father's murder. And with their favorite titan of industry gone, the media will scream for my head just as sure as the sun rises each morning—assuming security don't take a shot at it first, that is.

Come tonight, my life is over.

"Quit bullshitting me, Sarrah," Aja says. "I've seen your error logs. You run this code, it's gonna fry you."

"So I should run it *after* I take the Director out, got it."

"You should run it after you *talk to Ryder*." Her eyes narrow at the corners, her irises flashing red. Nice to see the protective instinct between them flows both ways.

Nice, but inconvenient.

"I can't do that," I say.

"Can't or *won't*? 'Cause that idiot deserves the truth, Sarrah. For some reason, he's decided to go and fall for you."

That's what scares me. I've spent the last ten years insulating myself from this feeling. I closed myself off from my family, from the Reggies, from the world. Until a week ago, I let exactly two people into my heart, and one of them has already gone and cracked it down the middle. So this . . . *thing* with Ryder . . . that was definitely not part of the plan.

Is it love? Christ-that-was, I don't think I'm naïve enough to believe I've fallen in love in a week. All I know is that being around Ryder makes me want to live to see *next* week. To figure out why my brain misfires when he's around, why the two of us keep gravitating towards each other, like magnets snapping together from afar.

And who knows, maybe that's what love is, a spark that builds to an inferno no matter how hard you try to smother it. Even when the flames don't make a lick of sense. Even when they're destined to fizzle down to ash.

"I'm not telling him because it won't change anything," I say. It would only make this harder. For both of us.

"You're wrong, Sarrah." With a sigh, Aja hits upload on the code. "Telling him changes everything. It means he'd get to say goodbye."

Aja's words stick with me the rest of the day, not only because she has a point, but because she keeps sending me increasingly barbed pings. They're disguised as status reports—hidden among the snippets of information she and Brin are feeding us about their part of tonight's plan—but I can practically see the face she's making as she sends them, the judgment dripping off every cheerful *only a couple of hours to go,* and *running out of time to pull this together.*

Or maybe that's my guilt talking and Aja's simply playing the world's most annoying alarm clock; a day *is* hardly long enough to coordinate a plan of this magnitude. Or at least, it would be, if we didn't have two CIPs and a Paxton on our side.

The hardest part of infiltrating Syntex is getting into the building and close enough to the right systems. A difficult feat on a good night, and nigh on impossible during an event—especially with zero time to indulge in the kind of bribery that facilitated the Analogs' last incursion. Lucky for us, Brin and Aja don't need to get inside for this to work, only Ryder does, and he's getting in thanks to Miles, who's added him to the guest list for tonight's dinner. And as for me, well . . . I'll also be walking in through the front door, though when I do it, they'll call it gate-crashing.

<ANONYMYNX> Last chance to get your affairs in order.

Aja's pings are growing downright blatant.

It's a good job Ryder's still at the hygiene station or else I'd crack and tell him everything. All day he's tried to engage me in talk of my exit strategy, which—with Miles on our side—he's decided is possible.

Mostly, because I told him it was.

As far as Ryder's concerned, Miles isn't just helping us kill his father; he's getting me out once the deed is done. Ryder doesn't know I've volunteered as scapegoat, and Miles has no idea I'll be causing him a few headaches on my way down.

I'm lying to them both.

Necessary lies, but they grate on me just the same.

Which is why I've been avoiding those conversations by excusing myself to go fix a piece of code, or swap important details with Jondi. So much has kept both me and Ryder so busy, we've found little time for anything else.

And I'm grateful for that, I think. Time for other . . . *distractions* would only make tonight more impossible. But in the quiet moments, when I let my mind wander, I find myself wishing I could spend my last day of life doing something other than staring at screens and making war plans. And that feeling only intensifies when Ryder returns to the safe house, wearing the designer suit Miles arranged for him.

Well, I'll be.

My commanding officer has impeccable taste.

The suit is coal-black with a hint of shine to the lapels, cut so well it might have been sewn right onto Ryder's body.

"Before you start, I'm perfectly aware of how ridiculous I look in this thing," he says, pulling at the collar of his shirt. Also black. A choice that lends him a dangerous air, the kind the other diners would expect from the son of a defense contractor—his alias for the evening. There's exactly one ridiculous thing about the suit Ryder's wearing, and that's how he's wearing it in the moldy back room of a bot-fighting bar.

"No, that's not—" I have to clear my throat, like a lovesick teenager. "You look . . . good," I say, though *good* doesn't begin to do him justice. The only change I'd make is to the slicked-back hair. It's too formal a style for him. Too stuffy. Every part of me itches to run my hands through it until it's back to ruffled normal.

I fight that urge with all the strength I have. If I touch Ryder now, I won't be able to stop.

"Careful, Sil Sarrah, that almost sounded like a compliment." He flashes me a smile.

Smiling in this suit should be illegal.

So should moving, for that matter. Heat creeps into my cheeks as he crosses the room, slinging his unused tie—made of the same shiny black material as his lapels—over his shoulder.

"You could still join me, you know," he says. "That store had some pretty nice dresses . . ."

And talking. Talking in this suit should be illegal.

"Would any of them go with electric cuffs?" I turn back to the snippet of code I'm studying, before I lose what's left of my self-control. "I'm thinking security will insist on those no matter how I'm dressed."

"Probably." Ryder drops down to the mattress beside me. "Unless we pack this all in and go lie on a beach in Hawaii."

"Hawaii hasn't existed since before the Annihilation," I say. "The only beaches left on the continent are on the wrong side of the Demarcation Line, and the ocean is radioactive."

And as for the rest . . . it's ten years, a botched mission, twelve million stolen documents, and one corrupt mogul of industry too late for that. I'm committed.

"See, there's that sparkling optimism that drew me to you." Ryder laces his fingers through mine. To stop me typing, I suspect.

"A 'Wanted' alert and a bar full of drunks is what drew you to me."

"Well, sure, that too." With his other hand, he covers the new screen at my wrist. "This is going to work, Sil. We'll make it work," he says, proving that I'm not the one suffering from an optimism problem.

Christ-that-was, I have to tell him.

I have to tell him right now.

Instead, I lean over and press my lips to his. Because I'm a coward, and I'm weak, and I'm terrified of what comes next, so before it does, I want to feel this weightlessness—this *wholeness*—one last time. I want Ryder's hands in my hair and on my skin; I want to run mine under all that expensive fabric.

I want to make *this* work, make *us* work.

I want to live. Not just survive.

But when I was eight years old, an impressive man sporting every mod I'd ever dreamed of convinced me to ignore my parents' wishes and sign my future away. And so this moment is all I get. One stolen moment in an android graveyard full of rusted metal and broken dreams. One perfect moment as Ryder's hands climb up my ribs and a groan of pure longing escapes his throat.

Then robot Jarvis pushes me Aja's latest ping and the moment shatters.

<ANONYMYNX> It's showtime.

Time to go meet my maker.

CHAPTER 26

We make our way to the Syntex building together, mostly silent, our fingers intertwined. The boy in the expensive suit and the Junker. A regular Holomark movie special.

I run the plan through in my head as we walk, going over each possible complication. For this to work, our timing has to be perfect. Ryder might have an invitation for tonight's event, but his alias is shaky at best. He'll need help getting inside.

That's where I come in.

Nothing gets a party started like the most wanted fugitive in the sector showing up.

"This is my stop," Ryder says when the glass monolith I used to call home emerges from between the buildings, shining like a gilded giant in the night. "I'll see you on the other side?"

"Yeah." I manage to smile without wincing, though it costs me the remaining piece of my heart. Because if all goes well, this will be the final time I see Ryder Stone. That's the choice I made, and it's too late to make a different one.

So I let him go, drinking in every last detail before his hand breaks free of mine and he turns towards the mouth of the alley, leaving my palm stinging at the absence. He's halfway down the block before I whisper an apology into the cold night air. *I'm sorry for not telling you the truth.* The words are a fraction of what I want to say, the opening line of a song I've not yet finished writing.

This is no time to sing about your feelings. I force myself to focus, locking the pain behind an impenetrable steel wall. "Jarvis, give me eyes on the entrance," I say, then a long moment later, the feeds from the security cameras pop up on my ocular display, offering me six different views on the arriving dignitaries.

During events like this, Syntex straddles the line between ostentatious and secure. So while no expense has been spared decorating the building with custom projection maps, rolling out the red carpet, and unleashing a thousand firefly drones to light up the street, security has also hired a whole squad of goons to man the doors, complete with clearance authenticators, facial scanners, and chip readers.

Our efforts will get Ryder past the first two; he'll use the code Miles generated him to beat the authenticator, and Jondi's uploaded his face to the guest database. His ID chip is the real problem. That information is stored on a government server we can't hack cleanly at such short notice. So instead, we'll have to distract security long enough for Ryder to sneak inside. The trick is doing it *after* they've validated his face and code, but *before* they scan his neck. With green lights across those initial checks, they'll likely overlook a missing chip scan when presented with a bigger prize.

Me.

That's the plan, anyway. If it were a sanctioned mission, Jarvis would probably give it an 83% chance of success. Maybe 85% once he saw how seamlessly Ryder blends into the river of arriving guests, swanning onto the red carpet with the cocky arrogance of a man who belongs. A muted rainbow of grays and greens flutters around him, high-ranking officials in sharp suits, military uniforms, and dresses that cost more than cars, all smiling politely for the army of news bots covering this illustrious affair. The sight hits me right in the gut, tugging loose a memory. Last time Syntex threw a party, I wasn't a fugitive, I was the main event. And I totally screwed up my life.

No, you didn't. I beat the feeling down. If Lena were here, she'd tell me to look at the bright side. *You uncovered a conspiracy, Sil! You're gonna save the company!* she'd say. She'd even get to the end of that sentence before bursting out laughing. Then she'd steal one glance at Ryder in that suit and send me a string of highly inappropriate pings for the rest of the night.

She's the reason I find the strength to step out of the shadows.

I'm doing this for her. And for Jondi. And for every other Walker the Director betrayed when he placed his greed before our lives. I only wish I could have done it sooner, back when the three of us could still walk away from it together.

I hit the red carpet right as security authenticates Ryder's code, but I keep my mouth shut for now. Not that I need to run it to draw attention; half the crowd immediately turns to stare at me, underdressed as I am for this occasion in my flimsy, vendo-bought clothes. Hard to tell if anyone's recognized me yet, but I'm not planning to keep them guessing long. The moment Jarvis confirms that Ryder's facial scan has also cleared the system, I put my hands up and yell, "My name is Captain Sil Sarrah of Walker Division Nine. I believe you've been looking for me."

Security's response is as swift and efficient as I imagined. It takes three seconds before every gun on the block is pointed at my chest. Another three and I'm on my knees, tasting metal. Then on go the electric cuffs, and a current-inhibiting halo to stop Jarvis registering my verbal commands. In ten seconds flat, they've cut me off from my tech.

But it's worth it because at the business end of the carpet, Ryder slips through the doors unchallenged. He doesn't look back, disappearing into the crowd exactly the way we planned. Trusting me to handle my part—even if security is a little rougher than I expected.

With a hand to each of my elbows, they haul me to my feet, a gun pressed between my shoulder blades to stop me doing anything stupid. I try to hold my head up high as they frog-march me into the building, but the cacophony of whispers and glares get to me in the end.

I shouldn't care what these bureaucrats think of me; I'm on the right side of this war; I have nothing to be ashamed about.

But it's hard to shake a decade's worth of performance-led conditioning. A week ago, I was the best Walker Syntex had ever seen, and these same people gathered around me to watch a show. Instead, they watched me fail. And the sharks must have gotten a taste for blood because they seem to enjoy watching it happen again.

They don't matter, only he *does,* I remind myself. If this works, and I get to the Director, then the sharks get to keep feeding, Syntex gets to keep developing the life-saving technology we need to survive this ruined planet, and idealists like Ryder, and Aja, and Brin, get to keep making sure they don't abuse that power.

Security rushes me through the lobby so fast my boots barely touch the polished marble. From there, it's straight into an elevator and down to the containment level—or the Boneyard, as we used to call it, back when I lived on a less notorious floor.

Syntex isn't a prison, and it doesn't *officially* have one on the premises, either. But hostile agents try to infiltrate this building every single day, and when they fail, security needs a place to stash them. Among . . . *other* things. Thanks to what Ryder would call *a very handy law,* the company doesn't have to report acts of espionage—it's free to extract mods and information from the culprits in any way it sees fit. And something tells me that status quo is even worse for agents it actually *owns.*

The room they take me to is a gray box. Literally. Gray cement floors, gray walls, industrial steel door. That's it. No windows, no chair, no cot. No expense spent on traitors.

I run my fingers along the peeling paint as the door slams shut behind me, swallowing a mouthful of stale air to steady the pounding of my heart. Next time that door opens, it'll be the Director on the other side. Next time that door opens, I'm going to kill a man.

Which is why the first thing I do is get to work deactivating my cuffs and this infernal halo. The hack comes courtesy of the tiny wireless transmitter I had Zell implant beneath my new keypad, and a tricky little snippet of code Jondi whipped up

special for tonight. We designed it to stay dormant and unde-
tectable until five minutes after I made it into the building. Long
enough that security will have finished running their scans for
malicious software, but not so long that I'd still be helpless when
the Director arrived.

Once live, the unit is set to respond to a simple voice command.
So I sink down to the concrete, drop my head to the wall and
mumble "son of a bitch", as though resigned to my fate.

If Jondi did his job right, that phrase will trigger a short burst
transmission that infects any unsecured piece of hardware within
five feet of me, rendering it defunct.

This theory of yours better work, J. I start counting the seconds.
A virus like this shouldn't need more than a few minutes to take
out such simple devices, and Jondi can program this type of bug
in his sleep. I've no reason to think it won't work. Which doesn't
stop me thinking it anyway. Hell, Ryder's prickly little hacker
was right, I do like being in control. And this is no control. None.
I'm entirely at the mercy of a sequence of ones and zeros.

Please let this work. Please let this work. Please let this—

I feel rather than see the virus take effect. The faint hum
buzzing at my temples dies, followed by the current dancing
across my palms. The lock on the cuffs disengages with a click.

Reliable as always, J. The breath I'm holding whistles out in
a rush. I should have known better than to doubt his skill.

I pull my knees to my chest, burying my face between them
so I can whisper a quick question without the cameras noticing.
"Jarvis, you there?"

"Yes, Captain."

Christ-that-was, I've never been happier to hear his stupid robot
voice. That, together with the fact my keypad is working again,
means at least one step of this plan went off without a hitch.

<FUGITIVE_AT_LARGE_SS> Code worked.

I risk a message to the others.

<UNKNOWN_USER> Like there was ever any doubt.

Jondi's reply comes instantly.

By now, he should have hacked into the building's emergency alert system, ready to swing the coming confrontation my way. Aja and Brin are—hopefully—in the suite of offices Miles arranged for them across the square, standing by to unleash some chaos once Ryder hijacks them an active node. And if all plays out as we planned, then the Director should be heading to my cell as soon as he can escape the party.

<RESISTANCE_RYDER> Perfect timing. Paxton Senior just left the hall.

Perfect timing indeed. I climb back to my feet, careful not to betray my newfound freedom as I type out one final message, ready for sending the instant the Director steps through that door. Then I take another breath and hold it, calming the storm brewing inside my veins.

I haven't felt this nervous for a mission since my first, when after a year of monitored simulations, I was suddenly expected to perform an extraction for real. Alone. No more guidance, no more supervision. I had to take control, make a plan, hold an actual life in the palm of my hand. So naturally, I fumbled my own name and asked Jarvis to initiate a neural lake instead of a neural link, over an open comms channel. That didn't exactly fill my host with confidence. Neither did the five minutes I spent running her in circles around the facility because I was too flustered to make sense of the blueprints. My simulations never prepared me for the pressure of melding with a living, breathing—*swearing*—host. They didn't prepare me for killing my boss, either, or for doing it in my own body, yet here I am.

Don't be a coward. I tell myself the same thing I did before that first mission. *This is far from the hardest thing you've had to do.*

The Director is pushing sixty; he left the military decades ago and hasn't seen any action since. Size may be on his side, but all the other cards are stacked firmly in my favor. I'm trained, I'm fast, I'm resourceful, and I have help. In this fight, I'm the safer bet.

None of which keeps me from flattening against the wall when the high-pitched scrape of metal announces his arrival.

"Hello, Miss Sarrah," he says, sweeping into my cell. "Welcome home."

Like the rest of tonight's attendees, he's dressed to the nines in a crisp suit, his thinning hair combed back against his scalp. Two large security guards flank him on either side, but much to my relief, he motions for them to wait out in the corridor. The tension in my shoulders eases a touch as they pull the door shut behind them. This was the one variable we couldn't control, and though Miles assured me his father would want to conduct this conversation in private, I couldn't help but worry about this fragile piece of our plan.

<FUGITIVE_AT_LARGE_SS> I have eyes on Paxton.

I press send on the message I drafted, giving the others the go-ahead to spring forth and incite a little mayhem. The second they do, lockdown protocols will engage, and thanks to Jondi, those protocols now include sealing the Director in here with me, where security can't reach him.

All I have to do is keep him talking until then.

"I must admit, Miss Sarrah, the timing of your return is most . . . inconvenient," he continues. "I assume that was your intent?"

<RESISTANCE_RYDER> Node going live now.
<ANONYMYNX> I see it. Two minutes out.

Two minutes. I can make small talk with the man who ruined my life for two minutes. No problem.

"I thought your guests would like to know who they're in bed with," I say, lacing my voice with accusation. "And what he's doing with their money."

"Ah." A flicker of annoyance crosses the Director's face, so quick and fleeting I might have imagined it. "You analyzed the documents you stole. That's a crying shame, Miss Sarrah." He reaches into his pocket for something I can't see. "I was so hoping to resolve this in a civilized manner."

The pain hits before he's done speaking, crashing through my brain like a joyrider on a stim-fuelled spree.

"Effective, isn't it?" The Director offers me a brief respite, holding up the device in his hand. "Your CIP makes you vulnerable to frequencies us lesser mortals can't hear. This takes those frequencies and amplifies them, causing pain without damaging your hardware." He hits me with a second sonic wave, sending me to my knees. "Now, Miss Sarrah, you're going to tell me exactly what you know, and who you may have shared it with, because believe me when I say that prolonged exposure to this frequency will not kill you; it'll just make you wish you were dead."

I'm doubled over by the time the sound dissipates, blood in my mouth from where I've bitten my tongue.

<FUGITIVE_AT_LARGE_SS> Hurry.

Another bolt of lightning thunders through my brain, setting my ears alight.

"You have the power to make this stop, Miss Sarrah." The Director crouches down beside me, placing a hand on my back.

<RESISTANCE_RYDER> What's wrong?

What's wrong is this asshole is touching me, and my skull is vibrating so hard I can't break his fingers, or wrap an arm around his throat and squeeze. What's wrong is we didn't plan for this.

I figured the Director would threaten me first. Rough me up a little maybe, nothing I couldn't deal with.

Nothing this . . . *incapacitating*.

"Tell me who you've spoken to, Miss Sarrah. Who else knows?"

<RESISTANCE_RYDER> Sil, talk to me.

But I can't say much of anything—to either of them—while this wretched device is tearing my eardrums apart. I can't even peel myself off the floor.

"Tell me and the pain stops."

<ANONYMYNX> Thirty seconds.

Thirty seconds. I scream and set my shoulders. I can handle another thirty seconds. Hell, I'll handle thirty more if I have to, because beneath the pain, something stronger is brewing. Ten years of my life I gave this man—my *last* ten years—and he barely spared me two words before stooping to torture. He spared me no words at all before trying to have me arrested, or putting a price on my head.

And just like that, any doubts I had about ending his life scatter into the ether. Because *he* made this necessary. He brought this on himself.

"What say you, Miss Sarrah?" The Director silences the device, affording me a chance to catch my breath. "Would you like the pain to stop?"

"Screw you." I spit blood over his shoes. "I'm not telling you jack."

"Very well."

Okay, so maybe being a smartass wasn't the best idea. A grunt rips from my throat as he sends a fresh wave of agony shooting through my temples. At least if he's focused on my screams, he's not watching my hands. I press them to my stomach, slowly slipping my wrists free of the cuffs.

Seventeen, sixteen, fifteen . . . I count the seconds down in my mind. If the Director thinks some white noise is going to break me, he's got another thing coming. His company grafted a computer to my brain when I was eight years old; I'm no stranger to pain.

"Care to re-evaluate that answer, Miss Sarrah?"

Eleven, ten, nine . . .

"Call me *Miss* Sarrah again," I hiss. "Go on, I dare you."

"I'm afraid you lost the right to your rank when you disobeyed orders."

And you lost the right to give those orders when you broke the law. I shift my weight onto my legs. Our distraction should be going live in *three, two, one . . .*

The world turns black as every light in this dazzling tower dies, plunging my cell into inky darkness. If Aja makes good on her hack, then when the electricity is restored, the gold projection maps decorating the building will have been replaced by the Analog Army's signature pattern. A honeycomb programmed to snap apart one hexagon at a time, in a way that'll have the powers that be fearing an explosive finale. Meanwhile, Brin will be wreaking her own brand of havoc by launching those oh-so-pretty firefly drones into the windows, creating the illusion that tonight's event is under attack. Even as the real attack takes place forty levels down.

The lights bloom back to full blaze, just in time for the Director to watch the door bolt shut with a clang. On the other side, security start working frantically to wrench it open, but they're too late. Jondi's already locked them out of this cell. And the Director's finger has slipped off the button.

One precious moment of silence is all I need.

I spring up and tackle him to his knees, knocking the device to the ground then crushing it underfoot. The Director makes to rise but before he can so much as think of fighting back, I plant myself behind him and wrap the cuffs around his neck, driving the metal into the soft flesh at his throat. Like a makeshift garrotte.

"You should have spent a little less time torturing me, and a little more wondering why I turned myself in," I say, tightening my grip. "Then maybe you'd have seen this coming."

The veins in his forehead bulge in response, his Adam's apple trembling as he battles to draw breath.

Christ-that-was. I stare hard at the ceiling, trying to block out the gruesome sounds escaping his lips. I thought this would be easy. I thought it would feel the same as doing it from afar, through somebody else's body.

It doesn't.

My arms won't quit shaking, for one, cramping as the strain of crushing a man's windpipe tears through my muscles. There's bile building in my mouth, salt leaking from my eyes. The smell of sweat and fear permeates the cell, his and mine, roiling my stomach until it's all I can do to keep from retching.

This is the right thing and it needs to be done. I think the words over and over, willing my nerve to hold firm. *It needs to be done.*

Except, something is desperately wrong.

Less than a minute ago, this man was interrogating me. He was resolute, cold, determined to get his answers. Now, he's barely even struggling. Instead of clawing at my hands as though his life depends on it, his arms hang limply at his sides, his fists clenching and unclench—

Oh fuck.

I lurch away from him, tossing the bloodied cuffs to the ground. I've seen this exact same motion before. I've been the cause of it.

<FUGITIVE_AT_LARGE_SS> Give me a total signal blackout in the Boneyard. No comms in or out.

I fire the message to Jondi while the Director gasps for air on the floor.

<UNKNOWN_USER> That's not part of the plan.

<FUGITIVE_AT_LARGE_SS> Plan's compromised. I need this, J.
<UNKNOWN_USER> You got it.

A moment later, Jarvis informs me I've lost both satellite and wireless connectivity. Which means whoever's driving this charade has lost it too.

"This entire level just went offline," I tell the Director, loosening his tie as I help him sit up against the wall. His face is a deep shade of puce, the vessels in his eyes blown bloody, an angry gash smiling across his neck. But he's still conscious, and breathing, and with any luck, I'm not wrong about this.

"I'm guessing you already knew that though, since we're alone now," I say.

He nods as much as the injuries I inflicted allow.

"Good. Then it's time you told me who's pulling your strings."

CHAPTER 27

Turns out, almost choking a man to death makes it pretty hard for him to speak.

"M . . . my . . ." The word rasps out as a broken fragment, barely more than a whisper.

"Your what, Sir?" I try to be gentle, to leave the impatience out of my voice seeing how I'm the reason he's floating in and out of consciousness in the first place. But the truth is, we don't have time to play twenty questions. Security has stopped hammering at the door, which means they've gone to find an engineer to hack it open. And even if Jondi manages to slow that engineer down, I doubt we have long before whoever I booted out of the Director's mind comes looking for his meat suit.

That's why I need to know *who* that someone is.

"My . . . son . . ." the Director breathes.

Well, that's just great. Hypoxia's gone and addled his brain.

"Sir, that's not possible," I say. "Your son runs the Mindwalking program; he isn't a Walker."

Or a psychopath, for that matter.

"What if . . . he is, Captain?" The Director's eyes meet mine, and for a moment, they're crystal clear. "Test your . . . assumptions."

Test your assumptions. When Ryder threw that phrase at me a few days ago, I ended up in a Faraday cage, breaking into his mind. But the chasm between *that* and *this* could swallow the universe whole. *This* doesn't make any sense.

"Please, Captain." The Director grabs my arm with surprising force. "Work it through," he begs.

So I do.

The first hurdle to becoming a Walker is securing the tech.

But even before Miles took over the program, he was a company stakeholder with his own dedicated R&D lab. If he wanted to get his hands on a CIP, he'd have certainly had the means.

Then there's the issue of blood compatibility, though I've no real reason to think Miles doesn't have the DNA markers required to survive implantation. Just because the children of billionaires don't normally sell their futures, doesn't mean they *can't*. And as for his ports and power button, well . . . they could easily be hiding beneath those longer-than-average blond curls of his, assuming that after installing the tech *illegally* he chose to put them in the usual place; they could just as soon be elsewhere.

No, the most obvious—and definitive—reason Miles can't be a Walker is because he's the wrong side of twenty; he'd have burned out years ago.

But if I remove that one limiting factor from the equation . . . if I accept the possibility that Miles found a way to implant the unit at a later age, or extend his CIP's life span . . .

It's like a door swings open in my mind, inviting a whisper of doubt to slither in.

I'm here because Miles allowed me to be.

I tried to kill his father because he insisted we *should*.

Because he promised me the one thing he knew I couldn't resist: research that would one day lead to there not being a wrong side of twenty, for any Walker.

Except, that's ridiculous.

This whole train of thought is ridiculous. I mean, this is Miles we're talking about. In the two years I've known him, he's only ever had my best interests at heart. He's trained me, he's encouraged me, he's comforted me. Why would he bother doing any of that? Why would he bother maintaining this lie, for *years*?

"Milford . . . manipulates, Captain," the Director says, watching the play of indecision on my face. "When he wants something. . .

he takes it. No matter the . . . cost. That's why I had him transferred to . . . the Applied Science division. I hoped he'd do . . .
less damage in . . . a lab."

"Sir, that's not—" *Miles*, I want to say. That's not the man I
know. It's not the man I trust. That man always puts his Walkers
first, even when it's the middle of the night and they're giving
him lip while beating a bag bloody, or when they're burning out
on the cafeteria floor.

But before I can get the words out, the Director's grip on my
arm tightens. "Think what he stood . . . to gain, Captain," he
says. "Just *think*."

It doesn't take a supercomputer to answer that question.

Ambitious men have done far worse than play a role for money,
or status, or power. A CIP and control of his father's company
would give Miles all three, with an army of faithful Walkers to
boot.

Walkers he trained himself.

Walkers more loyal to him than the law.

Walkers he could manipulate into running illegal ops.

Look how quickly he manipulated you into murder; the suspicious voice in my mind is fast growing loud. A little fearmongering
and a handful of documents was all Miles needed to convince
me to offer him what's left of my future—which he knew I *would*
because he knows *me*. He knew I would place the program before
myself. Preserve my legacy before my life. And hand him a tech
empire in the process. Hell, by throwing in a couple of choice
objections, he even made me think it was my idea.

Control the data, control the narrative.

What if the Analog Army weren't the only ones playing a long
game?

"I knew no one would . . . believe me," the Director continues.
"I got free . . . I tried to show you."

"That's why you sent Harper to that black site." The pieces
keep slotting together, no matter how much I don't want them
to. *He* sent her, not Miles. To *Miles's* black site, not his. Then

when Miles caught wind of the op and ordered a termination, he sent me in to extract her. To extract the truth.

"Yes." The Director's voice is beginning to wane.

"Why me, Sir?" I can't help but ask while he's still conscious, though the question makes me sound petty and dour. *Why did it have to be me?*

"Your . . . record, Captain. I knew you'd try to . . . preserve it."

So Miles twisted that narrative too. His father didn't assign me that termination because he thought I'd follow any order; he assigned it to me because he knew I wouldn't. He knew I'd fight to protect that stupid record more fiercely than I ever fought to protect my friends.

Rage sears through my blood, a heavy numbness that starts in my toes then seeps into every vein, and bone, and cell. The Director may not have broken the law, but he has plenty to answer for nonetheless. He made me this way, taught me to obsess over statistics so that I would keep performing for him, like an obedient child. Meanwhile, his actual child was out there destroying everything the rest of us sold our lives for.

"How long has this been going on?" I ask through clenched teeth. "How long has he been in control?"

"Two . . . years."

Two *years*? The number crashes over me like a radioactive tsunami. Miles has held his father prisoner in his own mind for *two years*. The entire time he's been running the program.

Christ-that-was, I can't even begin to imagine the horror of it, the helplessness. Whatever the Director's personal failings, no one deserves that. No one.

"Sir, I—" The lock disengaging saves me having to choke out an empty platitude.

No. My head snaps towards the door. *No, no, no, no, no . . .* Security can't have broken through yet. I need more time.

"Sil!"

"*Ryder?*" I'm halfway to my feet when he bursts through the door, lip split and fists bloody.

My heart stutters at the sight of him, as though finally able to beat properly again. "What are you—*how* are you—?"

"You didn't answer my pings," he says between shallow gasps. "I had to see if . . ." His eyes settle on the Director and he trails off, reaching for the gun—I assume—he acquired from the security guard he cut his knuckles on.

"No, wait!" I rush to block his way. "He's not responsible; Miles is. Miles is behind all of it." The words sting my tongue coming out, but what stings more is that they suddenly feel true. Never in a million years did I think I'd be siding with Paxton Senior over his son, but it's hard not to listen to a man forced to watch his own murder.

"Did *he* tell you that?" Ryder makes to step around me. To get a clean shot. "You can't trust him, Sil. He'll say anything to save his neck."

"Then why didn't he fight me?" I ask. "I was strangling him, Ryder. I almost *killed* him, and instead of struggling, he just clenched and unclenched his fists, like Aja did when I broke into her mind."

"So you're saying what? There's someone in there?" Ryder's hands clamp around my shoulders, his fingers digging into my skin.

"Not someone; Miles," I say. "Miles is a—"

I don't get to finish my sentence, because right at that moment, Ryder surges forward and slams me into the wall.

"Sil, Sil, Sil," he tuts, pressing the barrel of his gun to the underside of my jaw. "I so wish you'd stop sticking that nose where it doesn't belong."

"Miles." My stomach lurches into my throat, realization and dread mingling with the pain. And even if the threat of a bullet wasn't keeping me from screaming, I doubt I could find a string of curses colorful enough to do this feeling justice.

I've been the ghost in the machine hundreds of times; I built my career on it. Not gonna lie, I always wondered what this dance looked like from the other side, how people could not *know* that the person standing in front of them was being controlled by a stranger.

Except, I didn't know.

Not an inkling, not a flicker, not a doubt.

And I should have.

Because the elevators down to this floor are code-word acti-vated. My cell door was disabled. Only a universal override would have gotten Ryder into the underbelly of this building and through that lock. That kind of access isn't easy to come by.

Unless your last name is Paxton.

"That's right, Sil, boyfriend's not in charge anymore," Ryder says, though they're not his words, they're Miles's.

Because Miles is a Walker. The reality hits, cleaving me straight to the bone. Miles played me. He lied to me. He groomed me. Then he betrayed me. He betrayed us all.

"How?" The question rips from somewhere deep inside my chest, equal parts hurt and fury.

"Let's just say I made the most of my exile." Miles quirks Ryder's lips into a smile. He must have planted a portable trans-mitter somewhere on his body, because according to my sensors, the Boneyard is still a communications black hole.

"My father never did think big when it came to the Walker program," Miles says, glancing over at the Director. "Isn't that right, old man?"

Paxton Senior doesn't reply, having finally lost his battle with consciousness.

"But me? I had a vision," Miles continues. "If only you knew what your CIP was capable of, Sil. Once the training wheels come off."

Well, seeing how he's been wearing Daddy full-time while also running the program, my guess is losing those training wheels allows him to retain control of his body while he's melded. And given that he's been at this for *two years*, I assume it also lets him forge a stable neural link long-term. How, I have no idea. The degradation that would cause should have fried his system in days.

"So why not kill him yourself?" I hiss. "Why get me to do your dirty work?"

I'd understand Miles wanting to keep his own hands clean, but he was in his father's head; he could have easily walked him into an incinerator. Like he ordered me to do to Harper.

"Oh trust me, I've tried," he says. "It's the one kink I haven't ironed out yet. Use that supercharged brain of yours, Sil. Tell me why."

He's toying with me, drawing out this conversation far longer than necessary. We both know I can't fight him with a gun pressed to my chin, that he could have already killed me fifteen times over.

He's talking because he wants to talk.

He's been *dying* to talk; I can hear it in his voice—in Ryder's voice—the way it peaks when he's exhilarated. Miles has been living with this secret for two years, forced to play the role of kind commander and hide the true extent of his genius. He *needs* to share it.

And that I can work with.

"Because he fought back, you sick son of a bitch. He fought you."

"Very good, Sil." Miles rewards me with a smile that's almost wistful. "See, something happens when we're given consent: our hosts stop fighting. They don't like having us in their minds, but they allow it. They trust we know what we're doing, even as we walk them right up to the ledge. But if we force our way in, it's . . . different." He sighs, as though their refusal to cede control was designed solely to inconvenience *him*.

"It took my father a while to learn how to fight me effectively. I had to keep him alive at first; his standing and influence were pivotal to my plans. Then by the time they weren't, he'd learned to resist the Meld. He kept breaking the neural link—never for long enough to do any real damage, but long enough to stop me feeding him a bullet, among *other* headaches."

"Is that what Cole Risler was to you? A headache?" I ask. It's a gamble; Risler's the one piece of the puzzle I haven't quite placed yet, a risk Miles should have been too clever to take. But the pattern fits and I need to keep him talking.

"You really are the best I've ever seen, you know that?" A mix of annoyance and reluctant admiration flits across his face. "My father got loose while I was off-site, barricaded himself inside a wireless vault, and cut out his ID chip. I needed someone who could move around the building unchallenged to get him out of there and put it back. But since my forced Melds have been known to cause some . . . *residual side effects*, I figured it would be wiser to commandeer a recent host."

So the shrinks would dismiss Risler's ramblings as an adverse reaction to *my* Meld. So they wouldn't believe him when he said the ghost was still lurking inside.

Christ-that-was, that's why Miles peppered me with questions in the gym. He wasn't consoling me; he was making sure Risler didn't let slip anything incriminating.

"Do you even care that he killed himself, you arrogant piece of—"

"Careful, Sil—" Miles's voice takes on that tone I know so well, the barrel biting deeper into my flesh. "Best not say something your boyfriend might regret. He'll be most upset when I finally make him shoot you. Or at least, I think he will. He's gone rather quiet in here." Miles taps a finger to Ryder's temple. "Funny, he was just *filled* with rage when I first took over, but now that I've got a gun to your head, he's not fighting me at all. How does that make you feel?"

"None of your business, that's how." I hurl the words at him, though the real answer is *damn fucking happy.*

I don't need a knight in shining armor and Ryder's smart enough to know that. Smart enough to know that trying to fight the Meld while his finger is pressed against that trigger will only end one way, with blood on his hands and my brain splattered across the ceiling. More importantly, he's smart enough to know what I've already set in motion.

"Why'd you do it, Miles?" I ask while I still can. "Why'd you try to have me arrested?"

"I didn't get where I am by taking unnecessary risks, Sil, and

I've no use for a Walker I can't trust. The minute you disobeyed orders, you left me no choice."

Bullshit. The anger in my eyes threatens to spill over, the heat growing too hot to contain. Miles had nothing but choice. We both know I'd have given him the files I stole in a heartbeat. Back then, I wouldn't have even asked *why*.

"Honestly, Sil, you impressed me," he says. "I didn't think you'd have it in you to run. Then when you did, I reckoned you'd last a few hours before we tracked you down. I never dreamed you'd find a way to disable your trackers."

But I did.

That's why he sent me all those messages, imploring me to come in.

Then when that didn't work, he decided to exploit the opportunity I created when I ran. Two birds, one murder. By manipulating me into killing his father, he got to solve his wayward Walker problem, and his defiant Director problem both at once.

"Well then, I guess you're not as smart as you think you are," I spit, happy to have robbed him of those wins—and happier still that I didn't deign to bother him with every mechanical detail of tonight's plan.

Miles knew I'd be using code to disable my restraints, but I never told him the trigger phrase, so he never knew to keep an ear out for it, or else he'd have wrapped up this victory lap the moment I called him a son of a bitch. Instead, Jondi's virus should be disabling the transmitter he planted on Ryder's body right about . . .

Now.

I may not have noticed Ryder was mindjacked when he first burst into my cell, but I do notice the moment he's freed. It's like a spark ignites behind his eyes, recognition, relief, and revulsion rolled into one.

"Sil—" He scrambles back, making to drop the gun.

But I'm faster. And I'm done taking chances.

With a growl, I catch his arm, snatch the pistol, and sweep his legs out from under him, sending him crashing to his knees. "Convince me."

"Right . . . yeah . . . my name is Ryder Stone. My brother was Aiden Stone—"

"Do better." I give him a non-too-gentle prod with the business end of the barrel. "Nothing Miles could have found by running your ID."

"Okay . . . well . . ." He knots both hands behind his head and shakes it, as though trying to put straight the memories. "The first time you threatened to shoot me, I'd just kissed you— which was more enjoyable than trying to kill you—but the two things seem to piss you off about the same so . . ."

"That's not funny." I lower the gun, sliding down the wall to catch my breath.

"It's a little funny." Ryder loosens his tie as he shuffles over to join me, breathing equally hard. "I'm so sorry, Sil. I never saw him coming."

"Not your fault; none of us did. Except him." I point to the Director. "Two years he's been under Miles's control. We all missed it. A building full of employees missed it."

I missed it.

In every conversation and faraway stare.

In every gesture I misread and every act of perceived kindness.

I missed everything.

"So what do we do now?" Ryder turns to look at me. His eyes are tired, and wide, and for the first time since we met, entirely lost. Ryder Stone is the knife in the darkness. He's brains, and charm, and shadow, and stealth, he's the series of shallow cuts that overwhelms you in the end. What he's not is the guy you send into the world's most secure building without a plan. That isn't what he's good at.

Lucky for him, I am very, *very* good at it.

"Same goal, different Paxton." I shrug. "We kill Miles."

"How? You don't think he'll have locked himself somewhere safe and tight by now?"

"Probably."

In his father's penthouse office would be my guess. The most secure place in the building.

"Christ-that-was," Ryder swears and drops his head to the concrete. "He played us so perfectly."

"No. Not *perfectly*." The makings of an idea are already stirring in my mind, forming then re-forming as I mold them into shape. Miles did what all self-aggrandizing assholes do when they get too cocky: he talked too much. He told me exactly how to beat him.

"We need to get to the twentieth floor." I spring to my feet, dragging Ryder up with me.

"Sil, wait—" He cringes back from the door. "I can't go out there. If I leave this room, Miles could take control again." Fear colors his voice, lending weight to the truth he's too afraid to say. *He'll make me kill you.*

And though I long to tell him that he won't, that he's stronger than Miles, that this time, he'll fight him and he'll win, the words die on my tongue. Because this isn't a fairy tale and neither of us is that naïve. So instead of feeding him a fantasy, I take his hand and say, "I can think of one way to stop him." Though I doubt Ryder will like it much. "Do you trust me?"

"You know I do."

"Then pull down your collar and turn around."

CHAPTER 28

Lin's office sits twenty-four floors above the Boneyard. On a good day, it would take us a couple of minutes to get there. We'd hop an elevator to the atrium, cross the lobby to the residential banks, then hop another up to medical.

Today is not a good day.

Today, the man who secretly turned Walker and trapped his father in his own mind has a vested interest in keeping us down here; today, I helped the Analog Army hijack the company's most lucrative night of the year, ensuring every security guard on duty is standing in our way; today, my best friend blocked all communications to this level, so I can't call on him to lend a hand; and today, Ryder's still bleeding from the neck where I cut out his ID chip with a broken piece of plastic.

Today, the odds are not in our favor.

"What about Paxton?" Ryder points to the unconscious Director. "Do we just . . . leave him?"

"No safer place for him to be," I say, pulling the cell door shut.

If this works, and I convince Lin to help us instead of marching us back here in cuffs, I'll have her send a team to aid the man I almost murdered.

That's assuming we get to her office.

With connectivity jammed, I can't hack the elevators—they're controlled by a central matrix on the security floor—but the stairwell locks are localized and I learned how to crack those when I was ten. I didn't exactly love having a curfew back then, or being confined to the junior barracks—especially once Lena

272

discovered that if we snuck into the mess hall after dark, we could trick the food synthesizers into resetting our dietary quotas by spinning the clock forward and then spinning it back, as if it never happened. That girl kept me in candy cubes for years. She kept me sane much, much longer.

"Hey." Ryder's fingers brush against mine. "You okay?"

"Fine." I shove the memory away, barricading it behind a lock far more robust than this one. I thought killing a man would be the worst part of returning to this building. That's what I spent the day preparing for. But as it turns out, the hardest part is dealing with the ghosts.

The screams assault us long before we reach the atrium, heralding the commotion awaiting us beyond the stairs. Even from this side of the glass, I can see the honeycomb pattern projected on the windows, the countdown to a fictional explosion nearing its end. A cacophony of feral thumps and thuds punctuates the chaos; Brin having a little *too* much fun with the firefly drones, inciting a veritable stampede of bodies as the Director's guests ruin their finery in their rush to escape the danger. Proof that you don't need a bomb to cause a panic; the mere threat of one will do.

"Here, put this on." Ryder drapes his jacket around my shoulders and pulls me close to his side, so that we blend in with the other couples looking for an exit.

But we're not looking for an exit at all.

We scramble through the mayhem, cutting left towards the bank of elevators.

"You two—stop right there!"

We're a hundred feet shy of the doors when security spots us heading in the wrong direction.

"Keep moving," I tell Ryder. Then to Jarvis, I say, "I'll need those doors open in twenty-five seconds."

"Stop or I'll shoot!" the voice calls again.

I'd venture the only reason he's not shooting already is because he's not yet sure whether we're tied to the attack, or just a couple of Very Important People He Really Shouldn't Kill. And that question will disappear the instant he catches up to us.

"Do we take him out?" Ryder asks, discreetly cocking his gun.

"Not like that," I say. "It'll draw too much attention."

A quick and dirty right hook, though . . .

"On three, I want you to duck, okay?"

"Why? We starting a fight?"

"Not if I can help it."

This fight needs to end before it ever begins.

Which is why I wait until the footsteps building behind us draw close enough to ripple the air—only then do I push away from Ryder with a whispered, "One . . . two . . . *three!*"

He ducks, and I swing my arm around him in a wide arc, catching security by surprise. My fist connects with the man's jaw. Hard. Sending blood and a couple of teeth skittering to the marble. The guard grunts and doubles over, then before he has the chance to straighten up, I throw a knee to his groin and an elbow to his back. Once he's down, a blow to the head ensures he stays there.

"It's a little concerning how good you are at that." The elevator doors slide open and Ryder tugs me inside.

"Tell me about it," I mutter, shaking out the ache in my hand. Being able to floor a guy twice my size used to be a point of pride for me. Just another part of the job. But today, I actually *feel* the violence. Not a fraction of it, or some abstract picture viewed through a stranger's eyes. I feel the weight of my actions in every bruise and aching muscle. I'm finally starting to feel the human cost of what I do.

No worse time than the present. I mash the *close doors* button until the elevator inches shut. Guilt has no place on a mission like this. Neither does doubt.

"So what's our play here?" Ryder asks, tossing his blood-soaked tie to the floor.

"Remember what Miles said about my CIP having training wheels?"

He flinches, the lines in his body pulling tight. "Hard to forget much of anything a psychopath says while he's squatting in your mind."

"Well, we're going to see someone who can take them off."

At least, I hope Lin can. And that she *will*. Because the truth is, I'm in free fall, reacting, moving on instinct, pushing forward because if I stop, I'll have to admit that Miles is holding all the cards. My plan—the code I had Aja write for me—won't work if I leave him alive, with an army of loyal Walkers at his disposal and the keys to the Mindwalking program stored safely in his head. I need to lock those keys away. Every last one of them. In a vault so thick and impenetrable, Syntex can never get them out.

"Eyes up, Jarvis. Keep those doors shut until I tell you otherwise," I say as the elevator approaches the twentieth floor, setting Ryder's gun to incapacitate instead of kill. I left my taste for collateral damage in the cell with the man I almost murdered. "Follow my lead?"

Ryder nods and we both flatten ourselves against the elevator sides.

"On my mark, Jarvis." I track the guards until they're almost upon us. "*Now!*"

The doors wrench apart with a screech that would wake the dead. Both men whip around, reaching for their guns, but we've caught them unaware and out of formation, with one trailing several steps behind the other.

Sloppy.

I put an electric round squarely in the farther man's chest while Ryder rushes forward and tackles the closer one to the ground. A few wet thuds later, his knuckles have split open again, but he climbs back to his feet and the guard doesn't.

"Can't have you doing all the work." Ryder wipes the blood on his expensive shirt, then together we drag Twiddle-Down and Twiddle-Downer into an empty treatment room, shooting out the lock behind us. I'd worry about a second team showing up when they miss their scheduled check-in, but the girls' efforts should keep security busy a little longer. If we get this done fast, we might just pull it off.

Lin's office is exactly the way I left it a week ago: blissfully clean and tidy, the diagnostic chair at its center sterile and crisp. I run my hands along the soft leather, my fingers tracing the neat nylon stitching. Never thought I'd miss this thing. Never thought I'd miss the woman in charge of it, either.

"Sil!" Ryder snatches for the gun as Lin scans into the room a minute later, having received the alert that her office was in use.

Whoever she expected to see during a security breach, we sure aren't it. She freezes in the doorway, her eyes jumping from me, to Ryder, to the gun he almost drops at the sight of her.

"It's okay. She's why we're here," I say, and with an obvious surge of relief, Ryder lowers the weapon, though he still looks unnerved, sickened pale to a sheet, the metal trembling in his hand.

"Lin—" I start, but she silences me with a stern raise of her brow.

"Before you ask for my help, I want your word that the two of you aren't planning to detonate a bomb in a building full of *civilians*." Though Lin aims the words at me, she continues appraising Ryder, and the honeycomb tattoo beneath his rolled-up sleeve that marks him as a member of the Analog Army. The faction currently threatening to do just that.

"We're not," I'm quick to assure her. "The countdown is a hoax, I swear."

For a long moment, Lin only looks at me, like she has so many times before, when I was sat in her chair, lying about the pain of implantation, or how scared I was of the procedures still to come.

Lin knows exactly what I look like when I lie.

She knows me better than anyone.

"I had a feeling you wouldn't stay away." Her face softens. "What do you need?"

The knot in my stomach gives an inch, my eyes stinging with relief. Lin's been more a parent to me than my parents have these past ten years. It matters, what she thinks of me. It's always mattered.

"Access to my operating system," I say, blinking back the burn. "With unrestricted write permissions."

"Sil—" Lin cocks her head in that way that tells me I'm being unreasonable. That diagnostics aren't optional. That yelling at her over twilight won't slow the clock down any.

"I know it's a lot to ask, and how much trouble this could get you in. I wouldn't be asking unless it was important."

She sighs a sigh that's both exhausted and familiar. "I don't suppose you'd like to tell me why?"

"It's better if you don't know."

"You can trust me, Sil."

"I do." Which is why I have to keep her in the dark. Lin's already risked too much for me these past few days—the newly healed skin at her palm is proof of that. Proof that she'll do everything in her power to protect her Walkers—even when it means betraying her employer. But in order to do that she needs to be here, in this office, not dead, fired, or rotting in some cell. "It's just better if you don't know."

Another sigh, though this time, it's resigned. "Alright. Let's get you patched in." She folds the chair out flat. "Your friend should sit too. I'll take care of that wound."

"I'm fine," Ryder says.

"If you were *fine* you wouldn't be bleeding on my floor. Now please, sit." Her tone leaves little room for discussion, compelling him to jump up next to me.

"Be careful with this code, Sil," Lin says as she plugs a hard line into my neck, providing the biometric scan that will grant me admin privileges to the console. "It controls everything your unit can do."

And everything it *can't*. I mumble a quick thank you before getting to work. Somewhere in this mass of code is a limiting patch that stops my CIP from reaching its full potential. I'm going to find it and take it off.

"So." Lin shifts her attention to Ryder, snapping on a pair of gloves. "Is there a reason you decided to . . . remove your ID chip?"

"Not that I'm able to discuss at this moment." He hedges.

"I assume you're aware of the hardships associated with living off-grid?"

"It's a temporary measure." Ryder pulls the offending chip out of his pocket. "Plan was always to re-insert it."

"I see." The sour scent of antiseptic fills the room. "Would you like me to do that for you?"

"No—"

"—Yes," I cut in as the cluster of code I'm hunting flashes across the screen. It's small and expertly camouflaged—I only find it thanks to a targeted keyword search—but it's written to affect all my major systems, and once I scrub it from the database, the string of functions it unlocks answers a bunch of questions I didn't even know I had.

"Erm . . . Sil . . ." Ryder fixes me his best *what the hell are you doing?* look. Probably because I'm the one who clawed out his ID chip in the first place.

But that was then, and this is now.

And now I see a use for it.

"Please re-insert it," I say, turning back towards the console. Before I apply the changes, I want to add in a limiting patch of my own, a command that will optimize my system for neural links—and protect it from outside ones. No more hacks, no more database searches, no more monitoring security feeds in real-time. I'm diverting all power to this single function so that I might live long enough to trigger the one that'll kill me.

"Try to hold still."

Beside me, Ryder hisses, his fingers biting leather as Lin realigns his chip. A minute later, the mechanical click of a nanite injector rings out.

"That should do it."

"Thank you." I take the opportunity to say that properly. While I still have the chance. "I mean it, Lin. For everything." *For today,*

*and last week, and every month and year before it. For keeping
me together.*

"Oh, and Lin—" I reach for her arm, mustering the courage
for one final confession. "You should head down to the containment floor. You'll find Director Paxton there."

"In what condition will I find him?" she asks.

And this time, I can't bring myself to meet her eyes, ashamed
to admit that *alive* is the best I can hope for.

Lin doesn't linger after that. With a parting nod at Ryder, she
slips out of her office and out of my life, leaving another ghost
trapped beneath my ribs. A couple more and I can start my very
own haunted house.

"Not gonna lie, Sil, I'm a little lost here." Ryder rises from
the chair. "Feel like catching me up?"

"Right . . . sorry." I unplug from the console and slip the hard
line into my pocket, bracing to make my request. "I need you to
let me inside your head." I force the words out quickly, as if
adding speed might dull them of their sharp edge.

"*Sil*—" Ryder's said my name a hundred times before, but it's
never ripped from his throat like this, catching on his dismay.

"I know that's the last thing you want to do right now"—hell,
given what Miles put him through, I'd stake my life on him never
wanting to let another soul in there again—"but I have to make
sure this'll work," I say. I have to make sure *I* work.

And maybe Ryder senses my desperation, because he drops
back to the leather and says, "Okay."

"Yeah?" I'm not going in until I'm sure it won't break us.

"Yeah." His whole body tenses. Then when I hesitate, he adds,
"It's fine, Sil. I can handle it."

I've never tried to initiate a neural link gently, but I do my very best
to land this one soft. Though I guess there is no *soft* way to launch
an invasion. Ryder's breathing—already sharp and shallow—quickens
when he feels me there, treading on his free will, so before either of
us can think to say uncle, I raise his arm and take a swing at myself.

"*Sil!*"

It's an odd feeling, watching a movement happen from behind two sets of eyes. His fist, rushing towards my face, as if in slow motion. My hand, reacting on instinct, flying up to stop it connecting with my cheek.

"That's a new trick." Ryder's shock momentarily eclipses his unease.

"Yeah, it is."

It's the trick Miles won't be expecting because he thinks he's the only one who's mastered it. Because he doesn't realize I've cracked his secret to melding without consent. And because I doubt he'd suspect me of seeking Lin's help any more today than he did the night I escaped.

Why would he?

For the past couple of years, he's been the one I've turned to.

I play with the feeling, moving Ryder's fingers in mine, learning how to exercise control over both sides of the neural link. It's more instinctive than I imagined it would be, the way my focus splits as I maneuver our bodies around the room. Like watching two movies simultaneously. A touch distracting, sure, but it only takes me a few minutes to get the hang of it.

More importantly, the Meld is holding firm without putting an undue strain on my systems. The adjustments I made are working.

"So, Ryder Stone." I offer him my arm. "May I walk you to the penthouse?"

It's a terrible joke. A terrible, insensitive, inappropriate joke, but I swear, I feel Ryder's mind relax around me as he chokes out something between a laugh and a groan.

"That was in very bad taste, Sil Sarrah," he says, a smile in his voice. "Though I suppose if you're in my head, Miles can't be."

I flash him my teeth. "My thoughts exactly."

CHAPTER 29

<FUGITIVE_AT_LARGE_SS> Mission's burned. Aja, Brin: abort, now.
J: I need access to the penthouse.

I send the message on our way out of Lin's office, along with
the cheat-sheet version of everything that transpired in the underbelly of this building.

<UNKNOWN_USER> Sil, are you sure about this?

Jondi asks in a private ping.

<UNKNOWN_USER> I mean . . . this is Miles we're talking about . . .

So I point him to the security footage from my cell, then once
he's had the chance to watch it, I add, *I'll also need his ID number.*
And this time, Jondi doesn't argue.
The hack I've requested is no small thing—especially on a man
as insulated as Miles—but it's my only hope for getting within
a hundred feet of him. As an added bonus, it'll keep Jondi too
distracted to ask questions, or do something stupid, like wade
into the fight.
I can't have that.
I need him safe so he can act as my eyes and ears and hands.
I need him safe so he'll survive this.
But as it turns out, Jondi's not the one I need to worry about.
"Sil—!" It's lucky Ryder's panic is locked inside his mind, or

else he'd have already rushed the dozen-odd guards holding Aja and Brin in the atrium.

"I see them." A curse grits through my teeth. Security has both girls on their knees behind the welcome desk, their hands in cuffs and their faces bloody.

Damn. I should have warned them sooner. Miles knew where they were holed up; he's the one who suggested they set up shop in that suite of offices across the square. He must have sent a team after them the moment I banished him from Ryder's head, though by the looks of it, they didn't come easy. Aja's nose is broken, both eyes already on their way to swelling shut. And as for Brin . . . well, they really went to town on Brin. Judging by the burns around her defensive strips—and some of the guards' faces—she put up quite the fight before they managed to . . . *Christ-that-was* . . . rip the current regulator clean out of her wrist.

What's worse is it appears security was expecting us, too.

Despite the wrench I threw in his plans, Miles has stayed two steps ahead of us this entire evening.

<FUGITIVE_AT_LARGE_SS> I'm gonna need another ID number.

I ping my request to Jondi right as the head of security—a bully of a man named Dunner—bellows, "Show me your hands."

"Can you live with what I have to do here?" I raise Ryder's arms in mock surrender, tossing the gun to the floor. While all four of us can hold our own in a fight, the girls are cuffed and Ryder and I aren't bulletproof. If we want a chance at walking out of here, I'm going to have to level the playing field.

"Ask me that again when it's done," Ryder says, and since that's as close to a *yes* as I'm likely to get, it's going to have to do.

"Jarvis, on my mark, terminate this neural link and initiate a new one with user ID—"

<UNKNOWN_USER> 4382667368

Jondi's ping pops up on my display, supplying me the necessary information. Then with a hastily added, *I'm asking you nicely*, I'm propelled out of Ryder's head and straight into Dunner's.

There's no time for small talk, confusion, outrage, or lies. One second I'm staring down the barrel of a dozen guns, then the next, the cold kiss of metal is pressed between my fingers. A flick of my thumb shifts the weapon to stun and I whirl around, putting an electric round in as many of Dunner's friends as I can manage. I get five before the element of surprise wears off and chaos explodes around me.

"Get down!" Ryder pulls my body clear of a bullet as I throw my stolen one at Aja and Brin, tackling them to the ground.

"*Fuck*, Sarrah." Aja's the first to glean the truth behind Dunner's sudden change in loyalties. "You trying to get us shot?"

"Only a little." I free their hands from the cuffs. Across the atrium, I block a fist an inch before it hits my face. "Think you can hack us some cover?"

"Yeah, just keep them off me for a minute."

So together with Brin, that's exactly what I do.

We both charge around the desk, her towards the bruiser with the poor sense to train his gun on her girlfriend, me towards a man with a face as sharp as his knife. I use Dunner's speed and strength to my advantage, dropping him to his knees at the last second to slide beneath our attacker's outstretched arm. His knife hits air instead of skin, upsetting his equilibrium long enough for me to spring up and jam the blade into the soft flesh at his thigh. That should keep him screaming a while.

"Ryder—watch out!" A kick to Security Thug Two's leg elicits a crunch of bone that echoes down both sides of the neural link as I mirror the move in my own body, narrowly preventing a guy from slitting Ryder's throat. *Too* narrowly. Controlling dual minds was all good and well in the quiet safety of Lin's office. In the midst of a firefight, it'll get one of us killed.

"Brin, if I bug out, can you take care of this host?" I ask, eager to relieve the pressure building behind the Meld.

"You got it," she says, sweeping a man's feet out from under him. "Oh, and Sarrah—" She seizes his weapon and points it directly at Dunner's chest. "I ever see you pulling this shit again, I'll kill you myself."

It's not a heartfelt thank you, but she doesn't actually shoot me out of Dunner's head, so I'm calling it a win. What I'm not expecting is the pain that lances through my skull as I land back in my own body. Hard. The world bleeds black for a moment, the commotion dying down to a high-pitched squeal.

That moment is all the guard I'm fighting needs. The butt of his gun connects with my jaw, once, twice, again, sending me crashing down to the marble. Once I'm there, he doesn't waste any time ending the fight for good.

The gunshot rings out, the shock of it—the deafening crack— slamming into me before the pain.

That's because there is no pain. No blood, either, or bullet-shaped wound. Not in my chest, anyhow, but there's a dark stain spreading through the guard's shirt and a dribble of red escaping his lips.

"Go!" Ryder yells as the man falls to his knees, his mouth opening and closing but making no sound, as though he hasn't fully grasped what's happened yet. That someone beat him to the trigger. "Get to Miles. We'll be right behind you."

I nod, snatching a discarded switchblade off the floor as I scramble to my feet.

"And Sil—whatever you do, don't damage his unit," Ryder adds. "A guy like Miles doesn't put a bomb in his head unless he knows how to get it out again. The answer will be somewhere in his CIP. I'm sure of it."

A fresh torrent of guilt tugs at my resolve.

Ryder's still looking for a way to get me out of this.

He still thinks he can write me a happy ending.

At least I'm saved the pain of lying to his face again. With an audible snap, Aja's hack plunges the building into darkness and he disappears into the black.

I'll spare the tech, I make him a silent promise. I'll preserve Miles's unit so that Ryder can use it to help the others. So that something good might come from this deceit.

<FUGITIVE_AT_LARGE_SS> How's that access looking, J?

I ask, picking a path over to the executive elevator.

<UNKNOWN_USER> Show that pretty face to the scanner and find out.

And to my relief, the access light turns green and the doors beckon me inside.

<FUGITIVE_AT_LARGE_SS> Lock it down once I'm in?
<UNKNOWN_USER> Don't worry, I'll keep security off your back.
<FUGITIVE_AT_LARGE_SS> I owe you one.
<UNKNOWN_USER> You owe me two, actually. Here's Miles's ID: 4262223489.
<FUGITIVE_AT_LARGE_SS> Make that three. The Analogs could do with a hand in the atrium. Get them out safe?
<UNKNOWN_USER> On it.
<FUGITIVE_AT_LARGE_SS> Thanks, J.

If I weren't such a coward, I'd send him a proper thank you, something that will magically encompass all those things I don't know how to say. But when I try, my fingers stall on the keypad. I can't tell him goodbye any more than I could tell Ryder, and now that I've stopped moving, the ache in my skull is hitting me with a vengeance.

I lean into the wall, pressing my forehead to the metal, its cool touch a balm to the heat bubbling beneath my skin. A week ago, Lin would have told me to stop worrying, that it's a migraine, or dehydration, or too much adrenaline in my blood. *This is normal,* she'd have said. *Not the beginnings of a catastrophic failure.*

I don't think she'd say that anymore.

Not after the stunt I just pulled.

With a CIP already degraded to 34%.

"Stay with me, Jarvis," I mutter. "We're almost done."

I'm almost done.

I only need a little more time.

The executive elevator deposits me straight in the Director's office, an indulgence of a room that's both as large and as lavish as I expect. Every surface is a shrine to spun glass and polished metal, monochromatic save for the art on the walls—real classics from before the Annihilation, painted on canvas and displayed in gilded frames—a perfect complement to the sleek, white furniture, adding color to a room that would lack life without it.

"Annoyingly resourceful, aren't you?" Miles's voice greets me as I slowly circle the space. It sounds from over the loudspeakers, just as I suspected it would. A perk of having your own private elevator is that you always see company coming. So Miles has gone and locked himself inside the panic room his father will have had installed—behind one of the paintings maybe, or perhaps it's under the floor. Doesn't much matter where, to be honest; I'm not here to break him out of a steel box. When I'm through with my commanding officer, he'll come to me.

"I've been called worse," I say, heading over to the generously proportioned bar that sits along the back wall. There's a brandy here that's older than I am and probably cost the same as the hardware in my head. *Oh yes, this will definitely do.* I crack open the top and pour myself a drink. The amber liquid smells like wood and burnt sugar, and it's both hot and smooth going down. Rich. I fix myself another then settle on the soft, leather couch. It is my last day of life, after all.

"That's a very expensive drink you're nursing there, Sil," Miles says. "My father was saving that bottle for a special occasion."

"I think he'd agree this qualifies." I raise my glass to the camera, flashing him my most innocent smile. "He beat you today."

"Is that right?" Now that I'm in on his deception, the change in Miles is chilling and absolute. Gone is the mask of gentle kindness I'd come to know and trust. All that's left is the ruthless architect behind the biggest breach of consent law in history. A man with more ambition than conscience. And more ego than sense.

Which is why I'm confident my ruse will work.

"I'd say so." I take a long sip of liquor, savoring the pause and the flavor. Toying with him. Just as he'd toyed with me.

"You do realize security will arrive soon?"

"I do."

"I've already raised the alarm."

"I'm sure you have."

"They're going to arrest you, Sil. Then I'll be free to finish what you started. I'll kill my father, and you'll take the blame."

"What can I say, Miles, it sounds like you've got a real neat plan there." I shrug, downing the rest of my drink. "Except for one tiny detail."

"And what would that be?" A subtle edge creeps into his voice. Derision, certainly, but underscored by fear.

"You'll be dead before they ever get here."

"Will I?" Miles's laughter fills the room, arrogant and cold. "I'd love to know how you mean to kill me from out there. Please, Sil. Enlighten me."

Well, he did ask nicely.

So before the pain in my head grows unmanageable and the liquid courage loses its bite, I have Jarvis initiate one final neural link.

Melding with another Walker feels entirely different to melding with a naked mind. It's not a smooth change of state, like diving into water, but rather, like trying to walk through a solid brick wall. Like trying to break into the panic room in Miles's brain. And just like a real breaking and entering, my presence sets off a whole slew of alarms, triggering the emergency protocols our units are equipped with.

I do make it in, though, and for a brief second, the neural link holds firm, affording me a glimpse at Miles's modest-yet-comfortable surroundings.

"What the—" He pushes back against the connection, cursing me out of his head.

But I rattled him, I know I did; I heard the disbelief and shock in his voice, his unbearable smugness melting away.

I don't give him a chance to recover. The instant I land back in my body, I have Jarvis initiate the Meld again.

"No. You can't do this!" Miles kicks me out once more, though I last longer this time. Long enough to see that he's on his feet and pacing the length of his steel prison. That he's afraid.

"Sure I can," I say, launching a third attack. I realized it was possible the moment I got a look at my operating code, and the healthy list of functions the limiting patch was designed to block. Without the training wheels, it's not only *possible* to forge a neural link between CIPs, it *makes* possible the perfect threat. Because Syntex was so worried about the prospect, they built in a fail-safe, to ensure no Walker would ever survive an incursion by an outside mind.

"I figured out your secret catchphrase, Miles," I tell him, "though I'm sure you'd rather I hadn't, since we both know what happens if I hold the Meld for a full thirty seconds, don't we—?" My vision blurs as the neural link snaps and I'm forced to round-trip my way back in.

"—Or did you forget that Daddy wrote a kill-switch into your operating system—

—that will assume you've been compromised and trigger a catastrophic failure the moment I overstay my welcome—

—which is bad news for you seeing how I'm getting pretty damn good at holding it."

By the time I get the words out, Miles's terror is a creature I can see and smell and touch. The air inside the panic room hangs thick with his sweat, the whiskey he was drinking lying in a pool of shattered glass, his whole body shaking from the effort of fighting the Meld.

When he finally breaks free of my sixth neural link—after a full twenty-three seconds—I give us both a moment's respite, allowing the relief to drive him towards the door, but not yet wrench it open.

If I make this too simple, he might suspect I'm guiding his hand. I need him to believe that *this* is how I mean to kill him, even though I promised Ryder I'd preserve his CIP. That's the only way he leaves his impenetrable box, and I need him to leave it soon because the pressure in my head is growing with every Meld, filling my ears with needles and static.

"Jarvis, initiate neural link. I'm asking you nicely," I bark, gritting through the pain.

I regain control of Miles just in time to stop him disengaging the lock. "What's the matter, *Milford*? Suddenly wishing you'd bothered to rewrite that particular function?" I ask, though in truth, I was counting on the fact he hadn't. Miles made it clear that he doesn't take *unnecessary risks*. So why mess with his operating code for no reason? Why risk damaging his unit when he never expected another Walker to wield this kind of power? "Because guess what, *Sir*? I rewrote mine."

"Get. Out!" he seethes, and then I'm back in my own body, watching one of the wall-sized canvases swing sideward to reveal a door.

Here we go . . . My grip tightens on the stolen switchblade as Miles explodes into his father's office, a gun clasped between his fingers.

"Oh no you don't." I seize control and toss it to the ground. "You don't get to end this so easy. You want to kill me? I'm standing right there," I say, relaxing my grip on his muscles. "See if you can do it before I fry your brain."

"The hell kind of game is this?" He hesitates, looking for the trick, the lie, the hidden agenda.

"Tick-tock, Miles." The choice I'm offering him is clear: keep kicking me out of his mind in the hopes I won't hang on for thirty seconds, or spend the next twenty trying to finish me in the flesh. Either way, he's running out of time.

Which is probably why he doesn't waste more fighting me after that, and I don't risk giving away the game by talking too much like he did. Across the office, I hold myself statue-still, maintaining the charade that my body is powerless while I'm busy squatting in his. That I haven't discovered *everything* my CIP can do. Only once he's almost upon me do I finally break the illusion.

"Guess what, Miles, I took *all* the training wheels off." I freeze him mid-step, watching myself surge forward through his eyes.

"No, you couldn't have. It's not—"

"Oh, it's possible."

His fear spikes as I force him to his knees and press the switch-blade to his throat.

"You feel that?" A spot of red appears beneath the metal, staining his crisp white shirt. "This is what your father felt when I was killing him." I press down harder, letting my anger spill into the blade. "But you already know that, don't you? Because you were in there while I was doing it."

"You're making a mistake, Sil," he rasps, struggling to regain control. "I can—I can save you."

"Who's going to save *you*?" I hiss. Then with two seconds left on the clock, I break the neural link.

No more hiding behind my hosts. No more dampening my actions. When I slit his throat open from ear to ear I'll do it in my body. Using my hands. His death will be *my* burden to bear, and I'll happily carry that burden to the grave because if Ryder is right, and the answer to surviving a CIP removal is hiding somewhere in Miles's unit, then keeping that secret makes him responsible for every Walker who's burned out since he found the fix. It makes him responsible for Lena.

Which makes this justice. A wave of pure hate swells inside my chest. Miles was in that cafeteria, watching my best friend burn, when all along, he had the power to change her fate. Maybe if he'd done that, I'd have considered changing his, too.

But he didn't. So neither do I.

Warm blood soaks my hands, a geyser neither of us has any hope of controlling. Severed carotids spell death in a matter of seconds and even psychotic billionaires can't outrun the wind. Miles claws at the wound, his frantic gurgles filling the office. They don't last long before his body drops to the bloodied carpet, his eyes dimming as the final vestiges of life leak out of his ruined neck.

And just like that, Lieutenant General Milford Eugene Paxton is gone.

The knife slips from between my fingers, landing on the couch with a heavy thud. I double over and retch, the horror of what I've done gripping my insides like a vice, the pain in my head going supernova now that the fight's left me. There's blood on my skin, on my clothes, in my hair, wetness spreading down my cheeks.

I can't *breathe*.

But I have to.

"Jarvis, you still there?" I ask, hauling myself over to the desk.

"Es, 'aptin." His mangled words do little to reassure me. Losing Jarvis's voiceprint was a database error. An annoyance, sure, but ultimately harmless. Whereas broken speech means my processors are dying. Mindjacking Miles pushed my system out of its twilight phase and into the night.

"Load the SYN-HEIST program onto the central core. Get ready to execute on my command," I say, reaching for the hard line I took from Lin's office. The cable snaps into the port at my neck with an ominous click, connecting me to the Director's terminal.

At least Aja's code will have an easier time doing its work from here. We designed it to brute-force into Syntex's server—and the Director's private network—from anywhere in the building. But now that I'm physically patched into both, it'll be able to skip that step.

That should leave it enough power to do the rest.

This really is it then. I try to think through the panic. I want to go and pour myself another drink, to numb reality before stepping off this final ledge. But the pain in my head has graduated to *blinding* and when I look up from the monitors, the elevator is moving again.

I'm officially out of time.

I fist my hands against the desk, mustering every ounce of strength and courage I have. "Jarvis—" It feels right that his will be the last name on my tongue. That we get to run this final mission together. "Ex—"

"*Sil!*"

The command dies in my throat as the elevator doors slide open and Ryder springs from inside. *No, no, no, no, no.* My heart stutters to a stop, my resolve splintering like glass. In my life, I've never been happier to see someone. And I've never been more aghast.

"Christ-that-was, the hell did you do?" He freezes, glancing between me and the sullied carpet, where Miles is lying face down in a pool of his own blood.

"What I had to?" My thoughts are churning too slowly to make sense of Ryder's expression. Why he looks so appalled. He knew this story would end with a body—that was the entire point of coming up here—and I didn't destroy Miles's CIP, just as I promised.

"Not to him, Sil," Ryder says. "What did you do to your eyes?"

To my eyes?

"Nothing?" I run a hand across my cheeks, quickly wiping the tears away.

But instead of saltwater, my fingers meet blood.

Oh.

That red haze isn't in my head then.

It's leaching out of me.

"We need to get you looked at." Ryder makes a beeline for the desk. In a few seconds, he'll reach me, and I can't have that. If he gets any closer, I'll crumble. I'll lose the ability to do what I have to do. And I *really* can't have that.

Because Ryder was right, stopping the mindjackings isn't enough. If these past few days have taught me anything, it's that when you strip someone of options, there's little they won't do to survive. I'm proof of that. Ryder's proof of that. As is every agent who's ever granted me control of their mind. Proof that desperation is not the same as consent. That it can't be. And it's time we stop pretending it can.

"I'd have given it up, you know," I say, stepping back from the terminal.

"Given what up?"

"My CIP. I'd have given it up if there was a way."

I'd have changed the weather, let go of everything that makes me special if it meant we got more time. Truth is, if more time was an option, I doubt I could bring myself to run this program at all. I've never been selfless, not really. I say I sold my future for my family, but in truth, I did it for the tech. I've saved a lot of agents, but they never mattered to me as much as my stats. And this? I'm doing this for my friends, yes, but I'm also doing it because I'm out of life. If I had years left, or months—hell, if I had days left instead of minutes—I'd walk away and spend them with him.

"Sil, what are you—"

I spot the moment Ryder gets it, the sudden widening of his eyes, the fear that grips him as he realizes I'm saying goodbye. And in that moment, I know I made the right decision, not telling him my plan, because the heartbreak spreading across his face confirms that even if I only had seconds left to live, he would have still tried to stop me.

"I'm so sorry, Ryder. I never meant for you to see this." My voice sounds strangely removed, as though belonging to another time and place. As though I'm already gone.

"Don't—!" He lurches forward. But even if I were holding some kind of button he could knock from between my fingers, he wouldn't get to it in time. He still has to jump this oversized desk and I only have to choke out three tiny words.

"Jarvis, execute command."

CHAPTER 30

I am a scream, lost in space.

I am searing heat, and darkness, and pain.

I am a toy robot, broken beyond repair.

But I am not dead.

"Sil—"

Someone's shaking my shoulders, trying to claw me back from the edge.

"Sil, can you hear me?" Ryder's voice lands slowly, like an echo sinking through fog.

"The hell did she do?"

And that's Jondi's voice. Jondi's here too.

"I don't know, but she's burning up."

Out. I correct in my head. I'm burning *out.* Why else would it feel as though every cell in my body is on fire? Why else would it feel as though I've swallowed the sun?

"Sil, come on, open your eyes." Ryder sounds so worried I force myself to do it. Or at least, I think I do, but the darkness swirling around me doesn't give an inch.

"*Christ-that-was,*" both boys curse in unison, their gasps rending down into my bones.

"We have to get her out of here," Ryder says. "Go grab Miles's CIP."

"Grab his CIP—?"

I can practically hear Jondi's glare.

"—How am I supposed to do that?"

"I don't care how!" Ryder explodes. "Rip it out, download the contents, cut off his damn head if you have to. We need those files."

"Okay, okay." With another curse and a rustle of fabric, Jondi climbs to his feet.

"Sil?" Ryder's hand moves to cup my face. "Can you hear me?"

"I can't see."

"I know," he whispers.

Oh. It's bad then.

"How bad is it?" I ask.

"Don't worry about that."

"How bad, Ryder?"

His grip on me tightens, as though afraid I might bolt. "Your eyes are gone." The words stick on his tongue, telling me more than a detailed description ever could.

So that's how I'm burning out then. One piece at a time.

"I'm gonna turn off your unit, okay?" Ryder reaches for the button behind my ear.

"It won't help." If it were that easy, there'd be a whole retirement village of us walking around, unplugged and surly, but alive.

"It might until we get you to Sandria."

"Lin can't stop this," I say. No one can.

"She can *try*." The air hisses out from between Ryder's teeth, desperation and denial in equal measure. "Jondi," he barks, "how you doing with that CIP?"

"Working on it."

"Well, work faster!"

This is exactly why I didn't want him here when I pulled the trigger. Ryder's already lost a brother to catastrophic failure; he shouldn't have to watch it happen again.

"Hey—" I feel around for his hand, wracking my rapidly disintegrating brain for a way to distract him. "How are the others?" I ask. "Brin, Aja . . . are they alright?"

"Yeah." Ryder gentles as his fingers lace through mine. "Jondi helped me get them out, and now Aja's helping him keep security busy so we can get you out too."

"Helping a Junker save a Junker, huh? I bet Aja just *loved* that idea."

"She came around to it." The barest hint of a smile creeps into Ryder's voice. "I think she's starting to like you."

"Liar." I try to smile back, but it's getting hard to focus on anything but the heat building beneath my skin and the unease growing in my stomach. The feeling that I'm missing something. Something obvious. Something important.

"Will you tell her it worked?" I say while I still can.

"That what worked?"

"The program she wrote for me."

I don't remember much of what happened after I gave Jarvis the go-ahead to execute the code—the pain made it hard to do anything other than scream—but I do remember the progress bar hitting one hundred percent before the darkness took me.

The virus had broken through Syntex's firewalls.

Which means Aja's Frankenstein is now propagating through their servers, invisible enough to avoid detection until it infects their off-site backups as well. Over the next twenty-four hours, it'll systematically isolate and purge every last file Syntex has on the Mindwalking program. CIP schematics, Meld protocols, procedure notes, manufacturing instructions, our operating code; everything required to make us, train us, and put us to use.

And to ensure Syntex doesn't just rebuild the program from scratch, I've left the Director a warning in their place, letting him know what would happen if he tried. Because the final thing Aja's virus was designed to do was send out a few files of its own. Twelve million of them, to be exact—along with some pretty damning footage of the heir apparent confessing his crimes, which I added to the bundle in Lin's office—to be delivered to the Analog Army should my demands not be met.

If the Director doesn't make good on his son's promise to stop the burnouts, those files go public.

If Jondi suffers a catastrophic failure before he stops the burnouts, those files go public.

And my personal favorite: if he doesn't shut the Mindwalking program down within the year, those files go public.

How the Director will explain why he's dissolving his most successful initiative is his problem; call it the price for freeing him and sparing his life. Having spent the last two years locked inside his own mind, maybe he'll even welcome this development. Either way, the program's done. Whether the rest of his company goes with it . . . well, that's up to him.

"Christ-that-was, that's why you were plugged into Paxton's terminal." Ryder's tone hardens. "And you knew, didn't you? You knew what running that code would do to you."

"I'm sorry," I say. "I had to do it."

"Damn it, Sil," he growls. "You are, without a doubt, the most infuriating person I've ever met."

"No way I'm worse than Aja."

"You are so, *so* much worse than Aja," he mutters, leaning his forehead into mine. "Why didn't you tell me?" he breathes. "I could have done something. I could have helped you find another—"

"I've got it!" Jondi calls from across the room. "A full clone of Miles's drives."

"Good." In an instant, Ryder's pure business again. "Start filtering the data. Search for anything tagged *CIP removal*."

A ripple of pain shoots through my spine as he lifts me off the floor, so sharp and violent I gasp and fold in on myself.

"And ping Sandria," Ryder adds, cradling me tighter. "We'll be needing her help."

That's when I finally put my finger on what's been bothering me.

"How'd you know her name?" The question croaks out hair-thin.

"Whose name?" Ryder tenses.

"Lin's. I never told you her name was Sandria."

"Sure you did."

"No, I didn't."

"Then she must have." With a mechanical grind, the elevator doors slide open and Ryder steps us inside.

"You're lying," I say, thinking back to their conversation. The two had only traded a few clipped formalities; a query here, a brush-off there, all related to his ID chip. They never exchanged names.

Because they didn't have to. The answer hits me harder than the pain. They didn't have to because Lin and Ryder knew each other long before I dragged him into her office. That's why he looked so rattled when he saw her, and why they spoke like two robots following a carefully worded script. They were afraid I'd figure out whatever secret they've been keeping. Together.

Which doesn't make a lick of sense.

Except, neither does Lin.

Lin, the doctor on Syntex's payroll who believes that *just because we* can *implant technology doesn't mean we* should. Who chose to help me instead of turning me in—not once, but twice. Who is inexplicably on a first-name basis with the brother of the youngest Walker to ever burn out, and who has some sort of standing arrangement with a junkie modder and the tech-sparse friend he calls . . .

"You're Diet-Mod." The final piece of the puzzle clicks into place. "You're working with Lin and Zell." This must be how Ryder knew so much about the inner workings of the program, details about the medical staff not even his brother would have been able to provide.

"What's she talking about?" Jondi asks as the elevator begins its descent.

"Nothing. She's confused."

"No, I'm not." And now I'm sure I'm right because this is the first time Ryder's ever sought to minimize me. "You and Lin are—*ahhh*!" Deep inside my skull, something critical snaps. My hands fly up to cup my head, my groans turning to outright screams as the heat—which had been simmering at a blistering eleven—suddenly doubles.

"Sil!"

I can no longer tell whose voice is trying to reach me, but it's screaming every bit as loud as I am.

"You have to hold on, okay? You have to *hold on*."

But I can't.

I've already been holding on a week, dying in slow motion. From the minute Zell kicked my twilight phase into high gear, I've been counting down the days to this moment, and now that it's here, I just want the pain to stop.

I need it to stop.

"Let me go," I beg them. *Let me go, let me go, let me go.*

But no one is listening to me anymore, or maybe I'm no longer speaking aloud. And we're running, I think, each step a torment as I jostle in Ryder's arms.

Please, you have to let me go.

And then there's pain again, not just in my head but everywhere else.

And honestly, I don't know why they call it burning out, because in the end, all I feel is cold.

CHAPTER 31

Death is quiet.

Gone is the hum I've lived with since I was eight, the low-pitched buzz emanating from my processers that's become as familiar as breathing. It's so quiet, in fact, that it takes me hours—or maybe it's days—to adjust to the absence of sound. It takes me longer still to question it, how it's possible I'm contemplating the silence at all.

Around me, everything is draped in shades of blue and gray. Muted. As though I'm underwater, or watching the world from behind a cheap holoform.

But I am *watching* the world.

I can see.

The room I'm in is a sterile box, empty save for the bed I'm lying on, an IV stand, and a heartbeat monitor, which—much to my surprise—seems to suggest that I'm in possession of a pulse.

As far as dying hallucinations go, this one's pretty disappointing. My subconscious could have picked anything: a pre-Annihilation beach . . . the roof of the Syntex building, counting drones with Lena and Jondi . . . a room with a view of Ryder in *that* suit. Instead, it chose a low-rent version of Lin's office. Like I haven't spent enough of my life here already.

Too much of it. I peel the sensors off my temples. I have no intention of spending my death here as well.

"I wouldn't do that," a voice tells me from the doorway.

I don't need to ask who he is because his face is instantly recognizable, so much like Ryder's and yet different, somehow.

A little older. A little less carefree. A little . . . pixelated? I squeeze my eyes shut, trying to blink away the glitch. But when I open them again the effect persists, giving him an unfinished look. Like a half-res render.

"I know you." My voice is hoarse and whisper-thin. "You're Aiden Stone."

Which means I am dead.

I'm dead and in some Walker hell with my boyfriend's equally dead brother.

Super.

"You shouldn't try to stand yet," Aiden says. "You've been unconscious for almost a month. You need to go slow."

"Sorry. I don't take orders from ghosts." I slide the needle out of my arm, halting the flow of nanites to my blood.

"Alright, but if you fall, I can't catch you."

What an odd thing to say.

Then again, this entire dream is quite odd, so I decide to run with it.

"Whoa—" The moment I get vertical, my vision shutters at the corners, sending me stumbling down to the cold tiles.

"I did warn you." Aiden folds gracefully to the floor in front of me.

"You could have been more persuasive," I say, running both hands through my hair. But instead of slipping through my shoulder-length bob, the fingers on my left hand meet an inch of fuzz. *The hell?* I feel around my scalp. Someone shaved one side of my head, long enough ago that my hair has started to grow back.

But why would anyone—?

Oh.

Suddenly the silence makes all the sense in the world. And though I already know the answer, a broken question escapes my lips, "Jarvis, you there?"

He doesn't respond.

He can't respond.

Because Jarvis is gone.

"Breathe, Sil," Aiden says. "This is a good thing."

It doesn't feel like a good thing. It feels like I'm missing the only piece of me that's ever mattered. Like I've been stripped for parts and rendered obsolete.

"I don't understand," I manage between shallow gasps. "It was too late. I burned out." I remember it. The pain, and the heat, and the certainty that my CIP had broken in the most absolute way.

"You *were* burning out," Aiden corrects. "Quite spectacularly, I might add. Here, I'll show you." He projects an image into the space between us, of a brain with a computer grafted to both hemispheres. My brain. I'd recognize it anywhere.

"Your catastrophic failure began inside the main core." Aiden highlights the processor at the center of the array, turning it a deeper blue. "This kind of failure usually kills in seconds. The processor throws off sparks that ignite the charge in the backup power supply, and the resulting blast severs the brainstem."

It's the quick and lucky death Lena never got.

So how come I also didn't get it?

"But your backup had been inactive for almost two weeks," Aiden continues, rotating the image in place. "There was no charge left to ignite. Which meant that instead of kindling, it acted as a fire stop, sending the excess heat forward, not down. That's what saved you, the release of pressure when your—"

"Eyes melted," I say as the render zooms out to encompass my skull, complete with gruesome re-enactment. "So these are bionics then?" I point to the new pair I'm wearing. That would explain the blue tinge to the world; they're either an embarrassingly cheap model, or in need of proper calibration.

"Afraid so." Aiden offers me a sympathetic smile. "We wanted to save yours, but the tissues were—"

"Gone." My stomach turns as the render plays the moment over. *Your eyes are gone.*

"Shit, I'm sorry. Is this too much?" He makes to kill the projection.

"No—leave it please," I hurry to say. There's a comfort in knowing what happened to me. In understanding the silence. And maybe that's morbid, but the more Aiden talks, the more my panic wanes, my heartbeat finding its natural rhythm.

"Okay." He nods, refreshing the image. "The remaining heat continued to corrode your unit, causing your internal drives to warp and push against your pain centers. Luckily, that process was slow enough that inducing a hypothermic coma bought you a few extra hours, during which time, Lin removed your CIP."

Lin. The name pulls at a memory.

Ryder was rushing me to her office when the pain hit. Except, he didn't call her Lin, he called her Sandria. And then he lied about it.

"They know each other," I mumble. Ryder and Lin are working together. To what end, I have no idea. But I'm sure as hell gonna find out.

"Sil . . . what are you doing?" Aiden asks as I wobble back to my feet and break for the door. "No, no, no—" He lurches forward on instinct, trying to catch me as my legs buckle beneath my weight.

But he can't.

Just like he said.

Instead of clamping around my arms, his hands pass right through me.

"*The hell*—?"

We both curse as I crash back to the tiles, almost cracking my head open on the way down.

"Christ-that-was, you really do have a death wish," Aiden mutters under his breath. "I need you to take things *slow*, okay? Ryder will never forgive me if I let you hurt yourself."

"Then maybe he should be here!" I don't mean to yell; I don't even realize I'm angry until the words explode out from some deep part of my chest.

First he lies to me.

Then he lies about lying.

Then he leaves me to wake up in this strange white box with an eerily sentient holoform of his brother.

It's too much.

It *hurts* too much.

And I've about reached my limit for pain.

"He was here." Aiden stretches out beside me, as though lying on the floor is a perfectly normal thing to do. "Day in, day out, until I kicked his sad face to the curb. Your brain took an enormous amount of damage, Sil, and Paxton's removal procedure was something Lin had never tried before. We didn't know if you'd ever wake up, and it was killing him. It was killing him because the last time he spent weeks here, he was waiting to see if *I'd* wake up."

Despite myself, I turn to look at him.

"I thought that might get your attention." Aiden's smile is so similar to Ryder's, it sparks an ache inside my bones. "I'll make you a deal: I'll talk if you promise to take it *slow*."

"Fine," I say, since this dizziness seems intent on holding me hostage. "But talk *fast*."

He doesn't protest as I sit up and settle against the bed, though he does watch me with careful eyes, waiting for the strain of moving to ease out of my shoulders before he begins.

"I was sixteen when I realized I'd made a mistake, joining the program," Aiden says. "Ryder was twelve, and as angry a kid as I'd ever seen—not that I can blame him; he lost his brother when Syntex recruited me, then we both lost our parents when he was eleven. He was alone. I'd *left* him alone. And for what? A nice apartment he refused to live in? Better schools to get expelled from? Credits he wouldn't spend? I became a Walker to help my brother, not abandon him." Aiden's form flickers at the edges, as though blurred by his regret. "So I did what Syntex taught me to do when something felt wrong: I went to Lin."

"You asked her to take out your CIP?" I guess. It's not like I never thought of doing that myself, back when Lena's glitches started escalating—and then again the day twilight became my reality too, when my mortality began following me around like a dark cloud.

"I'm sure I wasn't the first," Aiden says, "but I was persistent. It took me six months to get her to agree. We both knew it was a risk. We both knew it would likely kill me. But I owed it to my brother to try."

And Lin owed it to *him*. I finally understand the good doctor's interminable will to help. By the time Aiden made his request, she'd have watched several classes of Walkers burn out. That's *dozens* of kids. Dead. All because some CEO decided the math on their lives didn't make sense. Faced with that kind of callous thinking, it's little wonder Lin took matters into her own hands.

"Waiting for my eighteenth birthday was her idea," Aiden continues. "She wanted ample time to plan for the procedure—where she would do it, *how* she would do it, how we would get me off Syntex's radar so she *could* do it—but she also wanted to attempt the removal before my unit degraded too badly."

"And it . . . *worked*?" My disbelief echoes around the room.

"It did," Aiden says. "And it didn't. Lin managed to get the CIP out without killing me, but the cost was . . . well, see for yourself." He projects a new image into the air. Of a man—a boy, really—lying in a vacutube, hooked up to a sickening array of IVs and machines. His skin is jaundiced and frail, his hair thin and graying. If not for the gentle rise and fall of his chest, I might have mistaken him for a corpse.

Christ-that-was. "Is that—?"

"My body? Yes," Aiden confirms. "The extraction damaged the connection between my brain and my spine. Irreparably. I'm still in there, but I'll never move again, or breathe on my own. This holoform is a projection of my consciousness and it's not a perfect solution. It only works in close proximity; it glitches and dies when I get tired; and more and more, there are days where I can't muster the strength to drive it at all. After so much time in stasis, my organs are beginning to fail. In a few months—maybe a year—I'll be gone."

The silence that follows sticks in my throat, the sight of Aiden's broken body searing a hole through my new eyes. It doesn't seem fair for his story to end like this. It doesn't seem fair for his story to end this soon.

"Oh no, don't you dare feel sorry for me." Aiden minimizes the image. "I don't regret what I did. I got to be there for my brother when he needed me most. I got to live long enough to watch him finish what Lin and I started." He flashes me another smile.

"You're our first real success, Sil," Aiden says. "For the past few years, Ryder's been working with Lin to develop a better—*safer*—removal procedure. She's heavily monitored, so they can't speak often, but she helped us set up this facility, and she smuggles out brain scans for us as often as she dares; we move them through a series of mod parlors in the Pleasure District. But without the kind of resources Paxton had at his disposal, progress has been slow. That's why Ryder's been trying to discredit the program. An overwhelming public backlash was the only way Syntex was finally going to fast-track the research Lin needed to keep you alive."

I guess that explains Ryder's single-minded obsession with mindjacking. What it doesn't explain is why he didn't tell me. Why he tried to sell me on an ethics debate instead of trusting me with the truth.

"He was going to come clean," Aiden says, reading my expression. "About me, about Lin . . . about all of it."

"But he didn't." My insides clench into a tight knot. Ryder chose to let me keep believing his brother was dead. He chose to leave this most important part of himself locked away.

"He wasn't ready yet," Aiden says. "You have to understand, Sil, what happened to me almost destroyed him. He didn't want that for you. He wanted to wait until we had a procedure that *worked*. And—in his defense—he didn't know you were planning to set your own CIP on fire." Aiden's eyes narrow at the corners. "You kind of blindsided him with that stunt. He thought you had months left, not days." A note of disapproval creeps into his voice. His big-brotherly way of saying, *you kept secrets too. Damn big ones.*

And he's not wrong.

I can be as mad at Ryder as I want, but what I did to him was no better. Worse, even. He was trying to spare me the heartbreak of false hope; I was only trying to spare myself.

"That program you ran *was* pretty genius though," Aiden adds grudgingly. "You should be proud, Sil. What you did will save a lot of lives."

Proud. The word ricochets around the space my CIP used to occupy. Maybe I will be *proud* one day, when the dust has settled and the shock of survival wears off. But right at this moment, I don't have it in me to care about the lives I *might* save. I only care about the ones I put in danger.

"Do you know if Jondi—" The question clings stubbornly to my tongue. Once I ask it, there'll be no turning back. I'll never un-know the answer.

But I do need to know it.

"—Is he alright?"

"Why don't you ask him yourself?" Aiden points to my keypad. "He's been pinging you every hour for the past three weeks."

He has too. A strangled laugh bubbles out as I open my inbox, flooding the screen at my wrist with a torrent of unread messages. Over 500 of them. I'm so used to Jarvis pushing alerts to my ocular display, I didn't think to check the notifications myself. I guess I'll be doing that more often now, manually checking my messages. *You'll be manually checking everything*; the thought damn near plunges me into another spiral. There'll be no more neural links, no more assisted hacks, no more private conversations with the computer in my head.

Because Jarvis is gone.

"Why don't I give you a little space?" Aiden rises to his feet. "Just please, take it *slow*. Oh, and Sil—" His holoform pauses halfway through the *closed* door. "Don't be too hard on that idiot brother of mine, okay? He really was here until he couldn't be." With that, Aiden's flickering form disappears, leaving me to drown out the guilt with Jondi's running commentary of everything I missed while I was sleeping.

There are messages berating me for not waking up yet, and those that threaten anatomically impossible things if I decide to go and die on him. I almost choke on my tears as I read through a particularly explicit string of them. I'd forgotten the mouth that boy has, and how creative he can get in running it.

Then there are the serious messages, assuring me that he's okay. That Lin's okay. That now I've stolen his favorite toy, the Director is playing nice. That he's announced an end to the program and authorized the first group of decommissioned Walkers to undergo the removal procedure. And hell, freeing him of Miles's control must have bought me a lot of grace, because despite my brazen act of blackmail, he's revoked my arrest warrant and paid out my contract in full.

You won, Sil, is how each of Jondi's messages ends. *You won, so you have to wake up.*

Hard not to when you're pinging me incessantly, I message him back. And just like that, my entire afternoon is lost as we trade another 500 messages, even while I avoid sending a single one to the person I long to speak to most.

It's early evening by the time I grow tired of taking things slow. Walking without the aid of a wall takes a few solid tries, but eventually, the dizziness abates and I sneak away from my room, my bare feet enjoying the kiss of the cold tiles.

The facility I'm in has all the charm I'd expect of a makeshift hospital. Pale walls, and glaring fluorescent lights, and paint-by-number art of pre-Annihilation flowers. A lone nurse sits outside the only other occupied room—Aiden's, I assume—and though she tries to bully me back to bed, I can't stand to be cooped up any longer. Which is what I tell her over and over until she relents and helps me to the roof for some air.

It's a clear night, dusk bleeding steadily into the sky, a tapestry of pinks and oranges my new eyes read as *blue* since without Jarvis, I've not yet figured out how to calibrate them. *That'll take some getting used to.* I ease myself down to the concrete. Living in a world devoid of instant answers. Learning to navigate it on my own.

At least the city looks the same as always, the giants of steel and glass shining like beacons in the night. Judging by their size, I'd say this facility is somewhere on the periphery of Sector One, far enough from the suffocating light-show that is the Tech District that once the darkness deepens, I can actually see the stars. That, together with the breeze, and the bustle rising from the street below, finally lifts the remaining pressure from my chest.

I can do this, I think.

Lead an entirely normal life.

No matter how much it scares me.

I feel Ryder long before I hear him, a physical presence stealing across the roof.

"Why am I not surprised to find you here instead of resting?" He sighs, dropping down beside me. Not too close, he leaves an entire universe of space between us, but close enough that I can feel the heat coming off his skin. I fight the urge to lean into it.

"I've been resting for three weeks."

"You've been in a coma for three weeks, that's not the same thing." Though Ryder says it lightly, an undercurrent of fierce emotion clouds his voice. The ghost of everything we haven't said yet. And everything we weren't yet ready to say.

"It was . . . quiet in there," I admit, since if we don't start somewhere, we'll never get anywhere at all. "I needed—"

"Noise," he finishes for me. "Aiden hates the silence too." His brother's name slides off his tongue easily now that it's not shrouded in half-truths and lies. "I guess we have some things to talk about, huh?"

"Yeah, I guess we do." I force myself to meet his gaze head-on. "But not tonight."

It took me hours to work up the courage to ping him, and even when I did, I only managed to say: *I'm not dead*, when what I should have said was: *you should be here. I want you to be here.*

Because I wasn't sure I did.

I thought I'd still be angry. That there'd be too much baggage left between us. Too many lies to overcome. Both his and mine.

I thought things wouldn't feel the same now that I'm not the same. That Ryder would look different through these bionic eyes, draped in shadows and shades of sapphire. That I'd look different to him now that I'm . . . *ordinary*.

I was wrong.

Ryder looks as good in blue as he ever did in color, and he's staring at me like I'm his own personal miracle. A miracle he fears he's about to lose forever.

"Sil—"

"I'm not saying no." I silence him with the urgent press of lips. "I'm saying *not tonight*." Because though there's still a mountain of secrets left for us to climb, the task no longer feels insurmountable. Because I think Ryder did try to tell me the truth, in his own way. *Would you give up the tech, Sil?* He was taking my temperature, trying to figure out if I'd even *want* to live without it.

He was asking for my permission.

And I pushed him away.

Because at the time, I never believed my answer would be yes.

I never believed it *could* be.

But Ryder did.

He believed it enough for us both.

Truth is, I'm not worried about us. We'll either keep falling now that we don't need each other, or we'll drift apart. This match will either spark an inferno, or it'll fizzle down to ash. Either way, I'm not afraid of the fire.

I was supposed to burn so bright and hot it consumed me.

I was supposed to succumb to the flames.

But now I can have any kind of future I want.

After 6624 days of life, I no longer feel the need to keep counting them.

ACKNOWLEDGEMENTS

So, first off, can I please take a minute to scream about how you're reading this in *English*! I know that may seem like a strange thing to say, but my journey through publishing has been more than a little strange, so just go with me on this.

These words have been four books, nine years, two agents, and a whole lot of heartbreak in the making, and even now, I can't quite believe I'm writing them. I won't bore you with the details of *why* I thought this book would never see the light of day, but trust me when I say it took a lot of help, trust, and relentless work to bring *Mindwalker* to your friendly neighborhood bookstore.

I'll start with my wonderful agent, Andrea Morrison, at Writers House. Thank you for taking a chance on this tricky little book of mine. YA Sci-fi is not an easy sell at the best of times, so thank you for falling in love with this story as hard as I did and championing it harder still (and for keeping me from melting into a literal puddle throughout the process, which was, arguably, the bigger job). Thank you also to Genevieve Gagne-Hawes, for making sure the manuscript found its way to Andrea and to Alessandra Birch (and Cecilia de la Campa!), who ensured it landed on all the right desks and worked tirelessly to find me the editor of my dreams.

Speaking of that editor . . . if you don't dream of being edited by Molly Powell at Hodder & Stoughton, then you're simply not dreaming big enough. By the time Molly got her hands on this book, it had already been revised to death, but somehow, she still found a way to push the story to new heights—and to make me excited about looking at it again. Thank you for taking this book under your wing and making it shine. I honestly can't think of a better home for *Mindwalker* than with you and the Hodderscape team.

And what a team it is! I owe an endless stream of thank yous to Callie Robertson, Natasha Qureshi, Claudette Morris, Andrew Davis, Will Speed, Sarah Clay, Fran Fabriczki, Sharona Selby, and Kate Keehan. Kate—publicist extraordinaire—you get an extra thank you for encouraging my . . . *enthusiasm* long before I officially became your problem.

But let's rewind a second, because in order to bamboozle my way into this dream deal with my dream team, I first had to get *Mindwalker* into fighting shape, and I couldn't have done that without Kat Dunn, who picked the manuscript out of the PitchWars slush pile. Thank you for helping me turn the book I never should have written into my debut, and for seeing the potential in my pages back when they still featured zero world-building, too many plot threads, pretty boys without faces or personalities, and a couple of totally unnecessary psychopaths (RIP Taz & Mason. It's safe to say you will not be missed).

To my whole PitchWars family: I could scream my gratitude at you every hour of every day, and it still wouldn't be enough. I love all of you awesome nerds, and I certainly wouldn't be crying over my laptop right now if not for you. Special shout outs go to Lani, Angel, Elora, Sami, Amanda, Gigi, Briana, Emily, Megan, Chandra, Alice, Sarah, Victor, and Lindsay, for cheerleading me through the down moments—of which there were many.

And to my extended publishing family: Naomi, Liam, Jocelyn, Madelene, Jesse, Grace, Shana, Natalie, and Sarah (yes, Sarah—I mean you), thank you for reading, and critiquing, and commiserating, and letting me whine at length about this book. I really do love a good whine.

Which leaves my pre-publishing family, who have had to deal with my book moods since I started this journey. Mom, Dad, Lee, Dani: thank you for your love, patience, encouragement, and support. For letting me follow my dreams no matter how odd or exasperating.

And to Pieter, my partner in all ~~knife~~ life-related crime. I wasn't a writer when we met. I didn't zone out for whole days at a time, or obsess over commas, or complain, at length, about em dashes (or timeline math or teenage fish). Thank you for giving me the space to become the author (!!!) I want to be—oh, and for enabling my ghost collection. It is a well-known fact that ghosts make the words go faster.

Finally, a massive thank you goes out to you, the reader. If you made it this far, I can only assume that Sil and the gang didn't make you want to claw your eyes out (or melt them out of your skull). It means the world to me that you chose to spend your time with my merry band of misfits. Without you, my story wouldn't have gotten the ending every author dreams of: an audience.